"I made a decision and a vow when I mated you with a bite and a mark, and I meant it."

He brushed his knuckles down the side of her face. "That hasn't changed, and we will mate again tonight. Completely."

She set her stance. No way would she let him sacrifice himself for her. Or even risk it. "No."

One of his eyebrows rose in a look she was becoming very familiar with. "Want to bet?" he asked mildly.

The shiver that took her had nothing to do with challenge or fear. She swallowed.

He smiled.

Also by Rebecca Zanetti

The Dark Protector series

The Realm Enforcers series

The Scorpius Syndrome series

The Deep Ops series

Guardian's Grace

Rebecca Zanetti

LYRICAL PRESS
Kensington Publishing Corp.
www.kensingtonbooks.com

LYRICAL PRESS BOOKS are published by

Kensington Publishing Corp.
119 West 40th Street
New York, NY 10018

All Kensington titles, imprints, and distributed lines are available at special quantity discounts for bulk purchases for sales promotion, premiums, fund-raising, educational, or institutional use.

Special book excerpts or customized printings can also be created to fit specific needs. For details, write or phone the office of the Kensington Sales Manager: Kensington Publishing Corp., 119 West 40th Street, New York, NY 10018. Attn. Sales Department. Phone: 1-800-221-2647.

Lyrical Press and Lyrical Press logo Reg. U.S. Pat.& TM Off.

First Electronic Edition: October 2020
ISBN-13: 978-1-5161-1075-9 (ebook)
ISBN-10: 1-5161-1075-7 (ebook)

First Print Edition: October 2020
ISBN-13: 978-1-5161-1080-3
ISBN-10: 1-5161-1080-3

Printed in the United States of America

This one is for everyone doing their best during the Coronavirus pandemic of 2020. A special thank you to medical personnel, first responders, sanitation workers, shipping workers, truckers, grocery store and assembly line workers, volunteers, and everyone else who's risking their health working right now while everyone else is self-isolating. A special dedication also to all the teachers working remotely with their students and trying to stay in contact and keep those kids connected, learning, and loved.

Acknowledgments

Thank you to the readers who have jumped into this new era of the Realm vampires. I have many wonderful people to thank for getting this book to readers, and I sincerely apologize to anyone I've forgotten.

Thank you to Big Tone, Gabe, and Karlina: for their love, support, for making my life better every day;

Thank you to my fantastic editor, Alicia Condon, as well as everyone at Kensington publishing: Alexandra Nicolajsen, Steven Zacharius, Adam Zacharius, Vida Engstrand, Jane Nutter, Lauren Jernigan, Elizabeth Trout, Samantha McVeigh, Lynn Cully, Kimberly Richardson, Arthur Maisel, Renee Rocco, Rebecca Cremonese, Alex Gendler;

Thank you to my wonderful agent, Caitlin Blasdell, and to Liza Dawson and the entire Liza Dawson Agency;

Thank you to Jillian Stein for the absolutely fantastic work and for being such a great friend. Thank you to Debra Stewart from Dragonfly Ink for the excellent proofreading edits;

Thanks to my fantastic street team, Rebecca's Rebels, and to their creative and hard-working leaders, Anissa Beatty and Margarita Coale.

Thanks also to my constant support system: Gail and Jim English, Debbie and Travis Smith, Stephanie and Don West, Jessica and Jonah Namson, Kathy and Herb Zanetti, and Liz and Steve Berry;

Finally, thank you to the readers who have kept the Dark Protectors alive all of these years. It's because of you that we decided to return to the world of the Realm.

Chapter 1

The vampire was late.

Grace Cooper twirled the straw in her half-finished ginger whiskey and tried to ignore the skunk smell wafting through the bar. Rather, the smell of pot, which two kids were smoking in the back corner by the lone pool table, seemingly uncaring that recreational use of marijuana was illegal in bars in Colorado. None of the few folks ambitiously drinking in the place paid them any heed.

She discreetly wiped snow off her jeans from her tumble in the snow right outside the door. Her wrist ached, and she tried to ignore the pain. How bad was the injury? Not that she had time to find a doctor, anyway.

Darkness had descended outside along with a blistering snowstorm, and the wind howled against the few windows in an effort to sneak inside. Mother Nature had decided on a brutal end to January, which might explain why so few patrons had ventured through the storm for cheap booze and a stereo system from the early nineties that only played Bon Jovi songs. *Renegade* was currently blasting at a slightly slower speed than she remembered.

Why in the world had the vamp wanted to meet in this dump?

The bartender, a sixty-something man wearing a ripped T-shirt, snow pants, and thick boots, tipped back a couple of shots of tequila as he wiped down the bar, ignoring everyone unless they approached him for more alcohol.

This was the closest she would come to Denver, where she'd lived before going into a coma and then becoming an immortal mate. Well, kind of becoming one. She'd promised everyone, especially her sister, that she'd never return to Denver. But persistent questions kept her up at night; she had to know the truth. Flashes of memory and warning. She'd go mad if she didn't find answers to the swirling vortex of questions in her brain. First, she had to survive for another week.

Grace turned her wrist, the healthy one, and read the time on her sports watch. She'd give Sebastian five more minutes.

The door opened, and wind blasted inside. A male wearing a baseball cap covered with snow kicked the door shut, looked around, and spotted her. He brushed snow off his long overcoat and strode toward her, his boots leaving a wet trail across the sawdust-covered floor. "Grace."

He was thinner than he'd looked in his picture. "Sebastian."

"I'm sorry I'm late." He pulled out the wooden chair across from her small table and sat, his eyes an odd bluish hue. "I can explain."

She held up her good hand, her temples starting to ache. "It doesn't matter. Do you have it?" She had to help that little girl lying sick in bed in the nearest hospital. No child should have to fight cancer.

He kicked back. "Yeah, but I thought we could maybe come to another arrangement." With the hat bill low over his face, and the bar so dark, it was difficult to judge his age. Or rather, what his age appeared to be, considering he'd supplied proof through email that he was over two hundred years old. "What's the hurry? There's a storm out there." He spoke with a very slight lisp.

She tilted her head. The overcoat was odd. "Take off your hat." Adrenaline started to hum through her veins.

His chest puffed out. "There you go. I knew we'd get along." With a flourish, he whipped off the cap with black fingernails, revealing thick blond hair—and black eyeliner rimming his eyes.

She blinked once and then again, looking closer. Were those colored contacts? Like the ones kids wore for Halloween? Yep. "You have got to be kidding me." How in the world had he fooled her? She'd asked for documentation, although records could be falsified. She began to stand.

He grasped her good wrist and tugged her down, leaning toward her. He smelled like cheap beer and even cheaper cologne. This close, he appeared to be in his early twenties. "I promise I'll give you what you want. My blood is all yours after I take a taste of my own." He opened his mouth, showing fangs.

Fake ones.

Anger snapped through her. "I can't believe this." Yes, she was a complete moron. The risks she'd taken for this meeting had kept her up for nights. She jerked free and started to stand.

The front door burst open, and a mammoth blond male strode inside just as a commotion sounded from the rear exit on the other side of the bar. The kids by the pool table snuffed out the pot, backing away and plastering themselves against the sole dartboard, their eyes wide and their chests sunken.

She stopped breathing. Damn it. Grabbing her bag, she moved toward the restroom behind her and the window she'd already scoped out—just in case this assignation went south.

"Grace?" The voice came from near the back exit. The low, dark, accented tenor stopped her cold.

She slowly turned, her body flashing to full-on panic mode. It couldn't be. *No, no, no, no, no.*

Yep.

Adare stood there, the surprise on his face quickly banked. The fury in his impossibly black eyes, however, glittered harsh and bright.

She edged backward.

"Dinnae even think it." In his anger, his Scottish brogue, the product of a distant time and place, broke free and strong. His black hair hung to his shoulders, dotted with snow that was quickly melting. For the raid, or whatever this was, he'd worn a jacket, cargo pants, and boots—all black and more than likely concealing various weapons.

"Holy shit," Sebastian muttered, standing and turning.

Grace nodded. If she could shove Sebastian toward Adare, she might be able to—

Adare's nostrils flared, and her body reacted, stopping her in her tracks. Then he started moving toward her, smooth and graceful, his six-foot-six height and broad chest making him look like the proverbial immovable object.

Sebastian swallowed loudly and backed to her side. "That guy is huge. Like huge, huge." He looked toward her, one fluorescent blue contact falling out of his eye. "What have you gotten me into?"

The lump in her throat nearly choked her. "Nothing. You're fine, but don't go around pretending to be something you're not. Trust me, Sebastian."

"Freddy," the kid croaked. "My name is Freddy. Not Sebastian. I thought that sounded more like a creature of the night."

The huge blond guy's mouth dropped open and then shut quickly.

Oh, this was so bad. She'd tried hard not to leave a trail. Fake name, fake email address, and she'd even moved around to use different library computers and IP addresses—in different towns. What kind of laws had she broken? As far as she knew, there weren't prisons for immortals, so what did that leave? Death for treason?

Not that she wasn't dying anyway.

The blond, his black eyes taking in the entire room, quickly stepped up to the bar and flashed a badge. "U.S. Government. We only want those two for federal crimes."

"Whew," one of the kids in the back sighed.

The bartender shrugged, still drying off a beer glass with a dirty towel. "Take 'em."

Freddy lifted his hands. "I haven't done anything. Really. The chick is nuts. She thought I was a vampire, and she wanted to buy blood, so I figured, why not? Freaky sex might be fun."

"Shut. Up." Adare manacled Freddy's neck with one hand, cutting off all sound. Without taking his gaze off Grace, he flicked his wrist and tossed Freddy toward the blond. "Nick? Take him, please."

The *please*, for some reason, sent shivers down Grace's back. Her legs weakened, but she lifted her chin, facing Adare. It had been nearly three years since they'd crossed paths, and he appeared even better-looking than she remembered. Meaner and bigger, too. A pissed-off expression on him was normal, but this one was new. All heat and fury. "I'll get going, too," she said, taking another step back.

Nick caught Freddy and leaned to the side, holding the human like a rag doll. "Adare? Do you know this female?"

Adare slowly nodded, his focus stronger than any hold. "She's my mate."

"I am not," she retorted.

"Yes. You. Are." Adare's face was as impenetrable as rock, even as the words rolled out with that brogue.

Nick's light eyebrows rose. He looked around the bar and, apparently satisfied that nobody was going to attack, returned his focus to Adare. "What's your mate doing trying to buy vampire blood in Colorado?" he whispered.

It sounded ridiculous. Heat spread up Grace's chest to her face, causing her cheeks to pound.

Adare's gaze followed the heat, making her even warmer. "We're about to get an answer to that question." He held out one broad hand, no leniency on his hard face. "Let's do this somewhere else."

It was an order, not a question.

"No." She said it softly but with authority. The bond of their mating was almost gone, and he had no hold on her. He never would, which suited them both just fine. "This was obviously a mistake, so let's just go our separate ways."

His lids half-lowered, slowly and deliberately, the deadly predator at his core fully visible. Not many people disobeyed the dangerous hybrid, and a human female, one whose life he had saved, shouldn't even have thought about it. But she was no longer his responsibility, and she was done being lost.

"Grace." One word, said in that brogue, with a demand that was absolute.

If she could run, she would. Instead, her body froze, her heart thundering. "I know I goofed up here, and I won't do it again." The appeasing note in her voice ticked her off, but she wasn't up to a physical struggle right now. This disastrous meeting had taken weeks to set up. "Let's just forget this and move on."

"Have you lost your mind?" He sounded more curious than angry.

Hope flared through her. "Yes, briefly. It happens." He'd never wanted anything to do with her, so giving him an out should work nicely. A simple apology—she tried to sound sincere—although she wanted to kick him in the shin instead. He'd always been a jackass, but there was no doubt he'd win any physical fight. Even at her best, which she wasn't close to right now, she couldn't take him. It was doubtful anybody could. "This whole thing was a mistake, and I'm sorry." She choked on the last word.

"Let's go." His hand was still out.

An electric shiver took her. "Adare, I don't think—"

"Exactly. You didn't think." A muscle ticked in his rugged jaw, revealing the effort his control was costing him. "Apparently that's something we need to discuss. At length."

Was that a threat? Yep. That was definitely a threat. "Not a chance," she snapped, drawing on anger to camouflage panic.

Nick turned Freddy and shoved him toward the door. "We need to take this somewhere else," he muttered.

"Not me," Freddy said. "Really. This isn't my fault." He pushed back against Nick, his voice dropping to a whine. "I just wanted to get laid. Whatever she's into, I'm not a part of it. Please. Let me go."

Nick opened the door and propelled him into the snowstorm. The wind shrieked, blowing snow inside.

Adare grasped her upper arm. "Now."

She tugged free. "Absolutely not."

"I wasn't asking." For a big male, he moved surprisingly fast. He ducked his head, and within a heartbeat, she was over his shoulder, heading toward the door.

Her chin hit his lower back, and her stomach lurched, the alcohol she'd consumed stirring around. She pounded against his waist with her good hand, not close to stopping him. This was a disaster. Panic grabbed her, and she tried to struggle but could barely move. "Let me go. Now."

"Hold on to your strength, Grace. You're going to need it." With that, he took her into the storm.

Chapter 2

Adare waited with supreme patience in the driver's seat of the SUV while Grace glared at him from the passenger seat and Nick delivered Freddy, not so gently, to his front door. Or rather, to his mother's front door, since the moron lived in her basement. By the time Nick was finished with his lecture, Freddy would not only forget they existed but would never try to pick up a woman on the internet again.

Grace huffed.

He held on to his patience because he was a patient male. Damn it.

"I could've taken my own car," she muttered.

"That was barely a car," he retorted, watching the snow billow outside. The female was lucky he'd allowed her to fetch her belongings from the death trap. He didn't have time for this, considering his mission commenced in less than twenty-four hours. "I'll have somebody pick it up tomorrow."

She crossed her arms. "I could pick it up tomorrow."

The tightness of his jaw was beginning to give him a headache, so he took pains to loosen it before answering her. "You have a bank account with a hundred thousand dollars in it as well as unlimited funds on various credit cards. Why you were driving that heap of junk is beyond me." She had to be smarter, since he probably wasn't going to make it past the week.

She turned toward him, setting one leg beneath her to face him. "I don't want or need your money."

"You're my mate," he said.

"Hah."

What the hell did that mean? He exhaled slowly. Out of all the females in the universe, why did this one small human get under his skin? "I understand it wasn't a conventional mating, but it happened nonetheless. You're my responsibility." By the widening of her eyes, he could tell she didn't like that. Too bad. It was the truth.

The back door swept open and Nick jumped inside the car, bringing snow and wind with him. "We're good. Let's get out of here." All pure-bred demons had rough voices that sounded like their vocal chords had been mangled; after the night they'd had, Nick sounded like he'd been eating gravel all day.

Adare owed him one for this. He backed out of the driveway, turning the vehicle toward the mountains. "Nicolaj Veis, please meet Grace Cooper. My...mate."

"It's nice to meet you." Nick slid to the side to better study Grace from the back seat. "Although you are a surprise. Adare? Why do you keep so many secrets?" The question in his eyes was more than obvious. How could Adare go on their mission the following day when he had a mate?

She twisted even more to face him. "It's nice to meet you, as well. I'm not really Adare's mate."

Nick rubbed his smoothly shaven chin. "Okay." He glanced from one to the other. "Proposed mates?"

Adare sighed. "No. We mated." He glanced in the rearview mirror. "Can't you sense it?" Normally the mating bond was easily discerned by other immortals, but what did he know?

Nick studied Grace. "Well, kind of, but it's not as strong as I would've assumed."

"We didn't really mate," Grace said, a slight pink flushing her cheekbones. "I was in a coma, about to die, and Adare bit me and marked me. No...well, ah, sex."

Nick's eyebrows shot straight up. "You can't mate without sex."

"We did," Adare said, ending the conversation. The fact that Grace was special, one of the three Keys who were destined to destroy evil, would remain a secret, even from his old friend. Adare believed that was why the mating had taken hold without a physical union. Speaking of which, the woman should be acting grateful and not like a pain in his ass right now. He had enough going on.

Grace rolled her eyes. "Are you a hybrid, too?"

Adare bit back irritation. She had lived in the immortal world for nearly five years, and she couldn't tell a pure-bred demon when she saw one?

"No," Nick said, smiling. "I'm all demon. You can tell from the blond hair and black eyes, as well as the weird voice." He jerked his head toward Adare. "Although I understand your question. Even hybrids usually take on the dominant aspects of only one species, except for your Highlander here. He's unique."

Whatever. Adare had the black hair of a vampire and the pure black eyes of a demon; sometimes, he felt his two halves fighting each other. Which was odd, considering both species were predators. "Nick? I apologize for taking you away from your family vacation. I owe you one." When the king had called saying his computer techs had discovered a possible Key in Colorado, he'd called in Nick as backup. Adare didn't need backup, but when King Kayrs meddled, he went all the way with it. Adare had agreed; he couldn't afford to have the king all up in his business with the mission into Kurjan territory happening soon.

"No problem," Nick said, almost cheerfully. "This has been entertaining. Also, it's getting late. Why don't you two stay in our extra room at the condo for the night? Apparently you have some things to talk about."

"No, thank you," Grace immediately said. "I need to be on my way."

Adare took a turn up the mountain road. He had to get some things straight with Grace before he died, and no doubt Nick's stronghold was well secured and far away from any humans. "We appreciate it, Nick. We apparently do have much to discuss."

* * * *

This night could not get any more embarrassing. The idea that she'd been fooled by some moron who wore fake vampire contacts would haunt Grace forever. She'd love to call her sister and get a laugh out of it, but then she'd have to tell Faith everything, and she couldn't do that. Faith had nearly gotten killed trying to save Grace before—it was time Grace stood on her own feet and stopped relying on her older sister so much.

Nick's condo was more like a spacious lodge than a typical mountain cabin. Warm and welcoming lights spilled out of a multitude of windows in a hand-sewn log building that faced the back side of an imposing ski mountain.

Grace followed Nick up the shoveled front walk to the double wooden door, her camera equipment slung safely over her shoulder.

Nick used a keypad to unlock the door and moved inside, turning left immediately into a dining room where three females sat playing poker with real money all over the table. One was a stunningly beautiful woman with green eyes and dark red hair, while the other two were kids, one probably eleven and the other a couple of years younger.

The youngest looked up, her eyes the green of pure emeralds. "Mom just lost your lake place in Scotland, Dad. You can start paying me rent, any time."

The woman rolled her eyes and stood. Even in jeans and a black sweater, there was something regal about her. "Adare," she breathed, smiling and moving toward him. "It has been too long."

He hugged her gently and then released her. "Simone Brightston, this is Grace Cooper, my mate."

Grace shook Simone's hand, feeling power surge up her arm in response. "Hi."

"Mate?" Simone shook, her eyes dancing. "Aren't you full of secrets?" She slipped an arm through Grace's and pulled her into the dining room. "These are our two monsters, Cadhla and Riona." Cadhla was the older girl, and she had Nick's black eyes and Simone's dark red hair, while Riona had Simone's eyes and white-blond hair. A definite mix of species, perfectly balanced.

"You're on the Coven council?" Grace asked, searching through her faulty memory. Hadn't she heard of Simone? The female was a rather notorious witch.

"Yes, but I'm on vacation now." Simone nodded toward the stacks of paper bills, which included currency from several different countries. "Currently, I'm about to lose one of my favorite motorcycles." She pointed a finger at the younger girl. "You had better not be cheating."

"How?" Riona snorted. "We all agreed that counting cards isn't cheating, and it's not like I can see through cardboard."

Cadhla stood and stretched her neck, her legs long and gangly. "Can I go shop online, now? I want to get Hope something cool for the Valentine's party she's gonna have next month after the grown-up symposium. She's a teenager, so I can't get anything babyish."

Simone waved. "Go ahead." She looked down at Grace, leading her gently beyond the table. "Would you like anything to eat? We finished supper a few hours ago, but I can drum something up for you."

"No, thank you." The whiskey still rumbled around in Grace's belly. "I don't want to put you out. There has to be a hotel somewhere around here." She didn't want to insult a witch, but she had to get out of there. "It's kind of you, but I should be going."

"We're staying," Adare said, walking up behind them. "If you could show us to our quarters, I'd be grateful."

Simone chuckled. "You have the subtlety of a walrus, Highlander."

Heat spiraled into Grace's face. The woman thought she and Adare wanted to be alone. Definitely not.

Even so, she let Simone lead them up hand-carved wooden steps and down a long hallway to a suite at the end. "Our guest suite is stocked with anything you could need, and you have a small kitchenette off the main room if you become peckish," Simone said.

"Thank you." Adare grasped Grace's hand and pulled her into the room. "Goodnight, Simone."

The witch shut the door, and Grace relaxed a little bit. She freed her hand and looked around. The suite held a quaint sitting area by the fireplace, with a king-sized bed in the far corner. One door no doubt led to a master bath, and the other to the kitchenette. "I don't see that we have anything to discuss."

"You're wrong. Sit down," he said, moving to the fire. The massive vampire-demon was all grace and economic motions. His grunt when he flipped a switch and the fire ignited was almost comical. "Fire should be fire," he muttered.

Grace set down her camera equipment, every bone in her body heavy. She sat by the fire and let the flames warm her freezing legs. "Listen. I'm sorry I inconvenienced you."

"Inconvenienced?" He turned, leaned against the stone mantle, and looked down at her.

She winced. "All right. Embarrassed you in front of your friends." No doubt a badass like him didn't want his mate running around trying to buy vampire blood.

"Embarrassed?" His brows came down into a fierce line. "I don't give a shite what anybody else thinks." He paused and then moved to sit in the other oversized chair, his bulk settling into it. He faced her, his bone structure solid stone, chiseled by a master. "I've tried to be as understanding as possible with you."

Everything about him was masculine and strong—and overwhelming. From his size to his intensity to his looks, Adare O'Cearbhaill was as male as male could get.

He took her breath away, and that was on a good day.

She cleared her throat. "I know I owe you for saving my life, and I've tried to stay out of yours, so let's just continue that way."

He looked her over. This close, tiny flecks of silver showed in his black eyes. "You've lost weight and you're pale."

Okay, so she looked like crap. "Thanks so much."

"Grace." Dark tone, definite warning. "I've given you the freedom you wanted, and this is as accommodating as I know how to be. If necessary, I will take you in hand."

Her head jerked and she stood, wanting to tower over him for once. Even so, they were pretty much eye to eye, though he was sitting. "You arrogant, back-in-the-dark-ages jackass." It felt damn good for fury to flow through her veins, so she let the heat have full reign. "I am not yours to do anything with. Not at all. This is not a zillion years ago, the time of the Highlanders, and I don't answer to you." In her anger, she put both hands on her hips, and then winced as pain rocketed through her left arm.

His gaze narrowed. "What's wrong with your hand?"

"Nothing," she snapped.

Quick as a whip, he reached out and grasped her belt loop, tugging her toward him. Then, slowly, deliberately, he circled her bicep and gently pulled her hand away from her hip. His head lifted slowly. "Jesus. What did you do?"

Chapter 3

Adare leaned in to look at Grace's wrist, which was a multitude of colors from yellow to purple and even black. Gingerly, he started to roll it, and she gasped, turning a frightening white. Her knees trembled so much, he could see the shaking through her jeans.

She swallowed. "I need to sit down."

He stood and gently prodded her into her seat, following on his knees in front of her. "I think it's broken." As lightly as he could, he ran his finger over the bones, wincing as he found the break. Maybe one of a couple. "What happened?"

"I fell on the ice on the way inside that stupid bar." She put her head back on the chair and closed her eyes, waves of pain cascading off her. "It happens."

The woman had been dealing with a broken wrist the entire night? Why? "I don't understand. Why don't you heal it?" He'd given her immortality five years ago, and no doubt she'd be fully charged with healing cells by now. This wasn't making sense. "This is why you were trying to purchase vampire blood in the middle of nowhere?"

"Of course not. I wouldn't risk a meeting like that just to heal a broken wrist. I could go and pay cash at an urgent care center." She spoke wearily and didn't open her eyes.

He sat back on his haunches, laying her injured wrist on her thigh, thinking through the entire night. "You are unable to create healing cells?"

She sighed and opened her eyes, the blue dark with pain. "Yes."

"Have you tri—"

"Of course, I've tried," she snapped, twin dots of red blooming and then disappearing in her pale cheeks. "I don't think I ever quite got the skill down, and tonight in that bar wasn't the right time to practice."

He shook his head. "Healing is a skillset, and I figured your sister would've taught you. This is my fault." He was about to die, and he hadn't prepared her to deal with life without the possibility of his protection.

Even in agony, she managed to roll her eyes. "This has nothing to do with you."

There were many things Adare disliked in life—tons of them, actually—and being in the dark about something topped the list. "Why were you trying to get vampire blood?"

She exhaled. "Since we mated, I've helped people whenever I could. If I saw an elderly man with an injury, I'd slip him some of my blood in his coffee and he'd heal quickly."

That was odd. Her blood should've been strong enough to stop an elderly human's heart. "All right," Adare said as calmly as he could. "You were trying to find blood to help old humans?"

"No." The look she gave him prickled irritation down his back. "There's a child at St. Bart's in Greentown, and she has leukemia. My blood hasn't been strong enough to help her."

Adare paused, staring at her. "You're serious?"

"Of course." She jerked her head, her nostrils flaring. "I know you immortals don't care about humans, but I do."

Sometimes he forgot what a complete sweetheart she could be. "Grace. Immortal blood can fix broken bones and wounds, but we've never been able to cure diseases in humans. Not even the common cold." How did she not know this?

"Oh." Her shoulders slumped. "I didn't know that."

What in the world? He'd give anything to erase that defeat on her pretty face. "However, we do have excellent doctors, and I'll make sure they take a look at the little girl. I promise."

"Thanks." Her smile was soft and barely there. "The girl's name is Janell Lewiston, and her prognosis is already good, from what I saw. I volunteer at different hospitals as I move around, and I read her chart. But still, I wanted to give her even better odds."

Grace's name fit her. Even so, this was all so odd. "Why didn't you go to your sister or Ronan?" His blood brother would've called him.

Grace sat up, cradling her wrist. "They're in Kurdistan right now, working on a diplomatic mission, and I didn't want to bother them." She cleared her throat, avoiding his gaze. "I can handle things on my own, Adare. My sister deserves some peace in her life."

Peace? Ha. None of them would find peace for a very long time. "Would you have taken some blood to fix your wrist?" His suspicions were confirmed when she blushed a soft peach. "Have you taken others' blood before?" His reaction to that notion was hot enough to burn him from within.

"No, but I saw Faith take Ronan's blood when she broke her ankle a couple of years ago, and it healed her faster than she could heal herself. So I thought I could take just a little."

"You were wrong. Another male's blood would've probably made you sick." Man, he'd neglected his duties here. That needed to stop and now. So he slid an arm beneath her legs, turned and twisted, sitting on the floor with her cradled in his lap and facing the fire.

"What in the world are you doing?" she gasped, her arm still safe against her ribcage.

"I'm going to help you heal your wrist, and then I'm going to teach you how to use healing cells." Obviously.

She pushed his chest with her good hand, not moving an inch. "I don't want your help. When are you going to realize that I'm not your responsibility? For Pete's sake. I haven't seen you in three years."

Did she sound hurt about that? It was what he'd thought she wanted. Plus, he'd known where she was the entire time, and he'd been on more grueling missions than he could count, some resulting in nightmares that would haunt him forever. "Why didn't you stay at the new Seven headquarters with your sister and Ronan? I wasn't pleased when you left." He kept his voice as level as he could, but the feeling of her soft buttocks against his thighs was heating him faster than the fake fire.

"I'm not concerned about pleasing you." Even her lips were beginning to tremble from the pain.

"Let's argue after we mend your wrist." He forced his fangs down, sliced into the fleshy part of his palm, and instantly drew blood.

Her eyes widened and she pushed against him again. "Listen, no."

"Yes." Careful not to jostle her injured arm, he gripped the back of her head and pressed the side of his hand against her lips.

She shut her lips tight, and her eyes narrowed, sparks all but flying from them.

Anticipation melded with amusement in him, rising up fast. "I have no problem going a round or two with you, *Leannain*, but how about we get you up to par first?" When she still fought him, he didn't relent. "You won't win, Grace." The last thing he wanted to do was bruise her pretty lips, especially when she was already hurting. So he relaxed the pressure and waited a beat. "After this, I shall have to lock you down in Scotland. Period."

She sucked in air through her nose, her temper igniting in front of his eyes. The second she opened her mouth to let him have it, he shoved the bleeding side of his hand between her lips and applied pressure with his hand on the back of her head. Then, just to end the scuffle, he reached around and pinched her nose so she couldn't breathe.

Her mouth opened, and he forced the liquid down her throat, making her take several drinks.

She struggled against him, keeping her injury immobile, and he could swear she growled. Finally, he relented, releasing her head and drawing his hand free to heal.

Her lips, coated in his blood, closed. She swallowed and color burst across her face. Then she gave a small moan and licked her lips.

This was why he'd stayed away from her. He shot from amusement to full on arousal so fast his ears rang.

* * * *

Grace's throat felt like she'd swallowed a sparkler from a fourth of July party. The heat flushed through her, uncoiling and landing in her abdomen. That fast, awareness of the incredibly hard thighs beneath her butt caught her attention. His blood tasted like fire tinged with something sweet. The throbbing in her wrist diminished almost immediately.

His eyes had turned a liquid onyx rimmed with silver. How did anybody coming across him think for a second that he could be human? There was nothing human about Adare. He was something more. Much more.

She moved to scoot off his lap.

"Oh, no." He wrapped an arm around her waist, holding her in place with almost no effort. "We're doing this. Put your wrist on your thigh."

The torture of pain turned to another, entirely different, torture. Desire rippled through her, stopping at every place she didn't want associated with the arrogant Highlander. "Fine." She set her damaged wrist on her thigh.

"Good. Now imagine my blood, full of healing cells, going right to that broken bone."

She closed her eyes to concentrate. As soon as she healed herself, she could get off his lap. So she followed his directions, imagining bossy marching little cells going toward her wrist. The bone snapped back into place, and she jumped, crying out.

"It's okay." His rough voice became soothing. "That was the difficult part. Now send more cells, and they'll take care of the swelling and bruising. Those won't hurt at all."

If she didn't get off him, she was going to turn and attack him full on, her mouth on his, and damn the consequences. He really had no clue how sexy he was, even though he was an ass usually.

Why did bad boys do it for her? Because of the coma, her memories of her prior life were hazy and still came in spurts, but she did remember more than a couple of tough guys in her past.

"Grace? You still with me?"

"Yes." Eek. Her mind had totally wandered. Heat from his body and the fire surrounded her, and the urge to snuggle into the safety of his iron hard chest was almost too much to resist. But he didn't want anything to do with her, and she had to keep that humiliating fact front and center in her brain. No self-respecting woman wanted a male only because his brother had mated her sister and he'd agreed to do his duty and protect her. Taking a deep breath, she utilized whatever the heck healing cells were and fixed her wrist.

"Nicely done." The approval in his tone washed over her skin, prickling awareness.

She opened her eyes. "For a weak and fragile mere human."

He blinked, his eyes back to the full dark of night. "Weak? No. Fragile, yes."

They really needed to get a couple of things straight. "Listen, Adare. I don't like being treated as an unwanted responsibility, and you have to stop thinking of me as such." She really should get off his thighs.

He studied her face, the impact of his gaze nearly physical. "You are my responsibility."

"I am not," she burst out.

He rubbed her shoulder, near her nape, probably unconsciously. "Of course, you are. I mated you, bite and brand, when you were in a coma. You didn't have a choice, and your current circumstances are a result of my actions."

What? She tilted her head. "You saved my life."

"Aye, but you might've wanted to move on to the next one, and I took that choice away from you. Probably for a long time. So you're here, in this life, and you can't be mated to another being, and you can't ever be physical with another male because of the mating allergy. It's not an easy life I subjected you to, without your knowledge or agreement." An emotion, a real one, glittered in his eyes for the briefest of moments before being snuffed out.

There was so much in that one statement, she didn't know where to start. He felt *guilty* about saving her life? "You believe in the afterlife?" Might as well start there.

"Of course," he said, moving to massage her nape and relieve the tension in her neck. "It's impossible to think that this is all there is, right?"

Wow. Okay. Hadn't expected that one. "As for the mating allergy, your facts are outdated." When one immortal mated another, they both ended up with some weird allergy that meant they couldn't be touched, for more than a few seconds, by a member of the opposite sex, or a devastating reaction occurred.

He sighed. "I'm well aware of the virus that negates the mating bond, but it has only been utilized in situations where a mate has been deceased for at least a century."

"So what?"

"The prevailing theory is that with the mate gone, the strength of the mating bond slowly dissipates, making it easier for the virus to finish it." He stopped the massage, and she wanted to protest.

"You've looked into it?" That shouldn't have hurt, it really shouldn't have. So why did her chest feel as if she'd taken a punch?

"Just in case you found somebody else you wanted to spend eternity with." The charm of his rueful smile was too much to take.

Rumor had it that Adare had had his heart broken a century ago or so by a female shifter who'd chosen somebody else, which just seemed impossible. "Oh. What about your finding somebody else? Some badass immortal who isn't so fragile?" She might have sounded a little bitter on the last part.

"No. The final battle, the one we're gearing up for, will result in too many deaths to be looking for mates."

She shook her head. "Your brother warriors, the Seven, are all getting mated, so they must have some hope of surviving."

The Seven were made up of seven vampire-demon hybrids whose mission was to kill a psychopath named Ulric. As far as she understood, Ulric was an immortal crazy bastard who, for some bizarre reason she'd never really studied, wanted to kill all enhanced female humans on the planet. Maybe it was time she figured all of this out. "The idea that the Seven will sacrifice their lives in the fight with Ulric is outdated, my friend."

"Even so, not all of us will survive. Somebody will leave a mate behind." He glanced at the clock above the fireplace. "Besides, the Seven were never meant to mate. Although that vow seems to have disappeared with time."

Oh. She moved to get off his lap. "Or is your reluctance to mate because of the shifter who broke your heart so long ago?" The spurt of jealousy that slammed into her didn't make a lick of sense. "She must've been strong and dangerous and deadly." Just his type, and just her opposite. "Are you still in love with her and mourning what you lost?"

"No." He stood along with her, effectively cutting off discussion. "We can practice with healing cells more tomorrow. It's a skill you must develop, and now that you're healthy, we can work on it."

She shook out her legs and looked down at her perfectly healed wrist. Oh, it must be nice to have that skill, but she would never have the chance to perfect it, although she wasn't going to give him the full truth about her health. There was nothing he could do, and it was too much having him near. Maybe it was because of the failed mating, or maybe he was just that sexy, but she couldn't *think* when he was around. "I appreciate your bringing me out of the coma and saving my life. Please don't feel guilty or responsible any longer." Absolving him was the least she could do.

He ignored her words and looked around the room, stopping at the bed. "For tonight, we need sleep."

She followed his gaze. In the same bed?

Chapter 4

Many years ago, during one of the earlier wars, Adare had been captured and tortured for a month by a psychotic shifter out of Alaska. Once he'd freed himself, it had taken a year to fully regain his strength. That was nothing compared to the agony of lying in bed next to Grace Cooper and not reaching for her.

He'd acceded to her wishes these past five years to let her live her life. That had seemed only fair, considering she'd had no say in being mated for eternity to him. But in order to grant her that freedom, he'd had to stay away, because the female was just too tempting. Now that he was headed into the lion's den in a day, he needed to let her go. Completely. Not that he'd ever really had her.

She lay on her side, facing away from him, her thick brown hair splayed out on the pillow, the mass naturally curly and enticing.

Her sigh echoed down to his balls. "For a guy who wanted to sleep, you're sure not sleeping." She rolled over to face him, resting her cheek on her now healed hand, her pretty eyes clear.

"A lot on my mind." Like taking that luscious mouth beneath his—he didn't want to leave this world with any regrets.

"Yeah, I get that." She stretched, barely making a lump beneath the luxurious covers. "It's weird. You and me and being in bed together. It's just so weird."

Weird wasn't the word he'd have used. "I left you alone these five years because that's what I thought you wanted." Why in the world was he explaining himself? "And, if I'm honest, I've been pretty centered on my mission."

"What have you been doing?" She yawned and covered the motion with her hand.

"Wasting a lot of time," he said frankly. He couldn't tell her about the fight to come, once the timing was just right, the suicide mission. She'd find out soon enough. However, she knew about the three Keys, so maybe he could try to keep the conversation going. "We've been trying to find the final Key before the Kurjans do, and so far, tonight was the best lead we've had." Which, of course, had led them right to Grace and not to the one missing Key. "You know you can't share details about yourself ever again on the internet, right?"

She nodded. "Yeah. Figured that one out on my own. Sorry."

Her own inability to heal her injured wrist still didn't make sense to him. "Perhaps we should make an appointment with the queen." Queen Emma Kayrs was the best geneticist, scientist, and doctor in the entire world.

"I'm meeting with her when she returns home. She's attending the same symposium as my sister and Ronan." Grace's gaze traced his face, a sadness in her eyes that caught him in the chest. "You seem even angrier than before, and that's saying something. What else have you been doing besides searching for the last Key?"

His gut ached. "The Kurjans have been taking enhanced females, and we've had to rescue several before they were either forced to mate or be killed." Often too late, unfortunately. The Kurjans were a powerful and frightening race that just needed to be put down, and he was willing to make the ultimate sacrifice to make it happen. If he could give his blood brothers and Grace a decent future, he'd do it.

"Since the Kurjans can't go out in the sun, I'd think you all would have a huge advantage," she murmured.

"You'd think." It was amazing how much evil could happen without daylight.

She shook her head. "I just don't understand why they want to kill all enhanced humans. After all, they need mates, too."

Adare's body thrummed at being so close to her, and he struggled to keep the discussion going. Vampires and Kurjans produced males only, unlike the other races. "There's a possibility they have a cure for their poison and can keep their mates safe. Plus, I think perhaps Ulric is the only one who wants enhanced females dead, because he's psychotic. Thinks he's some sort of religious cleanser. But don't worry. We have him contained in a separate world, and he's not getting free." Which was a falsehood. There was no doubt Ulric would eventually free himself, and Adare meant to make sure he had nothing to return to—no forces to use in a fight.

Grace snorted. "Not even I believe that."

Fair enough. Unable to help himself, Adare reached over and slid her shirt to the side, revealing a birthmark in the shape of an old-fashioned key on her upper chest. "He will be helpless, hopefully dead, before you have to get involved."

Her heartbeat increased beneath his finger. "You don't believe that. Fate dictates that the blood of three Keys is the only thing that can kill Ulric, and you know it."

Did she believe in legends? Fate? "You've accepted this?"

"Nope. I think you're all way too into history and the prophecies of the past, to be honest." She shook her head. "I don't believe in fate at all, in fact."

If that helped her sleep at night, so be it. He released her, his body aching. "I think I'll go for a run in the snow." Maybe it'd clear his mind.

"Wait." The feeling of her hand on his bare chest nearly snapped the chains around his control.

He stilled, tension cascading down his arms. "I'm doing my best here, but this is too difficult."

She frowned in confusion. "What is?"

"Being in bed with you." He gave her the truth, which was what she'd do for him. There was no coyness or subterfuge in

Grace Cooper, which only made her more intriguing. The woman wouldn't know how to lie with a gun pointed at her heart. "You're far too appealing."

Surprise widened her eyes. "Are you serious?" she asked. Did she truly not know how tempting she was? "Well, I guess it has been a long time for you, considering the limitations of the mating bond and all." Her voice was thoughtful now.

Was that guilt in her eyes? "What the hell is wrong with you, female?" he muttered. "You have no clue of your allure."

She chuckled, and there was irony in the sound. "Allure? Are you kidding me?"

"No." He frowned.

She shook her head. "Come on. Faith was always the beautiful one. I was her fun and goofy younger sister. The creative one with no curves and our grandpa's nose. I can promise you that nobody in my entire life has called me alluring."

"Your grandpa had a perfect nose, then." Straight and delicate, like the rest of her. Sure, Faith was pretty, but Grace was unique, stunning. Beautiful and filled with a light that had no doubt drawn people to her all her life. Since he'd known her, she'd been quiet, staying on the sidelines, often lost behind her camera taking photographs that now graced palaces in faraway lands.

She sighed. "Anyway, I lost the fun after the coma, and I think I lost the goofy part, too. Brain injuries change a gal." Her obvious attempt to lighten her painful circumstances made him sad. "You don't have to lie to me."

That was it. Just plain and simple *it*. He grasped her arm, rolled her so she was lying on top of him and settled back. "How's this for proof?"

* * * *

Holy crap, the immortal had a raging hard-on. Grace heated, head-to-toe. Lying on him was like spreading out on asphalt warmed by hot lava all day. With her core pressed against his, her mind tried to switch off and let her body take over. "Okay. That's proof."

His grin briefly relaxed the solid rock wall of his face. This almost playful side of him stole her ability to speak. "You're beautiful, fun, and no doubt still goofy," he murmured, his hand splaying entirely across her lower back. "I regret we didn't spend the last few years at least getting to know each other, but you will be taken care of in the future."

Did that sound like goodbye? Did he somehow know her plan? "I don't understand." She let her knees fall on either side of his hips, and he was so big, her thighs had to widen.

He groaned.

Her breath caught, and she watched, fascinated, as his eyes changed from black to molten silver. The color was still dark, deep instead of lustrous. What was happening right now? Her body tightened in need and her heartrate kicked up, while desire tore through her with a power she couldn't contain. "Why have you avoided me for five years?" Why the heck had that come out of her mouth? Where was her pride?

"There are many reasons, and most are work-related." His breath was minty with a hint of whiskey on it.

"If I didn't know better, I'd think you liked me," she murmured breathlessly, caught by the sensation of her clit rubbing against his erection.

"You're sweet and kind and wouldn't lie to save your life," he said, sliding his hand through her hair.

She blinked. Boy, had he read her wrong. "Adare, I—"

"We could've probably been friends," he continued, watching her curls play over his large hand. "If I had friends other than my Seven brothers."

Friends? Oh yeah. Internally, she deflated like a squashed grape. He had only mated her out of duty. Period. Where was her pride? She'd forgotten his type was badass killer cougar shifters, not fragile humans who broke their wrists falling on the ice. "Wait a minute. That was past tense." He must have figured out what she needed to do the following week. She was surprised he was so accepting.

Regret twisted his upper lip. "I should've told you before now. The mission we've been setting up for the last couple of years takes place a day from now. The chances of my survival are slim."

"Mission? What mission?" She pushed herself up on his chest with both hands to better study his face. Unfortunately, that motion pressed her core harder against his, and mini explosions rocketed up her body, tightening her breasts.

Red darkened his cheekbones. "We're taking out the Kurjan headquarters and saving what captives we find. Shock, awe, and destruction."

She blinked. "What? Ronan didn't say anything." Faith would be beside herself with concern.

Adare tightened his hold in her hair, slightly lifting her head back. "Ronan isn't going. It's Benny and me. Just us."

Panic clawed through her and she scrambled to sit up. He held her securely in place with just one hand. "Two of you taking on the entire headquarters of one of the most dangerous species on Earth? It's suicide."

"Aye." Almost causally, he twisted his wrist, tilting her head. "We can only afford to lose two of us in case we fail. They'll have to find two more members to make the Seven, and that's difficult."

Her chest ached. There were two unmated members of the Seven, Benny Reese and Garrett Kayrs. Well, three if Adare was counted, which he might as well be. The Seven were a secret group of vampire-demon hybrids tasked with destroying Ulric in some bizarre ritual that she was also to attend as a Key. Sometimes she wondered if the immortals had just lost their minds. "Why not Garrett?"

Adare shook his head. "Garrett's uncle is the King of the vampires and the Realm, and we need them on our side if Benny and I can't end things with our mission."

The Realm was a coalition of immortal species, excluding the Kurjans, and it was run by King Dage Kayrs. She would probably see the king the following week when she met with his wife, Emma. "I don't understand why it's just the two of you and not a whole contingent of soldiers. Why not take Realm soldiers?"

Adare nodded, rubbing his thumb across her cheekbone. "I think sometimes you forget that the Seven isn't part of the Realm, and they don't agree with our mission. Most of them don't even know about us or what we plan to do in the end. We're a secret, and don't ever forget that. If the king of the vampires started a new war with the Kurjans, without the approval of the witch, shifter, and demon nations, then the Realm would split apart. It was before your time, but not too long ago, that the Realm was at war with the demon nation. We can't let that happen again."

She would have thought immortal beings should have progressed to the point of not going to war, and yet it seemed they hadn't. "So you and Benny are going in as just two crazy immortals and blowing things up. Everybody else has plausible deniability." She'd heard the phrase on a Netflix television show.

"The King and the Realm dinnae know," Adare murmured. "They have no clue."

Well, that didn't sound like a complete disaster, did it? "This just seems like a bad idea." Her body was rioting with need, and her mind was fighting to stay in control.

His gaze dropped to her lips. "Sure, it's a bad idea, but it's all we've got. If we can take out Kurjan headquarters and many of their top soldiers, maybe we can avoid a final showdown, and you won't have to worry about it. Nobody will. If I'm gone, Grace, in about a century, you could take the virus. Maybe mate again."

Anger grabbed her tight. "I don't need a sacrificial lamb, Highlander." She pushed at his chest again to get off him.

He barked out a laugh. "I'm doing my job, little female. That's all." Still holding her in place with one hand tangled in her hair, he drew her inexorably toward him. "Though I wouldn't mind a goodbye kiss." With that, he pulled her down, and his mouth took hers.

Completely.

The kiss was hard and long, deep and seeking. Everything inside her quieted and then exploded, sparks flying throughout her body. She moaned and kissed him back, trying to keep up and feeling so much all at once that she just let go and let him lead.

Finally, he released her, his eyes completely dark silver, and desire stamped hard on his face. "That's why, Grace. That's why I've left you alone for five years."

Chapter 5

Adare could still taste Grace on his tongue. Sweet like honey with the spice of passion mixed in. Turning away from her after their kiss the night before had nearly killed him, but finally she'd dropped into dreamland. He'd listened to her soft breathing for hours, wondering what they might've been like together.

The morning came, hard and snowy, as he stood with her on the front porch of Nick's condo after having said goodbye to Simone and the girls, who had set out for the ski lodge. He kept Grace beneath the sprawling overhang, making sure she stayed dry as they waited. Clouds covered the sky, bringing a darkness to the day that matched his mood.

Nick walked outside and handed over a case. "You know how to use these?"

"Yes." Adare set the explosives down carefully.

Nick looked at him. "We've been friends a long time, and I know there have been secrets. I'm fine with that fact. If you need my assistance with whatever is going on, then let me know. With that kind of firepower, you'll need backup."

Yes, but his old friend had a mate and two young, rather wild children. "I appreciate the offer and will call if I need help." Adare leaned in for a hug. "Until then, have fun with your family." To see Nick Veis, one of the most dangerous demons in history, settled down with Simone and the girls warmed Adare through and through. "Stay safe, my friend."

"And you." Nick winked at Grace. "Take care of him." With that, he jogged around the cabin, no doubt running up the hill to meet up with his family. Hopefully they'd enjoy warm food at the lodge and not venture out into the oncoming storm.

Grace looked down at the innocuous metal box resting by her thick black boots. "I think this is a bad idea."

"I'm sure it is." He lifted her chin with one knuckle. "Before we leave, I want your promise that you'll learn how to use healing cells and that you'll stay out of danger. I have a car coming for you that will take you to the airport, where Realm transportation is waiting."

She stepped back. "The queen won't return until next week. I'll head to Idaho at that time so we can figure out why I was unable to heal my wrist."

Adare shook his head. "No. Sorry. With this campaign, I need you safe and protected in case the Kurjans take revenge."

"They don't know about me," she protested, her cheeks a healthier hue today and her eyes a sparkling greenish brown. "Nobody does. You made sure I had perfect new ID four years ago. And the Realm doesn't even know about the Seven—well, not much about you, remember?"

"Aye." He'd allowed her plenty of freedom as she'd regained her strength, knowing that Ronan and Faith were always nearby at the Seven headquarters. "You're staying at Realm headquarters until Ronan and Faith return from the symposium." If Adare had realized they were out of the country and Grace was arranging meetings with morons from the internet, he would've interceded sooner. "This is non-negotiable."

"Fine." She looked adorable all bundled up in a thick blue jacket with a matching hat.

A pang hit him, square in the heart. What might've been. "*A stream may fork, bend back, and rush along, but will always flow down in the end,*" he murmured.

She finished slipping on her gloves. "What was that?"

"A poem from my youth. It means that fate is set, no matter what we do." He often wondered about fate, about his calling, about the shield that protected his body from within his skin. Had there ever been a choice? "Promise me you'll go to Realm headquarters, have the queen take a look at you, and then stay with Ronan and Faith until your safety is assured." He'd never had a regret in his life, but one kiss the night before had him rethinking choices that were long set.

She studied him. "All right. I promise."

Good. His shoulders finally relaxed as much as possible under the circumstances. Oh, he shouldn't have kissed her the night before, but regretting the moment was impossible. He'd wondered how she would taste for years, and now he knew. Like perfection.

A light pink covered her cheeks. "So. Um." Her gaze cast around as if looking for somewhere to land. Then she frowned. "That box isn't big enough for a full assault, is it? Don't you need more weapons or something?"

Or something. "Benny is meeting with a source on the way here to get us what we need." It was a good thing Benjamin Reese had connections all over the world for all sorts of shady things.

As if on cue, a black SUV roared up the drive, spinning snow in every direction. The vehicle slid to a stop, and Benny Reese jumped out, all six-and-a-half feet of him. His abnormally large boots slammed through snow and ice, and he jogged toward them. "Grace Cooper, I've missed you." He grabbed Grace up and swung her around, setting her down before the mating allergy could grab hold and give him a rash. Mated people were unable to touch a member of the opposite sex. Ever. "You sweetheart, you." Benny's voice boomed off the mountains around them. He slapped Adare on the back. "Hey, brother. It's a good week to die, no?"

"No," Adare growled, his skin prickling. He had it bad. Benny was one of his best friends, and the hug with Grace was harmless. Even so, he had to force his fangs back where they belonged. "I'm hoping we live."

"Ditto," Benny said cheerfully, his barrel of a chest ensconced in a black leather jacket that must've been special ordered. His metallic eyes told another story. One of loss and absolution, tinged with sorrow. He wasn't ready to die, either. "Maybe we'll get lucky."

"Maybe." The chances weren't good. Another vehicle drove sedately up the road below—this one for Grace. "Did you get our, ah, supplies?"

"Yep." Benny motioned toward the darkened SUV. "The shifters in the area are excellent barterers, but I got a sweet deal. For some reason, they wanted to meet you in person before we go."

Adare frowned. "My name wasn't to be mentioned."

Benny shrugged. "They knew of you, knew of our connection, and that was that."

Odd. "All right." Adare looked toward the SUV, but with the windows shielded, he couldn't see inside.

The passenger door opened, and a streak of red jumped out, slamming it shut. A female strode around the vehicle, her curvy body protected by dark jeans and a red coat. "Adare. Good to see you."

He stiffened, his back straightening. "Jacqueline. This is a surprise."

"Jacqueline?" Grace asked, turning to face the newcomer.

Jacqueline stepped confidently through the snow.

Benny grinned. "Grace, meet Jacqueline, Adare's ex-fiancée. Jackie? Meet Grace. Adare's mate."

Oh, Adare was going to kill Benny for this.

* * * *

Grace held out her hand. "It's a pleasure." She shook the shifter's hand, seeing exactly what Adare had liked in the woman. She was freaking gorgeous. Long, tawny hair, straight and thick, hung almost to her waist. Her eyes were a strong topaz, sparkling and intelligent, while her features were slim and feline. She was almost six feet tall and perfectly curvy. Like, perfectly. The only flaw Grace could see was that the shifter had chosen another male over Adare. Man, she'd have liked to see *that* guy.

"Adare." Jacqueline leaned in and kissed him quickly on the cheek. "Congratulations on the mating."

"Thanks." Adare didn't move. "What are you doing here?"

The female purred slightly. Okay. More than slightly, and definitely sexily. "I wanted to see you and to ask why you need this amount of explosives. Also, several of these bombs are homemade, and you're going to need me to show you the correct detonation sequence. It'll be like old times, right? I'm available."

Yeah, Grace would just bet she was. She cleared her throat, ignoring the stomachache that had been her constant companion for almost six months as her strength drained away. Hopefully it was just some weird immortal—kind of immortal—virus. At least she wasn't throwing up constantly the way she had been last month. "You're a demolitions expert?"

Jacqueline chuckled. "I have a way with explosives, yes. We used to blow a lot of things up." How in the world did the shifter make that sound sexy? Must be a gift.

Grace kept her smile in place. "I understand you're mated?" Yeah, she really had to see the male Jacqueline had picked over Adare.

Jacqueline tucked her hands in her pockets. "I was, yes. He's no longer with us." Her voice softened, and she kept her gaze squarely on Adare. "We all did our duty in the last two wars, and the battles were hard on every species, some more than others. We're just rebuilding now, and sales of explosives like these definitely help my people."

Guilt swamped Grace. "I'm sorry for your loss."

Jacqueline smiled, finally turning to face Grace. "That's kind of you. Basel and I were a political match, and we made a good one. It has been difficult without him, but time moves on, and so do people."

A political match? What did that mean? Was the woman trying to tell Adare something? Not that it mattered. Adare hadn't mated

Grace for political reasons. It was a favor to her sister's mate, actually. She tried to watch Adare's reaction from the corner of her eye, but he was giving nothing away. No expression, no emotion.

Which meant there was a whole lot of emotion. Well, probably. It wasn't like she really knew him.

Benny watched the exchange and edged a mite closer to Grace. Was he actually offering support? For Pete's sake. She didn't need Benny's pity.

The massive hybrid brushed snow off his long black hair. "I told Jacqueline we couldn't take anybody with us on this mission, but she wouldn't sell me the goods unless I brought her to you."

Well. That wasn't obvious or anything. Grace shook herself. The only thing she'd ever blown up was a microwave, one of the memories she still had after her coma. What had she been like before? Would she have challenged the shifter?

Why? It wasn't as if she and Adare were together. What little claim she had on him was rapidly disappearing if the fading of her mark told her anything, and if he'd truly loved this chick, didn't he deserve happiness? Well, if he and Benny didn't die on the next mission. Although he could probably do better. If they stood in the snow any longer, the woman would start rubbing herself all over him. Grace bit back a smile. This catty side was new to her. Or maybe it was the old her coming back.

"Grace?" Adare said.

She blinked. "Oh. Sorry. I was in my head again. Did you say something?"

Jacqueline looked down from her impressive height, her brow furrowing and her eyes gleaming. "I asked you why you weren't going on the mission."

Direct hit. Everyone knew that fragile humans didn't go blow things up.

Adare frowned. "You obviously don't remember me well if you think I'd allow my mate on a mission that involved explosives from the Ledoni shifters."

So he'd known the explosives were coming from his ex-fiancée? He hadn't said a word. Wait a minute. *Allow?* He'd said allow. In front of his ex-love.

Benny groaned.

"Now wait a minute—" Grace started.

"No," Adare countered immediately. "Even if you'd learned how to heal yourself by now, I wouldn't let you go on a mission like this."

Heat blasted into Grace's face.

Benny peered down, his jaw going slack. "You can't heal yourself yet?"

Grace whirled on Adare. "Would you just shut up?"

He drew back, both dark eyebrows rising. "I didn't know that was a secret." Confusion clouded his gaze before quickly clearing. "It's okay. Sometimes the skill takes time."

Oh, God. Now Adare was trying to reassure her.

Jacqueline nodded, the glitter in her eyes cutting. "That's true. Did you just get mated recently?"

"Five years ago," Benny said helpfully.

For the first time, Grace understood the expression of someone wanting the ground to open up and swallow them whole. It had never made a lot of sense before. Now, she got it. "I haven't had much chance to work on the skill. My job doesn't get too dangerous." Yep. That sounded lame.

Benny nodded. "Grace is an amazing photographer. She captures moments nobody else sees."

Jacqueline patted her shoulder. Actually freakin' patted her. "So, you take pictures. That's nice." If any more condescension dropped from her mouth, it'd stain the snow.

"Well, there's a skill to getting the right angle and moment that are beyond many, ah, people," Grace returned smoothly. Yep. *Direct hit right back at ya, dumb animal.* Her phone buzzed, and she glanced at the face. "Um, I have to take this. Excuse me." She lifted the phone to her ear and dodged inside. "Hey, Doc," she whispered, heading for the kitchen. "Tell me you have good news."

"Nope," Dr. Palendrom said, his cheerful disposition gone. "Your bloodwork is worse, meaning the mating is completely disappearing from your body, which isn't a surprise since you mated without the sexual component."

Yeah, no kidding. She closed her eyes and pinched the bridge of her nose. "If my chromosomes unravel from mate to human, will I end up back in a coma?"

"I have absolutely no clue," the doctor said. "This is uncharted territory."

Okay. She'd never asked this, but she had to know all the facts. "What if we mate again?" Not that she'd ask Adare. But still.

"Again, I don't know, but it looks like his cells are attacking yours instead of strengthening them, so if I had to bet, I'd wager that a second mating would kill you." The doctor sighed. "You really need to see the queen—she's the expert in this situation. Well, with genetics. There never has been this *situation*." He coughed. "I'm totally guessing, but if you took the virus, negated the mating and somehow survived, you could conceivably mate some other immortal whose cells don't try to kill you."

It figured the best kisser on the planet would be unexpectedly trying to kill her on a cellular level. Time was not on her side. Adare wouldn't like it, but she had to finish what she'd started and get some answers in case she soon faced coma or death. Nobody understood how it felt to have blanks in your memory that tortured you every night. If she was going to die anyway, she'd die knowing who she'd been. Maybe who she could've been. She couldn't let Adare stop her. "Thanks, Doc." She hung up and hustled back outside, ready to say goodbye.

Her car and driver rolled to a stop, its headlights piercing the darkened winter day.

"Let's go, Grace," Adare said, reaching to pluck up her camera bag. Did he sound relieved? She could swear he sounded relieved.

With one last fake smile at Jacqueline, Grace stepped out from the protective overhang toward her car, wondering when she'd lost her mind. What did she care that a snotty feline shifter was making the moves on Adare? Would the old her have punched Jacqueline in the nose? It was doubtful.

Suddenly, all four doors of the black sedan opened at once.

"Grace!" Adare bellowed, turning and lunging toward her.

Chapter 6

Adare smelled the enemy a split second before the first boot hit the ground. Sour lemons. He dropped the bags and pivoted, manacling one arm around Grace's waist and twisting to shot-put her over the hood of the SUV. She flew high, her arms windmilling as she disappeared on the other side. Before she hit the ground, he turned and charged, head down, into the chest of the driver, smashing him against the rear door. Glass shattered and metal dented with a loud crunch.

Bullets pinged above his head, and he rolled the soldier over, punching repeatedly toward the bastard's face. Blood began to blend with his blackish red hair, and the driver struck up, slicing Adare's neck with a knife.

Blood arced and pain lashed through Adare's head. He growled, letting his fangs drop low, while sending emergency healing cells to the injury. The Kurjan beneath him, his eyes a swirling purple, struck up again.

Adare blocked the blade and went into a pure fighting state, which was where he belonged.

The Kurjan clapped a hand against Adare's ear, grabbed his hip, and rolled them across the icy ground. Thunderous pain clashed through Adare's head, but he reached down and drew his knife from his boot as they moved, slashing up and through the Kurjan's white skin from beneath his jaw to his brain.

The monster flopped down, and Adare shoved the heavy body off. The guy would be out for a while. Adare crouched against the vehicle to take in the scene. It was dark enough that the Kurjans probably didn't need the caps they'd donned, and there was no sight of the sun beneath the clouds. Damn it. He wouldn't mind the sun frying the bastards. Two Kurjans remained on the other side of the vehicle from him, shooting wildly at the SUV while Jacqueline leaned around the side and returned fire.

At the rear of the SUV, Benny fought hand-to-hand with the final Kurjan, their movements so fast they were only blurs. Blood spurted from them both, and the glint of silver could barely be seen through the storm.

Adare was too big to roll beneath the sedan, so he edged toward the front, planning to jump over and take down one of the shooters.

Two more vehicles burst up the road, traveling so fast the gravel beneath the ice spun up.

"Grace? Get into the SUV and lock the doors," he bellowed. "If you have to, drive out of here." It was doubtful she'd make it past the other two SUV's headed up the drive. He plunged his blade into the front left tire of the Kurjans' sedan and slid to the back to take care of the other one.

Benny punched through the throat of the Kurjan he was fighting and tossed the body to the ground, instantly stomping on the neck to decapitate the enemy. This Kurjan had red hair with black tips, and his pale skin melded with the snow as the head rolled away.

If there were eight more Kurjan soldiers in the oncoming vehicles, Adare had to get Grace inside the house and now. They could defend that position until reinforcements arrived.

Benny ran around the SUV, firing over his shoulder at the two shooters, no doubt deciding the same thing.

Adare took a deep breath, caught Jacqueline's eye, and she nodded, prepared to provide cover. She partially stood just as he bunched to run, sliding across the ice to the SUV and around it, landing behind her and pressing his back to the vehicle. "Thanks."

She ducked down, excitement dancing in her eyes. "Plan?"

Grace crouched on her knees, her hands on the SUV. "I need a gun," she said, her eyes wide.

He reached to the back of his waist for the Max-20, one of the Realm's most deadly firearms, and handed it over. "Aim for center mass."

She took the weapon and it looked far too large in her delicate hands, which were shaking. The cold had turned her skin pink, but her movements were deliberate.

Benny leaned around the rear of the SUV and fired as more bullets impacted the vehicle, shredding glass and metal in every direction. The tires popped with loud hisses, and the engine blew with the sound of metal shrieking. The smell of gasoline and other liquids morphed together into a warning that they should flee and now.

Adare grasped Grace's arm. "We need to run for the house." He had to cover Grace and fire, and he'd be faster carrying her than dragging her. "Just hold on to me." He looked toward Benny. "Provide cover until I hit the porch, and then I'll do the same for the two of you once I get Grace inside."

"I can shoot," Grace said, her voice harsh.

"Once we're inside the home," Adare said. The female had trouble healing an injured wrist; who knew what a series of immortals' bullets would do to her. "Get ready."

The first SUV rolled to a stop, and three Cyst jumped out. The elite soldiers and so-called spiritual leaders of the Kurjan nation rarely engaged in small skirmishes. In the eerie darkness, their creepy white hair and red eyes made it look as if evil had decided to join the fight.

"Shit," Benny muttered, firing rapidly.

A whoosh of sound penetrated the storm, an explosion cracked, and the entire area was lit by fire. Wood and debris flew in every direction through the snowstorm, falling fast. Adare grasped Grace and folded his body over hers, grunting as a coffee pot slammed into his back. Even though his torso was protected by his Seven shield, the impact still jolted his body. Heat flashed toward them.

Adare waited a beat to make sure nothing else was falling before turning to see what remained of the flaming cabin. The Kurjans had blown up the entire structure.

Benny ducked low as a multitude of shots slammed into the SUV and the trees behind them. "New plan?"

Adare pulled Grace up, keeping her pinned against the rear tire and safe from fiery falling debris. A hill, thick with snow and trees, rose behind them, leading to a mountain. If they went that way, they'd be easy to track, and the going would be too slow to find safety.

The second SUV came up on the other side, and three more Kurjans, their black hair visible against the snow, jumped out of the car. They were fully armed.

"Think we can get out of here with two tires blown?" Jacqueline twisted back to the sedan, her gun in hand.

"Not far," Adare said. "Ben? Can you get to the explosives in the rear of the SUV?"

Benny, blood flowing down from a cut above his eyebrow, nodded. "Might as well give it a try. They're gonna blow anyway."

He had a point. "I'll cover you." Adare looked at Grace, who'd gone stark white. "Keep your back to the tire so they can't shoot you beneath the carriage. I'll be right back."

She nodded, her eyes dark with shock, her hands surprisingly steady on the gun.

Jacqueline edged around the front again. "Feels like old times, right?"

Even in the old times, they'd never been outgunned like this.

The shooting stopped for a moment. Adare paused, looking at Benny, whose face was set in furious lines.

A loud voice, garbled yet strong, came through the storm. "Just give us the Key, and we'll go."

Well, shit.

* * * *

The Key? Grace held her position against the snow-covered tire, her mind swirling. This was her fault. Obviously the Kurjans had found her interaction with Freddy on the internet and had managed to trace her here. Now Nick and Simone's house had been blown up, and there was no escape from the fight. There was only one solution that would keep everyone from being killed. She swallowed, sucking in freezing air. "They won't kill me. Yet. I'll go."

Adare turned his head almost in slow motion to face her. Bruises mottled the left side of his face, and blood trickled from beneath his jaw. "Have you lost your mind?"

She clutched the heavy weapon with her gloves, even though her hands were freezing. Her stomach cramped, but her mind quickly calculated the odds. They sucked. "No. There's no way out of here, and we're definitely outnumbered. They have to have all three Keys to kill at once, and they'll only have me." She'd at least understood that much of the mythology. She knew her plan made sense. Her voice shook, but she couldn't stop it. "That'll give you time to find me." With a lot more soldiers at his back.

"No." He motioned for Benny to get the explosives out of the rear of the SUV. "I smell gas. We need to get away from this thing."

"You have five seconds to decide," the booming voice continued.

Taking a deep breath, Grace levered herself up to look through the broken windows. With one glance, every organ in her body froze. She'd never seen Cyst soldiers in real life, and they were much bigger than in the drawings Adare had shown her years ago. These were the religious leaders of the Kurjans, but they looked like the bringers of death. One stood in the headlights of the SUV, his stance wide, weapons visible against his black uniform. A strip of white hair down his head continued into a long braid; the remainder of his head was bald and paler than the snow. Despite the storm and distance, she could see that his eyes were an odd purplish red. He apparently stopped counting and reached for a glowing green gun at his waist.

"Wait," she called out. "Just give me a minute."

He paused, his gaze swinging toward her location.

"Stop it," Adare hissed.

Benny pulled the back hatch open an inch. Then another.

Grace panted as her heart rate sped up uncontrollably. In addition to the Cyst, there were at least seven Kurjans spread out, all armed, all waiting. They had either black hair tipped with red or red hair tipped with black, frighteningly pale skin, and light, purplish eyes. Most were closer to seven feet tall than six, and they were lean and muscled. The drawings she'd seen hadn't done justice to how frightening they appeared. She looked up at the sky, praying for a hint of sun to weaken them.

The clouds were too thick.

Benny pulled a long box out of the hatch and slid it back to Adare, who ripped it open.

It was ten Kurjans and Cysts to the four of them, and though she knew Adare and Benny were good, nobody was that good. Grace bunched her legs to run.

"You won't make it," Adare said grimly, not looking up from a set of six square gray blocks with silver pins. "But start bargaining with them as I set these."

Okay. She could do this. Her stomach rolled over and she forced herself not to gag. "Um, promise you won't kill me," she yelled, not having to make her voice shake since it did so on its own. They didn't answer, so she cleared her throat and tried to kick some ice loudly to give the impression that she was on the move. She had no clue what she was doing.

Adare pressed something on the gray squares and handed a couple to Benny, took several, and then pushed the box toward Jacqueline. "You still have an arm?"

The shifter nodded, her eyes gleaming. "Definitely, and you're gonna like these explosives. They're new generation."

"Okay." Adare crouched, one in each hand. "Benny, you throw at the group to the left, Jacki right, and I'll hit the bastard in the middle. Grace, the second these land, you shoot through the window at anything still moving, but keep your body down. On two."

She couldn't breathe. A buzzing set up between her ears, but she clutched the gun, waiting for the signal. Thank goodness she'd spent the last five years learning to protect herself.

"Two," Adare muttered, standing up and heaving the square toward the Cysts while the other two did the same.

There was a beat of silence and then a rush of movement. Three explosions echoed in a row, and a cry of agony came from the left. Grace lifted up, aimed, and fired toward the different smoldering fires. A series of gunshots instantly impacted the SUV from every direction, and she ducked down to protect her head.

Adare threw another square, while Benny and Jacqueline did the same.

A clink sounded, and then a larger explosion annihilated the stormy day. Shaking violently, Grace lifted and fired the gun again, sending green lasers that turned into steel bullets toward a burning SUV that had smoke and fire billowing out of its interior.

At least six soldiers were still standing, spread out and approaching from three directions.

Benny grunted. "I'll get another box."

A Cyst soldier threw something into the SUV, and it glowed in the back seat.

"Fuck," Adare shouted, manacling Grace around the waist and turning them toward the trees, running full bore through the snow.

The blast threw them into the air, and he tucked himself around her, holding tight. She screamed, her eyes shutting as they were propelled through the trees and landed in the snow, sinking several feet. Faster than she could blink, Adare was on his feet and shoving her behind a large spruce tree with icicles hanging from its branches.

She coughed snow out of her mouth.

Several more explosions detonated as the devices in the rear of the SUV all caught fire. He ducked as a wave of heat washed over the snowy land.

Grace tightened her hold on her gun. "There's only one solution," she whispered, the wind nearly stealing her voice. "I have to go with them." He'd saved her once, and she had to do the same for him. Even if she had to shoot him to do it.

Benny leaned up from a tree to the left, half of his face burning. "Not a good idea."

Jacqueline crouched to the right behind a spruce, her arm bleeding red onto the snow. "It's our only chance."

Unfortunately, it was a true statement. The wind blasted into the forest with the smell of burning metal and flesh. The enemy were advancing and fast, their heavy footsteps on ice echoing through the storm. "What the hell do you think I've been doing for five years?" she hissed.

Adare frowned.

"I've been training." Well, as much as she could with her schedule. "Yeah, I've taken pictures and worked, but I've learned to fight and shoot, just for this kind of situation. I'll go, stay alive, and you'll come for me." It was the only option.

"No," Adare said.

Grace lifted her gun. Adare's chest had been sealed with an impenetrable shield in the Seven ritual, but his head was another matter. He'd be out of commission for a while, but he'd survive a bullet.

"I'm not giving you a choice." She aimed right between his eyes.

Chapter 7

Adare jolted, the adrenaline flooding his system seeming to coagulate in his brain as he looked into the barrel of his own gun. Grace held the weapon high, her face unnaturally pale and the pupils of her eyes all but swallowing up the color of her irises. She looked small and determined against the tree with the wind whipping her hair around wildly and snow covering her from head-to-toe.

"Don't make me shoot you," she whispered, her voice shaking even more than her hands. She might just shoot him by accident if she didn't calm down.

The Kurjans were advancing, and he didn't have time for this. "Put the weapon down."

"No." Regret crossed her face and her shoulders went back. "I'll try not to hit your brain."

He turned and fired at a Kurjan who crossed around the burning heap that had been Adare's SUV. The soldier scrambled back for cover. "Grace? It took us three years to finally find one of the Cyst strongholds." It was easier to find the Kurjans, but to win this war, they needed to take out the Cyst faction of the Kurjan force. "If they get you, we might never find you."

She somehow turned even paler, and a thin blue vein showed above her left eyebrow. "Just do your best. I have to do this."

If she thought he was going to allow her to walk over to the Cyst enemy and disappear, she was crazier then he'd feared.

"It's the only plan that might work," Jacqueline hissed, two of her teeth missing.

Benny groaned and one of his bones popped loudly into place. He turned and fired toward the enemy with his good hand. "We'll never find her again, so no plan there. You guys run up the mountain and get as far as you can. I'll hold them off."

Adare quickly calculated the odds. There was only one answer. "Jacki? You have to shift. Take Grace and get to safety." As a cougar, Jacki would be faster than even the Cysts. He and Benny would fight these bastards as long as they could.

Jacki growled but set her gun down and shrugged out of her heavy jacket.

Adare knew the instant Grace made up her mind. She fired, and he ducked, charging her and securing the gun before he pinned her against the tree with one hand around her neck. The woman had shot at him. Actually aimed for his head.

Benny growled in pain behind him.

"Benny," Grace gasped, struggling against Adare's hold.

Adare partially turned to see a wound spurting blood from Benny's neck. Had Grace's bullet hit him when Adare ducked? The hybrid's eyes swirled a deep metallic bronze as he slowly healed the hole, the side of his face still abnormally bumpy.

Grace slapped ineffectually at Adare's hands. "Benny, I'm so sorry."

Adare leaned in, fury making his skin burn. "I'll deal with you later, mate." He turned and fired with both guns, shielding her with his body.

Jacki moved away as far as she could and her bones cracked as she began to shift. Adare covered Grace with his body as further explosions sounded, pushing him even harder against her. His ears rang, but he partially turned to find Jacki padding their way, her fur a tawny brown against the snow. She opened her mouth to reveal long canines and the gap of two missing teeth. One was already growing back in.

Bullets struck the branches above him, snow rained down, and an icicle cut down his temple. The smell of his own blood centered him.

"Grace, you're going to have to get on and hold on as hard as you can." He grabbed her biceps and shook her. "Lean low and make yourself the smallest target possible."

She shook her head, snow falling on her face. "We have a better chance if we're all here fighting. Two against that many isn't a good idea." She tried to pull away from him and failed, her gloved hands pushing against his chest. "This is my fault, and I'm not leaving you to die because of me."

"I'm not asking," he growled. If he knocked her out, she wouldn't be able to hold on to Jacki. He could just put her onto the moving cougar so she'd have to hold on. But there was a chance the stubborn female would just let herself fall off so she could turn around and sacrifice herself to the Cyst. There was only one other option. He looked over his shoulder. "Benny? You wearing a belt?"

Grace gasped and leaned away from him, not getting far with the tree at her back.

"Yeah." Benny yanked a huge brown belt from his jeans while shooting simultaneously with his free hand. He tossed it over.

Adare ripped his from his waist. "I'll knock your ass out and tie you to the cougar if you don't get on." He meant every word.

The snow lashed them, while the wind knifed through his coat. The Cyst and Kurjans had fanned out, advancing rapidly, even though Benny kept up a steady barrage of bullets. He hit a Kurjan in the head and the bastard went down hard.

The cougar growled in warning, its canines dropping low. The longer she waited to run, the more exposed she'd be to the Kurjans and their bullets.

Grace continued to struggle against Adare.

Regret filled him. He sighed and then tightened his hold on her neck. Her eyes widened, and she grabbed at his arm with both hands, fighting him. He couldn't bring himself to knock her out. "I will cut off your air, Grace. I don't want to, but it's going to happen. Obey me."

* * * *

Obey him? Come on. Grace pulled off her gloves, and freezing cold instantly pierced her skin. His hands were firm on her neck, but he didn't squeeze. She scraped her nails down Adare's coat and then reached for his face. He leaned back, out of reach, protecting his eyes.

They were a burnished silver, hot yet somehow still dark. His face was unyielding, matched only by his firm hold around her neck. She couldn't break it. For the first time with him, she felt real fear. Yet he didn't cut off her air. Maybe he couldn't force himself to do it.

The roar of a machine echoed through the air.

Adare leaned to the side, and his hold relaxed slightly. She sucked in a tiny amount of air. He released her and slapped the gun back into her hand. "Cover me."

She gulped in oxygen, filling her aching lungs with the frigid air. He'd threatened to choke her. Oh, she'd love to show him those fighting moves she'd learned, but she doubted she'd best him in any fight.

There was nowhere to go. If he decided to choke her out, she had no defense. Except the gun. She looked at the heavy object in her hands and then nodded. Yeah. She'd hit him instead of Benny this time.

She turned and peered around the spruce just in time to see Nick Veis, his face dark with fury, jump a snowmobile over the burning vehicle and smash right into two Kurjans with the skis, sending them spiraling across the icy ground. Before they could jump up, he was off the machine and slicing with a blade that looked sharp enough to take off several heads.

Right behind him, Simone Brightston executed a perfect flip on two skis over a burning porch swing, a plasma ball already forming in her hands. Her dark red hair flew in the snowy air, and the green of her eyes glowed with dangerous intent. She threw the ball at the nearest Kurjan, and he screamed, his uniform burning.

She landed, forming ball after ball and throwing with the precision of a major league pitcher.

Grace gulped and partially stood, aiming at a Kurjan running for the witch. She fired, hitting him in the neck, and he stumbled, going down on one knee. Simone turned, gave her a nod of what looked like approval, and then threw another ball of morphing fire at the downed enemy, who shrieked in pain.

Grace had heard that witches could create plasma balls of fire out of air, using an application of physics beyond her understanding, but she had never seen it happen in real life.

Nick and Simone fought in a deadly dance that appeared choreographed, each covering the other's back while delivering devastating blows with knife and fire. What would it be like to be so in tune with another person?

Adare and Benny ran out into the fray, firing until they reached the enemy and then going into hand-to-hand contact with punches and kicks, punctuated by blades flashing so fast, all Grace could see was the muted glint of silver through the storm.

The cougar, with a ferocious roar, leaped into the fray and snagged a Kurjan's neck in her jaw.

Grace shoved her feet through the heavy snow, keeping to the tree line and trying to see where to shoot. Her heartbeat clamored like cymbals in her head, making her ears ring. Her breath came in shallow pants, and her legs trembled in the icy snow.

The immortals all used such speed that by the time she could aim, everyone had changed position. The falling snow pummeled the various fires, smothering flames and creating immense clouds that rolled through the storm, further hampering visibility.

She blinked snow from her eyes, crouching to make herself a smaller target.

Adare took a Cyst down to the ground, his knife striking hard and fast, pinning the enemy to the earth through the neck. His movements were quick and economic, and all the more terrifying for their violent efficiency. He began to stand, looking around, blood flowing down his arm. In that moment, she saw the warrior, the immortal Highlander, that he'd always been. Not cold and calculating, but scorching and deadly.

Grace swallowed several times, forcing herself to stay in the moment and not drift into shock.

Jacqueline, her cougar snout covered in blood, finished off the Kurjan on the ground. A Cyst leapt over a pile of smoldering rubble, slicing wildly with a wicked knife. Jacqueline turned just in time to duck a head strike, but the knife slashed down her right front leg. She growled and turned, jumping for his neck.

He blocked her, pivoting and throwing her yards across the icy driveway, smack into Adare's back.

The impact threw Adare toward the burning sedan. He turned at the last second and pushed Jacki toward the tree line and away from the flames, right before he crashed into the molten-hot metal.

He fell into the fire, then rolled away, his coat burning. Steam rose from it as he landed on his back in the snow.

The Cyst soldier attacked immediately, knife swiping with a fury stronger than the storm around them.

Adare protected his face and neck with both arms, his boots fighting for purchase on the ice. The Cyst gouged deep wounds into Adare's forearms and hands, slicing mercilessly, dropping a knee onto Adare's stomach and stabbing down for his throat.

"Adare!" Panic sizzled through Grace, and she bounded out of the snow, running around the smoldering SUV. She slipped on the ice, regained her footing, and kept running, pointing her gun and pulling the trigger several times. Spurts of green laser fire shot out, turning into bullets upon impact as she hit the sedan behind them. Damn it. She tried to stop so she could shoot.

A strong arm caught her from behind and partially lifted her up. She twisted to see red hair tipped with black. "I've got her," her captor bellowed.

Her lungs protested as he squeezed the air out of her.

"Grace," Adare yelled, grabbing the blade slashing down at him with both hands.

She immediately let her arm drop and twisted the gun back, pulling the trigger at the same time. The Kurjan holding her screamed in pain and dropped her. Benny ran over two prone Kurjan bodies and slammed his fist into the soldier's head.

Grace hit the ice, rolled, and ran for Adare as fast as she could.

His hands bleeding on the knife, he slammed the hilt up and into the Cyst's face, quickly rolling them over and capturing the knife. In one smooth motion, he shoved the entire blade through the soldier's purple eye. The Cyst shuddered several times and then went still.

Adare backflipped to his feet, reaching for her.

Benny threw the now limp Kurjan into the burning SUV. "Dude. Did she just shoot that bastard in the balls?"

"I've been practicing," Grace gulped, searching for another target.

Adare tucked her behind him, looking wildly around. "We have to get out of here."

Grace swallowed down bile, her body shaking so hard she could barely hold the gun. The Cysts and Kurjans were all down, while everyone still standing was bleeding from several places.

Nick took Simone's hand and drew her near. "Before we arrived, I called for cleanup and a helicopter to take you wherever you want. Should be here soon. We need to fetch the girls and get the hell out of here, and then you can call and explain to me why the Kurjans and their religious fucking leaders just attacked my very nicely hidden condo."

Simone leaned around Adare to focus on Grace, her eyes gleaming and a pleased smile on her stunning face. "Nice shot, there."

"Thanks." The world began to waver around Grace.

Simone frowned. "Honey? I think you've been shot." Her voice came from far away.

Then, darkness.

Chapter 8

Adare held Grace as the helicopter sped toward his mission headquarters in south-western Colorado while the storm continued to batter the world outside. Benny sat next to him, the air popping as he healed himself. On his other side, Jacki had fallen asleep, her wounds slowly closing as she rested.

Blood continued to flow from the wound near Grace's neck, and he shook her again. "Wake up."

She blinked and then finally opened her eyes. "Adare?" Confusion clouded her eyes, then was quickly chased away by pain. "My neck."

"You were shot." His voice came out garbled, he was so pissed. As well as unwillingly impressed. The woman was a good shot. Where had she learned the skill? Aye, she was full of surprises. "You'll need blood." His fangs dropped fast and sharp, more than ready to sink into his hand.

"No." She pushed against his chest. "You were burned. I saw it, and you have stab wounds all over your arms."

His irritation must've shown on his face for a second, because she turned even paler and her body stiffened against his, still trembling with cold. "Where else are you injured?" He kept his voice as mild as he could.

"I don't know. Everything is frozen." A spark of temper finally lit her eyes. "Are you pissed at me right now?"

"Pissed doesn't come close to what I'm experiencing," he said, slashing into his palm and pressing the wound against her mouth. He'd deal with his new insight into her and how much that intrigued him at a later date. "I'm healing myself of other injuries right now. That means the healing cells will take over quickly, so drink before the cut closes." If she fought him this time, she wasn't going to like the results.

She glared but delicately pulled blood, careful to keep her teeth away from the injury. Even angry at him, even hurt and confused, she took care not to cause any more pain. Her kindness had drawn him from the very beginning, and now her determination and strength only made her pull stronger. Every second he stayed in her presence drew him nearer, and he'd avoided that temptation for years. It was a damn good thing he was so angry at the moment.

Color rose into her face like a finger painting on her cheekbones, and her eyes darkened to a deep green. She pulled away, and the wound along her neck slowly mended. "Thank you."

"Politeness isn't going to save you." He set his hand down and let the healing cells go to work.

"From what? You?" She snorted, reaching up to rub the spot where the bullet had sliced her. "You'll ditch me the second you can."

He blinked. "Sarcasm isn't a good tactic. Find another one." While her sweetness drew him, this sassiness challenged him, and he'd never been able to turn away from a challenge. "Fair warning, Grace."

She rolled her eyes. Actually rolled them. "I know I owe Nick and Simone an apology for stupidly leaving a trail for the Kurjans to find their condo." She wiped blood off her neck, scratching at the dry parts, her expression thoughtful. "How do you think they found us, anyway?"

Benny shifted his weight. "Your correspondence with that moron Freddy put up red flags everywhere. Why did you mention being a Key?"

"He mentioned fate and battles, and it seemed as if he knew about everything. I wanted to intrigue him enough to meet me in person." She felt so damn stupid about that, considering he'd probably just been reciting things from a fantasy novel or something. "I didn't say I was a Key. I just hinted about keys."

Benny coughed, the sound pained. "I think I got shot in the ass. Damn it." He took several deep breaths. "Your internet use was enough for us to track you, so no doubt it was enough for the Kurjans to do the same. I imagine once they caught your scent, they used satellite to find you. It was a good assault, actually. The Cysts have upped their game."

"They were lucky with the weather," Adare returned. He should've been more on guard.

Benny sighed, his eyes still shut and his head leaning back as he healed. "We're gonna have to buy Veis a new condo somewhere. I really don't want to piss his witch off."

Grace cleared her throat. "Speaking of which, I'm really sorry I shot you, Benny. I was aiming at Adare."

Irritation swept through Adare again. "Oh, we're going to talk about that at length."

Benny snorted. "No worries. I've been shot before because of the Highlander."

Grace shifted her weight on his lap. "Also, I'm sorry I brought the Kurjans and Cysts to the condo, and you all had to fight and get injured. I didn't realize how easy it was to track a person from internet use."

Oh, she wasn't getting it. "We've already dealt with that," Adare muttered.

She jerked her head back to better see him. "Then what are you so angry about?"

His ears heated. "When I tell you to do something, to get the hell away from a fight, you do it."

Her eyes widened. "Oh yeah. You threatened to choke me." She slapped him in the chest. "What were you thinking?"

"I was thinking I wanted you to obey me and get out of there."
He didn't give one whit that the word obey shot even more color
into her face. "Apparently that's a lesson you need to learn." He
settled his bulk more comfortably into the seat, and the storm
strengthened outside the small craft, batting them around like a
kitten with a ball of yarn. "We'll discuss it on the ground. I need
to heal now." Without waiting for her response, he set his head
back and shut his eyes, working on his arms and hands.

When she struggled briefly against him, he tightened his hold,
not in the mood.

"You bet we'll talk," she muttered. "Just wait."

* * * *

Grace slowly opened her eyes. She was in the back of an SUV,
leaning against Adare's side, as they drove up a snowy drive
toward a darkened cabin set amidst a thick forest. The moon
shone down, bright against the snow, sparkling like a fairytale
welcome. "Where are we?"

"The corner of Colorado and Arizona, kind of," Benny said
from the driver's seat. "It's our lair."

Adare shifted his weight. "I have asked you repeatedly to stop
calling it that."

"Huh." Benny pulled to a stop in front of the quiet porch. "We
had the demon nation's pilots drop us at a private airstrip an
hour away because we want this place to be public, right? *Not.*
We wouldn't even give them a hint as to where we're going, so
they'll have to sleep in the copter if they can't make it out. This
is our lair."

"It's not a lair," Adare growled, his Scottish brogue coming
out full force.

Jacqueline turned around from the front seat, once again in
human form with her clothes back on, her tawny hair flowing
down her back as if she'd spent hours in a salon. "Looks like a lair
to me." She caught Grace's eye. "You're awake. Good. You sure

faint a lot." She smiled, her teeth all back in place and perfectly white. "You've been here before, surely. Is it a lair?"

Grace hadn't even known Adare owned a place in Colorado. "I'm not entering this argument," she said, forcing a smile. No way was she admitting she didn't know a thing about her so-called mate. She pushed her curly hair away from her face, no doubt looking like she'd just been in a snowy battle before falling asleep in a military helicopter. Her life had gotten so odd since the coma.

Adare opened the door and stepped out into the cold. "Let's grab something to eat and some sleep. We can plan in the morning." He lifted his chin when Jacqueline exited the vehicle. "I don't suppose the Ledonis will give us a discount on replacement explosives?"

"Not a chance," Jacki purred, the moon highlighting her smile.

"I figured." Adare returned her grin.

Grace shoved her way out, elbowing him in the side, her chest aching. She was not jealous. Not at all. "I'm going to skip food and jump into a hot shower." The dried blood down her neck and chest was starting to itch, and she smelled like burnt soup. The shifter probably smelled like jasmine or orchids despite her battle with dangerous enemies.

Adare turned and led the way up the three long wooden steps, across the snowy porch, to a keypad near the door. He typed in a code, the lock audibly snicked, and he turned the knob. "You can shower, but you have to eat something afterward. Is this why you're so thin? You've stopped eating?"

If he made her feel any more unattractive, she'd just kick him in the knee. "Of course not. I haven't lost much weight." Which wasn't true. Whatever was happening with her, the fading of her mating mark had had several side effects, including nausea. The last Realm doctor had said she might end up in a coma eventually. So she had to take the virus from the queen and negate the bond. It was a risk, but it was also her only option. "Stop bossing me around."

He leaned to the side and flicked several light switches, illuminating a great room with stone fireplace, southwestern themed furniture, and a wide entryway to a dark tiled room with a stainless steel refrigerator.

Benny crowded in behind them. "Adare's rooms are to the left, mine the right, and the guest area is through the kitchen toward the rear of the house, Jacki. I'll get supper started with whatever we might have on hand. Everyone else take showers, get clean, and prepare for a culinary masterpiece." He flicked a switch by the fireplace as he walked toward the kitchen, and logs ignited instantly.

Grace looked around and gasped. Her photographs, ones she'd taken through the years and sold through an intermediary in Florida, adorned the walls. The black and white shot above the mantle had been taken in the aftermath of one of the Seven's headquarters being blown up, which used to happen with frequency. Rain poured onto the damaged mountain, giving a sense of finality along with longing. "Adare—"

"This way." He grasped her arm and led her to an entry hall before the fireplace. "Jacki? We'll catch up in a few," he called back.

"Can't wait," the shifter returned.

Grace stumbled down the short hallway to double doors that Adare opened to reveal a suite with bedroom, office alcove to the right, sitting room to the left, and another door that must lead to a master bath. The bed must've been specially ordered. Far larger than king-sized, it was topped by a photograph she'd taken of the lake edging Realm headquarters, right when fall turned to winter and the water shone silver with mystery.

The rest of the room was utilitarian with a dark blue bedspread and no personal objects, save for a smaller photograph above the desk that she'd shot of a fledgling deer near the lake. Why did he have her photographs decorating his lair? Her heart warmed.

"Your lair seems more like a retreat," she murmured, her eyes scratchy.

Adare moved to a heavy-looking mahogany dresser and pulled out a long-sleeved T-shirt, socks, and sweats. "Go take a shower, we'll eat something, and then we're having a talk." He handed her the clothing, his eyes a burning black, tension rolling from him with more force than the wind had blown earlier.

She opened her mouth to argue and then, her skin itchy, took the clothes and turned for the bathroom without a word. A shower would center her, and she needed all her faculties if she was going to argue with the badass Highlander. For one thing, they really needed to discuss the way he'd threatened to choke her out so she'd ride his ex-girlfriend, the cougar shifter, up a snowy hill while a fight to the death happened because she'd screwed up on the internet.

Life was just getting weirder and weirder. She also had to deal with the completely inappropriate and bizarre jealousy she felt for said shifter.

Adare wasn't Grace's. He never would be.

Chapter 9

Adare's body felt marginally better after a hot shower and clean clothing, although his temper kept pricking him from inside like a hot poker. He pushed his plate back, his stomach full and his limbs tired. Grace had been quiet during dinner, her mind seeming miles away. No doubt the human had never seen a bloody fight like the one they'd endured earlier, and she was probably in shock. His sweats had been too big for her, so she'd left them in their room. In his oversized shirt and socks, she looked adorably lost. He needed to get her into bed. To sleep. Just to sleep.

"Excellent, Benny." As always. Most people didn't realize the slightly crazy hybrid was an excellent cook who'd studied with the best through the years.

Ben, his long hair wet from his shower, nodded and swirled a glass of Scotch in one hand. "My pleasure. Let's get some sleep and we'll figure out how to acquire more explosives tomorrow." He winked at Jacqueline. "Perhaps I could use my impressive powers of persuasion to start bargaining tonight?" His eyebrows wiggled, but his eyes were soft and serious.

Good Lord. He was making a play for the shifter.

"Then you'd just owe me more money." Jacki winked and stood with her plate. "Adare? I would like a moment to talk and catch up, if you don't mind."

Grace finally looked up, and one of her elegant eyebrows arched.

Adare stood, taking Grace's plate with his to the sink. "Let's dicker over explosives tomorrow. Ben and I will pay ten percent more than last time, for the same order, because of the shorter timeframe. No more than that." He looked around the demolished kitchen. While Benny could cook, he liked to destroy every pan at the same time.

Benny waved him off. "I'll clean up. Whatever can't be salvaged, I'll just toss in the garbage. Again."

Adare didn't feel like arguing. "Thanks." He pulled back Grace's chair, and when she stood, almost woodenly, he guided her through the living room to his quarters. Once inside, he shut the door. "We need to talk."

She moved toward the bed, sitting and looking so incredibly small on its wide expanse that he almost reconsidered the discussion. Her hair had dried, long and curly down her shoulders, and without makeup, her skin was nearly luminous, enhanced by her pink lips. "She still cares for you, you know," Grace said.

He frowned, trying to figure out what she was talking about. "Huh?"

"Jacqueline. She wants to chat with you tonight because she still cares for you." Grace tilted her head, her voice soft and her eyes inscrutable.

He ran a hand through his thick hair. "I'm mated, Grace."

"So?" Grace tucked her legs up, crossing them. "That has nothing to do with feelings. What do you feel for her?"

Why the hell were they having this discussion? "She's an old friend who mated somebody else. I hadn't realized he'd passed on, but I haven't kept in touch with anybody except the Seven for a long time." Even if Jacki still had feelings for him, that was irrelevant. Forgetting the fact that he was more than likely going to die taking out Cyst headquarters, he had mated Grace, his eyes fully open. There could only be one mate.

Grace plucked at a string on her sock. Or rather, his sock, which reached above her knees. "You could have a second chance, you know."

He leaned back against the wall, crossing his arms. "I told you five years ago that neither one of us would ever take that damn virus." It'd probably kill them, and that wasn't an exaggeration.

"Love might be worth it," she said, facing him head on.

The kick to his gut had him biting back a growl. "I'm sorry you had to give that up, and that you didn't have a choice in the matter." It was the truth.

"I meant you," she countered.

The woman was worried about him finding love? Just when he thought he had pinned her down, she knocked him out of his head with her kindness. The female didn't know a thing about being coy or creating falsehoods. She'd probably pass out if she ever told a lie. He shook his head. "Grace, Jacki made the right choice back then. As a member of the Seven, my path was always destruction and death. My fate has made me who I am. There's no love in me. Anywhere." Although he'd never understood why Jacki had chosen Basel Ladoni out of all her suitors. The guy had a weak jaw, albeit a massive fortune.

Grace's shoulders straightened. "You and Jacqueline make a good match. You even fought well together."

"You fought like a champion—all heart," he said, his voice softening. "When that Kurjan lifted you off the ground, you thought very quickly and shot him right in the groin. That was brilliant." It was difficult to yell at a person while also trying to reassure and compliment her, damn it.

She blushed. "Let's not forget we were all there, in danger, because of me."

He straightened. "Excellent segue for our next discussion."

She sighed. "Wonderful. How about I just do it?" She cleared her throat and lowered her soft voice as much as possible to a growl. "Grace? You're still mainly human, and when there's a fight with immortal soldiers who've trained for centuries, and I tell you to get your ass on my ex-girlfriend's back and climb a mountain, you do it, damn it." Then she fluttered her eyes. "But Adare—" her voice rose to a falsetto, "I can take care of myself and don't need you telling me what to do. Butthead." Then she growled like an animal and pawed the bedspread. "Woman, obey," she snapped, her voice still a terrible imitation of his. "No," she said in her own voice. "In fact, bite me."

Amusement poked through his irritation like light through blind slats. "You really don't understand the freedom I've allowed you, do you?"

Her sigh was exaggerated. "Let's make a deal. You never use the words 'allow' or 'obey' again, and I'll do my best to stay out of immortal battles to the death?"

"No deal," he said. How, after all this time, did she not fear him at least a little?

She sighed. "Figured." Then she looked around, her gaze landing on her photograph of the deer. "How about this? Since you won't discuss your feelings about my taking the virus, or your feelings about your ex-girlfriend, the flirty cougar, how about you tell me what your plan is for this big attack?" She swung her gaze to him. "As your mate, don't I have a right to know?"

Well, she did have a point. He held out a hand and accepted her olive branch, not wanting to fight during this last time together. Her quickness and bravery in fighting earlier had pushed him off balance, and he wasn't sure what to do with that. For now, they could just get along. "I guess you do. Maybe it's time you saw why Benny calls this place the lair."

* * * *

Grace enjoyed the feeling of her hand in Adare's way too much. His easy grip was warm, firm, and protective. She'd hidden a lot about her health from him the last couple of years, but since he wasn't really involved in her life, she shouldn't feel guilty.

He led her to the side of the stone fireplace, reached up to the top, and inserted his finger in a crack. A section of the rock slid open to reveal a keypad.

"No way," Grace breathed, wishing she'd grabbed her camera.

"Yes. The door locks from either side with a keypad, and the code is 002241. Memorize it." He punched in the code, and the entire rock wall swung open like an ordinary door.

Adare flipped a switch, and lights ignited on the stone block walls, illuminating the stairs that curved down toward more darkness.

"This is so cool," she whispered, following him down the rough stone steps. "When did you build this place?"

"Two years ago," Adare said, reaching the bottom level and engaging the last switch.

Grace faltered, her head swiveling to take it all in. The room was massive, built of stone and concrete, extending far beyond the structure of the cabin above. One entire wall held different screens. Only one was lit up, showing an aerial view of a compound with heat signatures.

Adare caught her eye. "It's a Kurjan holding that hopefully houses some Cyst soldiers in northern Arizona."

"Satellite?" she murmured. The compound looked massive and well-guarded. Even from far above, the shapes of the guns were big enough to make out.

He nodded. "Three years ago, the Seven purchased a discarded satellite from the Chinese and then had the Realm experts update it. We try to keep it focused on this one place, for now."

She looked at the multiple computer consoles on wide tables down the middle of the room, and then to the opposing wall, where old-fashioned maps had been taped with different pins stuck in them. "Known Kurjans?"

"Known Cysts," he said, releasing her hand. "Our mission is to take out as many Cyst as possible, after extracting whatever information we can get from them. Ronan and Ivar are working on locating all Kurjans, while Logan and Quade are in charge of finding as many enhanced human females as we can before the Kurjans locate and kidnap them. The good news is that enhanced females are hard to find, as most don't know they're any different from other humans."

She studied the map of the world, noting that most locations of enhanced females were areas with high sun exposure. That made sense. "What about Garrett?" He was the only member of the elite Seven that Adare hadn't mentioned.

Adare didn't turn from watching the satellite feed. "Garrett's searching for the last Key. We have you and Mercy; now we have to find one more."

Mercy was a Fae mated to Logan, and no doubt she was helping with the search.

The room was chilly, and Grace rubbed her arms to keep warm. She felt a little silly in Adare's shirt and socks, but she was well covered. "Have you ever wondered if I'm really a Key?" Mercy was a powerful Fae, and it made sense she was one of the chosen. "I mean, what if my birthmark is just that? Just a mark? I'm not enhanced in any way." Enhanced humans, ones who could mate with immortals, had special abilities and were usually empathic, clairvoyant, or psychic.

Adare turned then, trapping her gaze. "Are you nuts? How can you say you're not enhanced?"

"Okay," she acknowledged. "I know we mated when I was in a coma without sex, so that has to be different somehow. But still. I don't have any special skills."

He shook his head. "Unbelievable."

Her face heated, and she shuffled her stockinged feet. "Fine. Let's change the subject. What's your plan?"

He pointed to the screen. "Go in there, get all the information we can on how close they are to pulling Ulric home, and then blow the place up."

Sounded simple. Crazy but simple. Adare and Benny would be far outgunned. No wonder he considered it a suicide mission. "If you die, all of that information goes with you," she said, her chest hurting for him.

"We'll transmit any information we can before carrying out the assault." He sounded so resigned to dying. "Plus, there's a chance we'll find a cache of kidnapped enhanced women, and we can save them before destroying the place. That kind of chance makes dying worthwhile."

"Mercy said there might be a chance Ulric will never make it home." Apparently, a zillion years ago, Ulric had made himself invincible, and the Seven had been created to stop him. They'd violated physics to build a prison world, far from Earth, and two of the Seven, Ronan and Quade, had sacrificed themselves to guard him. But when the worlds they inhabited were destroyed, they'd returned home, once again distorting the laws of physics, which was one of the reasons the existence of the Seven was a huge-assed secret. Supposedly, Ulric would soon find his own freedom and his way back home. At least, that was how she understood it all, although it was probably more complicated. "Maybe there's nothing to worry about."

Adare shook his head. "We screwed up physical laws by creating those bubble worlds, and we probably goofed them up even more by letting Quade and Ronan return home. Nobody can teleport any longer—at all." He frowned on the last.

She tilted her head. "I'd forgotten many of you used to be able to teleport. What was it like?"

"Convenient," he muttered, looking back at the heat signatures moving around the Cyst area. "For most of my life, it just was a way to travel. To close my eyes, imagine a place I'd been, and then fall into it."

Grace had once asked Promise, a genius physicist now mated to Ivar, how in the world anybody could do that. Promise had said it was an application of string theory, whatever the heck that was, bending time and other dimensions to cross through and end up elsewhere. "Do you miss the ability?"

Adare nodded. "It's like losing your sight or your hearing or any other sense."

She rubbed her aching temple. "Kind of like my missing memories. I'd do anything to get those back and remember what put me into a coma."

He lifted his chin. "We had the Realm guys look at all the evidence concerning what happened to you, you know. They concluded it was probably a burglar you caught in the act who attacked you in your apartment. A guy fitting that MO was caught several blocks away two months later. He turned on police and was shot."

She nodded. "I read all the reports." Even so, she didn't remember what had happened to her that one fateful night. That sucked. It was much easier to focus on her mate than her blank memories. Perhaps Adare's abilities would return the same way doctors assured her that memories could. "Maybe if Ulric makes it back, and if his prison bubble bursts, everything will align like it was before."

"That's doubtful."

"Or everything could just blow up, including our world," Grace whispered. Sometimes Promise didn't sugarcoat the facts.

"Maybe." He strode for the stairwell again. "Let's get some sleep."

Grace looked around the quiet room again. "Oh, this is definitely a lair. Benny has it right." She told herself the trembling in her voice was because of the chilly space and not the fact they were about to share a bed again. *Yeah, right.*

Chapter 10

Apparently he had some work to do before he sent her off to the Realm in the morning. He didn't think she'd tell them about the Seven, but she also didn't seem to care much about her own well-being. Adare followed Grace into his bedroom and shut the door. "We don't have a lot of time, but there are some promises I need from you before you go to sleep."

She started, her head going back, before turning and once again sitting on his bed.

He kept his distance across the room, just to stop himself from reaching for her. Her scent was unique, and one he'd always wondered about. A mixture of sweet lilacs and spicy oranges with a hint of the sea thrown in. Calming and peaceful. How odd that the one woman he'd loved, years ago, had been anything but peaceful. This one, the one he'd mated, had a gentleness to her that he would've liked to have known. In a different life.

"Well?" She crossed her arms and his shirt swallowed her up. "I am not promising to run from a fight if I can help."

"I'm going to try to survive our mission, but if I don't, promise me you won't take the virus from the queen for at least a hundred years," he responded. So far, that seemed to be the earliest anybody had taken it safely. "I need to know that you'll be safe if I'm gone."

She frowned and cocked her head. "You're totally confusing me. We've mainly lived apart these five years, and now you're worried about my safety?"

His chest heated. "I've watched out for you for five years, and I thought you'd be able to manage on your own when I was gone." The last thing he wanted was to sound as if he was lecturing a toddler. "At every second since our mating, I've known where you are and what you're doing. Did you honestly think otherwise?" By the surprise on her pale face, she definitely had. "After being in a coma and then being thrown unwillingly into immortal life, you needed some freedom, Grace. I owed you that."

"You took every mission you could to give me freedom?" Her incredulity was a little insulting.

"No. I took every mission I could because it's my job, and I'm good at it." He was the team expert in shock and awe, since he rarely lost his head in a fight. "I made a vow when I underwent the Seven ritual. I knew the sacrifices I'd have to make. I've made them." He waited a beat. "Now promise me."

She took a deep breath and looked him in the eye, not moving. "I promise."

Something inside him, deep and unfathomable, relaxed. "Good. Thank you."

"Anything else?" Her voice was just flippant enough to speed up his heart rate.

"Aye. Promise you'll learn how to heal yourself and that you'll see the queen when she returns. Just to make sure everything is okay with you." It wasn't too much to ask.

She nodded. "I already have an appointment scheduled. No worries there." She covered a yawn with her hand. "I can't understand how you're so casual about dying."

"I'm not." He pushed off the wall. "We're going to do everything we can to keep from dying, but the odds are great. When you're a soldier, especially one of the Seven, you weigh the risks against the possible rewards, and the rewards are worth it in this case. But I want you to be prepared." There was a great distance between them, and it was his fault. He could've spent time getting to know her, but he hadn't wanted to hamper her progress or muddy his path. Sometimes, life was what it needed to be. "Okay?"

"Sure." She didn't sound sure. "I really don't want you to die." She looked down at her knees as she said the words.

His heart took the hit. "I don't want to die, either. Benny and I are good at our jobs, and we work well together." The fact that Ben was nuts helped in battle, actually. There wasn't a door he wouldn't crash through. "One more thing." Adare moved to the desk and took out a black photo album he spent too much time looking at when nobody else was around to judge him. Or give him a hard time about it. Some things defied logic.

"What's that?" she asked.

He moved to sit by her on the bed, and his weight caused her to fall his way. She laughed and planted a hand on his thigh to keep from leaning. Lust, hot and brutal, rushed up his thigh to his groin. He laid the book on her lap and opened the cover. "Your sister sent this to me and sometimes she sends more pictures to update it."

She frowned at the first photograph. "I took that shot of her when she graduated from medical school. Long before we knew of this weird immortal world." Grace looked sideways at him. "Why do you have this album?"

He lifted a shoulder and turned the page.

Grace looked down and smiled. "This was last year at Christmas. See how happy she is?"

How was it possible Grace didn't see her skill? Her enhancement? "Compare the two pictures," he said quietly.

She pursed her lips and frowned. "Okay." Then she flipped back and forth, looking at the two pictures. "Well, she's older in this one, but she looks happy in both."

"Go deeper, Grace."

She stiffened. "I don't know what you mean."

"You know exactly what I mean. Stop hiding from who you are or thinking you're crazy." He planted a hand on her thigh. "We like crazy around here. You know how much everyone adores Benny."

Her laugh was small and unwilling, but then she nodded. "Okay.
I see your point, and I can also see the differences in the pictures.
My sister looks different with the passage of time."

Stubborn female. He grasped her chin between his thumb and
forefinger, careful not to cause a bruise, and turned her head to
face him. She was unique and special, and she had to know that
fact before he died. "You have the ability to capture who people
really are, and it's right there in front of you. You know it, you feel
it, and it's time you owned it."

Her small nostrils flared. "You're saying I capture the soul.
Through my camera."

A soul? It wasn't how he'd put it, but okay. "I'm just saying that
you're the only person in the world who could've captured that
essence of your sister, and deep down, you know it. Soul, essence,
being…whatever. It's a gift, Grace. One you could really hone if you
wanted. You look past the shield to who people are, and you use a
camera to do it, but probably don't need the device." She surprised
and impressed him, and both were nearly impossible to do after
his centuries upon centuries of living.

He saw the instant she decided to withdraw rather than deal with
the situation.

"Okay." She shut the book. "I'm ready for bed now."

He wasn't sure whether it was her stubbornness or her softness, but
he tightened his hold on her chin and leaned in. Her eyes widened.

His true nature took over, full force, and his mouth covered hers.

* * * *

The intensity of his kiss pushed her back on the bed, and she
clamped her hands on his T-shirt, pulling him down with her. With
a slight whisper, the photo album slid harmlessly to the floor.

Adare growled, low and deep, the vibrations resonating down
her throat to zing around her chest, tweak her nipples, then head
directly south to land below her abdomen. He kissed her with a

gentle but insistent strength, his tongue sweeping inside, and his lips curving over hers, possessive and demanding at the same time.

He dug both hands into her hair, holding her in place on the bed, partially rolling over her and landing on one knee, crouched above her and working her mouth as if he'd been starving for a taste.

She closed her eyes, kissing him back, letting pleasure and need fuse together and run through her unimpeded. Never in her life had she been kissed like this. While she might not remember her entire history, she'd remember anything that felt this good. Even so, there was a control in his touch, in his kiss, that she craved to let loose.

Her hands flattened over the hard planes of his chest, her fingers curving over his rock-solid shoulders and digging in, trying to draw him even nearer.

One of his hands released her head, and he brushed down the side of her arm, sliding up beneath the too-large T-shirt covering her. His palm, scalding hot, climbed her ribs, one by one, and settled on her bare breast.

She gasped and arched against him, her head going back on the pillow, her muscles tensing and her heart rate accelerating from zero to *OMG* in a second. This was actually happening. While she'd always been small-chested and a little self-conscious, all uncertainty sailed out of her head as he palmed her, gently squeezing her nipple between the base of two fingers.

The design on his hand, the one he'd marked her with, felt hot against her skin.

Air wheezed through her chest and she tried to breathe without panting. It had been at least five years, probably a lot more, since anybody had touched her, and this was exquisite. He moved to the other breast, his hand getting caught in the material of the shirt. Swearing, he reached down and ripped the material over her head, his head dropping at the same time and his mouth capturing her other nipple.

Electricity arced through her, and she bit her lip, her panties becoming wet and her hands frantic across his chest and down his abs, her fingers dipping into each ribbed muscle. She pulled his shirt up, making him duck, and then tossed it behind her. Everything was happening so fast, but she didn't want to stop. Or think.

His chest was amazing. Hard and angled, strong and powerful. His abs were a twelve-pack, each hard edge clearly defined as if somebody had drawn him. A tattoo she couldn't make out covered his left pec entirely.

He released her nipple and turned to place a soft kiss on the other one before looking up at her, his gaze a silvery black, his nostrils flared, and crimson darkening his rugged cheekbones. The warrior in him, the Highlander he'd always be, was in full force and on display.

She could *see* him. The real him.

"We can't do this." His brogue was a low rumble that caressed her aching nipples.

"I know," she breathed, digging her nails into his skin. "It's a huge mistake."

He kissed between her breasts. "Just one taste, Grace. That's all I ask."

The words didn't compute. "I don't—"

He slid her panties down with one finger, following with his mouth, kissing each hipbone and palming her thigh. Need and want and lust and every other feeling that was possible assaulted her, rioting through every nerve with a demand she couldn't fight.

He rubbed his five o'clock shadow across her tender thighs, stirring her desire hotter. He lifted up, his eyes pure silver. "Tell me I can have one taste."

Her mind rioted and her body pulsed. She was exposed to him, vulnerable and needy. She wanted to think of something clever, something flirty, something sophisticated to say. "Okay," she breathed.

He settled between her legs, driving her thighs apart to make room for his wide shoulders. "One taste," he murmured, as if to himself. His left hand planted itself on her thigh and he turned his head, striking with the speed of a true predator.

His fangs sliced deep into her thigh, and pain erupted through her lower half. She cried out, crashing both hands down on the bedspread and digging deep with her nails, her mouth opening in shock. Her body froze and then drifted into a warm numbness, followed by acute pleasure, sharp and direct, right to her core.

Oh, God. It was too much.

He drank her blood, and she felt the demanding pull deep in her sex.

Live wires uncoiled and sparked out, throwing her into an orgasm that had her crying out his name this time. In one smooth motion, he retracted his fangs and turned his head, sucking her clit into his heated mouth. The orgasm built in intensity, shooting sparks of pure white light behind her closed eyelids.

She whimpered, swelling and surging through a cyclone of battering pleasure that he increased by sliding one finger through her wetness and curling up, somehow caressing her clit from inside her. Her mind shut down as the ecstasy became too much, and she let it take her, until finally she came down and went limp.

Her breath panted, hard and fast.

He released her and gently pulled her panties back up, kissing her once right above her clit. His rough tongue then scraped over the wound in her thigh. To heal it? She remembered something about how that worked.

Then he looked up and licked a spot of blood off his lip.

She couldn't speak. Her body was satiated and on fire at the same time, and no words would come. What had just happened?

He reached for her discarded shirt and handed it to her, sliding back on the bed to stand. An obvious erection showed behind his jeans.

"Wh—what about you?" she asked, her voice barely coming out.

His smile was as gentle as it was rueful. "I'm fine—will take a quick run. It has to be this way." He turned, still shirtless, showing the black shield beneath the skin of his back where his torso had been made impenetrable during the Seven ritual. The words he spoke as he left were quiet but clear. "Thank you, Grace."

Then he was gone.

Chapter 11

Adare ran shirtless through the softly falling snow, his boots heavy and his head light. The taste of Grace, of her blood, would stay with him forever. Much like her scent, her blood tasted like a combination of sweet and good and pure sassiness. What in the hell had he been thinking to touch her? He was more than likely going to die, leaving her alone in this world, and he shouldn't have given in to his needs.

The sound of her climaxing, sweet and honest, drummed around in his head until he thought his ears would explode.

Finally, as dawn began to arrive, he ran back to the house. Maybe he could get some planning done in the situation room. Yeah. That was a good idea. He slipped inside quietly and kicked off his boots, brushing snow from his hair.

"You're a moron," Benny said, kicking back on the sofa, his boots on the marble coffee table, a protein bar half-eaten in his hands.

Adare wiped snow from his torso and down his jeans, striding in wet socks to stand by the fire. "Why?"

"I heard you earlier. Your lady isn't exactly quiet." Ben shoved the rest of the bar in his mouth and chewed with a sense of contentment most immortals never found, even at their happiest times. "Then you leave and go run for hours in the snow. Like I said, moron."

Adare flicked his temper off as easily as he'd gotten rid of the snow. "All right. How about you calculate our odds of surviving the raid we're planning?"

Benny steepled his hands together, watching the firelight play between his fingers. "I'd say we're halfway between screwed and fucked."

Yeah. That summed up the situation.

Benny looked up, his multi-colored metallic eyes narrowing. "Are you changing your mind?"

"No. We have to get what information we can, and we need to take out as much of their force as possible." The Cysts were becoming too insistent on gathering enhanced females, and the kidnappings of innocent women had to at least be slowed, if not stopped. "We might find prisoners to save. I still believe the risk is worth the reward on this one, Ben. You?"

Benny clasped his hands behind his head and stretched. "Yep. But I'm not mated, brother. You are."

"Not really." Adare could still taste her on his tongue. All of her. "That's a female who needs love and understanding and softness. She isn't going to get that from me." None of those things were in him now, and it was doubtful they'd been there even before he'd lost so many brothers in the Highlands. Hell. He'd dealt with loss his entire life, and that was after his parents and younger brother were slaughtered by the Kurjans in a long-forgotten war. A real connection with any female wasn't in the cards. Even with Jacki, there had been a sense of business about their courtship, and that had been before he planned to die for the Seven. "I have a path, Benny, and I'm gonna follow it."

Benny looked toward Adare's hallway and then back. "Sometimes the path forks on its own, my friend. Just keep that in mind." He stiffened, amusement glimmering in his eyes, and stood. "Incoming," he mouthed before turning and heading down the hallway to his room.

Adare looked up to see Jacki emerging from the kitchen, a glass of water in her hand. "Still get up at the crack of dawn, I see," he said.

She nodded, looking as if she'd healed all of her wounds from the night before. "Still go jogging without a shirt when you're struggling with a difficult situation, I see."

He kept his back to the fire, letting the heat dry his jeans. "Did you and Benny reach an agreement about a new sale last night?"

"Yes, and I've already received confirmation from my people." She crossed around the sofa and took Benny's seat, her jeans and shirt torn from the fight but looking freshly cleaned. The female must've found the laundry room last night. She never did sleep much.

"How much did said agreement cost me?" he asked.

She took a sip of the water before answering. "Seventeen million, plus half of the explosives you bought from the Bykovs and have stored somewhere in this so-called lair."

Damn it, Benny. Adare frowned. "Why would the Ladonis want the Bykov explosives?"

"Just half." She finished the water, her gaze steady on him, filled with a light he barely remembered. "They have some new product, and we need to figure it out." She shrugged. "It's part of the business, as you know."

"Right." He partially turned to let his left side dry.

She cleared her throat. "I should've chosen you, Adare."

He stilled, watching her. That's what she wanted to talk to him about? He was never going to understand females. Never. "You chose correctly with the information we had." Not in a millennium would he have thought Basel would've died before him. "My route has been bloody and dark, and it's going to become even more so very soon." Should he feel something other than exhaustion right now? He'd loved her once—hadn't he? Maybe even then he'd been incapable of love, although she'd helped him through the darkest times after the Highlands fell. For that, he'd always be grateful.

She shook her head. "No, I was wrong. I was hoping we could have a second chance."

His eyebrows rose. There was a time he'd wanted to hear those words from her—before he'd mated. "I'm mated, Jacki."

Her smile was all feline. "Barely. I've watched you two, and you don't fit. She's a human, Adare. You've always stayed away from weak humans, and you know it."

That was true. "She's stronger than you think," he said quietly. "She rushed right into the fight yesterday."

"You're defending her." Jacki's smile widened. "She almost got herself and you killed. I can barely smell you on her and vice versa. You can't tell me you love her."

He didn't love anybody.

"That's what I thought," Jacki said, twirling the glass in her hands, triumph crossing her angled face. "We were a perfect match. Strong and fierce, and you didn't have to worry about me constantly. I can take care of myself." She stood. "I've heard the virus to negate mating bonds works—my mate is dead and yours isn't connected to you. We could take the virus and be free to be together, just like we should've been. Just tell me you'll think about it." Her directness had always been one of her best assets.

He studied her for a moment, the fire at his back and the female he'd once wanted in front of him. "No."

* * * *

Grace awoke slowly, her body sated in a way she'd never felt before. She would've remembered that, right? She stretched, wincing as her thigh protested with a slight twinge. Desire flooded her, and she beat it back, trying not to remember the incredible orgasm Adare had given her.

Now her memory decided to work perfectly. That just figured. She stretched more carefully this time, noting that the other side of the bed hadn't been disturbed. Had Adare run all night?

How was she going to face him? She'd totally lost control the night before. Her temples thrummed with the headache that had found her nearly every day for the last year; she tried to ignore it.

The photo album on the desk caught her eye. He'd been right about her seeing angles nobody else saw, and she used the camera as a way to explore that gift. Did she even need the camera? It was time she buckled down and figured out who she was and who she'd been. If she was going to die the following week by taking the virus—and there didn't seem to be any alternative—at the very least she needed to try to figure out what had happened to her.

She couldn't go on without knowing, and she didn't want to end this life with unanswered questions if she could help it. Of course, she hoped the virus wouldn't kill her and she'd survive. There was a chance, and she'd hope for it. Why not? So she made herself get out of the comfortable bed and take a shower, dressing in her now dry jeans and sweater, although the coat was destroyed. Her limbs were heavy and exhausted, and that constant nausea was back. The deterioration of her health was speeding up. Darn it.

She had just finished finger combing her hair into submission when a knock came at the door. "Come in."

Adare entered the room, shirtless but with dry jeans and socks on. "We have to get going."

So much for flowers and love poems. She smoothed her sweater down. "Where are we going?"

He shut the door and tucked a thumb into his front pocket, looking so masculine and dangerous that her mouth started to water. "I have a car coming to take you to the airport, where a Realm plane will be waiting to fly you to headquarters. The pilot has already picked up a couple of shifter dignitaries who are heading over to meet with strategic leaders." No expression showed on his hard face.

She swallowed. This was so awkward. Should she tell him her plan and try to get him to understand? Something told her he wouldn't agree, and he'd have no problem ordering the Realm soldiers to take her to safety. She was tired of being safe and in the dark. The time for healing was done; it was time for answers. Whether she liked them or not. She should nicely say goodbye and thank him for the awesome orgasm. "Why do you have my photographs all over your house?" The question popped out before she could stop it.

He studied her, and for the briefest of seconds, his gaze softened. "They show who you are."

She sat straighter. What did that mean? The enlarged photographs adorning the walls were all of nature or scenes that didn't involve people, unlike the photo album Faith had sent to him. Those revealed something about the subject. Did the other ones truly show something about her? How was she supposed to respond to him?

He plucked the shirt he'd worn the night before off the ground and drew it over his head. "About last night—"

She held up a hand to stop him. "No. There's nothing to talk about. It's okay. We got caught up in the moment after the fight and everything." Considering she'd just decided to lie to his face and do something she knew would make him furious, she didn't want to talk about emotions. Not to mention the fact that the following week, she was going to the Realm to take a virus she'd promised him she wouldn't take for at least a hundred years. "Let's go on with our plans, Adare."

He nodded, his gaze intense. "If I survive the raid, which I plan to do, we can talk then. I'll meet you at Realm headquarters. Please remember that they don't know the truth about the Seven, or most of it, anyway. I trust you to keep our secret, as well as that of the Keys. The fewer people who know about you, the better."

"Of course." She slipped into her boots and strode past him to the door.

"If I don't make it, I wish you the best, Grace," he murmured. "Remember your promise to stay safe."

Oh, she remembered it; she just wasn't going to keep it. Time to change the subject. Her face was burning with embarrassment. "Did you get any sleep?"

"No, but I'll get caught up later. I ran, talked to Benny, and then I spoke with Jacki." He opened the door for her.

She paused and then walked through. Had he talked all night to Jacki? Not that it mattered. Probably. She moved out onto the porch, where Benny and Jacqueline were waiting. A black car idled by the steps with one driver in the front.

"We already checked him out," Benny assured her. "He's a hired guy from a good car service around here, but he's human, so don't say anything you shouldn't."

That was a relief.

Adare grabbed her pack and camera equipment and strode around to set everything in the trunk.

Benny lifted Grace up in a hug and whispered in her ear. "I'll make sure he comes back. Probably. Maybe. Well, anyway, I'll try hard."

Grace returned the hug, hit by the thought that this might actually be the last time she saw Benny. "I love you, Ben. You're a good friend."

He blinked and then hugged her again, gentling his squeeze when she winced from the pressure to her ribs. Then he released her.

She nodded at Jacqueline and waded through the snow to where Adare had her door already open. "Don't die," she said. Then, against her better judgment, she grabbed his coat lapels and jerked him down for a kiss.

His lips froze against hers for a brief moment and then he took over, growling deep and kissing hard. Her head was spinning when he released her, and his eyes had morphed to that deep silver color. "Promise you'll keep yourself safe."

She could only nod. Then, she slid into the car, and he shut the door. Within seconds, she was being driven away from Adare, maybe for the last time.

"To the airport?" the driver asked.

She sat straighter and tried to sound authoritative. "No. Please take me to a car rental place, not one of the ones at the airport." There were many cameras at airports, and she didn't want to be traced too quickly. She wasn't going to die without knowing what had happened to her seven years ago in Denver, what had put her into a coma. She had promised everyone she'd never return to Denver, but she had to know. It wasn't like she had anything to lose any longer. She had to do this.

No matter what it cost her.

Chapter 12

The kiss still tingling his lips, Adare watched Grace's car slide
in the snow and then correct before disappearing from sight. Why
had she kissed him? Probably as a goodbye. He'd always felt guilty
about mating her when she'd had no choice in the matter, so he'd
let her live her life. What if he'd spent five years getting to know
her instead? Well, then he'd be leaving a grief-ridden mate instead
of one who could move on if this campaign didn't go well. And
there was no way it would go well. At least her taste would stay
with him until the end.

"Adare?" Jacqueline asked.

He sighed and turned back to face her. It had been nearly a
century since he'd courted her, and she was as beautiful as she'd
been back in the days of long dresses and corsets. He'd meant
what he'd said the night before; he wouldn't go back. "You're not
coming on the raid," he said, remembering how much she liked
a good fight.

She rolled her eyes. "Give me a break. I'm not a fragile human.
We used to go on raids all the time."

"This is different." Was fate giving him a chance to say goodbye
to everyone who'd ever touched his life? Once, he'd thought he was
in love with Jacki. When she'd chosen to mate somebody else, the
loss had hurt a little, but he'd understood. Had the pain just been
ego? They'd seemed to make such a good match, and she'd been

insightful and a lot of fun. His world had certainly gone darker after she'd left. "It's good to see you, Jacki, but Benny and I have to do this one alone."

She shook her head, and her tawny hair scattered snow. "You're not still drowning in guilt, are you? Enough of that."

He'd forgotten how well she knew him. What he'd shared with her. Oh, he'd never broken his vow of secrecy to the Seven, but she'd figured some of it out on her own, way back when. He trusted her to keep his secrets. "I'll always have guilt." The cries of the dying at the Battle of Culloden reverberated in his soul, the pain so deep it could never completely dissipate. He was immortal and one of the most powerful of his kind, and even he hadn't been able to save his people or even his immediate family.

He wouldn't fail again, and that meant being prepared for this attack. "Benny? Let's get going, drop off Jacki, and pick up the explosives we'll need."

Ben nodded. "I know, I know. We have too short a time to get things into place, and based on intel I received a few days ago, the Cyst might know we're coming." He turned on his massive boot to head back to the vehicle. "I'm driving."

Adare looked down the empty roadway, where Grace had gone, and then strode toward the back seat of the SUV. "You can have the front, Jacki." He stretched inside, wincing as his knees hit the back of the front seat.

The door across from him opened, and she gracefully moved inside. "I'll sit beside you. We should catch up a little, don't you think?"

"On what?" He slammed his door.

She sighed. "You can't still be mad at me. It's been eons and eons." Her red lips pursed. "Perhaps longer. Time does fly."

A time they could've spent together if she'd made a different decision. The branding on his hand ached, and he glanced down, surprised. A marking appeared on a demon's hand when he found his mate, and his hadn't appeared until he'd held Grace. During all the time he'd spent with Jacqueline, the marking hadn't appeared.

Since he'd bitten Grace the night before, his hand had ached as if he'd never used the brand. There was so much about mating that he'd never learned. Did contact make the pain go away?

"Adare?" Jacqueline asked. "Answer me."

"What did you ask?" He had to get his brain back where it needed to be.

She tightened her lips. "I asked why you need this kind of firepower. Aren't you working with the Realm these days?"

He wiped snow off his shoulders. "No. We're not working with the Realm, and this mission is secret. That's all I can tell you."

Benny drove down the road with the finesse of a bulldozer, crashing through the median snowbank several times. "We gave you a good price for the explosives, and that was to ensure your discretion, as always." He looked into the rearview mirror and jerked his head. "Adare's mated, but I'm not, you know."

Adare barely kept from rolling his eyes. "You're propositioning her while we're supposed to be getting ready for a mission? Again?"

Benny lifted a mammoth shoulder. "We're probably gonna die, and you know it. I wouldn't mind a decent sendoff like you got last night."

He'd only gotten a bit of what he'd wanted last night. "Ben, if we're going to face death together next week, it'd be smart if I didn't want you dead." He said the last on a growl. Even though he didn't care what Jacki did, he didn't like Benny's teasing tone of voice. The time for levity had passed.

Benny lifted a hand in mock surrender, instantly piling the SUV into a berm of snow on the right side of the road. "Sorry. I give up." He used both hands to jerk the vehicle free, sending it bouncing over ice and rocks and forcing Adare to grab onto the door handle to keep from falling over.

Adare tried to regain control of the situation. "When are we going to transfer our explosives to the Ladonis? I'd rather everyone didn't know the location of our safe house."

"Oh, they're in the back of the SUV already," Benny said casually.

By all that was holy! Adare pulled the Max out of his boot and pressed the barrel against Benny's neck. "You've been driving like a maniac for the last ten minutes, and there are explosives in the rear of this thing?"

Benny's hands tightened on the steering wheel. "Well, yeah. Why do you have a gun to my neck?"

Hadn't there been enough explosions in the last twenty-four hours? "Stop the SUV and pull over, or I swear to all the fates that I'll shoot you through the head," Adare growled, his ears ringing with the heat rushing over his skin. "I'm driving."

* * * *

While the snow gently fell, Grace set out across the state of Colorado, letting the navigation in her phone direct her. Even though it was snowing, the sun pierced the clouds, brightening the day beautifully.

For five long years, while going through hypnotherapy, physical therapy, and mental exercises, Grace had avoided returning to Denver; now she had no choice. The Realm doctors she'd worked with had said that returning to the scene of her accident might jog her memory, but the soldiers had warned that the risk was too great.

Plus, she'd promised both her sister and Adare that she'd left that life behind.

They didn't know the full truth, and even if they did, they probably wouldn't like her plan. She'd seen pictures of herself before she'd gone into a coma. She had looked lively and fun and extroverted. Had she completely lost that woman?

Memories of her childhood, teenage years, and early adulthood had slowly returned, but the night she was injured, she couldn't remember. In fact, the months leading up to that night were hazy and only came back in spurts, often right after awakening.

Right now, her stomach ached and her head throbbed with a low pulse of pain, her constant companion since her health had started spiraling down.

Her phone dinged, and she pulled into the parking area of a community park to answer. "Hello?"

"Hey, sis. Just checking in," Faith said.

Grace winced. "Everything is fine. How's the Baltic?"

"Amazing and beautiful. You really should've come with us," Faith said, sounding relaxed and happy. "Speaking of which, Adare called and said you're on the way to Realm headquarters. I'm flying home with the queen and will meet you tomorrow."

Grace froze. "You're coming home early?"

"Yeah. Something's up and Dage has to return home, so Emma, Ronan, and I are going, too. Before you ask, the king doesn't share, and I have no idea what's happening. Could be anything."

King Dage Kayrs had always been an intimidating figure, and Grace was fine not hanging in his inner circle. "It'll be good to see you." Relief filled her that she'd get the appointment with Emma sooner rather than later. Her energy was definitely ebbing and not returning. "I'm glad you're coming home."

"Me too. How are you feeling?"

"I'm fine," Grace lied. She never should've let Faith know that her mating mark was fading. It was a darn good thing she hadn't mentioned the broken wrist. She'd come clean when they were in the same room once again. "Don't worry."

"If you're fine, why do you want to meet with Emma next week?" Faith's voice held a mix of irritation and sisterly concern.

Grace flipped on the windshield wipers as the snow began to pile up. She might as well tell Faith some of the truth. "I'm going to take the virus and end this mating." She'd been getting weaker and weaker for about a year, and she'd rather make the transition happen more quickly so she could get on with her life. "It's my choice, Faith. I don't want to argue about it."

Her sister was silent for a moment. "You know the risk of that. Even if you could negate the mating bond while Adare is still alive, we don't know what will happen in your case. You were in a coma and you could very well return to that state. This is an enormous risk you're taking."

Her life force was fading anyway, and the excruciating slowness of it all was terrifying. "We don't know that. It's possible I could be fine. Maybe even human again."

"We're going to talk about this before you do anything. A lot," Faith warned. "I'll support whatever you decide, and you know it."

She did know that. Finally, Faith was happy, and Grace hadn't wanted to worry her about her own decline, since there was nothing that could be done. It wasn't like she'd just accepted her fate. She'd met with several Realm doctors, and they'd all been stumped. The queen was her last option. "I agree about talking." At that point, she'd have to tell Faith everything.

"Okay. Have fun at Realm headquarters and I'll see you soon. Love you."

"Love you, too." Grace ended the call. She reached for the manila folder on the adjacent seat and flipped through the police report of the night seven years ago when she was injured by a burglar who'd broken into her home. Though Realm soldiers were satisfied that the burglar had since been caught, it didn't feel right to her. According to the report, the neighbor had heard the sounds of a struggle and pounded on the door. The guy had taken off out the back door, and she had been found injured inside. Yet Grace remembered none of it.

She took a sip of her strawberry milkshake and dropped the file. The contents were memorized by now.

Okay. She could do this. Taking in a deep breath, she opened her window and tossed her phone out into the park garbage can. Though it was Realm-issued and couldn't be hacked, she was sure the Realm soldiers could trace her through it.

Rolling up the window, she headed back onto the main road for a six or seven hour drive. She had to do this.

Finally, after too many mental debates to count, she reached the outskirts of Denver. Her heart rate picked up, and she practiced her breathing exercises, trying to ignore the constant headache. She turned the car's ancient navigation back on and drove through the quiet streets, maneuvering between neighborhoods with stately brick homes to an area of apartment buildings surrounded by mature trees.

Her temples ached and her stomach clenched.

She looked around, but nothing seemed familiar. Finally, she drove up to her previous apartment building and parked in front of Unit L, staring at the blue doorway on the first floor. The walk had been shoveled, and hints of greenery poked out through the snow on either side.

Breathing in through her nose, she counted and then breathed out through her mouth, calming herself. The area was quiet with the snow falling, and a couple of apartments still had Christmas lights twinkling.

She took another deep breath and forced herself to cut the engine and step out of the car. It would be dark soon, and she wanted to do this while it was still light outside. For some reason, that felt safer. The sun shone down, not really warm but making everything look bright and alive. She shut the door and stood there, taking in the deep red brick, wrought iron railings, and tall trees that combined into an aesthetically pleasing picture of peace and calm.

How many times had she sat on that porch during the spring or summer, sipping her tea and looking for the perfect camera angle? How many pictures had she taken of this neighborhood?

Why couldn't she remember that night?

The wind picked up, scattering the snow, and she shivered, her feet going numb. Enough with the procrastinating. Throwing her shoulders back, she strode along the walkway to the door, stepping over a couple of small sleds that looked as if they'd been dropped on the way to the door. Hopefully the residents would allow her inside to look around.

Right. Who wouldn't welcome a stranger who claimed she'd been so viciously attacked there that she'd fallen into a coma? She lifted her hand but hesitated before knocking. This was crazy.

She knocked anyway.

A sound came from inside, then the thumping of something rolling across the floor and a soft curse, before the door was opened. A man stood there, tall with light brown hair and glasses showcasing brown eyes. He hopped on one foot with a child's toy right behind him, spinning wildly as if he'd tripped over it. "Sorry about that. I—" His eyes widened and he reached for her. "Grace!"

Chapter 13

Grace froze as the stranger embraced her and then let go, the force of his hug pushing them both out onto the porch.

He leaned back, his eyes wide. The sun shone down on them, highlighting streaks of natural blond in his hair and showing freckles across his face. "I don't know what to say," he said, rubbing her arm. "You're alive. You're awake and here." He smiled and then started. "Crap. Sorry. Come inside where it's warm. I'm just completely taken off guard."

"Ditto," Grace said, tripping over her own feet as she followed him inside. Who was this nice guy?

"Oh, watch out." He kicked a couple of toy trains out of the way and led her to a faux leather sofa. "Here. Sit down. Um, would you like a drink?"

"No, thanks." She looked around the small unit that contained a living room, cute breakfast nook, and open kitchen separated by a granite island covered with what looked like Legos. Colored pictures of puppies had been proudly taped to the refrigerator, the crayon lines more like scribbles. "So. Um, you know me?"

He frowned and slowly lowered himself to a chair facing the sofa across from a coffee table that held a couple of magazines. "You don't remember." He said the words slowly, as if realizing her situation. "Oh. Okay."

Vulnerable and feeling unsure, she nodded. "Yeah. Who are you?"

He took a deep breath, his gaze wandering the apartment and then coming back to her. "Brian. I'm Brian." He ran a hand through his thick hair, which was cut short and stylish. "Okay. This is so strange. I'm Brian, and we dated for about three months before, um, the attack."

She blinked. He was cute and tall, and she could see herself dating him. Well, before she'd met someone like Adare. "My sister didn't like the guy I was dating." In fact, Faith had moved Grace to a hospital across town and hadn't allowed anybody to visit her until they found the criminal who'd hurt her.

Brian winced. "Yeah. Your sister couldn't stand me." His grin was rueful. "I don't blame her, not completely. Seven years ago I was a struggling musician and not really worth much. I also partied a lot and could have been considered an asshole, and she was this famous neurosurgeon and you were getting really successful with your photos." He looked around at the assorted toys. "I grew up, I guess."

It looked like it. "We dated?"

"Yeah." His voice softened. "I really liked you, and I tried to visit you in the hospital, but your sister nixed that idea. Then you disappeared, and I never found out what happened."

"I'm sorry." That had to be so weird. "So, you rented my apartment?" That was kind of strange.

He chuckled. "I was living with you, and for a while, I waited for you to come home. Then, I met someone else, but I'm still here. For now. We just closed on a house across town, a cute bungalow with a fenced back yard, and I'm procrastinating with packing." He leaned down and picked up a stuffed animal that looked like a cross between a dog and a unicorn. "I guess I've moved on, but I had to in order to deal with your loss. I'm sorry if that's hurtful. Where have you been?"

She relaxed her body and took a couple of deep breaths. "I came out of the coma five years ago and have been, um, in rehabilitation. In Europe." Yeah, that sounded like a good story.

He smiled again, his face lighting up. "I'm so glad. I really am."

She stared at his handsome face, her headache intensifying. "I wish I remembered you."

He breathed out. "Well. Maybe I can help. Is this the first time you've been back home?"

She no longer had a home. Not really. "Yes. I thought coming to Denver might help shake loose some memories, but so far, nothing."

"Okay." He leaned forward. "What if I showed you around town? Like went places we used to go? Maybe that would help?" When she didn't answer, he chuckled. "Sorry. This is all just so much. I'd like to help."

She could see what she'd liked in him.

A door to the right of the kitchen opened, and a woman walked out with a toddler in her arms. "I fell asleep with her again, and apparently nap time is now over." She looked around and started, her green eyes widening. "Grace. Oh my God. Grace!" Wonder danced over her pretty features.

Brian stood and took the little girl, hugging her.

Grace partially stood, staring at the blonde. She was on the tallish side with pretty features, dressed in yoga pants and a T-shirt with the word "NOPE" across her chest.

The woman looked at Grace and then Brian and then back at Grace. She grimaced. "So. We ended up together." She held up a hand. "We didn't plan it. You were gone, and we tried to find you, and somehow…"

"We found each other," Brian said over the toddler.

The little girl had green eyes and blond hair, like her mother. She looked at Grace and sucked her thumb, her eyes sleepy.

"I'm glad," Grace said, turning back to study the woman. They must've been friends. Who was she? Trying to remember was increasing her headache, so Grace sat back down, deflated.

Brian sat. "Grace doesn't remember us. This is Bobbi. You two were good friends."

Bobbi stepped over a couple of stuffed animals to sit on the sofa with Grace, facing her. "You don't remember? But you're out of the coma. That's amazing." She reached out to touch Grace and then pulled her hand back. "We tried to visit, but your sister—"

"Can be a little overprotective," Grace said, her mind reeling. How many friends had she left not knowing what had happened to her? Darn Faith. She had always been so focused on school and career and probably hadn't even thought of friends. "I'm sorry I just disappeared. I'm okay now." Not even remotely true. "I'm glad you found each other, and your baby is adorable." She really was cute.

"Her name is Rose. After my mom," Brian said, settling the little girl on his lap. "So. We were thinking of showing Grace around town to maybe jog her memory. What do you think, honey?"

Bobbi shrugged. "Let's give it a shot. What could go wrong?"

* * * *

Adare finished loading the new explosives in the back of his vehicle as darkness began to fall and the dropping temperature turned the snow to ice. The metal doors of the storage units around them creaked from the cold.

Jacki handed him the last box and stretched her back, rolling her neck and tossing her tawny hair. Her car was parked beside the opposite units, gathering snow across the windshield. "You know, one of the things I always liked about you was your sense of loyalty," she said.

"Thanks." He tucked the box into a gap, wedging them all in so they wouldn't detonate, even if Benny drove.

"But don't you deserve to be happy? How can you be when you're mated to a woman, an actual human, whom you don't love? How does that make sense, considering you might live forever?"

Jacki's tenacity could be an asset sometimes, but right now, it was grating on his nerves.

He shut the back hatch. "I don't love you, either." It was time for harsh truth. "It's not in me to love anyone."

Jacki snorted, apparently not insulted in the least. "You've cut yourself off, and that makes sense, but you can love again. Stop being a moron and let yourself."

He'd forgotten how direct she could be, a fact he'd once appreciated. "I have more important concerns right now than love." Like not dying on the raid he and Benny were planning.

"Good point." Jacki leaned against the vehicle with the snow falling softly onto her hair. "If you survive, which I could help you do, you should think about it. Grace seems like a nice woman, but she doesn't challenge you. She's like milk toast in a spicy enchilada world."

Milk toast? Grace was sweet and honest, and she needed to be protected. Although she had an impressive sense of calm and strength that he hadn't realized until the fight with the Kurjans. "I have enough challenges in my life," he muttered. "I made a vow to her, Jacki, and that's final." It made zero sense to think about what might've been, because reality always won in the end.

"You kept your vow, and she's alive. Now it's time to move on," Jacki pushed.

It was time for him to shut this down. "I haven't seen you for a century, feline, and that's okay. We were close once, and I'll keep those memories, but all we can be now is friends. So stop pushing me and accept those parameters." There was no need to stop and consider her suggestion, because he was mated, and that was absolute. He nodded as Benny loped around the corner of the farthest storage unit.

Jacki sighed. "You used to like my tenacity."

"Still do," Adare said, dusting snow from his coat. "Doesn't change the situation."

Jacki huffed out a breath. "You don't even see that woman for who she is. You have her on this stupid pedestal, thinking she's so perfect, impressed that she managed to shoot toward an enemy without hitting you."

"Actually, she hit me," Benny said cheerfully, his overlarge boots leaving heavy tracks in the snow. "Not the first time a female has shot me, by the way." He frowned. "That happens a lot, actually. Maybe I should take stock." He was silent for a moment, studying his boots. Then he shrugged. "Nope. I'm good."

Adare was done with the two of them. "Jacki, it has been a pleasure. Thank you for the explosives." He held out a hand to shake hers, and she followed suit, rubbing her thumb on his palm. He released her. "Benny? I'm definitely driving." Without waiting for an answer or an argument, he strode around to the driver's side and slid inside, igniting the engine in an unsubtle way to get Benny on the move. They had to go back to the cabin and prepare.

Benny barreled into the passenger seat, flinging snow as he settled in.

Adare drove sedately down the drive between storage units.

Benny kicked out his boots, thunking them on the rubber floor mat. "I like that feline shifter. Would it bug you if I asked her out?"

"No," Adare said. Benny had been hitting on Jacki for two days, so why he was asking now was a mystery that Adare couldn't be troubled to solve. "Feel free."

Benny flipped on the switch to heat his seat. "She was all over you. I know you have a history, so are you tempted?"

"No. I'm mated." Adare leaned forward and peered at the snow before increasing the speed of the wipers.

Benny sighed. "That's logical. But what do you feel about all of this?"

Adare turned the SUV out onto the main road and increased his speed. They could make it back home by dawn if Benny didn't insist they stop to eat too often. "I don't feel anything."

"Yeah," Benny drawled. "That's something we need to talk about. Now is a good time."

Adare partially turned, keeping an eye on the road. "You want to talk about my *feelings*?" Had Benny been watching too much daytime television again?

"Sure. I understand that you don't think you have any, and I'm sure that's an excellent survival tactic after everything we've all been through." Benny turned and looked out at the night. "Maybe I should get rid of feelings. That'd be nice. I mean, I feel everything all the time, and it's exhausting." He was quiet for several moments, no doubt continuing the one-sided conversation in his head. Finally, he nodded. "Nope. I'm good. Feelings make life worth living and give us a reason to fight the way we do." Apparently satisfied, he turned back to Adare. "We have to work on you. You'll never find happiness this way."

Happiness? That was merely a construct of idealists. "I like my life and my job. That's all I want." An image of Grace spread out before him on his bed flashed through his mind and called him a liar.

Benny huffed out air. "Sometimes it's difficult being your brother."

They'd become brothers, bound by blood and bone, during the Seven ritual. Adare turned down the heat. "I'm sorry about that, Ben." He really was.

Benny's phone buzzed, and he dug it out of his pocket, pressing it to his ear. "Go for Benjamin." He listened and then straightened. "When? Where?" He cut a look toward Adare, losing the lazy amusement normally glowing in his eyes. "Do we have allies nearby? Okay. Great. They need to find that driver, right now, and lock him down. We'll be there as soon as possible." He clicked off.

Adare slowed the vehicle, adrenaline flooding his system. "What's happened now?"

"That was Talen at Realm Headquarters. Grace wasn't on the plane."

Chapter 14

Grace lay back in the surprisingly comfortable bed of the motel, the pain behind her eyes so great she had to close them. During the last several months, she'd tried over-the-counter pain meds, alcohol, and even sugar combined with caffeine, but nothing touched the pain. So she let it take her, sometimes into a deep sleep she feared could turn into a coma.

Every instinct she had told her that was where her brain was heading.

Brian and Bobbi had taken her to several of the old restaurants and bars they used to frequent, but nothing had jogged her memory. She'd done her best to keep her face averted from any surveillance cameras, since the Kurjans knew she was in Colorado. At least she was far away from where they'd attacked, so maybe they wouldn't look immediately in Denver. Once she'd started to feel sick, Bobbi had taken her back to her rental car, offering to put her up for the night.

She wasn't ready to spend the night in the place where she'd been attacked. Plus, she could use a little bit of space from Brian and Bobbi.

There was something familiar about Denver and the snow and mountains, though. Like a wisp of thought she couldn't quite grasp. Man, she wanted to call Faith and talk. It was possible no one yet knew about her detour to Denver. She'd paid off the driver with a hundred dollar bill, and it was unlikely the Realm would contact Adare when their plane arrived.

Maybe.

Either way, since she'd tossed her phone several counties to the south, she wasn't calling anybody. So she kept her eyes shut and breathed deep, using the exercises one of her many doctors had taught her. Soon, she drifted into sleep, her body relaxing completely and her mind going dark.

Until light flashed in, jolting her system and flooding her with energy. She slept deeper, turning on her side.

The night came into focus, and she stood in her kitchen in Denver, cookies cooling on the rack and photographs spread across the island. The smells of chocolate and something different, something metallic, filled her nostrils.

Almost in slow motion, she turned to see red dripping down the cupboards. Red against white, a spectacular combination. Where was her camera?

Pain flashed in her head, and glass cut into her back when she rolled over shards, somehow on the floor all of a sudden. Fight. She had to fight. More red dripped down. Was that her blood? Her vision clouded, and she hit back, fighting with everything she had. Blows rained down, one after another, and a voice tried to cut through the pain.

The pain was excruciating, and blood dripped into her ears, partially deafening her.

"You need to stop fighting." The voice was garbled and angry. She didn't recognize it. The hands hitting her were strong and bigger than hers. "Just stop. We must go."

Go? She wasn't going anywhere. She punched up hard and screamed, her body arching with the effort of her lungs.

He punched her square in the mouth, and she went silent, the hazy room swirling around and darkness trying to take her down. She blinked several times, and saw purplish red eyes. She screamed again, and another punch took her into nothingness.

She gasped and sat up in the bed, her muscles tightening with panic. Coughing, she pressed her hand against her diaphragm, her heartbeat galloping dangerously, her ears ringing. Okay. She was safe. It was just a dream.

Or was it?

Shit. Was it a memory or just a nightmare after the fight with the Kurjans the other night? If it was a memory, they'd found her before she'd even known about immortals.

She shuddered, chilled from head to toe.

Closing her eyes, she breathed deep to calm herself. Was that just a dream? She truly didn't know. If the Kurjans had found her seven years ago, how had she survived an attack all by herself?

God, she hated not remembering what had happened.

The land line beside the bed rang, and she jumped, yelping. She swung toward the phone, her body trembling. Only two people knew she was in this motel. Still, her hand shook when she answered, and she lowered her voice in a lame attempt to disguise it. "Hello?"

"Oh, shoot. I woke you up. I'm sorry," Bobbi said, her voice cheerful despite the early hour. "Rosy wakes up early, and sometimes I forget the rest of the world might want sleep and that dawn isn't a normal time to call. I gave sleep up two years ago." She laughed.

Grace relaxed, although her heart still beat so hard her chest ached. "I'm up. Had a weird nightmare, but I'm thinking that's probably a good thing."

"About the night you were attacked?" The baby giggled in the background.

"Yeah. Well, maybe. It's pretty fuzzy." Grace pushed hair away from her face.

There was a muffled sound and then Bobbi came back on. "Sorry about that. Rose wanted down. You probably don't remember this about me, but I'm a planner. I came up with a list last night of everywhere you and I used to hang out, and then I made Brian do the same. He's young. He can sleep when we're in our fifties."

Apparently Grace had made good friends before disappearing. "So the three of us didn't do a lot together? I mean, you have different lists?"

Bobbi was quiet for a moment. "Well, yeah. It's kind of weird, but Bri and I met through you. We didn't really know each other until you disappeared, and well, this is awkward. You're being really cool about it, though."

Considering she didn't remember either one of them, it was easy to be cool. "That was seven years ago." Anticipation rippled through her, although she'd need to be mindful of surveillance. Cameras were everywhere. "What's this great plan you've come up with?"

Bobbi laughed. "You used to say that before. That I had great plans, and you said it with just a hint of humor, just like that. I've missed you."

The words meant something. Grace bit her lip. If she was in danger, everyone she brought into her world would also be in danger. She'd take this day, this one day, and try to rediscover her life. If she failed, she'd move on before any harm could come to the little family that she'd helped to bring together. "I wish I remembered."

"You will. The plan is for you to grab lattes on the way here, and then we'll go step by step. My sister is coming to babysit Rose, so we'll have all day. Don't worry. By the end of it, you'll surely remember something, right?" Bobbi asked.

"Yeah." If not, Grace would leave. The feeling of time counting down weighed on her, and not just because of her illness. If Adare knew she was gone, he'd be hunting.

Hopefully he had no clue.

* * * *

Night was falling by the time Adare and Benny made it back down south to the airport.

Adare drove as if a hell beast snorted on their back bumper, barreling toward a metal hangar set far back from the others in the private part of the airport. "Somebody has taken her." He couldn't believe it. He'd just put her in the car, believing the Realm officials knew what they were doing. "There's a fucking reason we haven't aligned with anybody." The Seven were the best of the best and didn't need complications or connections.

"This isn't your fault," Benny said, grabbing onto the handle above his door to keep from crashing through the windshield.

Of course it was his fault. He never should have trusted a human chauffeur to take Grace to the airport.

"Um, not for nothing, but we still have explosives in the back of this thing," Benny said.

Adare didn't care. Not a bit. He slid to a stop in front of the metal building, slamming into a snowbank. The vehicle hadn't stopped moving before he was out and striding through the darkness and snow, followed closely by Benny.

A figure stepped out of the shadows, long and lean, smooth danger in every line. "Hey, Benny."

Benny stepped up, his face splitting in a smile. "Jordan Pride. Damn, it's good to see you." He shook hands and then jerked his head toward Adare. "Have you guys met?"

"No," Adare said shortly, although he'd heard of the leader of the feline nation. The guy was deadly and fiercely protective of his people. He also didn't know about the Seven, but somehow knew Benny. Of course, everyone knew Benny. "Have you acquired the human?"

Jordan studied him, his topaz eyes gleaming through the darkness. As a lion shifter, he was probably used to a bit more deference.

Adare didn't give a shit.

Jordan nodded. "Talked to the Realm, and they IDed the guy, so we searched for him all day. Finally found him, stoned out of his gourd, playing video games in some moron's basement."

"What did you tell him?" Benny asked.

"Nothing," Jordan returned. The shifter wore cargo pants with a black long-sleeved T-shirt and thick boots; no doubt he was armed. Although a lion like him probably didn't need much besides his claws. Even in human form, there was something feral and predatory about the male. "He was starting to cry when I tied him up, so I came outside. The noise was annoying."

Benny winced. "I hate it when they cry."

Adare rolled his shoulders back. The bastard would do a lot more than cry by the time he was done with him.

Jordan lifted his head and sniffed. "You boys have explosives in the back of that vehicle?"

"Yep," Benny said. "Your sense of smell is amazing. It's good to stock up once in a while."

One of Jordan's sandy blond eyebrows rose. "Interesting. You've never been part of the Realm, Benjamin, and I know O'Cearbhaill here has kept his distance as well. Why would you be using Realm transportation and sending Adare's mate to headquarters?"

Adare needed to get inside the hangar and now. Yet the shifter nation could not learn about the Seven. The cats wouldn't like it. Not at all.

Benny came to the rescue. "Well, now. Adare's mate hasn't been feeling all that well, and he thought the queen could take a looksee at her. You know that Chalton, my nephew, is the head of the tech arm of the Realm, right?"

Jordan turned his attention on Adare. "You didn't accompany your mate?"

"No." Adare wasn't going to explain.

"I find that odd," Jordan said, his chin lowering.

It probably was odd to the leader. "Even so, I don't have time to chat. If you don't mind, I'm going to go interrogate the crying moron," Adare said, stepping around Benny toward the door.

"I do mind," Jordan said mildly.

Benny sighed. "Jordan, this is what it is. I'm calling in a favor."

The cat looked at Benny for several long beats. "We're even, then. Also, don't think I'll let this go for good. Just for tonight."

"Fair enough." Benny clapped Jordan on the back. "Say hi to Katie, Menace and Mayhem for me, would you?"

"Sure." Jordan turned, and silent as death, disappeared into the darkness.

Benny watched him go. "That always creeps me the hell out. I mean, we move silently, but feline shifters are just too quiet. Nobody should be that quiet."

Adare paused. There was a chance they'd just made an enemy if Jordan dug deep enough to find out about the Seven. What he and his brothers had had to do to become the Seven wouldn't be tolerated by the shifter nation. Or the witch nation. He'd heard of Katie Pride, Jordan's mate. "Who are Menace and Mayhem?" he asked, heading for the door.

"Jordan's twin girls, Samantha and Sydney. They have to be in their early twenties by now. Jordan gave them the nicknames when they were born, and they just stuck. Fun kids but definitely wild."

So Pride had a weakness. Good to know.

Adare shoved open the door to find a lone figure duct taped to a chair in the center of an empty airplane hangar. He had to appreciate the aesthetics of the situation.

The guy's head hung down, and he sniffled, his hands behind his back. When he lifted his head, Adare saw he was in his early thirties with dilated brown eyes, shaggy brown hair, and a trimmed brown goatee. "Who are you guys? Come on, dudes. Why am I here?"

Adare studied him and drew the knife from his left boot, walking slowly and purposefully across the smooth concrete floor. He let the light glint off the blade and made sure that the idiot could see it. "I'm the guy who's going to cut you into ribbons, pretty ones, and then decorate this entire hangar with your entrails."

The human's eyes widened and he turned his head, puking what looked like pepperoni and pineapples all over the floor.

"Gross," Benny said, halting. "That's just gross."

Chapter 15

Adare twirled the knife in his hand, careful to avoid the vomit. "You picked up my woman earlier today." It wouldn't hurt to let the jackass know the sense of possession Adare was feeling.

The guy snorted snot up his nose. "My name is Gilbert. I'm thirty-two, and I want to be a champion gamer. I'm working hard on it."

Adare glanced sideways at Benny.

Benny shrugged.

Gilbert coughed. "What's your name? Let's talk."

Benny frowned and drew back. "What are you doing?"

Gilbert shrugged, his bony body barely moving in the thin gray T-shirt that covered his sunken chest. Visible goosebumps rose on his skin, and he shuddered, even his nose getting red from the cold. "I thought we could get to know each other."

"Why?" Adare growled, keeping the blade front and center.

"I, um, saw it on television. That you should try and personalize yourself to sociopaths if they kidnap you." Tears filled Gilbert's dilated eyes. "I'm not into guys, man. It's totally okay if you are, but the BDSM thing has never interested me. I like chicks and have never spanked one. I mean, not one time." His eyebrows lifted. "In fact, I have a girlfriend named Peggy. She's blond with dark eyes and she likes slow kisses and no bondage."

"You do not," Benny muttered.

Gilbert deflated. "You're right. I don't have a girlfriend." He struggled briefly against the bindings. "Just let me go. I won't tell anybody about this. I promise."

Adare cocked his head, studying the human. "I don't want to kill you, Gilbert."

"Good." Gilbert breathed out and nodded wildly. "We're on the same page. I don't want you to kill me. This is good, dude. What's your name?"

Adare shook his head. He was losing control with this twerp. "Obviously you're not the mastermind here."

"Nope. Not at all." Gilbert smiled, his head bobbing. "I'm not. Not even close."

Just how high was he? Adare dropped to his haunches so they were eye-to-eye. "Who did you deliver my woman to?"

Gilbert blinked. "Huh?"

Adare drew the knife forward and set it on Gilbert's knee. "I asked you a question."

"Oh. Okay." Gilbert stared at the blade as if he couldn't look away. "The pretty lady with hazel eyes? I didn't deliver her to anybody."

Adare grasped the knife. "You didn't take her to the airport, and that's where I paid you to take her."

"Wait. Okay. Wait." Gilbert shuddered. "She gave me a hundred dollars to take her somewhere else."

"Liar." Adare stood, flipping the knife around to more easily plunge the blade into Gilbert's thigh. Grace had promised him she'd go to the Realm, and she'd looked him right in the eye as she'd made the vow. The only way she wasn't where she'd said she'd be was if somebody had taken her. "The first time I stab you, it's really going to hurt. The second time won't be as bad, and the third will feel like a twinge." He lowered his chin. "I could stab you at least a hundred times before you lose consciousness. Is that what you want?"

"No. That is definitely not what I want," Gilbert gasped, trying to push his chair backward on the concrete. He didn't move.

"Okay. Then I'll give you one more chance. Tell me what happened to Grace." Adare kept his voice soothing to throw off his prey.

Gilbert's mouth dropped open and he stared at the knife. "Okay, now listen. I know I was supposed to take her to the airport, but when she got into the car, she asked me to take her to a car rental place that was far away from the airport. I wasn't sure what to do, and then she gave me a hundred dollar bill, so I figured she should go where she wanted, you know?"

Adare plunged the knife into his leg, careful not to slice an artery or anything that couldn't be easily fixed. For now.

Gilbert cried out and gasped, his chest moving wildly as he absorbed the pain.

Adare pulled the knife free, and Gilbert fell forward as much as his bindings would allow, hissing in agony. "Dude. That was so uncool," he coughed.

Adare wiped blood off on Gilbert's good leg. "I'm going to ask you again."

"No." Gilbert shook his head wildly. "Don't ask me again. Don't ask me anything. You don't want the truth. I'm done. I'm done talking."

Adare smiled. "No, you're not. You're nowhere near done."

Gilbert whimpered.

Adare lifted the knife.

Benny held up a hand. "Just give this a second. Gilbert, what was the name of the car rental place?"

"Romeo's Reasonable Rentals," Gilbert said, his back arching and pain etched into the lines of his pale face.

Benny pulled his phone from his back pocket. "That's a rather detailed response." He lifted the phone, pressed a button, and quickly spoke into it. "Hey, Chalton. Do me a favor. Hack into the surveillance system of a Romeo's Reasonable Rentals outside of Durango, would you? Probably around nine this morning. I'll wait."

Adare stared at Gilbert. How many times would he need to stab this idiot before he told the truth? It was frankly surprising he'd lasted this long.

Benny waited a few beats. "Perfect. Thanks." He clicked off and moved toward Adare, holding the phone so they could both see the screen. "He sent me the feed."

Adare looked down at the video to see Grace enter the facility and approach the counter, sign documents, and then walk out with the kid from behind the counter. He frowned. "Play it again." Benny did so, and he watched again, searching for the threat. Bright sunlight cascaded in through the windows, so no Kurjans or Cysts could've been outside with weapons. What in the world was Grace doing?

Benny's phone buzzed, and he brought up a video outside the car rental place. The sunlight sparkled off the snow and Grace's hair as she walked with a dark-haired kid to a rental car, got inside, smiled at him, and drove away.

Benny cleared his throat. "Looks like she took off on her own."

Adare lifted his chin. "Not a chance. I don't know where the threat was or who made her do this, but I will find out."

Gilbert sniffed. "Does that mean I can go?"

Adare sighed. Jesus. He'd just stabbed the moron for no reason. "Yeah. Let me bandage your leg, and you can go. If you want to notify the authorities, feel free, but they'll never find me."

Gilbert's eyebrows lifted. "Maybe. Or not."

Benny sighed and pulled out his wallet to reveal several bills. "I have about a thousand."

"Now we're talking," Gilbert said, smiling through his tears. "I knew we'd become friends."

* * * *

Grace delivered the lattes, stepping over a princess castle on the way into her old apartment. This time, there were boxes lined up in the kitchen.

Standing in the living room, Bobbi accepted her drink and nodded toward the boxes. "Think he'll get the hint? I packed a week ago, and he's driving me nuts with the procrastination, you know?" She took a big drink and then pushed the castle to the side with one tennis shoe. "If we have time, maybe you'd like to see the new house? I mean, just if you want to."

Why couldn't Grace remember this friend? "I'd like that, Bobbi."

"Cool." Bobbi picked up a purse big enough to use as a weekend bag. "Bri? Let's go."

Brian emerged from one of the two bedrooms, a tablet in his hands. "I've calculated the best route to see everything, and—"

Bobbi sighed. "I already did that."

"Yeah, but you went by location, and I went by drive time." He grinned, this time wearing fashionable glasses. "My way is twenty minutes faster."

They were a cute couple. Maybe something good had come out of Grace's coma, and maybe that knowledge could help her move on, even if she never regained her memories.

Bobbi angled toward the furthest bedroom. "Sis? We're taking off. Okay?"

A blonde woman in her early twenties emerged from the bedroom with Rose in her arms. She was slight, and her movements were halting, as if she'd injured her back. "Sure. No problem." Her voice was soft and timid as she pulled at a T-shirt sporting the logo of the Denver Broncos. "Have a nice time."

There was something off about the woman. Grace studied her, itching for her camera. Her temples pounded and the room went in and out of focus, so she held perfectly still until the attack stopped. Her stomach felt hollow, and the coffee gurgled into an acidic mess inside her. She hadn't had an attack like this one for a week, but that was sooner than the last interval. Time was definitely running out.

"You okay?" Brian asked, concern drawing his lips down.

She nodded. "Yeah. I'm fine." She tugged her older camera out of her bag. "Could I take a couple of pictures? Rose is just so cute."

Bobbi's sister's eyes widened, and she took a step back.

"Sure," Brian said smoothly. "This brings back memories, big time."

Grace clicked off several shots of the toddler with her aunt and then quickly reached for her digital camera to do the same. "The film shots will turn out better, but they'll have to wait for development. For now, this'll have to do."

"You always were a snob about film versus digital," Brian said.

Bobbi laughed. "That is so true. I forgot about that." She moved and reached for Rose. "How about a family picture? Do you mind, Grace? I've missed your shots."

"Sure." Warmth filled Grace. "Why don't you sit on the couch? The color of the wall behind it is a nice background." Had she chosen that paint color way back when? Something told her she had.

"Excuse me," the sister said, turning and heading for the bathroom.

Bobbi watched her go and sighed. "Don't worry about her. She's going through a rough time." Rose, dressed in a cute pink outfit, fussed, but Bobbi sat and settled the toddler on her lap. Brian sat next to them and put an arm around them both, smiling for the camera.

Grace adjusted her angle, lifted up, and snapped several shots. "I'll send these to you once I get on a computer and tweak them a bit. Maybe as a thank you present for all you're doing for me." It was the least she could do.

"Let's go." Bobbi stood and walked to the back bedroom, returning without the baby. "She's ready for a nap. Didn't even complain." Moving past Grace, she opened the door and tucked her arm in Grace's, looking up at the clear blue sky. "Oh, it's a pretty day. Are my sunglasses in the car, Bri?"

Brian followed them, shutting the door before zipping up his leather jacket. "I don't know. Last time I saw them, they were on Rose's stuffed pig." He picked up the sled and set it against the house before striding into the sun, squinting at the sparkling snow. "I think mine are in the car. You can borrow those if you don't find yours."

Grace relaxed for the first time in days. These had been her friends, and she'd helped bring them together. Kind of. The sun brought out the blond highlights in Brian's hair, and he grinned, looking boyishly handsome. Yeah, she could see why she'd been attracted to him. There was a lightness in him that Adare had probably never had, even in his youth.

The thought of Adare just wouldn't leave her mind. He'd kissed her. Well, she'd kissed him. That hadn't felt like a duty—even on his part. Maybe she'd been a dreamer way back when.

She followed the couple to an older SUV and sat in the back, next to a sparkling clean baby seat.

The two sat in the front, and Bobbi searched for sunglasses.

"Your car is so clean," Grace murmured.

Brian snorted. "No comment."

Bobbi smacked him. "I do not have OCD. Okay, maybe a little, but not enough that it affects my life."

"It affects my life," he said on a laugh, driving quietly out of the residential area. "Where to first on this lovely Saturday, my lovely wife?"

"To the Purple Plate for breakfast." Bobbi partially turned, her eyes sparkling. "You and I used to meet there once a week, Grace. Let's see if you remember the place, or if you order the same thing you used to." She grinned. "It's like an experiment."

Yet another one, but maybe this time it would have better results. "What's up with your sister, Bobbi?"

Bobbi lost her smile. "She's been dating this total dickhead and finally broke up with him. I think he was pushing her around, but she won't talk about it. Yet."

The memory of Grace's nightmare flashed through her head. Had it been a memory of somebody hitting her? Or was her subconscious just messing around? She frowned.

Bobbi leaned back and patted her hand. "I know we're going to figure something out today."

Just so long as no cameras caught them, they were okay. She couldn't let her friends get hurt. Grace forced a smile. "I hope so."

Chapter 16

"We've been driving all night and have no clue where to go once we get to Denver," Benny protested, once again. "The satellites caught her heading toward Denver but then lost her. I'm hungry."

Adare's fury grew as the sky began to lighten. "This is the only place she could've gone, right? I mean, where else would she be?" If she was on her own. Except she wasn't, because she had to have somehow been forced into renting that car. "I don't believe Grace would've lied to my face like that." The woman didn't have it in her.

Benny scrolled through the information on his phone. "She asked for an older vehicle and they had those at this crappy dealership." He looked up at the snow hitting the windshield. "The car she rented isn't chipped in any way and doesn't have GPS, so it was a smart move if she didn't want to be followed."

"This still doesn't make sense," Adare muttered, pressing harder on the gas pedal. "If somebody has her, she could be anywhere. If she's following her own plan, then she has to be in Denver, right? It's where she used to live, and it's a town she once knew."

Benny blew out air. "Yeah, but why go back to Denver? She knows she can't return to her former life."

Adare lifted a shoulder. "If she went willingly, which I'm still not buying, then maybe she wanted to regain those lost memories?"

"Does she have lost memories?" Benny asked.

"Aye," Adare said. "I haven't talked to her about it, but the last time I checked, her memories about her old life were still hazy. Although if she wanted to return to Denver, why didn't she just say so?"

"Would you have let her?"

Adare slowed his pace to drive around a bus painted a bright purple. "Sure. Up until a month or so ago, I would've let her. Before we really started planning for our op." But she hadn't asked—hadn't even reached out.

Benny stared at the morning outside. "I don't know, brother. We find Grace in the middle of nowhere trying to buy vampire blood, then we get attacked by Kurjans, and now she's broken a promise and rented a vehicle in Colorado so she can disappear? What is up with your mate?"

That was a damn good question. Adare had been too busy with his fangs in her thigh to question her; apparently he shouldn't have been satisfied with her explanation of why she couldn't heal herself. "I'm not easy to fool," he muttered.

"No shit. You can detect a lie a mile away," Benny agreed. "If she lied, she must be good at it."

Anger spiraled through Adare so quickly his hands tightened on the steering wheel. "There's no way Grace is a good liar."

"I guess we're about to find out." Benny looked down at his phone. "Chalton and the Realm computer experts are trying to catch her trail again with traffic cameras and other surveillance, and they're looking at downtown Denver as well as the neighborhood where she used to live."

Adare swallowed. "She's been gone for nearly twenty-four hours, Benny."

Ben sobered. "I know."

"If we're looking for her, so are the Kurjans." It was too much to hope that the Kurjans had just given up after the fight the other day. They probably had a satellite feed searching the state of Colorado at that very moment. Adare took the next exit. "Give me directions."

Benny read off the route to Grace's former apartment.

Adare banished emotion, letting his brain take over. The only feasible explanation was that Grace had chosen to drive to Denver, chosen to lie to him, and chosen to put herself and the entire Seven in danger of exposure. He exhaled slowly, shackling the beast at his core that wanted loose.

Nice subdivisions slowly swallowed them on both sides until he parked in front of a brick building covered with snow. They were looking for Unit L.

"There it is," Benny said.

Adare stepped out and made sure none of Gilbert's blood remained on his clothing. The dork had seemed happy with the two grand they'd given him, once Adare had added his money to Benny's, so hopefully he wouldn't go to the authorities. No blood. Good.

He strode across a shoveled path being warmed by the sun and knocked on the door.

A woman answered, looking way up; she held a cute blond girl in her arms. She took a step back, her terror apparent.

He stepped away and shoved his hands in his pockets, trying to look casual and unthreatening. "Hi. I'm so sorry to bother you, but I'm looking for my friend. Her name is Grace, and she used to live here."

The woman's gaze went behind him to Benny, and she turned even paler.

Benny remained in place. "Howdy. I know I'm huge, but I never hurt cute women like you. I'm as harmless as a puppy." He clapped Adare on the back. Hard. "My buddy here is harmless, too, but since he's Scottish, it's harder to tell. I'm not Scottish. I'm kind of Russian and a few other things melded in, and that makes me mellower than most guys my size. Maybe all guys my size. I can't tell you how hard it is to find shoes."

What the hell was he doing?

Adare studied the woman. The more Benny talked, the more she visibly relaxed. Maybe she related to buckets of crazy.

Benny must've thought the same thing. "Shoes are one thing, but have you ever thought about socks? Normal socks, even the big ones, don't fit my feet. It's a true challenge. My ma used to knit my socks, but she passed on to the great beyond, and now I'm caught trying to scrabble material together to cover my big feet. I like the fabric of potholders, but they just don't make them big enough, you know?" He leaned in and lowered his voice. "I'm not wearing socks right now, which is fine, except when I take my boots off, everyone yells at me."

Her lips pressed together as if she was trying to hide a smile.

Adare nodded. "Yeah, he stinks. So, about my friend Grace. Has she been here?"

The woman slowly shook her head. "No. I'm sorry." Her voice was soft with a hint of an accent. What was that? Her scent was unfamiliar as well. Sugar and lemons? Something sweet? "I don't know any Grace." Pink infused her cheeks and she dropped her gaze.

The woman was a terrible liar.

"What's your name, beautiful?" Benny tugged his wallet out and scribbled something on a piece of paper. "My name is Benny, and this is my cell phone number. Call me if Grace comes by. Please."

The woman's hand trembled, but she took the paper. "K-Kim. My name is Kim," she whispered, taking the paper. "I shall call you if anyone named Grace visits." With one last look at Benny, she stepped back and shut the door.

Adare looked over his shoulder.

Benny shrugged, his gaze remaining on the closed door. "Do you sense your mate near?"

Adare tuned into the area. "No, but I've never sensed her." He turned and followed Benny to the vehicle.

"Why do you suppose that woman lied?" Benny asked.

Adare slipped into the vehicle. "I don't know. Let's check in with the satellite guys. If they can't help, we might need to go back in." The woman had seemed terrified of him, but she'd lied.

"I'll call my nephew and see what he's found," Benny said, uncharacteristically serious. "You've stabbed enough people today."

* * * *

"You used to eat more than that," Bobbi said, munching happily on a taco for lunch.

Grace pushed her enchilada around her plate, taking a few bites and trying really hard not to throw up. "I've lost weight, but I'm feeling better now." Which was a total lie. She looked around the brightly decorated restaurant, feeling as if she had been there before. The margarita in front of her was delicious, but she was careful not to drink too much. Alcohol didn't agree with her any longer. Not much did.

They'd been all around town, and oddly enough, she had ordered many of the same items she used to, according to Bobbi. Some of the places had seemed familiar, but no memories were jogged loose. She'd learned that Brian had become a real estate agent and that Bobbi still worked as a bank teller.

"I really appreciate you two doing this all day with me." She took a sip of the drink.

Bobbi's green eyes softened. "I wish a memory would just hit you."

Brian tossed down the rest of his drink. "Maybe that'll happen tomorrow. Like your subconscious will work on it and then boom. You'll remember us."

That'd be great. Grace's vision blurred, and she waited it out, accustomed to the experience. The headache that followed was as normal as breathing for most people.

Bobbi pulled out a photo album. "If you're finished eating, take a look at these pictures. I thought maybe they might help." She slid a dark blue album across the table. "Since Brian hasn't packed yet, it was easy to find." She nudged him in the ribs.

He rolled his eyes. "I will pack. Tomorrow."

Grace flipped open the top page to find a picture of herself, about seven years ago, smiling next to Brian with a cake in front of her. "My birthday?"

"Yeah," Brian said. "I brought you here and had a cake waiting. I gave you a bracelet."

She had no idea where that bracelet was, darn it. "Who took all of these pictures?" There were some cute ones, but they were obviously taken by amateurs.

"Different people," he said, reaching for another taco. "You always were a snob about phone shots, but I liked the pictures."

She grinned. "Fair enough." She flipped through, seeing photographs of them with other people, all smiling. "You're not in here, Bobbi."

"Nope." Bobbi took a healthy drink of her blended margarita. "The three of us didn't hang out. We were from different parts of your life, until you got hurt. If you want, we can check out our new house tomorrow, and I can dig through boxes for some pictures I have of us."

A waiter brought over three cupcakes with sparklers.

Bobbi laughed. "You have to remember these. Blow yours out."

Grace's stomach lurched. She'd been up for too many hours, and her limbs were becoming heavy. She blew, having to try twice to extinguish the flames.

Bobbi leaned toward her. "I hope you made a wish." She closed her eyes, took a moment, and then blew hard. Sparks flew around and dust from the sparkler settled across the table as it was extinguished.

Grace sucked in air and coughed.

"Sorry." Bobbi opened her eyes and plucked her sparkler free, reaching for the cupcake to eat. "I wished for you to remember."

Brian blew on his sparkler, scattering even more of the dark dust. "Me too." His phone chirped a cheerful tune about mermaids, and he lifted it to his ear. "Brian Banks," he said, licking frosting off his fingers. He listened for a moment. "I'm only a few blocks away. I can be there in a couple of minutes." He clicked off and leaned over to kiss Bobbi on the cheek. "We just got a counter-offer on the Samuelson property. A good one. I have to head to the office, I'll grab an Uber home." He stood and winked at Grace. "Maybe tomorrow we should go skating."

She smiled and nodded, her jaw beginning to ache. A migraine was on the way, and though that wasn't unusual, she didn't even have aspirin. "Sounds good." She'd be long gone by morning. The day hadn't revealed anything new, but maybe Brian was right, and her subconscious would go to work now.

Either way, she had to leave before endangering the friends she wished she remembered.

Brian left, paying the waiter on the way out. That was nice of him.

Bobbi finished her drink. "I guess it's just us girls, like old times."

The room went dark. Grace grew still. She hated it when that happened.

"Grace? Are you okay?" Bobbi's voice came from far away.

"Yes," she slurred. "A migraine is coming. Just a second." She wavered but held strong, and soon the wave passed. "Sorry. That happens sometimes." Her vision cleared, and Adare stood in the doorway. She blinked as he walked inside. He had to be a hallucination.

His gaze caught hers, and the fury in his eyes was a physical burn. Crap. He was real.

He strode toward her, and people at nearby tables paused in conversation to watch him, their eyes wide. A waitress actually licked her lips. He reached their table.

Grace had the oddest urge to laugh. "Adare? This is my friend, Bobbi. Bobbi, this is my, ah, boyfriend? Yeah. I guess. His name is Adare." The darkness pressed in from every direction, and she closed her eyes, letting it take her. "I think we're gonna have to see the queen sooner rather than later."

Then, blissful nothingness surrounded her, taking away the pain along with everything else as she passed out completely.

Chapter 17

After a rushed two-hour flight from Denver to Realm Headquarters in northern Idaho, Adare was about to lose his mind. Grace hadn't awakened. It had been three hours, and she was still out. She looked pale and fragile on the examination table—which was more of a plush bed—in the infirmary of Realm headquarters. He cleared his throat. "Queen Kayrs? Shouldn't we do something?"

"Emma. For Pete's sake, call me Emma." The queen turned from the granite counter and a series of medical records that she'd requested about Grace. "She's seen quite a few Realm doctors, and the records are fairly complete."

What? Grace had been seeing multiple doctors and hadn't said anything? Adare crossed his arms.

The queen nodded, looking very unqueen-like in ripped jeans, ratty tennis shoes, and a T-shirt with Sheldon Cooper on it saying his mother had him tested. Her black hair was smoothed back in a ponytail and her deep blue eyes were serious. An intricate golden cuff encircled her left wrist, and she kept fiddling with the heavy-looking metal. "I've taken blood already, and we'll have those results soon." She waved her hand toward a bunch of spinning medical instruments on the far wall. "She's really been out for three hours?"

Faith hovered near the bed, her fingers on Grace's wrist. "Is this her first episode of hypotension with concomitant bradycardia?"

Adare shook his head. Sometimes he forgot that Grace's sister was a world-famous neurologist. "What?"

Faith released Grace. She was taller than Grace, and her mahogany hair was straight instead of curly, but they shared similar bone structure. "What has been happening with my sister?"

"I don't know. I tried to awaken her on the transport here, but she's out." As if she were in a coma.

Faith looked at Emma, concern bright in her gaze. "We need an MRI."

"Let's bring her out of it first to get some answers." Emma opened a drawer and pulled out a syringe. "Pure adrenaline—the immortal kind. This should do it." She turned and plunged the liquid into Grace's arm.

Grace gasped and sat up, her eyes wide. She slapped a hand against her chest and took several deep breaths, looking around the room and focusing on Adare. "Ah, shit."

"Nicely put," the queen said dryly.

Relief flooded Adare so fast he couldn't speak. So much for having no emotions. Then anger spiraled in faster than a hurricane, and he thought it better not to say anything. Right now.

"So." Faith pressed both hands on her hips. "You lied."

Grace blanched. "I didn't lie so much as decide to tell you in person."

"Tell her what, Grace?" Adare's voice was so garbled it surprised even him.

Grace shifted her weight on the bed, drawing her legs up to sit cross legged. "I haven't been feeling so well lately, and I lost the ability to heal myself."

Adare straightened. "You once had the ability?" At her nod, he didn't move. She had lied to him. Exceptionally well. Just who was this female? Whatever showed on his face had her wincing and looking away.

Faith grabbed the back of Grace's shirt and pulled it up.

Grace grasped the bottom of the shirt in front to keep herself covered. "Faith? Knock it off."

Faith's face turned pale and she angled her head, looking at Grace's back. "The marking is almost gone."

What? Adare shoved off his chair and strode around the side of the bed, forcing the queen to jump out of his way. He looked down at the perfect imprint of his marking across Grace's back. It was several shades lighter than it should have been. Sure, the one on his hand had faded, too, but that was to be expected after it had been transferred. It should never have faded on Grace. "I don't understand."

Grace pushed her sister away, red blooming across her face as she pulled her shirt back down.

Faith pulled a guest chair over and dropped into it. "You said the marking had stabilized."

Apparently Grace had lied to everybody. Adare retook his seat, watching her as if he'd never seen her before. "Why didn't you say anything?"

"Because there wasn't anything you could do," Grace said quietly, gesturing toward the several manila files spread across the counter. "Those must be my medical records. Right, Emma?"

Emma nodded. "Yeah. I've been reading through them." She pushed a stray strand of hair away from her face. "Your mating was unconventional, to say the least. We never knew what the consequences would be." Two of the machines buzzed across the room, and Emma hustled over to a printer that began spitting out documents. She gathered several and read them, recrossing the room to the other records. "Huh. Interesting."

Adare growled.

Emma looked up. "Oh. Sorry." She turned toward Grace. "As you know, when an enhanced human mates an immortal, her chromosomal pairs increase from those of a human at twenty-three to those of a mate at twenty-seven pairs, thus granting immortality, except in the case of beheading or extreme fire."

Grace nodded.

Emma read the page in front of her. "We tested you right after the mating, and your pairs did increase. However, now they're decreasing. You're at twenty-five right now. It's sort of like you're unraveling from within."

Grace frowned. "That's what it feels like."

Adare had to keep a calm head. He'd lose his temper later. "Because we didn't have sex during mating? That's why?"

Emma bit her lip. "There's more to a mating than sex and an exchange of bodily fluids. It's a bonding of some sort beyond the physical and one we can't quantify or understand, really."

Grace plucked at the blanket beneath her legs. "What if I take the virus to negate the bond? It'll speed up the process, and then maybe I'd be okay? The slow unravelling is too hard to experience."

Emma shook her head. "I really don't know. If you ended up human again, then you might be fine, or you might end up in a coma again, since that was the state you experienced before being mated." She looked at Faith, who just sat still, shock on her face.

Adare swallowed. "Absolutely not. We'll mate completely this time." To him, the answer was so simple.

So when Emma blanched, he nearly stood. "Well now, that's a problem," she murmured. "Since you half mated, for lack of a better term, Grace's system has developed antibodies to yours, and basically her cells have defied you, while yours are on the attack. It'd be a war inside her, and I can't tell you what would happen. She might survive or you might kill her."

"That's why I didn't tell you," Grace said, facing him directly. "There's nothing you can do."

* * * *

It didn't take an empath to decipher the multitude of emotions bombarding Grace from every direction in the room. Faith was concerned and angry, Emma was concerned and confused, and Adare was just out and out pissed off. She might as well take advantage of the fact she was looking all helpless on a hospital bed. "I'm sorry I lied to everyone, but there wasn't anything anyone could do, and I had a few things to take care of before ending up here."

Faith patted her arm. "It's okay, Gracie. We'll figure it out."

"We will," Emma said, obviously trying to sound encouraging.

Adare didn't say a word. Just stared at her with those deep black eyes, his jaw clenched so hard he had to be getting a migraine.

Grace swallowed. "I've given this a lot of thought, and the unraveling is happening no matter what I do. I think the best option is to take the virus and end up human again." Then she could figure out where to go from there. If she was in a coma again, then there wasn't anything to do. If not, she'd proceed.

Adare tilted his head. "You're a Key, Grace. That's how you survived the coma initially." His voice was silky and thoughtful, rough and dangerous.

Grace's abdomen warmed and her heart rate picked up. Big time.

Emma pursed her lips. "That's true. Perhaps it's time you shared what that really means, Adare." She gestured to the medical records. "Not one of those doctors knew she was a Key, or even what a Key is. Neither do I. There's no way we can create a good medical plan without all of the facts."

Adare kept his gaze on Grace but spoke to Emma. "Could anybody else have survived that coma for two years?"

"No," Faith answered before Emma could. "It was a medical mystery, along with the fact that Grace's body didn't atrophy in the slightest, and her breathing and heart functions remained in the healthy range for nearly two years, until she started to decline rapidly and almost died."

"That's when we mated," Adare said quietly. "The fact that she's a Key kept her alive much longer than normal." He finally released Grace's gaze and looked directly at Emma. "I can't tell you much, but you've studied your three prophets, right?"

Grace leaned up. "I've heard of the prophets but don't know much about them."

Emma picked up a pen and twirled it between her fingers. "There are three prophets, supposedly determined by fate, and they're kind of the spiritual leaders of the Realm. They have a marking down their necks and backs, and when one dies, another takes his or her place." Her nostrils flared. "They're psychic and powerful, and we have no idea how they're chosen, to be honest."

Grace tugged the front of her shirt down to reveal the perfect mark of a key set between her heart and clavicle. "I have this birthmark, but I don't believe in fate and all of that."

"Why?" Adare asked. "Obviously there's an entire world you didn't know existed and can't explain, so why not fate? Do you really think this path, any path, is arbitrary?" His gaze burned as he looked at the birthmark. "How do you explain your surviving the coma? Becoming immortal? Seeing things in other people nobody else sees?"

She couldn't explain any of it. "What's your point?" She went with irritation instead of uncertainty.

"My point is that we know for certain what happens to you as a human. You go into a coma and eventually die." He stood, looking powerful and determined. "Taking the virus to negate the mating bond will only land you back in a coma. Your dying is not an option."

Because they needed her as a Key? She swallowed, her stomach now doing flip-flops. "Listen, Adare—"

"No. I'm done listening, since all you do is lie." The anger in his eyes would scare a charging grizzly bear. "We don't know what would happen if you mated, but I believe that being a Key will save you. It's the only thing that will."

She sat straighter on the bed. He was actually saying what she thought he was saying. "This is my decision."

"No. It really isn't." His expression showed absolutely no give. "It would've been your decision if you'd been honest years ago when all this started, when you might have had more options. Right now, there is only one. As a Seven, it's my duty to make sure the Keys survive until the ritual."

She tossed her head, anger finally sparking through the fuzziness in her brain. "Oh yeah?"

"Yeah. And as your mate, one you've left in the dark for far too long, it's my duty to make sure you dinnae die. The best way to keep you alive, the only option really, is for us to mate." He jerked his head at the medical records spread over the counter. "You can go over those for hours, and when you're finished, you'll reach the same conclusion."

Emma cleared her throat. "Maybe. Maybe not. I need to study your blood. Not for nothing, but you look pale for yourself, Adare. How are you feeling?"

"Fine," he growled.

Was he pale? Grace studied him. Yeah. He did look a mite under the weather. What the heck did that mean?

Faith sighed. "Doing nothing isn't an option. Obviously, Grace, you are declining, and since you just passed out for three hours, I worry that a coma is next. You don't have a safe option. Taking the virus or mating completely are both risks, and I have to admit, the risk seems slightly lower with mating for you. Probably. Returning to human form would be worse, I believe."

Grace let her shirt fall back into place. "I could take the virus, become human, and then mate another immortal." Then maybe she'd get rid of this torturous attraction to the furious Highlander.

Faith's eyebrows rose and Emma smothered a cough, both looking toward Adare.

"No," he said. He spoke so softly she could barely hear him, but she felt his tension along her skin, at the edge of every nerve ending. Her lungs heated and seized, and her breath caught painfully.

Emma held up a hand to stop the explosion Grace wanted to let loose. "Before you do anything, I want to take your blood and make sure all is well with you, Adare. Then I need to study your genes in various combinations. Maybe something will become clear."

"That's allowable," Adare said, moving for the door. "Yet I already know the outcome. If my cells are at war with yours, Grace, it will benefit you to get more of mine by mating. I have no doubt they'll win any war, overcome any antibodies, and you'll survive." He looked over his shoulder, the impact of his gaze harsh. "Then we'll discuss your future. *Mate*."

Chapter 18

The one time Adare had visited Realm headquarters before, he'd been shown the gym in the basement of the main lodge. He headed there now. If he remembered right, there were punching bags mounted around the sprawling basement. He needed to beat on something, and right now.

He turned the corner, his boots quiet on the heavy mats, and stopped short.

Two young girls stood facing each other, one with her hands on her hips. "I have no idea where he is. What is up with Pax lately, anyway?" the taller one asked.

As one, they turned toward him. The taller one wore her dirty-blond hair in a ponytail and despite her youth, her shifter ancestry was obvious. Cougar shifter? Probably. "Hi."

"Hi," he said, turning toward the other girl. She had to be in her early teens, with intense blue eyes and light brown hair. A blue marking, swirling and intricate, danced down her neck and disappeared into her worn T-shirt, showing her to be one of the three prophets walking the earth. Hope Kayrs-Kyllwood. The only female vampire, or part vampire, in existence…and the Lock. A fact she probably had no clue about.

The girl studied him right back. "Adare. It has been a long time."

Three years, actually. He was surprised she remembered his name. "It's nice to see you, Hope." He should probably leave the girls to whatever they were doing.

"This is my friend, Libby," Hope said, reaching down for a couple of black strike pads sitting by her tennis shoe.

Libby nodded. "Hi." She moved, or rather bounced, to the door. "Sorry I have to go. I'm sure Pax will be here soon, but there's something up with the shifter nation, and we're having a family meeting. I'll be back." She smiled, showing impressive canines, and then jogged down the hallway.

Hope tossed him the pads. "Do you mind spotting me until my friend arrives? Pax isn't usually late, so he should be here soon."

Adare caught the pads with one hand, curious about this young prophet. "Sure." He slid his hands into the pads and held them up. The girl looked more human than anything else, which was a surprise.

She pulled on small boxing gloves and took position, bringing her wrists to cover her face. Her first few hits were tests, making sure he was holding the pads tight, before she started punching for real. Her form was good and her aim perfect, but the lack of strength in the hits concerned him.

"How's Grace doing?" Hope asked, spinning and adding a surprising kick.

He kept the pad in place and took the impact. "She's with your Aunt Emma doing some tests." Or great-aunt Emma, but why get specific?

"Uh huh." Hope kicked again. "It'd be nice to keep her alive, since she's a Key. Right?" Her next punch held more force.

Adare looked down at the small female. What was she now? Thirteen or so? "What do you know about the Keys?"

"More than I'd like to know." She bounced back on her feet, lifting her gaze from the pads. "I also know more about the Lock than you do." Her eyes held a depth and seriousness beyond those of a thirteen-year-old. "Do you even understand my role in the ritual?"

He took a step back, his impenetrable chest heating. "Who told you?" Garrett and Logan, both new members of the Seven, were Hope's uncles, so maybe they'd been talking? Their vow had been one of silence and secrecy, and he'd believed they'd meant it.

Hope rolled her eyes, looking for a moment like any other teenaged girl. "Relax, Sparky. Everyone around here tries to forget the fact that I'm a prophet with a destiny, yada, yada, yada. Nobody has said a word."

Goosebumps rose along his arms. "You're psychic." Like the prophets were meant to be.

She lifted a slim shoulder, dropping into a fighting stance again. "Who knows. I see things, I feel things, and sometimes fate talks to me." *Hit. Hit. Hit.* "Or, there's some break in the time continuum, and certain people get glimpses into the future." She turned and kicked again, her foot making a decent slap on the pad. "In the end, does it really matter?"

"Aye," he said, falling back into his brogue. "How this all ends definitely matters. Can you see the ending? Do you know who wins?"

Her smile was small and rueful. "That's not how fate works, as you should know. We're not there yet. The blocks that lead up to the battle are still falling into place, and nothing is certain. Fate doesn't have the control we think she has."

Maybe there wouldn't even have to be a ritual. If he and Benny succeeded in their mission, was it possible they could end all of this now? "Why do you think fate is female?"

Hope executed a decent roundhouse kick. "Female power is more natural, and definitely stronger than male."

He couldn't argue with that. "What is the role of the Lock?" He'd never known—none of them did. The blood of the three Keys, combined, could kill Ulric, according to legend. He had to ingest it somehow. But what of the Lock?

She sighed and shook her arms loose before sneezing several times.

"Bless you," he murmured.

She grinned. "Thanks. Allergies are rough in January, for some reason."

An immortal with allergies? He frowned.

She nodded. "Yeah, I know. It's a concern to my folks, too. But we have bigger things to worry about, don't you think?"

"Yes. What's your role as Lock?" He needed answers.

She tilted her head to the side, studying him. "The ritual to become one of the Seven. When your torsos were fused. How did you become brothers?"

"Through blood and bone," he said automatically.

"Exactly. It always comes down to that, right? To pain and sacrifice…to blood and bone." With that, she took off her boxing gloves. "Thanks for spotting me. I'm staying with my grandparents, Talen and Cara, until my folks get home later tonight, and Talen gets cranky if I'm late for lunch. Gotta go." She walked to the doorway, graceful and fragile. She partially turned, her eyes an impossible blue that didn't occur in nature. "Good luck, Adare. Your path isn't set, and you have more power than you know."

* * * *

It was nice to have her folks home, although everyone seemed to be buzzing around in a wild commotion. Having Adare at headquarters definitely threw off the vibe, especially since there was so much mystery still surrounding the Seven.

It was interesting that nobody asked her about it. Why did her parents and grandparents try to act like she didn't have a window into the future sometimes? Not that she could help much here.

She hustled through Cara's kitchen and finished putting in the new amber earrings her parents had purchased in the Baltic. Why hadn't Pax showed up to spar? Her mom had brought him chocolates, and she tapped her finger against the ribbon on top of the box.

"Cara?" she called out, waiting a moment. Then she sighed. "Grandmama?" Though immortal kids called their grandparents by their first names, because one day they'd look the same age, sometimes using the grandma name with Cara got instant results.

Nothing.

Everyone was out of the house. She bit her lip. They were on a high alert right now, which meant she couldn't leave without the coordinated effort of a guard and a scouting of her destination. Which she usually had to have if she visited Pax, anyway.

But that was silly. She wanted to see Pax, and he only lived a short distance down the lake walk. It'd be fun to surprise him for once.

Yeah, she'd get in trouble. But there was so much going on, it'd be brief. Hope pushed open the rear sliding door that faced the lake. Her boots slipped on the icy deck before she found purchase. Oh, Pax was going to get it for not showing up to spar earlier. After she gave him his candy, of course. Pax's mom had been a demon but had died during the last war. His dad was a vampire, so Pax lived at the Realm headquarters subdivision close to Talen and Cara, just a mile down the lake from the demon headquarters, where Hope usually lived with her parents. That didn't keep Pax from visiting all the time, though. He didn't stay at home much.

Being there had to be difficult for him, because his dad didn't like demons. Apparently, his mating to Pax's mom had sucked. Which meant that his dad didn't like half of Pax, since he was half demon.

Although Pax would never talk about it.

She walked along the lake, nodding at different soldiers on patrol, letting the snow brush her hair and land on her eyelashes. Winter was her favorite time and always had been.

When they were younger, Pax, Libby, and she had spent hours upon hours building snowmen. They should get together and build another one while the snow was still thick and fluffy enough to make it easy. She hummed as she meandered along the brick sidewalk, past the back entrances to several homes, just as the lights inside began to flip on and illuminate the sparkling snow.

She reached Pax's house, which was darker than most of the others, showing very little light through the windows. Was Pax even home? What was going on? The icy snow crunched when she walked by the side of the house and around to the front to knock on the wide door. While Pax would normally just come into her house, she didn't visit him enough to feel comfortable doing that, especially since her bodyguard hadn't scoped out the place. Even she knew the limits. She knocked again.

Nobody answered.

She tensed and knocked again. Pax usually told her if he was going anywhere, and he hadn't said anything. Maybe he was sleeping. Or sick. She knocked even harder, leaning in to listen for any sound.

A crash vibrated inside and a raised voice suddenly echoed through the house.

She stepped back, her heartbeat speeding up. Was Pax in danger? "Paxton?" She rang the doorbell several times and looked around for any patrolling soldiers, but the snowy street was quiet.

The door swung open and Pax's dad stood there, scowling. He was big and broad with metallic copper eyes, and his black hair was ruffled around his shoulders. His face was wide and his cheekbones sharp, kind of like Pax's. "What are you doing with the damn doorbell?"

Hope paused. "Hi Paelotin. Is Pax here?"

"I'm here." Pax pushed past his dad, his lip bleeding. His dark hair was long and wild around his shoulders. "Let's get out of here."

"I'm not done with you." Paelotin grabbed his hair and pulled him back inside, twisting and throwing him toward an end table. The sound was loud and frightening. Pax crashed into it and rolled, coming up on his feet as if it was no big deal. "I'm leaving."

"The hell you are." Paelotin turned and backhanded Pax across the cheek, throwing him over the sofa to land on the other side. Pax hit the coffee table, and glass shattered, cutting his throat.

"Pax!" Hope dropped the candy and reacted without thinking, rushing around the torn sofa to her friend. Her best friend.

Paelotin slammed the door shut, and she jumped, grasping Pax's uninjured arm.

Pax shoved to his feet, his hands bleeding, his cheek already darkening with a bruise. "Hope. What the heck? You run from danger, not into it." His smile showed bloody teeth and his pupils were dilated from being hit. He pushed her behind him and stood straighter than she'd ever seen him. "Hope is leaving. If you want to finish with me, that's fine. But she needs to go first."

When had Pax gotten so tall? He'd gone through a growth spurt when he'd turned thirteen, and now he had to be at least six feet tall and thin. The boyish chubbiness he'd always lamented was gone, leaving him gangly and wiry. No match for his father, who was at least eight inches and a hundred pounds or more bigger than Pax.

Her voice shook. "Come with me, Pax." She'd known he didn't like his dad, but he'd always said there was no physical hitting, and she'd never been allowed to just drop in before. He'd lied. "You can stay with me." Her dad would never let Pax be hit like this.

"My boy stays here," Paelotin snarled, his hands curling into beefy fists.

Hope's legs shook.

Pax lifted his chin, even though blood was dripping from his neck to stain his T-shirt. "Hope? Take the back door and go home to your grandparents. Tell Cara and Talen that everything is fine here." His voice cracked.

"No," she whispered, her voice trembling. She moved over the broken glass around him and slid her hand into his, facing the threat. Her uncle Garrett had taught her always to face the threat. "I'm not leaving you."

Pax's hand tightened over hers.

Paelotin smiled and his eyes looked kind of funny. He burped. Was he drunk? How much did a vampire have to drink to actually get drunk? "Aren't you the loyal little bitch?"

Her eyes widened and her stomach cramped. Nobody had ever called her anything like that. "Um."

"And a prophet. A freaking lunatic prophet who'll ruin us all."
He took a step toward them, and she gasped, tightening her grip
on Pax's hand. She should've run to get help. Now what were they
going to do? "You're more dangerous than any Kurjan enemy
alive, and you have demon in you," he slurred, kicking the broken
table out of the way. "Maybe I should do what needs to be done."

Pax shoved her behind him again. "Run, Hope. Now."

Chapter 19

After a bland dinner of chicken noodle soup, Grace barely contained her irritation as she sat on the examination table and listened to Emma and Faith discuss her test results, which were spread over the wide counter, using terms that might as well have been in another language. In fact, some of them were Latin. Probably. She leaned to the side and drew her trusty old Pentax out of her bag, snapping several shots of the two women.

Emma, now wearing a white lab coat over her casual clothing, looked over her shoulder. "Sorry. That probably didn't make much sense."

Grace took several more pictures before setting the camera on her leg. "No, and none of it sounded good."

Faith turned around and leaned back, rubbing her eyes. "No. Interesting but not good." She brushed her hair away from her face. "We tested your samples with several others."

Emma stuck her hands in her lab coat. "We let the virus attack your cells in a Petri dish, and it's clear that if you took the virus, you'd be back in a coma." She shook her head. "There's something odd in your blood that I can't identify, and it probably has to do with being a Key. I don't understand the Key marking, by the way. But taking the virus will change you almost into a plant."

Well, that sounded terrible. Grace braced herself for more bad news. "And?"

Faith looked at Emma and then back. "We used an agent that speeds up the life of a cell exponentially, as if you just did nothing and let your body do what it's doing."

Grace cradled her camera. "That was encouraging?"

"No," Faith said, fine lines spreading out from her pretty eyes. "The cells died. Which means—"

"I'd be in a coma for a while and then I'd die." Grace drew air in through her nose. She had to appear brave for Faith. "No matter what, you gave me five more years of living, Faithie. Never forget that. I enjoyed these years." She'd learned of people she'd never imagined, and she'd gotten so see her sister happy and mated to a great male. "This has been good." She swallowed several times, her body heating. "I'm sure you also combined my cells with more of Adare's. As if he mated me for real this time."

Emma nodded. "Yes. Your other doctors misinterpreted the tests because they didn't know about you being a Key. I do and set the parameters for the tests accordingly. Um, your cells, the antibodies you've developed, destroyed his. Completely. I've never seen anything like it."

Not what she'd been expecting. Grace stiffened. How was that even possible? "Are you sure?"

"Yes. I ran the test three times," Emma said.

Grace deflated, sitting back on the bed, her mind spinning. Her antibodies were that strong? What the hell was it with being a Key? "I thought, deep down, that maybe—"

"Mating him, full on frontal nudity, would be the only answer to saving you?" Faith murmured, her gaze understanding. "I know. I've seen how you look at him."

Grace sputtered. "Look at him? What are you talking about? I can't stand him."

Emma snorted. "Right. Ha. The same way you can't stand an ice cream sundae with extra sprinkles. I may be lost in my own world a lot, working on these experiments, but even I can see that. You want that badass. Like bad."

Grace frowned, lowering her chin. "You really don't sound like a queen."

Emma grinned. "Like I haven't heard that before." Her blue eyes sparkled. Once again, her mass of dark hair was piled high on her head, escaping in tendrils in every direction. "We also combined your cells with genes from a couple of unmated males, and the allergy sprang forth fast and bright. No option there."

"Wow," Grace said slowly. "My options are death, death, or... death." She breathed out. Well, it was nice to have answers, right? No. Not right. "This sucks."

Faith clasped her hands together. "Well, not death. Whatever is in your blood, in your cells from the Key marking, ensures you'll live for a while. Maybe not consciously, but that would give us time to find a cure? Maybe?"

Emma shuffled her feet. "I really want to agree with you."

But she didn't. The most knowledgeable geneticist in the entire world, human or immortal, thought Grace was going to drop back into her coma and then die. Grace pressed her fingers against her eyebrows to try to stall the oncoming headache. "Okay. What I learned from the science class I took in college was basically how to listen to music and balance a checkbook at the same time. But if I've developed antibodies to Adare, can't we get rid of those somehow?"

"No," Faith said slowly. "There's no way to get rid of antibodies. I mean, they can diminish over time, but you don't have time." She winced on the last. "Your only option is to mate Adare, Gracie. After your antibodies destroy his, you may recover."

Grace let the words sink in. "You just said my cells destroyed his. If we mate, and I'm saved, what happens to Adare?"

Neither woman answered.

Grace shook her head. "We know that mated couples both change, or there wouldn't be a mating allergy for both. There must be something about being a Key that takes over." It was getting more difficult to deny the supernatural element of fate in her life, but she'd figure that out later. "And whatever that is, it's gotten stronger in the last five years, developing antibodies to Adare. I can't save myself and kill him."

"The hell you can't," came a low voice from the hallway.

Grace sighed and turned to see Adare taking up all the available space in the doorway. "You saved me once, and now I'm going to save you." It totally sucked, but maybe somehow Faith or Emma would find a cure before the coma killed her. "If I do die, then you could eventually take the virus and mate again." It was the least she could do for him. Plus, Jacqueline was free now, and she had to admit, the shifter wasn't so bad.

Adare looked at Emma. "You said my cells were demolished when mine and Grace's combine, but in the other tests, Grace's cells were just changed."

Emma nodded.

"Perhaps mine changed as well and combined with hers, thus appearing demolished," Adare said quietly. "You don't know that mating would kill me."

Faith stepped forward, her eyes earnest. "That's true. We truly don't know. Mating would change your genetics, too. Her cells are stronger than yours right now, and you could very well die."

Emma cleared her throat. "You haven't been feeling well, have you? And you've told no one, just like a typical male. Why didn't you call me?"

Adare's frown darkened. "I'm fine. We've been on mission after mission, many bloody, and I figured I just needed a break. My cells are perfect."

"Your cells are deteriorating," Emma countered. "The mating mark has faded, and your blood is changing. You'll survive if the mating completely disengages, but if you mate Grace again, you might not. You probably wouldn't, actually. We've never seen anything like this. You do understand that, right?"

"I do," Adare said, focusing on Emma. "Mercy is a Key, and she and Logan successfully mated. Have you tested their blood?"

Emma nodded. "Of course, but after they mated. Their results were like those of every other mated pair."

"As ours will be." He focused on Grace. "We will mate tonight. Wrap your head around that, because the discussion is over."

Fury zapped through Grace so quickly she could barely breathe. "You'd sacrifice your life for me, but I can't do the same for you, you arrogant ass?"

"No." He turned on his heel and strode away.

"Well," Faith said, pressing her lips together.

Emma chewed on her lip. "That's that, then."

The hell it was.

* * * *

Adare returned to the gym just as Benny finished knocking one of the punching bags off the ceiling. Good. Anticipation rippled through his veins, inciting the need to hit. "You want to spar?"

Benny partially turned, sweat forming a V down his shirt. "Sure, but why aren't you with Grace?"

Adare ducked his head and charged, hitting Benny mid-center and lifting him up before slamming him down on the mat.

Benny landed on his back and struck up, rolling away and flipping sideways to his feet. "Okay, then. You really want to spar." Using his teeth, he tore the tape off his hands, his eyes glittering. "Let's do this right." He toed off his boots. "No boots. I don't want you to wear my tread for the next week."

Adare grinned, letting his fangs drop. "Fair enough." He reached down and pulled his boots off, tossing them over his shoulder. The second he let them fly, Benny kicked, nailing him beneath the jaw. Stars exploded in his head, and he stumbled back, dropping to one knee and sweeping out of pure instinct.

Benny back-flipped, landing easily on the mat. "So. Where's Grace?"

Adare went full out, hitting and dodging, while catching Benny up on the news of the day. Benny asked questions, made comments, and showed no mercy with his strikes.

After two hours, they were both bleeding and bruised, flat on their backs, coughing and wincing. It was the best Adare had felt in weeks.

Benny hacked up a lung and groaned. "Man, I feel good. You?"

"Much better." Adare sent healing cells to his skull, which had been split into two or maybe three parts. "I appreciate the sparring."

"Me too," Benny said, stretching his legs out. A bone popped back into place, and he sucked in air. "That was a great kick, by the way."

"Your left has gotten stronger. I think you broke my eye socket." Adare sent healing cells to his socket.

"Gee. Thanks." Benny panted heavily, staring up at the high ceiling. "Maybe if you admitted you loved her, then her cells wouldn't eat yours."

Adare winced as his broken fingers slowly mended. "I don't love her."

"Well, you at least like her. I mean, you've surrounded yourself with her photographs for years, and it's not because you've always had an appreciation for the arts. Right?"

"I like her art." Okay, maybe he liked what he saw in her photographs. Her. She was insightful and kind, strong and adventurous. And a calculating liar who'd deceived him. "She's not who I thought."

Benny chuckled, the sound slightly pained. "Right. She pulled one over on you." He kicked out a foot and rolled his ankle. "That only makes you want her more. I know you, Highlander. Have for centuries. You can fool yourself, but you can't fool me."

How screwed up had Adare's life become that Benny was making sense? "I've wanted her since the first time she opened her eyes and started defying me," he admitted. "But I've always been afraid to hurt her."

Benny laughed. "To think it's her cells that will eat yours like miniature Pac-men."

Adare grimaced at the image. "I didn't survive the ritual of the Seven to be taken down by mating a fragile human, Benny." Even one who'd surprised him with her bravery the other day.

"I know, Brother. But she ain't a fragile human. Well, she might be fragile and she could've been human, but she's a Key. We don't even know the full implications of that fact." Benny exhaled slowly as healing tingles wafted from him. "By the way, you've been a good brother. I hope you don't die."

"I love you too, man," Adare returned, chuckling along with Benny. "Seriously. It has been an honor, Benjamin Reese." He stood and reached down a hand to help Benny up.

Benny grabbed him in a hard hug, smacking his back with a force that echoed through the quiet. "It has, and you need to live through this." He stepped away; his gaze serious. "I think you're gonna have to let go that hold you have on emotion to do it. It wasn't your fault the Highlanders died, and it wasn't your fault that your family perished." He scratched his chin. "In fact, a lot didn't die. You know that."

Adare nodded. Many of his brethren had gone into service with the British, but the clan system was destroyed. "My way of life ended."

"Yeah, but now we have running water. Clean clothes. Netflix." Benny grinned. "It's a better world, and mine will go dark if you leave it, so how about you grow a pair and hit the emotion hard?"

Adare cut him a look.

Benny set his stance. "If you don't, she'll say no, and we both know you won't force her. Even if it means she dies."

Adare couldn't argue with that. He'd never force a woman. "Did you just tell me to grow a pair?"

"Yep."

"You want to go again?" Adare muttered.

Benny shook out his arms and rolled his neck. "Sure. Let's do it."

"Knock it off." Grace walked into the room, her face pink, with both Emma and Faith on her heels. "We, um, may have found a solution. Maybe." She wouldn't look him in the eye.

The riot inside him settled, hard and fast, definite and sure. "Unless it involves us mating, I don't want to hear it." He said the words as gently as he could.

Grace's head snapped up. "Stop being bossy and just listen, damn it."

He raised an eyebrow. "Are you going to tell the truth? Finally?"

She rolled her eyes. Actually rolled her pretty green eyes at him. "Yes. The truth is, we think you can create some antibodies to me. At first, the doctors didn't think so, but then we did a whole bunch more experiments that included my giving way too much blood. I think this'll work. You just have to agree and not be all growly and a pain in the butt about it."

If she was trying for his cooperation, she was failing. He looked sideways at the queen. "Well, doctor? Want to explain?"

The queen cleared her throat. "How do you feel about taking Grace's blood?"

His own blood began to hum. Strong and sure. "I'm all for it."

Chapter 20

Paxton Phoenix had one goal in life and that was to keep Hope safe. That was it. Nothing more. He'd never stood up to his father before, but when faced with the choice, there wasn't one. "Get out of here, Hope. Now." He wasn't big or strong like his father, but he could hold the male off long enough for Hope to run.

"I'm not leaving you." Her voice shook as hard as her hand in his, but she tried to step up to his side again.

His father gave a smile, the mean one he only got after he'd been taking the white powder and drinking alcohol. "It's time we got rid of the threat she represents. Show me you're a man, boy. Let's do this."

Hatred, the kind with ice, scraped down Paxton's body. "No."

His father's face hardened even more. "You'd choose that little freak over your family?"

Pax lifted his chin, looking way up, making sure he made eye contact. "Every. Single. Time." He tried to push Hope behind him so he could back her to the sliding glass door, but she wasn't making it easy. She didn't understand the threat here, but he did. He always had. Right now, his only chance was his brain. He couldn't take his father. Not yet. "She's Zane Kyllwood's only child and Talen Kayrs' only grandchild. If you touch her, if you even scare her, they'll tear you apart piece by piece. You know that." Could he get through to the monster? Sometimes his father was beyond reason.

"She's evil," his father hissed.

Paxton ignored Hope's gasp and finally got her to move back a little. "She's not. You are. If you touch her, the vampire nation, the demon nation, and the entire fucking Realm will be after your ass."

His dad started, as if shocked by the language. "You little shithead." He swung full force, hitting Pax in the side of the head with a sound that echoed through history. Pax fell into Hope and pushed her as hard as he could toward the back door before he hit the ground. "Run."

Hope screamed, high and loud, and ran for the back door.

Pax's dad jumped over him, going for her, and Paxton kicked up with all his strength, even though the world was going black. His foot nailed his dad right in the groin, going so far he felt something stretch and pop.

The sound his dad made defied description. He fell to the side wall, grabbing his groin, panting in pain. "I'm going to kill you for that."

Yeah, probably. The back door opened and Hope ran for freedom, still screaming at the top of her lungs. Paxton closed his eyes, letting some of the darkness in. He'd done his job. She was safe, and he didn't have any more fight in him. Not now.

His dad pushed himself away from the wall, his big boots crunching glass. "I'm going to kick your fucking head from your body." He lifted his leg, and the boot started to fall. Paxton watched it come.

A growl sounded at the back door and a dark blur tackled his dad back into the wall. Paxton blinked. Zane? A strong hand gently touched his shoulder, and he turned to see Talen Kayrs bending over him, his golden eyes concerned. Oh, shit. They were going to hate him for getting Hope into danger like this. "I'm sorry," he whispered.

Talen leaned down to pick him up, and Paxton pushed his hands away. "I can walk." Whatever they were going to do to him, he would take it standing up. Especially since Hope hovered in the doorway, tears streaking her cheeks. He stood, his stomach rolling over, his legs wobbly.

Zane and his dad fought, but it was pretty one-sided. Within seconds, his dad was unconscious on the floor, bleeding from the nose. Zane turned toward him, his green eyes nearly black, fury across his face.

Paxton's legs shook but he stood straighter, even though his face felt caved in. He deserved whatever they did to him.

Hope ran for her dad, who enveloped her in a hug, looking so big and dangerous that Paxton knew she'd be safe without him. At least for now.

Talen put an arm over his shoulders and turned him toward the door, standing even taller than Pax's dad. "We'll have somebody else clean up this mess," he rumbled, letting Paxton lean on him as they exited the house. "Your face looks damaged. I'll give you some blood to heal it as soon as we get back to the warm lodge."

"I can heal it," Paxton said, letting the chilly air wash over the heat bombarding him from within.

Talen started. "You're young to be healing yourself."

"I've been doing it for years," he mumbled, letting the cells go to work. Had Zane just growled at that? Talen stiffened and then relaxed as well. Pax shook his head, trying to concentrate and fix his face. "Where are we going?"

"To get you checked out and have a talk," Zane said from behind him.

Paxton exhaled, the movement hurting his entire side. He'd fallen harder than he'd thought. That talk was probably going to hurt worse that he did right now, but he deserved it. Maybe they'd let him still be friends with Hope afterward, if he didn't fight back, but probably not. He'd almost gotten her killed, and now she was crying. "How did you know she was in danger?"

"We didn't," Talen said, taking more of his weight easily. "We discovered she'd left without the proper precautions, and we figured she went to see you. Why didn't you let us know *you* were in danger?"

There it was. He'd lied to them all for years. His ears heated and he straightened his back, continuing along the lake toward the lodge. There wasn't anything to say, and Talen didn't push him for any more answers.

They entered the lodge and Hope's mom made a beeline for him, fussing over his already healing face. "I'm okay, Janie," he mumbled, wondering if she'd still talk to him after learning the full truth. She was the nicest lady he'd ever met, and she'd always treated him like he mattered. "Please stop fussing." The kindness was too much, and he was afraid he'd start bawling like a baby.

Zane and Talen spoke for moment and then Zane walked toward him. "Do you need to see a doctor?"

"No," he said, feeling his face heal completely so he could send cells to his side. "I don't." They might as well get this over with.

"Okay." Zane slid an arm over his shoulder. "Let's go for a walk." When the head of the entire demon nation wanted to go for a walk, things were about to turn bad.

Pax swallowed and looked over his shoulder and saw Hope, her eyes wide and worried, tears still on her face. He wanted to tell her goodbye, but the words wouldn't come. So he smiled, and when she smiled back, that was good enough. She'd grown even prettier lately, and her smile was a good image to remember before dying. "Let's go." He went with Zane, walking through the main lodge to the rec room, where he'd spent countless hours playing games with Hope and the other kids.

Zane released him and went to grab two root beers from the fridge before motioning toward the outside door. "It's a pretty night."

This was weird. Pax took the soda and followed Zane out the wide doors to the covered deck and wooden chairs facing the snow falling lightly over the lake. Zane pressed a button on the table in front of them, and a full fire sprang to life, warming Paxton instantly. Almost in a dream, he opened the soda and took several gulps, letting the sugar take hold.

Zane kicked back with his drink and put his boots on the table near the fire.

Pax swallowed. "I'm sorry I put Hope in danger." His voice cracked, but it had been doing that for months, so hopefully Zane wouldn't think he was scared, even though he was.

Zane drank, the expression on his face thoughtful. "I've asked you before if your dad was hurting you. I didn't know if it was regular training, or what, so I wondered when I saw bruises and cuts on you. Every time, you said he wasn't."

Pax wanted to throw up. "I know. I lied."

"Why?" Zane asked quietly.

Pax opened his mouth but nothing came out. What was the right answer?

Zane sighed. "You thought it was your fault."

Pax jerked. Did Zane know it was his fault?

"You thought you deserved to get hit." Sadness and an odd understanding filled the demon's garbled voice.

Paxton held perfectly still. "I was fat and slow, and now I'm too skinny and still too slow. I'm not very smart." He didn't know why he was telling Zane all of this. "I——"

"You're none of those things, Pax," Zane said quietly. "I know words won't help, but someday, when you look back, you'll understand that the problem was with your father, not you."

Right. "How do you know that?"

"I was there. Right where you are now." Zane finished his root beer and crumpled the can. "We were raised by my uncle, and he hated us. It was—hard. I blamed myself, and I was wrong. Just like you are now."

Somebody had hurt Zane? He was the strongest demon alive. How was that possible? "Where is your uncle now?" Why had Pax asked that?

"I took off his head." Zane turned to look at him. "I'm not suggesting you do that with your dad." He grinned.

Paxton laughed, shocking himself. They were actually joking about this? He relaxed a little bit. "Hope was very brave in there. You should be proud of her."

"I am. I'm proud of you both." Zane turned serious again. "You risked yourself to save my daughter, to protect her, and I'll never forget that, Paxton Phoenix. Never."

Well. That was definitely a different way of looking at the night. Maybe there were different ways to look at every situation. Pax drank more of his root beer, his body finally healing, although he struggled a little bit with his hip. It'd heal soon enough. "Thanks for coming in when you did."

"You bet. We're going to have to send your dad away. Maybe put him on mission in Antarctica or something."

Pax nodded, closing his eyes. "I'll miss this place, but I understand."

"You're not going with him." Zane's voice was firm. "Not a chance."

Pax frowned, even as hope leaped into his chest. "He won't give me up."

"He doesn't have a choice," Zane said. "What do you think of your Uncle Santino? Your mother's brother?"

Paxton watched the snow fall to cover the ice over the lake. "I don't know him very well, but my memories are good. My dad didn't let me spend time with him after my mom died." He barely remembered either of them, to be honest.

"I've talked to him through the years, and Janie is calling him right now. He's been studying butterflies somewhere in the tropics, but he'll come home and do some work for the Realm. He's a little eccentric, and he travels a lot, but last time I talked to him, he said he'd be here if you ever needed him. I'd say you need him right now."

Pax finished his drink, his mind reeling. He didn't have to live with his dad any longer? Was he dreaming? Maybe he'd been knocked out again. "You sure he wants me?"

"Definitely. You could also live with us, if you want. You have choices, and you're welcome anywhere you want to be," Zane said quietly.

Paxton winced. "I don't think that's a good idea." The temptation was so strong he almost took back the words.

"Because of Hope?" Zane asked.

Pax nodded. She was his best friend, but she was more than that to him. He couldn't stop thinking about her, and the last thing he wanted was to end up as her brother. They might always be friends, and that was okay, because he could protect her as a friend. She had a different destiny from him, and they both knew it. But he needed some distance to stay her friend and not wish for a whole bunch of stuff that he could never have. "Yeah. I don't want to be her brother. I'm sorry, Zane."

"I appreciate the honesty, my friend," Zane said, settling back to watch the snow again. "Girls can sure complicate things."

Oh, the demon leader had no idea how complicated Hope's life really was these days. It wasn't Paxton's job to tell him, since Hope wasn't in danger. Thank goodness. "I'll always be her friend and I'll always protect her," he vowed.

Zane looked over at him, his green eyes gleaming through the darkness. He was quiet for several moments, taking measure, just relaxing into the night. Whatever he saw in Pax's face, he must've liked, because he slowly nodded. "We make our own fate, Paxton. Never forget that."

Chapter 21

The fire crackled and warmed the luxurious suite as Grace perched on one of two chairs, separated from Adare by only a round wooden table. "The more I think about it, the more certain I am that this is too risky. You took a huge chance to save me, and I'm going to do the same. It's okay, Adare. Really. I got five more years than I should have, and I'm happy with that." She started to relax as she made her decision, although she couldn't help but wish for a different path.

He steepled his fingers beneath his chin, facing her, relaxed in his oversized chair with his legs partially extended and his ankles crossed. "No. I'm intrigued by the idea of taking your blood, and I'm willing to sample a little bit to experiment here." He hadn't shaved in a while, and the thick scruff around his chin made him look like the marauder he'd probably once been. Tonight, relaxed after his match with Benny, his eyes were deep pools of black. Even so, a sense of alertness, of intensity, flowed from him and entwined around her, sensitizing her skin. "Weakening you further isn't an option."

"I'm not weak," she retorted.

"I didn't say you were," he said mildly. "Yet you remained unconscious for a worrisome amount of time earlier, and I assume that losing blood wouldn't help you regain your strength."

Now he had to sound logical? She wiggled to find a comfortable position on the plush chair. "You're not listening to me."

"Let's talk about it, then." He watched her, the potency of his gaze unnerving. "If you can remain truthful, that is."

He was still all tied up about her lying to him? She groaned. "You have to let it go, for goodness sake. Enough with the digs. I swear, sometimes I just want to kick you in the balls." He wanted honesty? She'd give it to him.

His smile was slow and challenging. "That'd be one way to get things going."

Amusement attacked her, and she laughed, her body finally letting go of some of the tension. "How can you joke about this?"

"I enjoy your laughter," he said.

She paused, pleasure heating her. "Oh." Her hands started fluttering, so she flattened her palms on her jeans. If he was finally going to open up to her, she was going to take the moment and enjoy it before she left this world. "I guess in your day there were many arranged marriages or matings?"

"Aye," he said softly. "It was a way of life, and frankly, more people stayed together in those days than they do now."

She wrinkled her nose. "Getting intimate with a stranger would be difficult, don't you think?" At least she and Adare had known each other for years, and the attraction was there. Oh, was it ever there. The idea of his impossibly hard and naked body had kept her up for more than one sleepless night.

He shrugged. "I don't know. I don't think we'd have to worry about that."

Was he flirting with her? Why not daydream a little? She swallowed. "We wouldn't?"

His grin, this time, was more wolfish than boyish, but it was endearing nonetheless. "Oh, I've wanted you for years. Based on your reaction the other night, I believe it's mutual."

Yeah, there was no reason to deny that fact. "Aren't we so adult discussing this?" It was too bad they couldn't just find a couple bottles of wine to get sloppy drunk and then naked. But it was not to be.

He exhaled slowly. "Thus far, I've kept my distance from you, and it has probably appeared that I'm easy-going. I'm not."

She burst out laughing. Full out, relieved to deal with the tension, belly laughter. "This has been you *easy-going*?"

Both of his dark eyebrows rose, instead of the usual left one. "Well, yes. Why are you laughing?"

She quieted. He was *serious*? "Dude."

He frowned. "Maybe this is a good time for you to express what you'd like out of this mating, and then I'll do the same."

Express? Seriously. "We are not mating. You really need to listen to me." She lifted her hands, gesturing.

"Huh. All right. Before we argue, how about you hypothetically tell me what you'd like if we did decide to trust fate and science and mate again?"

Oh, she wasn't strong enough to resist playing along. "Well, hypothetically, I'd like for you to pull the stick out of your ass and show some real emotions." She leaned forward, on a roll, losing the battle to be an adult. "This brick wall you've built around yourself has to end. I can't break through it, and I would not beat my head against it for eternity. Or even for a while."

"Meaning?" he asked, his rough voice silky.

She swallowed and fidgeted. Might as well give him the full truth. "Well, we're talking about options, so there might be a couple we haven't discussed. If we got crazy and did fully mate, and if I regain my strength and don't kill you, then we'd be like any other mated couple. Physically, I mean." When he didn't respond, she continued. "In that case, I'd be strong enough to take the virus, as would you, and then we could go our own ways." Yeah, the virus would be risky since they'd both still be living, but it was necessary to discuss all options before they made a commitment. He remained silent, which wasn't a shock. "Speak," she snapped.

"All right," he said. "Let's start with the beginning of that statement. I'm not an emotional person. Never have been."

It was like pulling teeth with a tweezer. "I don't want you to start sobbing about losing your virginity, Adare. I just would not be able to mate you without knowing you. There would have to be something intimate between us." She bit her lip. "I think it was Billy Crystal who said that women need a reason for sex and men just need a place."

"We have both a place and a reason," he murmured. When her eyes widened and her temper was about to burst out, he lifted a hand. "I understand. I will work on the emotions. I actually quite enjoyed losing my virginity. It was with a wolf shifter who was several centuries older than was I." He smiled.

"What is it with you and shifters?" she muttered.

"They're wild in bed," he responded instantly.

So now he decided to open up. Wonderful. She had to turn this conversation. "You know I think we shouldn't mate. I don't want to kill you."

"You won't. I'm glad you're discussing it now."

She sighed. "Yeah, I want to live, but not at the expense of killing you."

He rolled his eyes, just like a typical male. "You won't kill me. You're a Key, I'm a Seven, and that means more than science. You have to believe that."

She was starting to, at least a little. But there was always a balancing of the scales, right? If she lived, did he have to die? Or were they both so necessary that they wouldn't die? Sometimes she longed for the days when she was just human and not aware of all of this insanity. She swallowed. All right. They were talking about this for real and not hypothetically now. "How do you feel about mating me?"

"I'm committed to you and will be a good mate so long as I live." It wasn't wine and roses, but there was something sweet about the statement.

"What does being a good mate mean to you?" she asked.

"Keeping my patience while being questioned," he retorted instantly. Then he exhaled. "I will protect you, provide for you, and learn to express emotions with you. Even if it kills me. If I live after the raid, that is." His gaze softened. "I like you, Grace. Your insights and depth intrigue me, your beauty draws me, and your spirit challenges me."

She sat back, stunned. That was a lot from the Highlander. She'd had no idea he considered her anything but a responsibility. "I like you, too."

"That's fortunate," he said dryly. "Especially since there will be no taking of the virus after mating. That's nonnegotiable."

He'd been pretty adamant about it before. "What do you think happens if one mate takes the virus? I mean, to the other mate?" she asked.

He looked toward the fire and then back. "That's the risk, right? That's why it can never happen, and I assume a law will be put on Realm books soon enough. There's no other option."

Immortal laws seemed a little too rigid. She cleared her throat, needing to lay out all the cards. "You might have a second chance with Jacqueline." Another shifter, who no doubt was a wildcat, literally, in bed. "You need to think about whether mating me is really what you want."

The fire crackled, the light dancing off the hard planes of his face. "I said goodbye to Jacki a century ago, and I meant it."

"But how to you feel about that?" she pressed.

He looked as if he wanted to roll his eyes but prevented himself somehow. "I don't feel anything. It was a long time ago, and it's over. When it's over, it's over."

"You can just cut people out like that?" Boy, were they different people.

He nodded. "Yes. I'm all or nothing, according to Benny. It's not a bad way to live."

If they actually survived this, she hoped he never cut her out completely. That would hurt, more than she'd realized until right this second. How she wished she could've known him when he was young. What was he like way back then? "Do you believe in love?"

"No. Do you?"

"Yes." She was right and he was wrong. Did she want to prove it to him? She was so busy pushing him to have feelings that she hadn't really examined her own. How did she feel about this immortal badass? He was hot, sexy, strong, stubborn, and protective. Her body felt alive when he was near, and she felt stronger in his presence. Even when they were arguing. Oh, he was emotionally stunted, probably from being a soldier his entire life, but he had depths. She could see them. Could she plumb them?

"Grace?" he asked. "Are you still with me?"

She nodded. "I'm just thinking through the matter." He was talking her into taking a risk.

"Take your time." His shoulders were even wider than the back of the chair. "The conclusion is foregone, but do what you need to in order to get there."

How could he sound so certain? "You understand that you're risking your life by mating me? That the doctors might be wrong about my blood helping you to survive?"

"I risk my life every day. This is a much more pleasurable way than most." His eyes glittered.

A shiver ran through her, delicious in its journey. "Aren't you afraid to die?"

"No."

She believed him. This was not absence of emotion but absolute truth. Had he faced death so many times during his long life that dying was just the next step? She felt sad at that thought. Great. Now she wanted to save him. To show him that life meant everything and that he should fight to keep it. To enjoy it. She sighed.

"What?"

"Nothing." There was no way to explain her thoughts to him.

His gaze turned piercing. "Do you trust me?"

The question hit her dead center. "Yes," she whispered. She truly did.

"Then do so now. I know what I'm doing—we will both survive this mating. I'm asking you to trust me completely, Grace." His eyes changed to the rare dark silver hue.

She couldn't breathe. "I've wanted you to let me make my own decisions about my life, and I guess you deserve the same. If you want to risk your life, so long as we try everything we can to preserve it, then you have that right. If we do this, I'm all in. You need to understand that."

He frowned. "You have to be all in. We both do."

Oh, he had no clue what she meant. "If we mate, things will change." If they survived, she had to get to know him, maybe love him, whether he liked it or not. Whether he was prepared for all of her or not. The idea thrilled her to a degree that was surprising. So much for being self-aware.

"Agreed." His expression lightened. "I'm pleased you understand."

She swallowed. "Come on, Adare. Neither one of us knows exactly what we're getting into, and that's a fact. You think you can handle me, and I think I can handle you, and neither one of us likes to be handled."

"Grace, I admire your sense of adventure, but make no mistake, you will be handled. After your escapades in Colorado, you're on the Kurjans' radar again, and we'll have to take additional measures for your safety. That needs to happen whether we mate or not, and if we do mate, it becomes my duty." He paused. "Not that there's a choice in mating. We've both agreed it's the only path to take, and now we're just wasting time waffling."

Waffling? Take her in hand? Oh, he had a harsh reality coming his way. "What? You just want me to take off my clothes and bend over?"

"If I want you bent over, I'll bend you over." He straightened in his chair. "However, I'm willing to follow the queen's two step, two night plan."

"Meaning what?" Grace snapped.

"Meaning, come over here. Tonight, I'll bite. Tomorrow, I'll mate."

Chapter 22

Hope settled down in her bed, her head hurting from crying. Libby snuggled next to her, already sound asleep, while Paxton lay in a sleeping bag across the floor. They didn't have sleepovers much anymore, at least not with Paxton, but his even breathing relieved her. Why hadn't she known about his dad?

She'd been so dumb. At the very least, she should've made Pax tell her the truth. He was a much better liar than she'd thought, and that just made her sad.

It was her job to protect him; to protect everybody. She was the prophet, even though she didn't know exactly what that meant. She was also the Lock, and sometimes nightmares revealed what that might mean.

For tonight, she needed sleep. So she let herself drift off, keeping a firm hand on her imagination and her mind, knowing tonight was the night. With Libby and Pax in the room she felt safe, and somehow, she was stronger.

Sleep took her, or maybe she took it.

She was soon standing on tall cliffs, watching a gray ocean throw up spray before her. The sky was dark and the water mysterious. She rubbed her hands down her chilled arms and took a step back, her bare feet scraping across rocks. There'd been a change in the air, in her body, the day she'd turned thirteen, and power flowed through her in a new way. She'd figured this would be part of it.

"Hope?"

She partially turned, not surprised to see Drake emerge from a cave in the rock. She blinked, looking up the cliff to high above. Huh. She hadn't realized she stood on a ledge. The dream world used to include pink sandy beaches and warmth. *"Hi."*

Drake looked around, his greenish-purple eyes taking in the area, his body tense. He'd grown, a lot, since she'd last seen him. His hair, all black, was cut shorter to wisp at his shoulders, which had widened considerably. The new play of muscle was nice. Interesting. He was a full Kurjan but his skin wasn't as pale as most, and his features were more human. Even his eyes could pass for green if one didn't look too closely. Now that he was a teen, he looked even more human, except for his height. *"How are we in a dream world again? Weren't they destroyed? How did you do this?"* he asked, moving closer, his gaze on the ocean below.

"I turned thirteen," she said, looking way up at his face. He was even taller than Paxton, but he'd filled out with muscle, too. They had met in dream worlds as little kids until the dream worlds had disappeared along with the immortals' ability to teleport. It was because Quade Kayrs, another greatish uncle of hers, had returned from a world far away—somehow that had screwed everything up. *"I didn't create this dream world, though."* It was too cold. Too scary looking.

Drake watched the water spray up from far below. *"Can your people teleport again?"*

"No," she said. *"This is different."* She didn't know how, but she felt the truth in her bones. She looked up, way up, to another cliff and saw the edge of her book. The green one she could never reach but had always been with her.

Drake followed her gaze. *"Have you figured out what's in that weird book?"*

"No," she said quietly. They'd agreed, years ago, not to tell each other the secrets of their people, and that was one of them. The book was for the Lock, and only she could open it. That was all she'd figured out so far.

He looked at her, his eyes filled with a light she'd never seen. "Thirteen, huh? You wear it well."

She'd heard the expression on a television show, and she blushed, her face heating. Flirting was new to her, and she was a dork about it. Man, he was cute. Like the boys on television but taller and stronger. She kicked a pebble. "You got a lot taller."

He nodded, sweeping an arm out. His hands had gotten bigger, too. "What do you think this means? That we can meet again?"

"I'm not sure." For a while, they'd tried to communicate over the internet, but the grownups had found out and shut them down. It had been nearly two years since they'd talked. Were they still friends? Their people were enemies, but they were going to change that someday. Somehow. The wind whipped up, feeling unfriendly.

Drake grasped her arm and tugged her closer to the rock wall. "Let's sit."

She sat with her back to the rock and her legs extended, watching the churning water spread out to the far distance. Drake sat next to her, and for the first time in a long time, she felt right. Was he gonna hold her hand? Should she grab his? What if he didn't want to hold hands?

He took her hand in his, and her stomach got all squishy. "How are Pax and Libby?" They'd all met once, and all had gotten in trouble because of it, too.

"They're both good." Pax wouldn't want Hope telling Drake about Pax's dad, mainly because Pax didn't like Drake. At all. Hope held very still so Drake wouldn't let go of her hand. His was big and warm, and really nice. "Do you think it's bad that I'm a prophet?" She'd never forget the look in Pax's dad's face when he called her names. He'd hated her. Really hated her.

"No. Why?" Drake asked.

"Some people don't like it. They think I'm a freak," she whispered. Was she? She could do a lot of things others couldn't, and fate talked to her.

"You're not a freak." Drake stiffened. "Who said that to you?"

The anger in his voice made her feel all warm. "It doesn't matter. I just wanted to know what you thought." How many people out there hated her just because of a marking she'd been born with?

"I think you're special, and that's a good thing." He didn't look at her. "Hope? Our lives aren't gonna be easy, and we've known that for a long time. We're gonna have to make hard decisions that other people might not like."

Yeah, like ending the war between their peoples. Like finally finding peace. Some people didn't want peace. "But we're still friends, right?"

"Always," Drake said, tightening his hold on her hand.

Her mom and dad had met in dream worlds, and they'd ended up saving everybody. Now it was her and Drake's turn to make things even better. Or it would be when they were grown up. "Promise me we'll always be on the same side," she whispered.

He sighed. "I'm not sure we'll always be on the same side, but we'll end up on the right path. I'll make sure of it."

A scraping sounded over by the cave, and they both turned to see a figure come out.

Hope jerked her hand away from Drake's, her face burning. "Uncle Sam?" Her dad's younger brother looked around as if he didn't see them. He shook his head, his dark hair flying, his eyes blazing green. Then he disappeared. Her mouth dropped open.

"That was weird," Drake said, nudging her in the arm. "Let's wake up now."

She sat upright in bed, her heart beating hard against her ribcage. What had her uncle Sam been doing there? In a freaking dream world? He wasn't anywhere near Realm headquarters, but she'd have to contact him the next day. He always took her calls.

Sucking in air, she looked around her bedroom to see Libby on her side, facing away, sleeping soundly. But Pax wasn't in his sleeping bag. Instead, he was sitting on her window seat, his arm around his legs, looking out at the snow.

"Pax?" she whispered, slipping from the bed. "Are you okay?"

Pax turned, his eyes blazing in the darkness. "You went back to a dream world."

She stiffened but kept approaching him. "Yeah. How did you know? Did I talk in my sleep?"

He shook his head, and his long hair flew. "No. I've always known when you go in. There's a change in energy or something in the room. In my head." He sounded disappointed but not angry. As if he was too tired to be angry. "When did you start traveling in your sleep again?"

She licked her suddenly dry lips. "Tonight. It's the first time in a couple years."

"Great." He rested his head back on the wall and closed his eyes.

Her hand shook, but she reached out to touch his arm. "Don't be mad at me."

"Did you see the Kurjan?" Pax muttered.

"Drake. You know his name." She shook her head. Why did Pax have to be so stubborn all the time? "Yeah, I saw him and he said to tell you hi."

"Bullshit," Pax said.

Hope jumped. Paxton never swore. Like never. "Paxton Phoenix. We're all gonna be friends someday, and you know it."

"The Kurjans don't want to be friends, and you know it," he returned. "They hate us, Hope. That can't change, no matter how strong you think you are as a prophet."

"My mom and dad—"

Paxton opened his eyes and held up a hand. "I know they met in dream worlds and saved the Earth and lived happily ever after and had you. That's not what's going to happen with Drake. You need to open your eyes and see what's in front of you instead of what you think fate has in mind. There is no fate, there is no destiny, and there is no path that has already been set for you. For any of us."

Wow. That was a lot of words from Paxton at one time.

He grabbed her hand, his own warm and calloused. Maybe even bigger than Drake's. "Do you love him?"

She nearly swallowed her tongue. "No. I don't love him. Geez, Paxton." She'd never even kissed a guy before, although she was thirteen. On television kids kissed and fell in love at her age, but that seemed weird. If she did fall in love when she was really old, then it probably would be with Drake, the way it happened with her parents. But maybe they'd all just be friends and save the world.

Although, she had liked holding his hand. "You know that you and I are always going to be best friends, right?" No matter what, she and Pax would last.

He sighed, his bony shoulders dropping. "Yeah, I know. Best friends."

If they all had to get mated, maybe Paxton and Libby could be together. A weird shiver went through Hope, hitting her in the stomach. She didn't want Libby to have Pax. But she loved Libby—they were like sisters. Shouldn't she want Libby and Paxton to be together?

He was watching her, still holding her hand. "What?"

"I don't know," she said, wishing things were as simple as they used to be.

Then, Paxton kept her hand and leaned forward. His mouth was on hers before she could take a breath, and she blinked, shutting her eyes. Curiosity kept her still, and when he moved his lips, she moved hers too. Tingles swept along her mouth and through her arms, even to her fingers.

Paxton leaned back, his eyes dark now.

Wow. She'd just kissed Paxton. Or he'd kissed her. "Um, I have to go back to sleep." She let go of his hand and turned to go back to bed, settling in and watching as he moved off the window seat and slid back into his sleeping bag. It took a long time, but he finally started breathing smoothly, falling into sleep.

Libby rolled over, her eyes wide open. "Did Pax *kiss* you?" she whispered.

Hope nodded. "Pax kissed me and I held Drake's hand in a dream world."

Libby's head jerked and her jaw kind of dropped. "You have *two* boyfriends?"

"No." Hope pressed her hand against her mouth to keep from giggling. "I don't have any. We're all just friends."

Libby snorted. "Girlfriend, you've had a big night." Her accent copied a girl from television and sounded like she was from the South.

Hope giggled, unable to stop. It had been a *weird* night.

Libby smacked her arm. "Shhh. You'll wake up Paxton." She stopped smiling. "You're gonna have to choose one of them. They already don't like each other. This will only make it worse."

Hope shook her head. "I'm not choosing either of them. We're friends, and that's all. You know I can't date until I'm sixteen." Her dad had been more than clear about that, and for the first time, she was actually glad. She didn't have to make a choice.

Libby snuggled down, her face in the pillow. "Did you like kissing?"

Hope thought about it. "Yeah. It was nice."

It really was.

Chapter 23

When Grace didn't move fast enough, Adare reached over and plucked her from her chair. "Are you always going to be this difficult?"

"Probably." She perched on his lap as if she wasn't sure where to put her hands. A lovely flush slid from her neck up to the smooth skin of her face, turning her pink and making her green eyes shine. "Before we go through all of this, don't you think we should discuss this suicide raid you insist on undertaking?"

It was a fair question, and a topic he'd like to get out of the way. "My job is dangerous and my path is bloody. That isn't going to change."

"I understand." She let her body relax into his heat. "It's just, why not take more of a force with you?"

"Strategically, two of us makes more sense. We're not starting a new war—it's more of a random attack. I mean, the Seven know we're at war, but many of the other groups don't, and we'd like to keep it that way." Her scent wrapped around him, awakening nerves and an awareness that caught him off guard.

"Why?" she whispered, leaning back so she could meet his gaze.

He held her securely. "The ritual we created to become the Seven violated several laws and twisted the heck out of physics. Many people would want us put down for breaking those laws." It was a fact he'd always known, one that had made keeping the vow of silence pretty damn easy. "The longer we keep the Seven a secret, the longer the Keys are safe, too."

She rubbed her nose. "This all seems so farfetched, although I've seen your back and know your torso is fused. But why Ulric? I mean, why does he want to kill all enhanced females? Are you even sure that's his plan, if he ever makes it back here?"

"Yes." He didn't want to frighten her, but she had to understand the gravity of the situation. "Ulric killed a hundred enhanced females and used their blood to fuse his entire body. It was an abomination of the worst kind, which is why one of his early victims created the Keys before dying. A psychic witch who saw the end but couldn't stop it."

"But why kill all the remaining enhanced women?" she asked.

"So he can never be killed." Adare shook his head. "Our theory is that all of the Keys have some enhanced blood in them. Even Mercy. If all three of you die at the same time, legend says the Keys will end. Legends are often wrong. But if all enhanced females die, then…"

"No more Keys for certain," she murmured, rubbing her right temple. "Life was a lot easier when these kinds of stories happened just in books and not in reality."

He grinned, smoothing her hair away from her tempting neck. "Where do you think fairytales come from?" Every fairytale he'd ever read had been rooted in history, even if the author got most of the facts wrong. Like vampire legends. In real life, vampires didn't sparkle, they didn't hide under the cover of darkness, and they didn't take blood to survive. But still…they did exist. "We've talked long enough. Are you ready?"

She swallowed. "Yes. Just one more question. If the Cysts want to get rid of all enhanced females, why are they trying to kidnap them all across the globe?"

He should've shaved, but it was too late for that. "There are a couple of possible reasons that we're exploring, and I'll share those when I know more." He didn't want to discuss it.

"No." Her teeth played with her bottom lip as she thought through the problem. "Do you think they have some sort of cure or protection for their own mates from whatever Ulric has in mind? That would make sense, right? They could gather as many enhanced females as they wanted." She cleared her throat. "Um, can a human be mated without consent? I mean, completely?"

"Yes."

"Oh." She turned pale. "I didn't know that."

"It's against the Realm laws and the laws of all the other nations, except the Kurjans," he said, needing her to understand the danger out there. "I think the Cysts have spent the last centuries trying to figure out how to save the females they wanted and destroy the rest of us. If our mates die, we might as well, too." He brushed a knuckle down the side of her face, marveling at the delicate bone structure. How had she survived that coma?

She leaned into his touch. "So that's why?'

"Yes." He really was finished discussing this topic.

Her gaze narrowed. "There's more you're not saying."

He exhaled. Was she trying to stall his bite? "Do you want to do this or not?"

She ignored him, a variety of expressions crossing her face. "Wait a minute. You said Ulric killed a hundred enhanced women and used their blood to create true immortality for himself."

"Yes." Man, she was like a dragon with a bucket of gold. Although, he did admire how quickly her mind worked. Every moment he spent with her made her more intriguing.

"Immortality would be lonely," she whispered. "He's going to make more immortal Cyst soldiers—by killing hundreds more enhanced women."

Adare didn't need to reply. It had been his theory for a while, and it made sense. "So you see why we need to take out the Kurjan base in Arizona."

She nodded. "Yeah. I see."

He leaned back, stretching his legs further. Apparently there would be no biting tonight. Fine with him. Although, with her tight butt on his legs, his body was getting other ideas. Fast. "How are you feeling?"

She wiggled a little. "Tired, concerned and a little aroused." She bit her lip again. "Maybe a lot aroused."

His body woke up with a growl he felt to his toes. When the woman decided to be honest, she sure as shit did it with a vengeance. The biting was back on. He shifted her slightly for better access. "You sure about this?"

Gulping, she nodded, angling her neck toward him. "Take a lot. I really don't want to kill you."

Sweet words, really. His fangs dropped, and before she could ask any more questions, he struck.

* * * *

Adare's fangs struck deep into Grace's neck, and she gasped, her eyelids closing instantly. Pain and numbness and pleasure collided inside her, spiraling out in every direction. Sparks flashed behind her eyelids and she moaned, leaning into his touch. Into his heat and hardness.

Smoothly, with his fangs remaining in place as he drank, he turned her to face him. One hand twisted in her hair to pull and elongate her neck even more, and he went deeper, overwhelming her.

Her blood electrified and rushed through her veins faster than ever as if to get to him.

Her thighs gripped the outside of his, and she pressed herself against the obvious bulge in his jeans, crying out as electrical shocks zinged across her engorged clit.

His fangs retracted and his rough tongue scraped across her neck, sealing the wound.

She partially lifted herself away. "You didn't take enough."

His hand twisted more, and his mouth crashed down on hers. The tip of a fang caught her lip as it retracted, shooting hunger through her every nerve. He went deep, hard and fast, kissing her with indescribable ferocity. He tasted of male and spice and a hint of sweet metal.

She moaned, opening her mouth, taking more of him.

His free hand gripped her hip, pulling her even closer against him, forcing her to ride the hard ridge of his erection. Pressure built inside her.

Wait a minute. Wait. She plastered a hand against his chest and pushed, wrenching her mouth free. "Stop."

He stilled.

She panted, tried to get herself under control, and then groaned. "We have to stop. Emma said you'd need twenty-four hours to assimilate the blood you just took." Her hands shook with the need to rip off his shirt and go to town on his magnificent chest. Instead, she pushed away, sliding across his thighs to stand. Her sex ached for him, and she partially bent over, trying to ease the pressure from her own jeans. "This is so hard."

"That's what she said," he rumbled.

Her head snapped up. Even in pain, she stood, her mouth agape. "Did you just make a joke? A real joke?"

Lust sizzled in his eyes and agony darkened his high cheekbones. "I'm very funny."

She chuckled. "I didn't know that." If she didn't die from lust, it was going to be interesting getting to know him better. Getting to see a side to him that nobody else ever saw. The side that cracked a joke when they both were so aroused the air thickened around them. The desire slowly ebbed so she could at least walk. "I'm, ah, going to go eat something. A lot of something."

He chuckled. "Fair enough. There's a burner phone over by the desk. Take it with you and call your friend Bobbi. She promised not to call the cops on me if you phoned before midnight."

Bobbi and Brian. Crap. Grace had forgotten all about them. "After I passed out in the restaurant, she must've been terrified when you just took me."

He nodded. "She was, but I assured her you'd be okay and promised that you'd call. Did you remember anything while you were with her?"

Grace shook her head. "No. A lot of places and things felt familiar, but no memories came back." Did it even matter any longer? "If this mating works tomorrow, I guess I'll have plenty of time to remember."

He sat forward and groaned. "Why don't you go take care of that before I throw you on the rug and kiss you from head to toe?"

Her body jerked with a *hell yes*. "Okay. Concentrate on making antibodies somehow." She had no clue how that worked, but if she didn't leave, she'd rip off her own clothes. "I'll see you tomorrow." There had to be another room in this huge lodge where she could sleep. Leaving him in pain, she grabbed the phone and all but ran from the room. She hadn't had sex in at least seven years. No doubt that explained this crazy hunger for him.

Yeah, right.

She tried never to lie to herself. It was Adare. She might not remember her entire life, but she'd never wanted anybody so badly. She was sure of it.

When she reached the game room, she fell into a chair to watch the snow falling outside. Quickly, she dialed the number she'd memorized for Bobbi.

"Hello? Hello?" Bobbi said breathlessly.

Grace winced. "Hey, Bobbi. It's Grace. I'm fine."

"Grace! God, I've been so worried. Bri and I are sitting here watching the clock and were about to call the police. I never should've let that humongous guy take you, but you said his name, and then you passed out, and he kind of took over."

"He does that," Grace said dryly.

Bobbi exhaled loudly. "Okay. You're all right. That's all that matters." She was quiet for a moment. "You were out cold. What happened?"

Oops. She should've thought of an excuse. "Um, well, after the coma, sometimes I pass out for a while." So much for being an accomplished liar. "I'm usually fine, but Adare panicked and brought me to the hospital."

"Are you in the hospital now? We can come visit tomorrow morning," Bobbi said.

Grace shook her head, trying to slam some sense into herself. She needed to focus. "No, I'm with Adare now. Just fine. Don't worry."

"He's very, um, a lot," Bobbi said tentatively. "Though seriously good looking. Like wow."

"Hey," Brian said, his voice carrying through the phone.

Bobbi laughed. "You're seriously good looking, too. So, Grace? We were talking. Rosy is getting baptized in a few weeks, and we were hoping you'd be her godmother. You probably remember that neither one of us has family, and it's so nice to have you back in our lives. It would mean the world to us. If that's not weird." She ended the last on an uncertain note.

It was definitely weird, considering Grace would soon be immortal. But her past life, or rather her former life, had helped shape who she was and that mattered. These people mattered. "I'd be honored." She'd have to figure out how long she could stay in their lives, without aging, before it was time to say goodbye.

This immortal situation took a lot of thought. Thank goodness her sister was immortal, too. It was too bad their parents had died when she was in her teens.

"Good. I'm so glad. I'll give you a call in a couple days once we have the schedule set. I'm glad you're okay," Bobbi said.

Grace swallowed. "Thanks." Hopefully she'd remain that way, and so would Adare.

Chapter 24

"This is ridiculous." If the woman weren't the queen, Adare would've told her to go jump in the freezing lake outside. Instead, he sat on the examination table after he'd showered, waiting for her to finish looking at his blood through the microscope across the room. He'd left on his shirt when she'd taken blood so she couldn't see the marking across his back. Even though Garrett Kayrs was her nephew, and a member of the Seven, he'd taken a vow to keep the shield a secret, and Adare was sure he'd kept that promise. "I need to go, your highness."

"You're cranky." Emma straightened and partially turned. "So far, no antibodies. It looks like Grace's cells are flattening yours."

Adare didn't much care. "Looks like? Perhaps they're both mutating." Either way, he needed to find Benny and make a plan for their upcoming raid.

He stood, his legs already touching the floor. "Thanks for checking, but I'm good."

Heavy footsteps ran down the hallway outside, and Adare immediately put himself between the doorway and the queen. Benny came into view, grabbing the door frame to stop himself. "Hey. We have to go. Now."

Adare stiffened.

Benny looked down at Emma and then back up at Adare. "Um, our project? The one we've been working on? Yeah. The contractor is there now."

"Okay." What in the holy hell was Benny trying to say? Adare smiled at the queen. "Thank you for trying, but I'm sure my mating will go as planned."

"When we get back." Benny grabbed his arm and yanked him out of the room, right into Grace. Her face was freshly scrubbed from her shower and her hair was drying softly in cute tendrils.

Adare reached for her before she could hit the opposite wall, lifting her with one arm and swinging her free of Benny's barreling body. "You okay?" He set her down gently, his senses humming to life.

"Fine." She blew hair out of her eyes. "What's going on?"

Benny hovered, moving from one foot to the other. "We need to return to the cabin." He leaned in toward Adare. "Right. Now."

Shit. Something had gone wrong. He had to get Benny alone to find out the details, but it appeared they were on op. Right now. Adare forced a smile for Grace and Emma, who'd just emerged from the examination room. "Looks like we're taking a trip, but I'll be back as soon as I can."

"No," Grace protested, putting her hands on her hips. "You took blood last night, so we need to, you know, tonight." Color burst across her face, but she kept eye contact.

Emma nodded vigorously. "If you hope to have any chance of surviving a mating, it has to be tonight."

"I'll take your blood again when I get back," Adare said, "and then we'll go the next night."

Emma frowned. "That's a good plan, but Grace is fading, too. Time is of the essence for her, as well."

Shite. If he didn't return, then she was as good as dead. "Give me a minute." He jerked his head for Benny to follow and hustled out the front door, stopping on the porch. "What is going on?"

Benny scouted the area. "Satellite feed just popped up from our lair, and the Kurjans have a new crop of females at their site.

Right now. We don't know where they ship them next, but it'll be fast like always, so we need to go. Now. We can actually save this bunch."

If they waited, they'd lose those females. If he stayed here, the women would perish or face terrible fates. But if he left Grace right now, he was leaving her to possibly die as well. There was a good chance he wouldn't be able to bring her out of another coma. "How many females?" he asked.

Benny stepped back, his eyebrows rising. "Looked like about ten of them from the heat signatures."

Adare looked up to find that Grace had silently joined them on the front porch. She wore a blue sweater and had her hair piled on her head, even after crashing into Benny.

She nodded. "When do you have to go in, Benny?"

"First light," Benny said grimly.

Grace took a deep breath. "Okay. We all go to the cabin, we do our, ah, thing tonight, and you guys head out in the morning."

Adare shook his head. "You are not coming."

Benny cleared his throat. "The security at the cabin is excellent. It's not any of my business, but she'd be safe there. If something goes wrong, Ronan will fetch her." He leaned in, whispering loud enough that the neighbors surely heard. "You can get laid, Bro. It's a good way to face death."

Faith ran out onto the porch. "Emma said you guys are leaving."

Her mate, Ronan, filled the doorway behind her. His gaze was somber. "The timeline for the op has changed?" As a member of the Seven, he was well versed in the plan.

Benny nodded. "Yes. The rewards have increased."

Ronan's eyebrows rose as he deciphered Benny's not-so-subtle code. "Confirmed rewards?"

"Yes." Benny looked at his watch. "We need to go. Now."

Ronan stepped toward them, close enough that eavesdroppers couldn't hear. "If there are hostages, I'm coming, too. This just changed from a search and destroy mission to rescue...and destroy.

You'll need another soldier if there are that many confirmed captives."

He was right. They'd only thought to find a couple of captives. The idea of more was breathtaking. Adare nodded. He, Benny, and Ronan had suffered the Seven ritual together centuries ago, along with Quade and three members who were now gone, and he trusted Ronan not only with his life but with Grace's.

Ronan turned and looked at his mate. "I'll be back, Faith. In a few days."

"Oh, no." The woman stepped forward and put an arm around her sister's shoulders. "If Grace is going, so am I. While I don't know exactly what's going on, something tells me you guys might need a doctor sooner rather than later. I'll get my supplies, and then we can leave."

"This is turning into a caravan," Benny muttered, looking up at the cloudy sky. "I mean, I want to be a decent wingman and get you some sugar, but this is getting ridiculous."

* * * *

After a turbulent helicopter ride with Adare piloting the craft, Grace sat on the kitchen counter of Adare's cabin while Faith set medical supplies out on the table. It was disconcerting, to put it mildly, that everyone knew she was about to play crazy vampire-demon bedroom rodeo that night.

Adare was down in the basement with Benny and Ronan, coming up with updated battle plans. She'd been surprised to see the helicopter hangar set into the rocks at the back of the cabin. What other surprises did this place hold?

Faith finally finished and turned around, her eyes a shade darker than Grace's and a lot more somber at the moment. "We've already had the sex talk. A long time ago."

Grace grinned. "Yes. That's one of the memories I still have. I believe you called it 'putting a banana in the fruit salad.' Thank goodness for her sister. When their parents had died, Faith had stepped in and become everything to her.

"You called it 'bone storming.'" Faith laughed, the sound soothing.

Grace kicked her legs. "Immortal sex can't be that different."

Faith's eyebrows rose past her hairline. "Oh, girl, do you have that wrong. It's…" She shook her head and blew out air, obviously searching for the right words. "A box of dynamite times a thousand. The biting and marking are just part of it, as is the immortality. I totally want you to do this to stay alive with me forever, but you have to understand, hybrids aren't, well, casual about mating."

Grace swallowed. "I don't think it's casual, either."

Faith gave a half-shrug as if lost for words. "You'll be connected in a way I can't explain. Mates can communicate telepathically, and you become a part of each other."

"Can you?" Grace asked, perking up.

Faith nodded. "Yes. It's not easy, but it's possible."

"Huh." Grace hadn't had a clue. Must be a secret mating issue. "I guess Adare and I never tried. Well, we never really mated." She couldn't help but be curious about the changes she'd face. "I'm looking forward to knowing him better. If we live through this."

Faith reached for a glass of water. "Be careful what you wish for. These guys get a little intense, and you've always had a bit of wanderlust. That'll change."

Grace smiled. "You're in love with Ronan, and that makes a difference. I'll wander all I want."

Faith lost her amusement. "No, you won't. Make sure you understand who he is. What he is."

"He's a demon-vampire hybrid," Grace said. "I already know what he is."

"Grace, you're from this century. Never forget that he isn't." Faith wet her lips and moved to stare out the window at the snow falling softly around the secured cabin. "They seem all tough and unemotional, but when those emotions are tapped, they blow hurricane force."

Adare barely had emotions. "You're happy though, right, Faith?"

Faith turned and smiled, her whole face lighting up. "Definitely. Ronan is everything." Contentment looked good on her.

"I'm glad." Grace didn't want to discuss sex any longer. "I never heard the results of today's blood tests." No doubt Adare had built lots of antibodies. He was immortal, after all.

Faith turned and busied herself with reorganizing supplies that were already organized.

Grace stopped moving. "Faith?"

Her sister turned around, her lips set in a stubborn line. "I'm sure Adare will be fine."

Oh, no. Grace slumped against the counter. "There was no change? My cells still killed his?"

"No, your cells kind of swallowed his. Not killed," Faith said, grimacing. "We don't know what it means. But I think you should mate him, and Adare knows the risks. It's his decision to make."

Adare popped his head in. "Grace? Do you have a minute?"

Faith turned away.

Grace hopped off the counter and pushed her sister in the arm before approaching the kitchen doorway. Well, so much for having sex with the hard-bodied badass. She'd tried to have faith in the process, but so far, it wasn't looking good. "Sure. What's up?"

He took her hand. "I'll show you."

Was that supposed to sound dirty? Or was her mind just in the gutter? "Okay." Curious, she followed him through the main room to the hidden stairwell, climbing down as they had before. They reached the cavernous underground room, and she nodded at Benny and Ronan, who were studying a map over at the far table.

Adare drew her around the consoles to another doorway, pushing it open and leaning in to flip a light switch.

She gasped as she moved inside. "You made me a darkroom." She looked around. He'd set up the wet side and the dry side perfectly, and there was even a running sink. A huge fan was mounted against the exterior wall for ventilation. She took in the three trays and tongs as well as the chemicals stored on the shelf above them, including neatly labeled hydroquinone and sodium hydroxide. Her chest swelled, and surprising tears pricked the backs of her eyes. "It's perfect."

"Good." He stepped back. "I had it installed after we left the other day, after I saw the Pentax you lug around." He turned and pointed to the nearest desktop computer. "That one is yours for editing digital pictures."

"Thank you." Her throat was clogged, but she turned and slid her palm over the hard ridges of his bicep. "This is really nice of you." She didn't know what to say. So she levered herself onto her toes and kissed him beneath his whiskered jaw.

He grinned. "I figured you'd like this more than diamonds."

"Always." Her hands itched to get in there and start developing some of the film she'd taken lately.

He gave her a gentle nudge. "You have a couple of hours before supper. Why don't you break in the room? I'll fetch your bag from upstairs."

"Wait." She stepped away from him. "I can't do it, Adare. I just can't." She'd been fooling herself, thinking he was immortal and would survive whatever they did. "Emma said your antibodies haven't changed from taking my blood. I can't save my life by risking yours." Even though her limbs were heavier than they'd ever been, and a peculiar darkness kept edging in from the far reaches of her vision, the facts were the facts.

"Grace," he murmured. "We are mating. I'll be fine."

She could play dumb and accept his words, even though science said otherwise. Or she could face things head-on and take control of her destiny…and his. "No."

He sighed. "The queen admitted she didn't know or understand the Seven, the Keys, or the effect of your blood on mine in a Petri dish."

Grace nodded vigorously. "Exactly. She doesn't know. Why would you risk your life on an uncertainty?"

He brushed his knuckles down the side of her face. "I made a decision and a vow when I mated you with a bite and a mark, and

I meant it. That hasn't changed, and we will mate again tonight. Completely."

She set her stance. No way would she let him sacrifice himself for her. Or even risk it. "No."

One of his eyebrows rose in a look she was becoming very familiar with. "Want to bet?" he asked mildly.

The shiver that took her had nothing to do with challenge or fear. She swallowed.

He smiled.

Chapter 25

"Getting her drunk seems like dirty pool," Benny said, scouting the outside perimeter of the cabin along with Adare.

"I know." Adare had made sure Grace's glass was full of very good wine during dinner. "But she's determined to save me from myself, and I'm determined to save *her*, and that's the end of it."

Benny chuckled. "You have it bad, and so does she, and you're both being morons about it. You've wanted her since you met her, and I've seen how she looks at you. If you both admitted that shit, maybe the mating would be stronger and take hold. Genetics and all that crap never made sense to me."

The wind whistled a sharp tune, scattering powdered snow in every direction.

"You're more a fate and *what the fuck* kind of guy," Adare agreed. "Think you'll ever get mated?"

"Sure. There's a wildcat out there waiting for my mark on her ass, but let's be honest. She'd have to be at least half-crazy to fall for a hybrid like me, and that's gonna take some energy on my part. We have too much going on for crazy right now. Well, more crazy than we already have."

Sometimes it was impressive how self-aware Benny could be.

"But," Benny continued, "at least I won't face possible death or mutation to mate. Like you."

"Possible mutation?" Adare eyed the next camera, satisfied it was shielded from the falling snow.

Benny nodded. "Sure. If she has these, what are they, antibodies? Say they attack your cells, meaning your immortal cells, and hers somehow win. Maybe they don't kill your cells but just turn you into a human. Can you imagine?"

"No," Adare said shortly. There was no force on earth that could turn him into a human.

Benny clucked his tongue. "Yeah, you're right. Your cells would die before letting you become human. Probably. I mean, cells are an enigma to me, but that sounds right."

This pep talk from Benny was giving Adare a headache. "You're a good brother, Benny."

"I know." Benny reached up to move a branch out of the way of camera three. "I am the glue that holds us Seven together."

Well, okay. "You've done a good job so far."

"True. As such, I feel we need to get serious for a moment. You mated Grace out of duty to Ronan and Faith, and you could be talking eternity if not death here. You have to take a moment and ask if you really want Grace. If she's worth the risk."

Adare nodded. "She's a sweetheart, and she'll sacrifice her life so as not to risk mine. It's my risk to take."

Benny kicked a couple of branches out of his way, snow falling on his dark hair. "Think you'll die?"

"No." Adare angled around a tree to make sure the security lines were still solidly in place. "She's a Key, and that's powerful, but I'm one of the Seven, right?"

Benny nodded, tapping a tree trunk and looking up at one of the many cameras. "Sure, but the power of the Seven comes from fighting and our shields. The power of the Keys comes from their very blood." He paused, looking at Adare. "And hers swallows yours."

"True," Adare allowed, turning back toward the cabin. "Bottom line, if I don't mate her, she'll return to a coma state and then eventually die. I can't allow that to happen."

"Because she's a Key or because she's Grace?" Benny asked, his boots sinking deep into the snow.

Adare thought about the question, listening for any threats in the vicinity. "Both."

"Good on you." Benny clapped him on the back, and the sound echoed through the air. "I wish we had invited that shifter back here with us for the night. I'm the only one going to bed alone." He frowned, opening the back door. "But I guess at least I know I ain't gonna die tonight. Good luck, Adare. You've been a good brother."

"You too, Benny," Adare said, meaning it. "On the off chance that I don't make it, would you—"

"Of course. I'll make sure Grace is safe and taken care of." Benny toed off his boots inside the mudroom by the back slider. "Don't you worry about that." He paused, his metallic eyes darkening. "No shit for a moment, brother. I feel like you're not taking the threat seriously enough. It's real. I don't want to lose you."

Adare's chest filled. He and Benny had been brothers longer than many species had survived on earth. "I'm taking it seriously, but my mind is already made up, so why wallow in what might happen?" He drew Benny in for a hard hug. "You're a good brother. You've done your job, and now I have to do mine."

Benny nodded, hugging back before letting go. "Fair enough."

Adare leaned down to untie his boot.

Benny stretched out a calf. "You scared?"

"No." He hadn't been scared of anything for longer than he remembered. "I don't want to leave her alone, though." So he'd survive the night and then the next day. He had to make sure the mating took hold this time and she was healthy and strong.

"Huh." Benny glanced at the control panel by the back door where several lights blinked. He flipped on a screen and keyed in a string of numbers, stiffening when code began to scroll. "I don't want to cause any problems, but I think your female is making a break for it."

Adare paused and read the screen. "Damn it." Leaving his boot alone, he jogged through the house to the garage, only to see the door open and the taillights of his SUV disappearing down the drive.

Benny reached his side. "I don't suppose you told her about the landmines and electrical shields we have guarding the property?"

"No." Why would he have? Adare flipped open the garage control panel and quickly disengaged the landmines and shields, leaving only the main gate in place.

Benny nodded. "Good job. It'd probably be a bad idea to blow her up before mating her."

Adare cut him a look.

Benny shrugged. "Maybe going it alone isn't so bad tonight. Good luck, brother." He turned back for the house.

The surprise flowed out of Adare, leaving irritation to swirl around and then bubble into anger. Grace had been about a half mile from driving over a mine that would've tossed the SUV in the air like a frisbee. She very well might've died.

He jumped down to the main level of the garage and followed her into the night, steam rising from his skin when he strode into the snowy air. His steps were sure and purposeful, and he tried to let the storm calm him as he walked down the driveway toward the gate.

Grace wasn't going anywhere.

* * * *

Safely in the SUV, Grace stared at the wide metal gate through the windshield as the wipers struggled to keep the snow cleared. She put the headlights on bright. Just wonderful. Okay. Maybe it was only shut and not locked. She pulled on her gloves and stepped into the rapidly increasing storm, struggling against the wind to reach the gate. The cold sliced into her, burning the skin on her face.

There was no latch. No lock. No area where it looked like the gate would split in two and open.

Okay. So the entire thing must swing one way or the other. She grasped two of the prongs and shoved. It didn't move. So she pulled. *Nothing.*

"It's a biometric device that can't be moved by hand."

Grace yelped and jumped, hitting her shoulder on the fence. She whirled around to find Adare standing in the snow, a dark figure in a dangerous storm. "You scared me."

"Good." In his position by the vehicle, his face was veiled by the darkness.

She set her stance, her left boot slipping in the snow. "We both know you can open this gate."

"Do we?" His voice was low. Silky. Aggressive.

Her lungs froze. The lump in her throat suddenly kept her from swallowing. "I hadn't realized there was a gate in place," she said lamely.

"There are quite a few things you've failed to realize." His low voice carried easily through the blistering wind. "For one thing, we have land mines as well as target missiles protecting the property, in addition to electrical currents that could fry a buffalo." He strode closer, all casual grace and powerful threat. "Not to mention the fact that you're intoxicated."

"Oh, please." It was too cold to roll her eyes, but she gave it a try. "Every time you filled my glass, I poured the wine into Faith's when you looked away. She was loaded. Didn't you see her try to take Ronan's clothes off as they left the kitchen?"

"Get into the vehicle, Grace."

She looked around. Running was just foolish, so why the hell was her heart beating so fast and her skin sensitizing? She didn't like him all growly like this. Did she? Yeah, he was kind of sexy in a demolish-the-world kind of way, and the guy could kiss, but she was trying to save his life. He could at least be a little bit appreciative of that fact. Yeah. He definitely should be thanking her instead of ordering her around.

"Grace." The edge to his tone sharpened.

Dang. She'd gotten caught in her head again. Must be some kind of defense mechanism. She shook herself out of it. "Open the gate, Adare."

"I'll give you the count of two."

Oh, he did not. She slapped snow off her gloves instead of throwing a snowball at him. "I'm not a wayward toddler, you arrogant jackwad."

"More like an errant mate," he retorted. "I'm done with it. Get in the vehicle, now, or I'll put you in it."

It had been freaking torture sitting next to him at dinner thinking about having sex, wanting to have sex, and if he put his hands on her right now, she'd probably just give in and take him down to the snow. Or at least try to. He was making it a lot easier for her to forget the risk to him if they finally gave in and had sex, so he should probably lose the attitude.

"That's it." He lowered his chin and strode directly at her.

She jumped. "Fine." Without waiting for him to stop, she tried to run for the passenger side door and slipped on the ice.

He caught her by the arm to keep her from falling. Then he dragged her back toward the driver's side.

She tried to pull back, but her boots couldn't find purchase and just slid along where he wanted. He jerked open the door, lifted her inside, and shoved her over with his hip as he sat in the driver's seat.

Scooting over, she glared at him. Yeah, she could open the door and run, but she'd end up right back here. There was no way she could outrun an immortal hybrid. "Did you say landmines?" Her head jerked as the conversation came back. Landmines and electrical currents? On the fence she'd tried to move?

"Yes." His voice was grim as he set the vehicle in drive and turned around in the storm, crunching into snowbanks on either side of the driveway.

"You didn't think those were facts I might want to know?" Her voice rose.

His head turned, in slow motion, and his gaze captured hers. "I didn't think you'd be foolhardy enough to venture out at night in a storm with the entire Kurjan nation on your ass."

Well. Since he put it like that. "I'm trying to save your life."

"That's not your job." He turned back to drive over the thick snow piling up on the driveway. "There's a simple truth you need to get into your stubborn head right now. I know you were raised human, but my world is simple. No soldier, no immortal male, would ever let his mate risk her life for his. Period." He lifted a hand. "I don't care if that's politically incorrect or not how the humans live these days. That's fine for them. But it's in our very nature, *my* very nature, to put your life before mine. Before almost anybody's, in fact."

They weren't true mates. "We didn't really mate," she reminded him.

"I did." He pulled the vehicle into the garage. "And you're about to. Get inside the house, Grace. Now."

Chapter 26

Grace slid out of the car and stomped her boots to get rid of the snow before climbing the stairs and bursting into the kitchen. His view of the world was kind of sweet, and if they were in love and mates, she'd understand. But right now, they wanted to smack each other. Or get naked. Why those two feelings were intertwined when she thought of him, she had no idea. "I really don't see—"

He lifted her, flipped her around in the air, and caught her. She yelped and grabbed on to his coat, instinctively smashing her thighs around his hips to keep from falling.

His mouth was on hers before she could make another sound. Hard and demanding, his lips were cold from the snow and his tongue so hot it burned. He went deep, one hand on her ass and the other stabilizing her back. His tongue took hers, conquering, as he strode through the cabin, his steps soft and sure.

She couldn't breathe. She didn't want to.

With a low moan, she returned his kiss, tunneling both hands through his hair. Snow fell all around them.

All that existed was Adare and his mouth. His hand scalded her butt, even through her jeans. His heat and his energy, his anger and his desire. His powerful determination.

He kicked the door to their small suite shut with one boot and let her slide down his body to the floor, still kissing her.

She stepped back, her mind reeling, her body aching with a need so great it had to be unnatural. Or immortal. "Adare."

Keeping her gaze, he drew off his coat and dropped it on the floor. His shirt was next, and all of that smooth and impossibly hard muscle played as he reached for his belt.

"Wait a minute." She held out a hand, trying to think. Tried to rationalize what was happening and use her brain instead of her body. The pull he had on her was unreal, and it was more than just need or want or lack of sex for years. There was something between them; something big and real that she couldn't explain. The marking along her back, the faded brand that he'd put there years ago to save her life, began to tingle until it burned.

He paused, his eyes dark pools of burnt silver. "There's only one way this works, and it's if we both decide it'll work. That much I know. All in, Grace Cooper. We control our cells, our DNA, not the other way around."

The truth in that statement dug deep inside her. Where she wanted *him* right now. "You're telling me you believe in mind over matter?" she asked breathlessly, the craving she felt for him making her voice shake.

"No. I believe in fate and our ability to decide for ourselves what our ultimate destiny will be. You're a powerful Key, I'm a member of the Seven, and if we decide to mate and survive, we will. There's no other way life makes sense, and it's time you stopped running and faced what you need to face." He released his belt and drew it through the belt loops, the sound making an erotic wisp she felt in her core.

"I don't want you to die," she whispered.

"I won't." He unclasped the button on his jeans.

Oh, she wanted her mouth on those abs. "I don't want to die either," she admitted, her legs trembling with a combination of need and fear.

"You won't." He reached for the front of her coat and slowly unzipped it, giving her plenty of time and room to take another step back. "I won't force you, and you know it. I won't hurt you, and you know it. This is your decision, and it's time you made it. You either trust me to protect you, to protect us both, or you don't." He released the zipper but didn't make another move.

He was asking for what she'd never given anybody but her sister. Absolute trust. The woman she'd been before the coma would've made the leap of faith. Of trust. Would've believed that Adare was as powerful as he seemed. Was she still that woman? "What if you're wrong?" she breathed.

"I'll have no regrets." He drew her coat down her arms and dropped it next to his. "Not a one. You're going to have to trust me on that, too."

She did believe in mind over matter. There was a lot about the immortal world she didn't understand, and there was no doubt Adare did. "All right. I trust you." She gave it all to him, letting go of doubt and the fear of risk. Of failure. If they both went all in, as he'd said, then they'd survive and deal with the problems of tomorrow...tomorrow. "So. I haven't done this in a while."

His smile held charm and amusement. "I'll guide you through it."

Why was she suddenly so nervous? Oh yeah. The hottest male on earth was about to see her naked. Thank goodness she'd shaved her legs that morning. "I think I remember what goes where." She tried for humor but her words came out breathless.

"Good to know." He unbuttoned her sweater, his gaze scorching.

Finally giving in to temptation, she flattened her hands across his abs, letting the hard ridges fill her palms. "Were you like this before you underwent the Seven ritual?" According to Faith, the ritual was a near death experience that involved fire, blood, and traveling between worlds.

"Like what?" His thumbs caressed her arms as he drew her sweater down them and let it go.

"Airbrushed," she whispered. "Hard as steel." Each ridge was powerful muscle, tight and strong.

The pads of his fingers skimmed across her clavicle, heating and sparking. "I was a fighter before the ritual, although it did make us stronger, I think."

She gently tried to twist him around. "I want to see."

He paused, and then with a soft sound of regret at removing his hands from her body, he partially turned to face the fire.

She breathed in sharply. His back was incredible. The black form of a shield, a tattoo way deeper than his skin, covered him from neck to waist. A solid form that could never be penetrated. No matter what, his heart was protected.

From the outside.

He turned back around, just as impenetrable from the front but lacking the tattoo. She felt vulnerable standing there in snowy jeans and her bra, but the flare in his eyes gave her confidence. "I'll try not to hurt you," she whispered, meaning every word.

* * * *

God, she was cute. A rush of emotion, hot and determined, swelled through Adare's chest. The thought that she could hurt him was sweet.

With a flick of his finger, the front clasp of her bra sprang open, revealing small, high breasts. His fangs started to drop, and he retracted their sharp points, wanting to get his mouth on her as soon as possible. He traced from her collar bone down over one pretty pink nipple, smiling at her gasp. She was so honest in her responses. Finally. No more concerns or doubts.

When Grace Cooper went all in, she did it with a vengeance. He really liked that about her.

Even so, her expression showed a vulnerability that he needed to handle. "You're beautiful, Grace."

As expected, she rolled her eyes. Fair enough. He'd have to show her. He settled both hands at her waist, easily spanning the width, and lifted her toward the bed. She'd lost too much weight while fighting the decline of the mating mark, and the first thing he'd do after the op was make sure she ate healthy and continued to train. She needed to know how to fight, and she'd taken that on herself admirably, but he was done ignoring his duties.

Plus, he wanted to spend time with her. It was unexpected, but he fell into the truth. He laid her down, tugging off her jeans and boots as he stood to remove his own. Her panties were pink with lace along the edges, sexy and sweet at the same time. Like the female herself.

She reached for him, and he set a knee on the bed, leaning over to meet her mouth. He let her take control of the kiss, her lips soft and seeking, curiosity in the hands skimming across his shoulders.

He'd waited five years for this, so he tried to slow down. Her statement the other night kept running through his head; that females needed a reason for sex. To give that kind of trust. He moved his mouth from hers, kissing along her delicate jawline to nip the fragile cord along her neck. "I won't ever let anybody harm you," he murmured, his hand caressing her breasts, enjoying her gasp of pleasure.

"You're making promises?" she arched against him, her tone raspy.

"Yes." He grazed his fang along her skin enough to bite but not scratch.

She moaned and dug her nails into his biceps, cutting erotic pain through his arms. "Then promise you'll let me photograph you any time I want. Anywhere I want."

He stilled. "I promise." If that's how this was going, he was on board. "Promise me you won't take off by yourself and put yourself in danger again. That we are honest about our plans and locations." Not that he wasn't going to keep a close eye on her in the future, anyway. He sucked a pouting nipple into his mouth.

She grasped his hair, arching even farther into his mouth. Her promise was breathless and garbled, but she made it nonetheless.

He laved her nipple and moved to the other one, his cock so hard he was losing feeling in his legs. But it was fucking worth it. The taste of her went to his head, and he kissed lower, dipping over her navel to those satiny pink panties. He tucked his thumbs in the sides and snapped them free.

Her laugh was free and pained. "I liked those," she said.

"Me, too." He tossed them over his shoulder, settling down to what was becoming his favorite treat. The other night had been way too fast, and he hadn't had a chance to play. He was taking the time now and would worry about the danger tomorrow.

The sight of his mark on her thigh, from when he'd bitten her, arrowed satisfaction through him with a shocking intensity. Unable to resist, he leaned down and nibbled.

She jerked. "Oh, God."

He chuckled against her, watching her abdomen roll in response. "Pray all you want, *Leannain*. I'm still doing this my way." Which meant nice and slow so he could enjoy himself.

"You called me that before," she moaned, her thighs widening on their own. *For him*. "What does it mean?"

"Sweetheart. In the language of my people." He kept his mouth close to her clit, so his heated breath brushed her. The strangled moan she gave nearly made him laugh.

But he'd never been able to resist temptation for long, so he slipped one finger inside her, testing her. Ah. Nice and wet, but incredibly tight. Way too tight. He'd have to see what he could do about that.

He licked her once. Twice. And she detonated like a Bykov explosive, crying out, her abdomen undulating as she rode the waves. Chuckling again, he enclosed her clit with his mouth, sucking hard and prolonging her ecstasy until she pulled his hair and tried to get away. Disgruntled, he lifted his head. "Are you ever going to let me play?"

Chapter 27

Grace couldn't breathe. Her chest heaved and her thighs trembled. All from a couple of kisses. "Is your mouth magic, or what?" As reality returned, she realized her precarious position and tried to close her legs. A little.

His massive shoulders prevented the movement. At the realization, hunger shot right to her core, heady and hot.

"Magic, no." He moved up her again, a huge shadow in the light from the fire. "Hungry, yes. Someday, I'm going to do that all day until I'm satisfied, no matter how many times you orgasm."

She couldn't breathe. "Well, okay," she whispered, grinning even though she was aching for him. In a million years, she never would've thought sex with Adare would be fun. Oh, wild and crazy, erotic and intense…but not fun. "We'll go ahead and put that on the calendar."

He smiled a second before he kissed her again, going slow, taking his time. Was he being deliberate in taking as many cells as he could, or was he getting as lost as she was? She had to know. So she tightened her hold in his thick hair and jerked hard.

He lifted up, his gaze dark and disgruntled. "What?"

"Just making sure." Oh, he was as into it as she was.

"Oh yeah?" His fangs glinted and he sliced into her neck, the points going deep. Pain shimmered and edged to pleasure almost immediately as he drank. A flash of electricity arced right from her neck to her sex, and she rolled into another orgasm so quickly she could only grab his shoulders and hang on, shutting her eyes.

As if sensing her need, he pressed a knee between her legs, the friction and hard pressure deepening the waves until she gasped, her ears ringing.

She came down again, her mouth gaping open.

His fangs retracted and he closed the wound, leaning up and licking his lips clean. "You taste sweet. Like honey with sass."

For answer, she leaned down and tried to shove off his boxer-briefs. He helped her, finally as nude as she was, and holy crap he was big. She wasn't surprised. She'd sat on his lap enough times that she knew his sex was in proportion with the rest of his magnificent body. Twisting her body, she reached for him, running her fingers along his impressive length.

His eyes flashed to full silver, bright this time. She went still, entranced.

He pressed against her sex, and she released him, settling back with her head on the pillow. She swallowed at the pressure. "Relax," he murmured, balancing on his elbows and dipping his head to kiss her, his lips firm and his tongue teasing.

She softened against the bed, breathing him in, widening her thighs to make more room.

"There you go," he whispered, licking along the shell of her ear. "We have all night, Grace. No hurry." He pushed in another inch, stretching her and shooting sparks of painful need throughout her body. He waited, kissing her nose, her eyelids, and her chin before easing in another inch.

Her body protested the invasion, even as she wanted more of him. Confusion filtered through her, and she grasped his hips.

He lifted up. "We can stop if you want."

"No," she exploded, lifting her knees to trap him and then wincing at the ensuing pain. "If you stop, I'll kill you. For real." She meant it, damn it. They had to fit somehow, right? They were meant to fit. "Maybe you should just go for it." So far, her body had accommodated his.

"I'm not gonna hurt you if I don't need to." He lowered his forehead to hers, his arms visibly pulsating as he held himself back.

The protectiveness in the statement, spoken in his garbled and pained voice, eased her as nothing else could have. She took a deep breath and relaxed her body, going soft, letting him take over. He'd asked for trust before, but she hadn't completely understood how all-encompassing that might be. Now she gave it to him. "I'm all right." She reached up and drew his head down, kissing him and licking along his firm lips.

He kissed her back, taking over, diving them both so deep she forgot about the pain and the pressure. Slowly, he took her, kissing, nipping, and licking her neck and ears and mouth until finally, he was fully embedded inside her.

She caressed his chest, her legs wide, her body overtaken by his. "Wow," she whispered.

His chuckle against her neck was pained.

She bit the top of his ear. "I'm ready, Adare," she whispered, scraping her nails down his back and nipping them at the small of his waist. Indulging herself and challenging him, she reached lower and drilled her nails into his tight butt, making her own marks.

He lifted up, his gaze soft, his body impossibly hard. Then he started to move.

Finally.

He went slowly at first, his gaze intense, watching her reactions, trying his best not to hurt her. The pain was delicious, melding with pleasure, his restraint driving her need even higher than it had been before. He increased his speed and his thrusts, and the thrill took her, pinning her in this one moment in time that felt too good to ever leave.

The blood rushed through her veins, pounding in her head. Her muscles tightened in every extremity, with an ache that wasn't even close to enough. She climbed higher, her body floating, sparks shooting in every direction. Her hands were frantic on his back, on his ribcage, over his chest, trying to find purchase somewhere. *Anywhere.*

He growled and grabbed her hands, pinning them to the bed and planting his over them. He hammered into her, driving the headboard against the wall and caressing nerves inside her with a raw demand her body could only heed.

She caught her breath, tightened her muscles even more, and went over the cliff. She cried out, her eyelids shutting, as the orgasm overtook her with a power she'd never even imagined. The firestorm of pleasure burned her from within, forcing her to peak at several crests, and finally released her to go limp.

Gasping, her body shaking, she slowly opened her eyes.

And realized he was still hard inside her.

* * * *

Adare's entire body tightened and heated, power surging through his veins. He pulsed inside her, the feeling of absolute possession and truth strengthening him in a way he'd never imagined.

Grace's eyes opened and she blinked. He caught the moment she realized he was still inside her. Still not done. Still unmated.

Her eyes widened, the blue mysterious and so deep he could get lost forever. A hint of trepidation lingered there, as well. Good. She needed to understand the significance of the mating.

He slowly withdrew from her delicious body, enjoying her gasp of protest. "My way, *Leannain*," he reminded her. This time, he wanted to see the marking take hold. He was going to ensure it did so. His hold was gentle but unrelenting as he grasped her hips and flipped her over on the bed, rising to his knees to do so.

She fell onto her stomach and instantly pushed up. "Hey," she breathed.

He helped her, lifting her to her hands and knees, facing the headboard.

"Oh," she murmured.

He palmed her cute butt and reached between her legs.

She mewled, already wet and swollen. "Adare," she breathed, tossing her hair back.

"Say my name again." He leaned over her, his hand still playing, liking the sound of his name on her lips.

"Adare." The sound was soft.

He grasped her hips and eased inside her, careful to go slow and not harm her. His body rioted and wanted to pound, but he held on to control, easing in again. She accepted him more quickly this time, and he pushed the last few inches, knowing without a doubt this was as close to heaven as he would ever experience in this life.

Holding tight, he pulled out and pushed back in, setting up a rhythm that kept him in control. Anticipation built up inside him, combining with a rush of heat that burned him from within. Every stroke made him more sensitive and ready, and he was nearing the point of no return.

There was no going back.

For either of them.

Tremors started from inside his knees and shot up to his thighs and groin, landing hard in his cock. He pounded harder, leaning over her, taking everything he could.

She dropped down, her head on the pillow and turned to the side. Open and vulnerable to him, trusting him like she'd promised. That trust, that surrender, quieted the world around him until there was only this moment, only this female, only the two of them. *Forever.*

He hammered, his body taking over, his entire being filled with Grace. Her scent, her skin, her essence. A surge of electricity shot throughout his cells, going deeper, into a part of him he hadn't known existed.

His fangs dropped low and sharp, and he clamped onto her shoulder, slicing until he marked bone. She cried out and tried to pull away, but he held her in place, letting her blood flow into his mouth. The sweet spiciness exploded on his tongue, and he drank more, the beast at his core taking over in the thrill of mating.

He edged to the side of her, lifted his burning palm, and placed the marking flat across the spot where his hand had been before. This time, energy ran through his palm, scalding in its intensity and sparking through his veins to clamp around his heart. He felt—actually felt—strings tie around his heart, all bearing her name. Who she was and who she'd always be.

They entrapped him, taking him, settling into his being with the certainty of belonging he'd never felt before.

His world was filled with her, with their future together and the knowledge that he was hers. Forever hers to protect and defend, to keep safe during an immortal lifetime.

To do that, he made her his.

The marking sizzled, and he removed his hand, driving harder inside her, his fangs still in place. His balls drew up tight, and live wires uncoiled up his spine. He came in a rush of power and strength, stilling and jerking several times inside her, his mind soaring and his body filling with an invincibility that stole his breath.

He panted, his sweaty body attached to hers. Slowly, he retracted his fangs and closed her wound, his vision fuzzy. Taking a deep breath, he withdrew from her body and turned her on her side, curling around her and yanking the comforter over them both.

Nobody had prepared him for this.

He held her tighter, against his chest, feeling her heartbeat race wildly. "Are you all right?" he managed to gasp.

She nodded, the back of her head hitting his chin. "Yes," she breathed. "That was just a lot."

That was an understatement, to say the least. "I didn't hurt you?"

"No." She snuggled her butt into his groin and pressed her face into the pillow. "Tired. My shoulder aches a little." She yawned, the sound exhausted. The marking on her back heated his stomach, and a sharp sense of possessiveness ran through him. "I hope I didn't just kill you," she mumbled sleepily.

"If you did, it was definitely worth it." He kissed her on the back of the head, holding her close, meaning every word.

Chapter 28

Morning came too early, but Adare had a job to do and couldn't snuggle down with Grace for the entire day, as he would've liked. The urgency of this day shot adrenaline into his muscles. They had a one-shot chance to save those women; destroying the facility was secondary.

Yet he'd still get it accomplished if he could.

Adare kept the helicopter along the tree line and out of radar range of the Kurjan stronghold, his head aching but his mind clear. He'd had a headache all morning, but that was probably from lack of sleep. His hands were easy on the controls as he scoped out the landing area they'd chosen more than six months ago.

Seeing no threats in the surrounding forest, he set down and had barely cut the power before Benny and Ronan jumped out, hauling their backpacks full of weapons and explosives.

He powered down completely and stepped into the thick powder, catching the tarp Benny threw at him from the other side. They camouflaged the copter with a white tarp that would blend into the snowy landscape. He jogged around and lifted his pack onto his back. "It looked like there was an avalanche to the northeast, or at least some sort of rock slide, so let's go with Route B."

"Affirmative," Benny said, all business while on op. With his winter-camouflaged coat, pants, and hat, he probably didn't need the paint on his face. With it, he blended into the environment as well as Adare or Ronan did, even though he was a couple inches taller than their six feet six inches.

Ronan jogged up, his face painted as well. "I took a look at the last satellite feed, and the kidnapped women are still in place. Although, I didn't see the van that was there last time."

Shit. They'd need a way to transport those victims out, and there was no way to haul them to the helicopter, even if there was room in the craft for that many people. "We'll have to improvise. I'm guessing they have trucks in the metal building to the south of the stronghold, right next to that power station we're taking out second." There was a bigger power supply to the north they'd blow up first.

At least the weather was on their side. The snowstorm had finally moved on, leaving a cold blue sky and merciless sun. The Kurjans wouldn't be able to venture outside, which definitely gave the Seven an advantage.

Benny clapped him on the arm. "Congrats on the mating. Can't wait to see you all moonfaced around the campfire like the rest of these guys."

Adare grinned. "Thanks, and that isn't going to happen. I like her, she likes me, and we'll make a good match. That's what lasts." He'd been honest when he'd said he didn't believe in love, but he believed completely in promises and doing his duty. Grace understood that.

"Right," Benny said. "Okey-doke, then. Back to business. You're on lead, brother."

Adare turned and jogged through waist-high snow into the forest and up a mountain, his boots heavy and his left leg aching at the ankle. What had he done to his ankle? Ignoring the pain, he ran for fifteen miles with Benny and Ronan behind him, just like old times.

They reached the outskirts of the Kurjans' forty acres and an innocuous dilapidated wooden fence that looked like somebody had forgotten about it. He donned sunglasses that enabled him to see the electrical current running through the wood, between the planks, and about a foot above the fence post. Impressive security, that was for sure.

He backed up and made a run for it, jumping high and curling to summersault over the electricity to the other side. Ronan quickly followed, his boots barely making a sound as he landed. Benny watched them both, made sure they didn't blow up, and then followed exactly in Adare's footsteps.

Adare motioned toward the tree line. "Let's keep to the trees."

Benny nodded and fitted sunglasses on his face. He dug a circular device out of his pack and pushed several buttons on it. "Hold for electricity overload." Taking a breath, he tossed the disc at the fence. Blue waves immediately blew out in every direction, sizzling over Adare's face.

He stepped back, his eyebrows rising.

Benny clapped his hands together. "Oh, yeah. Chalton said that'd work, and what a rush, right? That should've knocked out every camera in the trees. Maybe even the electricity for the main buildings."

Ronan set the alarm on his watch. "We're on go."

Adare jogged toward the trees, keeping out of camera range until he reached the first backup generator he'd identified via satellite. He had it disabled within seconds, silently and with his knife, while Benny and Ronan moved down the tree-line, taking out the other generators.

His glasses identified landmines, and he stepped around them easily, noting the grid pattern he'd assumed would be in place. Oh, there'd be a couple not in line, but the new Realm glasses would identify them. The Realm had always been lightyears ahead of the Kurjans when it came to security and modern science, and apparently that hadn't changed any. Yeah, he'd stolen them last time he visited, and someday he'd be held accountable for that. Not today, though. Within minutes, the three of them reached the end of the trees and faced the several buildings, concrete and metal, that dotted the landscape.

Benny wiped snow from his hair. "Their cameras are disabled. They must know that—"

Gunfire erupted from the nearest metal building, and bullets plowed into the trees all around them. They scattered, taking cover, the plan firmly memorized.

Benny returned fire, while Adare went left and Ronan right, zig-zagging across the snowy landscape and utilizing everything from machinery to the metal buildings as cover. Adare reached the second building to the north and pulled out his gun, keeping his back to the exterior wall. He reached the door, took a breath, and dodged inside, gun first. The large shop held vehicles and fuel. His boots were silent as he cleared the building. Most of the Kurjans had probably been sleeping since it was bright out, but now they'd be awake and firing from the buildings. He had to find those women.

He turned to exit the building and continue east, but his vision faded. Pausing, he dropped to his haunches, taking several deep breaths. What was going on with him?

His vision cleared, and he shoved to his feet, setting several of the explosives he'd purchased from Jacki on his way out. The cold air centered him, and he continued on his way, having full faith that Ronan was doing the same on the other side of the property.

Finally, he reached the largest buildings as gunfire erupted all around him.

He fired back, careful to aim for guns and not people, in case the women were there. His watch dinged. Ducking against the building, he drew the detonator out of his pocket and put more distance between himself and the bomb, crouching in the snow and letting it provide cover.

He frowned. Ronan's explosives should've detonated already.

Damn it. He flipped the cover open and pressed his button. *Click.* The shouts of soldiers echoed, and the wisp of a missile being fired from the main lodge hissed through the air. It landed toward the tree line and exploded, sending debris raining down. He glanced down at the detonator and pressed it again.

Nothing happened.

*   *   *   *

Grace worked in her darkroom, letting the familiarity of developing pictures distract her from worrying about Adare. He'd seemed fine as he set off with Ronan and Benny that morning. Maybe he'd been right, and the mating wouldn't cause him any harm. Perhaps her cells would even make him stronger.

She hung up a picture of him to dry. She'd taken the shot back at Realm headquarters when he'd been relaxing, his hair down, his gaze thoughtful. His black eyes expressed so much, it was difficult to look away. She then developed several pictures of Faith, a couple of Faith and Ronan, and then some landscape shots she'd taken of the lake during the storm.

Humming softly, she lifted a photograph out of the water. It was one of the shots of Brian she'd taken with her Pentax. He stood in the sun, smiling toward Bobbi, his face partially hidden by shadow. It was a good shot. It was nice to have found her friends again.

It'd be even nicer if she remembered them. She hung it up to dry and then quickly developed the pictures of Bobbi and her family before moving on to the sister and Rose. There was something odd about that sister, and maybe Grace could figure it out when she saw a photograph.

Was Adare correct? Did she have sight that was special? Could she see things nobody else saw?

Her burner phone buzzed, and she lifted it to her ear, cradling it with her shoulder. "Hello?"

"Hi, Grace," Bobbi said, her voice chipper. "How are you feeling?"

"Good." Grace clipped the pictures into place and leaned back, taking the phone in her hand and rolling her neck. "I'm much better. How are you guys?" It was nice to talk about normal things. She'd had a stomach ache all day, worrying about Adare being shot at by the Kurjans.

Bobbi chuckled. "We're great. Want to meet for lunch?"

Grace grimaced. "Um, we're not in town any longer. We're visiting family in Montana." She hated lying to her friend, but she'd learned five years ago to be careful on the phone, even burner phones. "We should be back in a week or so."

"Shoot," Bobbi murmured. "Well, okay. Brian and Rosy are outside right now building a snowman, and we thought you'd like to help with the rest of the fort later today. You used to love the snow. Do you still?"

"Yes." Grace warmed, imagining little Rose in a snowsuit. It was nice that Bobbi remembered so much about her. Why couldn't Grace's memories return? Maybe now that she'd mated, she'd get stronger, and she'd be able to remember. It was something good to hope for. "I'll call you when we get back to town." She had to figure out a way to stay in Bobbi and Brian's life without causing them any danger. Was it possible for an immortal to be friends with humans—at least for a little while?

How odd to think that she might know Bobbi and Brian's great-great-great grandkids someday. The marking on her back pulsed with energy, but Faith had assured her that would dissipate.

The picture of Bobbi's sister and Rose caught her eye from where she'd hung it to dry. The little girl was pale and her eyes wide. She held on, but sadness and fear lingered in her pretty eyes. The sister held tight, a hardness or maybe a secret in her eyes. Something off. "What's your sister's name, Bobbi?"

Bobbi was quiet for a moment. "Kim," she sighed. "Our mother was a hippie from the old times. Why do you ask?"

"I don't know. She just seemed quiet and kind of shy," Grace lied.

"Oh, she is," Bobbi agreed. "She's never talked much, and frankly, she's not a lot of fun."

Was that darkness in the sister? There was an aura around her, a sense of shadow that Grace couldn't place. How could she warn Bobbi? What was there to say? Um, there's a strange shadow around your sister in my picture, and even though you've known her forever, I think she's weird? No. That wouldn't work. Maybe if Grace spent more time with them, she could put her finger on it. For now, she'd develop all of the pictures. "Any plans on the baptism?"

"Oh, yeah. I know it's short notice, but we were able to get the hall for the celebration next Sunday. It's five days away, and I know you're out of town, but could you please come? It'd mean a lot to us."

Grace stared at the picture. At Kim and innocent Rose. "Yes. I'll definitely be there." Every instinct she had told her to look out for that little girl, whose innocent eyes were already telling her something. What, she didn't know. But she'd figure it out, and hopefully Adare would want to help.

A ruckus sounded on the other end of the line. The sound was muffled, and Bobbi's voice was filtered. "Hey, hon. I'm on the phone with Grace, and she can make it on Sunday."

"Awesome," Brian said, his voice coming through clearly. "Is her head all right? That was kind of weird."

"Yeah, I already told you that her head is fine." Bobbi came back on the line. "Watch out, or he'll make a lame joke about your brain. I apologize preemptively."

Grace smiled. She could do this. Live in two worlds for a while, until other people started aging and she didn't. If she survived the mating. "There probably is something wrong with my brain," she joked, not really joking. She'd give anything to remember the good times with her friends. Well, almost anything.

She glanced at the clock on the wall. It was too early to hear from Adare. Her stomach clenched. "Bobbi? I'll give you a call in a couple of days and set things up, okay?"

"Sounds good. Stay safe, my friend." Bobbi hung up.

Grace set the phone down. Could she have a somewhat normal life with Adare? For some reason, she couldn't see him joining a bocce team with her. She sighed and turned on the light, leaving the darkroom and heading upstairs to spend time with her sister. No doubt Faith was as worried as Grace about the soldiers.

They had to be okay.

Chapter 29

Adare's head swam. Snow pinged up around him from laser bullets, and he rolled out of the way, using the metal shop to cover his ass. The explosives weren't working? What the hell? He grabbed one out of his bag, ripped the pin, and threw it toward the empty building. It hit the side with a small clank and dropped to the snowy ground to disappear.

Harmlessly.

The explosives were duds. He swallowed and kept his gun loose, running through the snow and zinging bullets to another building.

He arrived at the doorway just as Ronan made it around the other side, blood flowing from his arm and a pissed off expression on his ancient face. "The fucking explosives don't work."

Adare nodded, his head hurting as if he'd taken a bullet between the eyes. "Yeah. I can't explain it."

Ronan leaned back against the building, blending almost into it, his gun in his right hand. "The Ledoni shifters are for sale to the highest bidder, but I thought you had an in."

"I thought so, too," Adare growled, his brain pounding. Had Jacki set him up? He couldn't believe it. But it wasn't possible that every single one of the explosives had been faulty. "A problem for another day."

Ronan nodded.

A whoosh sounded, and they both ducked as a missile crashed several yards to the left, exploding. Heat flashed over Adare, and he stood, wavering slightly. "Ready?"

"Yes." Ronan grasped the doorknob, crouched, and yanked the metal door wide open to reveal a long hallway with red doors set several yards apart down its length.

Adare went in high, shooting a Kurjan guard between the eyes and then sweeping left.

Ronan went in left and swept right. They kept their backs to each other, maneuvering up the hallway and kicking in doors. A Kurjan squad burst in through another door, well protected with hats and skin guards, their movements still slowed from exposure to the sun.

They fired immediately, and Adare flattened himself on the concrete, shooting up. He took out two while Ronan took out the other two. The concrete heated and then cooled beneath him, and then the red doors spun around and around. Nausea filled his belly and blood echoed through his ears.

Ronan tapped his shoulder and stood.

Adare forced himself to stand and sucked down bile, blinking until his vision cleared.

"You good?" Ronan asked.

"Yes," Adare snapped, hurrying down to the last doorway. His body ached as if he'd been dragged behind running horses, but they had to find those women. More Kurjans would be coming, and only the sunny day outside had helped him this time.

A missile flew through the wall and continued through a red door, detonating in the exterior wall.

"Shit," Ronan bellowed. "They're trying to take out the whole building."

Adare ducked his head and kicked in the final door. The women huddled on what looked like sleeping bags on the other side of the concrete room, except for two who stood in front of the others, their faces dirty and bruises on their arms. He didn't have it in him to smile, but he tried. "We're here to get you out. We have to go. Now."

The women in front of the others appeared a little older, maybe mid-thirties. The first one spoke. "Who are you?"

The room wavered.

Ronan stepped forward. "US Army, ma'am. We're under attack, and we really need to move. Now."

The women nodded and helped the others up, edging warily toward them.

Adare could feel their power, their enhancements, especially with all ten of them in one place. It was lucky they'd been found so quickly. Not one of them had been mated, or he'd sense it, so at least they'd been spared that, although being kidnapped and held in a cell like this one would surely cause some nightmares. He tried for a smile again. "We're going to get you to safety. I promise."

Ronan turned and led the way toward the undemolished part of the building. "Plan D?" he yelled back, shooting a Kurjan who ran in from the outside front door.

"Affirmative," Adare said, taking the rear and turning to fire at another squad that came in through the back. Their enemy's equipment was top of the line, allowing the Kurjans to be outside so long as they stayed covered. He followed the last woman out and slammed the door, edging to the side.

Benny barreled up in an FMTV that looked like it had been stolen from the US military. "Let's go," he bellowed from the driver's seat.

Ronan hustled the prisoners to the back and helped them up.

The door to the building opened, and a soldier emerged, machine gun first. Adare grabbed the barrel and jerked him out, ripping off his headgear and shoving him into the sun before turning and firing into the building again, hitting one soldier in the neck and another between the eyes. It wouldn't kill them, but they'd hurt for a while. The fourth soldier ducked back into the room that had housed the women.

The Kurjan in the sun screamed, his skin frying. He struggled to get back inside, but Adare turned and kicked him in the face, sending him sprawling across the snow. The sun beat down, eating him alive.

Benny tossed a black bag out the window at him. "Explosives I found in the rear building. These work."

Adare yanked out a black hand grenade and ripped the pin off before throwing it inside the building. Then he jumped onto the back bed of the vehicle, setting the women in the middle. He fired from one side, while Ronan fired from the other, and Benny drove crazily, dodging Kurjans and land mines with his glasses on.

Adare threw hand grenades as they moved, blowing up as many buildings as he could. He threw several at the main lodge, which no doubt held more Kurjans. He hadn't seen a Cyst. Not one. Had they known of the attack? Jacki had a lot of explaining to do.

He threw two grenades in the main lodge, ducking as they exploded. The Kurjans probably were underground, but he'd hurt them.

A guard ran out, letting the sun fry him, and fired toward them. Adare made his body as big as possible to shield the women behind him. Several bullets turned from laser to metal and impacted his leg, moving up his arm and piercing his neck. He'd had much worse injuries.

But the world halted, and he bent over, fighting the darkness. Then, against all odds, he passed out completely. The last thing he heard before his head hit the bed of the truck was Ronan bellowing his name.

* * * *

Grace's tea steamed as she watched Faith take a phone message from Ronan. Her sister jumped up. "Got it." She ran for the control panel by the garage door and quickly released a bunch of buttons. "They're coming in hot, whatever that means."

"Sounds like fast?" Grace stood and moved to the window to watch the drive. "Did Ronan say they were okay? Are they all okay?" She stood closer to the window, trying to look down the snowy drive. How far away would they have called? "They must be close, right? Did Ronan say anything?"

"He just said to turn off the security and right now." Faith moved to the window to watch as well. "He sounded stressed."

Well, yeah. They'd just fought a battle. Of course he sounded stressed. That didn't mean anything had gone wrong. Grace hugged herself, mumbling a prayer that had come back from her childhood.

A dented blue truck, low and small, came into view, spinning snow as it bumped over the ground. It slid to a stop in front of the door. Grace ran over and opened the door, running out to the front porch with Faith on her heels, both of them sliding across the wood decking.

Ronan leaped out of the driver's seat and yanked a still form toward him, ducking and lifting before hustling around the car.

"Adare?" Grace said, her chest hurting. He was slung over Ronan's shoulder, his body limp and blood dripping onto the snow as they moved.

Ronan's face was a grim mask as he maneuvered up the steps and into the cabin, flipping Adare over onto his back on the oversized sofa. "He passed out about an hour ago and won't awaken, and he's not healing himself while sleeping." Ronan wiped dried blood off his forehead. "I don't know what's wrong with him."

Faith ran back into the kitchen.

Grace hurried around the sofa to the table, reaching out to push Adare's hair away from his bloodied face. More blood poured from his head, arm, and leg, pooling on the sofa in bright red. "Adare?" Her voice shook.

Faith hustled back in with supplies in her hands. "We need to stem the blood if he can't heal himself. Was he knocked out by a head shot?" She handed Grace scissors. "Cut away his shirt and pants while I examine his head."

Ronan stood by the end of the sofa, his face cut into harsh lines. "I don't think so. He was hit several times, but he was off all day. I think he just passed out." Ronan reached down and pulled off Adare's boots, grunting as he did so. "He can't take blood while he's unconscious, so we might need to give it to him intravenously. Do we have any medical equipment for that? We've never needed it before."

Faith finished examining Adare's head, which looked enormous in her slender hands. "He's been cut and has bruises, but no bullet or knife wounds to his skull. Although he has a cut above his eye, probably from shrapnel." She sat back, pursing her lips. "He should not be unconscious from these injuries."

Grace finished cutting away his jeans, fighting not to vomit at the damage to his leg. "It's because we mated. Right?" She knew it.

"Maybe." Faith poked at one of the bullet holes. "He didn't even expel the bullet." She reached for a black package and ripped it open with her teeth, her gaze worried. "He needs surgery and a lot of blood. We have to get him to the Realm hospital, Ronan. Like right now."

Ronan nodded. "We split with Benny before stealing the truck. He ran to get the helicopter."

Faith started wrapping Adare's injuries. "This is a blood clotter that will help until we can get him to a trauma unit." She finished with his leg and moved up his arm, working until she could place a bandage on the cut above his right eye. The white pad immediately turned red from the blood.

Grace took his limp hand and held it tightly. "He's getting too pale." An unnatural hue glowed beneath his skin.

Ronan swore and ripped open his wrist with his fangs, leaning down to press it against Adare's mouth. "This will help, but I can only get so much down him while he's unconscious."

Tears filled Grace's eyes. "This is my fault. My blood or cells or whatever are attacking his." Deep down, she hadn't really thought it was possible. Adare was just too strong for simple blood cells to harm him.

Ronan wiped more blood off his cheek. "I can't imagine that. The threat honestly didn't seem real." Bewilderment showed in his world-weary eyes for a moment. "I don't think any of us thought he was in real danger, not just from a mating."

Grace squeezed Adare's hand tighter. He felt cold. Even his palm, which was always hot, was chilly against her fingers.

Faith checked his eyes and then felt his wrist, counting out loud. She frowned. "His heart rate is too slow. This isn't good."

Ronan looked out the window at the sky. "Benny should be here any minute."

Faith nodded, feeling Adare's head. "Did you save the enhanced females?" She didn't look away from her patient.

"Yes," Ronan said. "We dropped them off at the local police station and got out of there to steal the truck and get Adare help. We have no idea what they saw or what they'll say, but at least they're safe. We notified the Realm, and they should intercede soon with the women. Dage will make sure they're safe, which is what matters."

Well, that was something. Grace grabbed Adare's hand with her free one. That was what he had wanted.

Ronan straightened, looking out the window. "I hear the copter. Let's get everything ready to go."

Grace and Faith had already packed up, just in case. Grace leaned in, skimming her lips across Adare's. "Wake up," she whispered. "Please."

Her big, strong, immortal warrior didn't so much as twitch, and the wound in his arm started bleeding again.

Chapter 30

Grace sat in a small waiting area outside the trauma room at Realm headquarters as the doctors worked to remove the bullets from Adare's body. Benny sat on one side of her, while Ronan took point on the other.

"It's a miracle we survived the trip here," Ronan growled, his head in his hands. "Where the hell did you learn to pilot a helicopter?"

"Who said I ever learned to pilot?" Benny growled right back. "How hard can it be? I got you here, didn't I?"

Grace pressed her palms against her eyes. How was any of this happening? She turned toward the television quietly droning in the corner. The screen showed a newscaster in front of several burning buildings with snow starting to fall on them. "Was that from you guys?"

Benny turned and grabbed the remote, turning up the volume.

"We have a developing story here, Martha," said a blond guy with earnest blue eyes. "Apparently the women were kidnapped from different western states, their ages ranging from thirteen to thirty-two, and they were kept here for days. None of them saw their captors, who always wore masks."

Martha, the anchor in the studio, tapped her earpiece. "Did they say anything about their rescuers?"

The guy on the scene shook his head. "No. So far, all we've been told is that a special force went in to rescue them and then disappeared. It might be some sort of vigilante justice, because nobody has claimed credit for the daring rescue that destroyed this entire encampment. According to my sources, nobody was apprehended. By the time the local police force made it out here, everyone was gone."

Martha shook her head. "Sources say it was some kind of trafficking ring. Do you have any more information on that?"

The snow billowed around the blond guy's head while the fires behind him sent dark smoke into the dusky sky. "Not yet, but this is a developing story. I'll keep you up to date."

Benny set the volume on mute. "Well, there's at least that."

Ronan sat back, wiping dirt off his hands. "Why weren't any Cyst there? You had them on satellite up until the day before. They had to know we were coming."

"I'm sure it has something to do with the explosives not working," Benny muttered.

Grace started. "Are you serious? The explosives were faulty?" She knew they shouldn't have trusted that damn shifter.

The door opened, and Faith walked out in scrubs, taking the hat part off her head. Her eyes were tired and her movements slow.

Grace stood along with Benny and Ronan. "Faith?"

Faith reached her. "We got all of the bullets out and have patched him as best we can to stop the bleeding. He's hooked up to an IV with saline and blood, so he's covered there."

Ronan towered over his mate, his gaze uncertain. "He still hasn't regained consciousness?"

"No." Faith twisted the cap in her hands. "It looks like he's in a coma. I want to do another MRI to make sure, but it's like…" She shrugged.

"My cells put him in a coma?" Grace's voice rose.

Benny planted an arm over her shoulders. "Now calm down, Gracie. He'll be okay. He's Adare." Then Benny winced, lifting his arm, where a spreading red rash had appeared where he'd touched her. "Oops. Forgot you're freshly mated and dangerous to my pretty skin."

Grace scratched at the skin on her shoulder. The mating had taken, obviously. Or Adare wouldn't be in a coma. "Do immortals even go into comas?"

"Rarely and only to heal themselves," Emma said, emerging from the trauma room. "But he's not healing himself."

Grace's legs wobbled, but she kept upright. "What now? What do we do?"

Emma and Faith shared a look.

Grace fixed them with a glare. "Knock it off, you two. I want to know what we do next."

Emma shuffled her tennis shoes. "I have an idea, but it's a risk." She exhaled. "If your blood is causing the coma as we think it is, then maybe we could create antibodies from your blood to give to him. That might save him or give him more fighting power for the war that's going on inside him on the cellular level."

"Or," Faith said quietly, "Giving him those antibodies from your blood might kill him. Right now, in a coma, maybe he can fight. We just don't know, Grace."

Melted snow from Benny's boots was spreading all over the floor. "Let's give him more blood. More is always good."

"Agreed," Ronan said.

Grace took a deep breath. "When do we have to decide?"

Faith reached for her arm and rubbed it reassuringly. "Not tonight. We don't have to make any decisions tonight."

"Not true." Looking pissed, the king of the Realm strode down the hallway, his gaze an intense silver.

Grace took a step back out of pure instinct. Dage Kayrs wasn't somebody you wanted mad at you. Ever. She'd only met him a couple of times, but the guy was as intimidating as anybody could ever get.

He stopped near his mate. "Ronan and Benny? Would you care to explain what you were doing in an unsanctioned Realm op this morning that pretty much blew up an entire Kurjan compound?"

"Wasn't us," Benny said, moving slightly to shield Grace.

"We don't work for the Realm," Ronan added, also shifting his weight to protect her.

The king watched the interplay without expression. "Yet here you are, asking for help." His voice was so low and silky that the room chilled several degrees.

Ronan straightened. "We're family, whether you like it or not."

Dage stepped right up to him, toe-to-toe, just as big and broad. "Then you be the king, Great Uncle."

Huh. That was weird. Sometimes Grace forgot they were related, although Dage had never heard of Ronan or the Seven until recently. Well, five years ago.

"But you're so suited to it," Ronan returned, his back teeth grinding.

"All right. Enough, boys." Emma grabbed Dage by the arm while Faith set her hand on Ronan's elbow, each woman taking her mate in hand.

Grace sighed, her legs shaking.

Benny nodded. "That's why I don't have a mate. It's way too complicated."

"Right, Benny," the king drawled. "*That's* why you don't have a mate."

Grace edged out from behind Benny, the tension in the room giving her a headache. "Can I see Adare?" she asked her sister.

Faith nodded. "Go ahead. We'll handle things here."

It might have been cowardly, but Grace took the out and all but ran inside the trauma room. Adare slept in a bed at the far end, hooked up to liquids and medical equipment. It was a sight she'd never imagined seeing. The bed was extra-large and long, no doubt created for the immortal soldiers.

Her legs faltered, but she approached the bed, taking a chair close to his head. Somebody had cleaned him up. No dirt or blood remained on his skin, and he wore a thick white T-shirt over his immortal chest. His lashes were dark against his skin, and his dark hair pillowed around him. Even his lips were paler than usual.

The soft beeping of the machinery made her want to cry. She took his hand, slipping hers into his, but he didn't curl his fingers around it. He didn't move at all.

The door opened, and Hope Kayrs-Kyllwood slipped inside, holding a pretty plant in her hands. Grace had met her a couple of times, and the young teenager had always been polite and ready with a smile. "Hi."

"Hi." Hope set the plant on the granite counter by a sink and took the other chair. "I thought you might want some company. Everyone seems so mad out there, and as usual, nobody tells me what's going on, so I thought I'd bring you a plant." She stared at Adare. "Immortals aren't supposed to go into comas."

"I know." Grace sat back, keeping Adare's hand. The young girl was supposedly a prophet, whatever that meant. "Do you know anything? I mean, can you read his mind?"

Hope didn't laugh at her. "No. I can't read minds, and I don't know anything about Adare. Sometimes fate whispers to me, but it's usually not helpful, not anything I want to know about. I honestly just thought I'd check on you."

It was a kindness, that was for sure. The girl seemed older than thirteen. Maybe it was her pretty blue eyes. There was an ancient wisdom in them, tinged with a sadness most people probably never noticed. Her slim shoulders also looked as if a heavy weight pressed down on them, even though her posture was good. Perhaps Grace did see things nobody else did. She should probably spend more time on that skill, after Adare got healthy. "I want to help him, but I don't know how."

Hope rubbed her nose. "Has he ever asked you to help him?"

"No," Grace whispered. "Well, I guess he asked me to trust him completely. That's the only thing he's ever asked of me."

"Then maybe that's what you should do," the girl said, turning toward the doorway as raised voices filtered through. "Wow. Uncle Dage never yells. He must be super mad." She stood. "I'll go out there. Even if they stay mad at each other, they won't yell with me nearby." She patted Grace's shoulder. "Trust him. I can see he's a good one." Then she was gone, and she was right, the yelling stopped.

"I can see you're a good one, too," Grace whispered.

Her sister walked in with her bags in one hand and deposited them next to Grace. "I don't know what to tell you, but you know I believe in science. Maybe giving him more of your blood, right into his veins, would help." Faith kissed her on the head and left quietly.

Maybe. Grace set her chin on the bed and stared at Adare. He was so big, it was weird to see him just lying there. Almost absently, she plucked her digital camera out of the bag and took several shots, trying to get the right angle on his face. Her instincts started to hum. She stood on her chair, finally, with one foot on the bed, and pressed the button. As always, a sense of peace ran through her at getting the perfect shot.

"What are you doing?" Emma asked from the doorway.

Grace stepped down. "Trusting Adare, and in doing so, trusting myself." She sat and scrolled through the pictures. "Or vice versa. Trusting myself and thus trusting Adare?" She pondered the question. "One of those, anyway." She looked at the pictures, stopping at the final one and enlarging it on the little screen. "Ah." She sat back, relaxing, her shoulders finally going down.

"What?" Emma stepped her way, leaning over to look.

"What do you see?" Grace asked.

Emma leaned over her shoulder. "Adare in the bed." She studied it for a moment. "It's a good angle?"

Yeah. It was the exact right angle. Grace enlarged the shot even more, zooming in. "What about now?"

Emma squinted and leaned even closer, her face almost touching the screen. "I don't know. The air around him looks a little bit fuzzy. Is it because you zoomed in so far?"

"No." Grace zoomed out, her eyes growing heavy. "Those are healing vibrations, I think. I've heard immortals talk about healing cells and feeling that energy next to somebody healing, and while we don't feel anything from Adare, I think that's what we see. It's what I saw."

Emma drew back. "Interesting. All right. I take it you don't want to give him more blood tonight?"

"No. I don't." Grace set the camera gently back in the bag and toed off her shoes. "He's taking care of himself, and more of my blood would only hurt. We can trust him." She slipped into the bed with him, curling into his side. "'Night, Emma. Thank you for getting the bullets out of him."

"You're welcome," Emma said, turning off the lights as she headed out the door. "Have a nice night. Call for me if you need me. I'll check on you tomorrow morning if I don't hear from you."

"Thanks." Grace settled in, putting her hand over Adare's beating heart. When she'd thought he might be gone, she'd hurt deep down with a sense of futility and panic. Their mating had been explosive and incredible, and she wanted more of him. In fact, she wanted all of him.

He'd been so adamant that love didn't exist, and she wasn't one to convince people to like her. To love her. In fact, she wasn't even sure what her own feelings were, except that they were deeper than she would've imagined.

Maybe love did exist.

If so, she'd have to prove it to him. How hard could it be?

Chapter 31

Adare woke up to a raging headache and the scent of his mate. He opened his eyes, his body instantly alert. Grace was curled into his side with her nose in his neck and one knee thrown over his groin. Ah. That explained the erection. When he moved his head, just a bit, he spotted a packet of blood and one of what looked like water leading down to his arm.

What the hell?

Without jostling her, he reached down and plucked the catheter out of his vein and then sent healing cells to the wound. They moved sluggishly through his system, but at least they were moving.

Monitors beeped above his head, and he looked around. When had he been brought to the infirmary? Based on the smell of the place and the ambient sounds from outside the door, he was at Realm headquarters. Had he been shot in the head? He didn't remember being shot at all.

His arm and leg hurt, but he didn't want to disturb Grace.

Raised voices caught his attention, from down the hallway a bit. At least his immortal hearing was working. That was something. Gingerly, he eased out of the bed, settling Grace back down and making sure she was covered. She didn't move and her breathing remained even.

When he looked down, he saw thick white scrubs and bare feet. Bandages covered his arm and his leg beneath the cotton material.

Man, he needed to take a piss. He wandered out of the infirmary and down the hallway, finding a restroom near the main entrance. Thank goodness. After he'd taken care of business and removed all of the bandages, he went in search of something to eat.

The gnawing in his stomach wasn't going to abate until he found protein.

Wait a minute. The fight came back to him. He had been shot. Arms and legs, and then nothing. Had he passed out? More memories, flashes really, hit him hard. The explosives. They'd been duds.

He turned into one of the guest offices he remembered from his last visit and shut the door, reaching for a secured phone. He didn't give a shit if the Realm knew he was calling Jacki. Anger ripped into him, and he took several deep breaths to keep control.

She answered on the first ring. "Hello."

"What the fuck was wrong with the explosives?" he growled, leaning against the wall to ease the odd ache in his leg.

She sputtered. "What do you mean?"

"Don't lie to me. You always were a rotten liar," he said, his temples pinging again. What was up with this headache? More importantly, how could someone he trusted send him to battle with defective explosives? "Why, Jacki?"

She swallowed. "Come on, Adare. Don't ask stupid questions."

It was like a blow to the balls. He'd trusted her. "Say it. Tell me why you set us up."

She sighed. "Fine. It was for the money. The Kurjans offered us a lot more, so we did what we had to do. Don't be angry. You know how business works."

Yeah, and he was suddenly realizing why he'd been okay when she'd mated somebody else. "The Kurjans? If they offered you money to give us duds, then they had to have had an idea of where we were striking. In other words, they didn't go to you, did they?" The sense of betrayal burned.

She was quiet.

Oh, he couldn't believe this. She'd actively set out to betray him. The money-hungry bitch. "You went to the Kurjans for a better deal after we used those first explosives." It was a damn good thing she was in Colorado somewhere right now. "How could you? We barely got there in time to save those women."

"You saved them. I saw it on the news." Her voice turned coy. "I really am sorry. Maybe we could get together and you could show me your displeasure."

His stomach rolled over. No matter how long he lived, he'd never forget this betrayal. There were so few people he trusted. "I'd rather be shot in the eyeball."

"Whatever. That human will never make you happy." Now she just sounded whiny.

"We're done, Jacki. No more business." He'd make his own explosives before he bought from the Ladonis ever again. "I'm also sending out the word that you're working with the Kurjans. By the time I'm done with you, they'll be your only client." She should have known him well enough not to want him for an enemy.

Her hiss sounded very catlike. "Oh, I think you're going to have more important things to worry about. You should've said yes to me when I asked so nicely the other day. We could've been something together." She disconnected the call.

He stood there for a moment, mourning the loss of a long friendship. Maybe they'd never really been friends. Good riddance. His stomach growled again, so he left the office to find the kitchen. Last time he'd been there, fresh muffins had been available all through the day.

The voices he'd heard earlier rose again, and he turned down the other hallway, headed to the conference room. He made out Benny's voice and walked faster, turning into the third room, which was the biggest, if he remembered right. The king of the Realm, Dage Kayrs, and the king of the demon nation, Zane Kyllwood, sat on one side of the table. Benny and Ronan sat on the other. A live feed appeared on a screen covering an entire wall, and Jordan Pride, the king of the shifter nations, was center stage.

He didn't want to deal with three kings.

Benny looked over his shoulder, and his eyes sizzled with what looked suspiciously like panic.

Adare stepped inside, the concrete floor chilly on his feet. "What's going on?"

Jordan Pride looked at him through the screen. "Another member of this mysterious Seven. Is it or is it not true that you twisted the laws of physics, thereby threatening this world? That you screwed up teleportation and maybe other elements of our natural laws that we haven't even figured out?"

Adare went expressionless. Oh, God. Their secret was out? Or at least a good portion of it.

How in the hell had the lion leader figured that out? Jacki. Jacki had apparently pieced together more than Adare had ever realized, and she'd been right earlier. He was now facing a whole new set of problems. It was a smart play on her part, because nobody would care what he had to say about the Ladoni shifters and their faulty product. He'd have to take his revenge on that front later.

Dage straightened. "Jordan? The Realm isn't involved in any of this."

Jordan sighed, his topaz eyes going dark. "Three members of the Seven are standing in your conference room, Dage."

"He didn't know," Benny said instantly. "The King has no clue about the Seven."

Adare barely bit back a wince. If Jordan ever discovered that Garrett Kayrs and Logan Kyllwood were members of the Seven, he'd never believe Dage and Zane were in the dark. War would be declared. Without question.

"Wait a minute," Zane said quietly. "Let's talk this out."

A ruckus sounded from the front door, and Adare stepped into the conference room just as Nick Veis strode inside, accompanied by Simone Brightston.

"Ah, shit," Dage muttered.

Jordan smiled through the screen. "I felt it necessary to notify the witch and demon nations of this threat to the Realm."

Zane stood. "I am the demon nation." He faced Nick directly, his jaw hardening. "Nicolaj?"

Nick nodded, his white-blond hair tied back at the nape. "I'm with you, brother. Always have been and always will be." He kept his arm around Simone's waist. "I am getting calls for your head, however. There's a chance the demon nation will split in two if you decide to align with the Seven and the Realm."

Simone nodded. "The Coven Nine is holding a special meeting to discuss the matter and take a vote on whether or not we stay in the Realm. I'm flying out in an hour."

Dage held up both hands, his eyes a dangerous silver. "Several members of my family are mated to witches. You can't split families apart. Let's discuss this."

Jordan cleared his throat. "I'm sorry, old friend. We've already had a meeting of the shifter leaders, and the nation is withdrawing from the Realm. The vote of feline, canine, bear, and even our friends on Fire Island was unanimous." Sorrow darkened the leader's eyes. "I hope someday things will be different, but my hands are tied right now. Our natural laws must be obeyed, and anyone who fucks with physics and threatens our home can't be an ally. You're too entrenched with the Seven, since Ronan and Quade are your family." He clicked off.

Emotion swept through the room. Dage sat back down, his look one of death.

Nick sighed. "I'll keep you informed. We have to go now." He turned and strode out with Simone at his side.

Adare shut the door and leaned against it, trying to keep from puking.

Dage glared at Ronan. "What the hell have you gotten Garrett and Logan into?"

"They made their own decisions," Benny said quietly. "If you have a problem with them, talk to them."

"Oh, we've called them both back," Zane said, looking like the predator he was rumored to be. "The question at this point is whether or not I declare war on the Seven. You think you can take on the entire demon nation?"

"Would you really set brother against brother?" Ronan said quietly. "You might want to check with Sam, as well."

Zane's nostrils flared, and a burst of power choked the air. It was obvious the leader knew his youngest brother, Logan, had become one of the Seven. He apparently had no idea the role his middle brother would play. "What are you telling me about Sam? He will not become one of the Seven."

"No, he won't," Benny agreed. "That's not his role."

Zane looked as if his head was about to explode, and Adare could relate.

Benny leaned forward, no doubt trying to help when he should probably remain quiet. "Sam has a path, and it's not one of danger," he said. "Well, probably. Okay. There might be some danger involved."

Zane turned his dark gaze on Benny. "What is Sam's path?" His voice lowered several octaves and sounded like he spoke through shards of glass.

"Can't tell you," Benny said, turning to Ronan. "This is why we've tried to remain hidden through the years."

The situation was deteriorating too rapidly. It was time for the Seven to regroup alone, and figure out what to do. The Realm shouldn't be involved.

"We should be on our way," Adare interrupted. "Thank you for your hospitality. The sooner we leave, the sooner you can fix the Realm."

"If it can be fixed," Dage said grimly.

Adare had never been one for politics. "You need to know that whatever we did, we did to save the world. Our intentions were good."

"You perverted the laws of physics and destroyed our ability to teleport," Dage returned. "Intentions don't mean squat when the results are disastrous." Energy cracked through the room. "It's time you told us everything about the Seven, what you did, who you are, and what your plans are for the future."

Ronan stood, his gaze tortured. "We took vows of silence."

"It's too late," Dage said, standing and facing his ancestor.

Adare studied them. This close, he could see the resemblance. It was quite striking, actually. "You're family," he reminded them, speaking before he could stop himself. He'd do anything to see any of his family again. He had no one. They were all gone.

Dage cocked his head. "Family? Family is honest and puts family first. You skulk and hide. You lie."

"No," Ronan said. "We've never lied. We took a vow, and we've kept it."

"Guess what?" Dage growled. "The vow is over. We know about the Seven, we know about the Cyst, and we know about other worlds that we can no longer access because of your actions. What we don't know is why the secrecy." The king leaned forward, power in every line of his body. "What is it you don't want me to know?"

The king was smart—there was no question about that. As was Zane Kyllwood.

And both men would do anything, absolutely anything, to protect Hope Kayrs-Kyllwood, the Lock. They could never know the role she was to play in the end. Even Adare didn't know, but experience told him it would be one of danger and sacrifice. If they had a clue of the danger she'd someday face, they'd try to dismantle the Seven, regardless of the cost to the Realm or to their family.

Ronan stood tall and took one last look at his great-nephew. "It was nice getting to know you, Dage. Good luck."

Adare exited the room before his brothers, heading down the hallway to awaken Grace. They needed to take their leave and now. Besides, he could use a nap.

He was exhausted.

Chapter 32

Too many people were scrambling around the lodge at Realm headquarters. Hope ran into the rec room, where Libby was sitting, crying with a gift basket in her hands.

"Libby," Hope said, grabbing her best friend for a hug. "I don't understand. What is happening?"

Libby sniffled and handed over the bag. "We're leaving. Going to my mom's family in Montana for a while. I guess the shifter nations have all left the Realm. We're enemies now," she wailed.

"No," Hope said, setting the bag on the couch. "We're not enemies. We'll never be enemies." She held Libby's hand. "I'll go get my dad. He'll make it okay." There was no way the shifter nations would just leave the Realm.

Libby shook her head. "It's too late. We're all leaving today."

Paxton ran into the room, his hair long and wild around his shoulders. "Is it true? Do you have to leave?" He grabbed Libby's arms.

"Yes." More tears fell down her face and she leaned in to hug Paxton. "I'll miss you guys so much."

Pax hugged her back and pulled Hope in for a group hug. "It won't be for long. I'm sure the shifters will rejoin the Realm soon. They have to." He was tall and solid holding them, even though he was so skinny.

Tears filled Hope's eyes and she let them fall. Things weren't supposed to change. Not like this. "I don't understand," she said, her voice muffled against Pax's T-shirt. "Why do you have to leave?"

Paxton let them go, and Libby wiped off her face. "The Seven broke laws of nature or something like that. They're super bad and the Realm and demon nations have aligned with them, I guess, and the shifters want out. My dad said something bad is going to happen because of the Seven. Do you know anything about them?"

Hope shook her head. "What do the shifters know about them?"

"Not as much as they want to," Libby said.

Hope blew out air, her stomach hurting really bad. Her uncles were part of the Seven. A lot of people were, and she was the Lock and now she couldn't tell Libby. Well, it wouldn't be fair to tell Libby. She wouldn't want to keep that kind of secret from her parents. "I don't think the Seven are bad. What I know of them, anyway," she whispered.

Libby looked up. "Can you tell me anything else about them?"

"No," Hope said, biting her lip.

Paxton's gaze narrowed, but he didn't say anything. Instead, he patted Libby on the shoulder. "Promise we'll still talk every day. Do you think we can FaceTime still?"

Hope nodded, feeling lost. "Your parents will still let you be friends with us, right?"

Libby shrugged. "I don't know what they'll say, but the three of us are friends no matter what." She grabbed them both for another hug. "Right?"

"Right." Hope wiped her face off.

Paxton's eyes swam, but he didn't let any tears fall. He held them back, and his nose turned red. "I wish you didn't have to go, Libs."

Libby sniffed again. "Don't forget the business we're gonna start. Then we'll all be together again. When we're eighteen."

"The ice cream store," Paxton said.

"No, the movie theater," Hope said, trying to sound happy and not like her heart was breaking.

Libby smiled. "No. The three spies, remember? We're gonna be spies." She wiped her nose. "Except now we might have to spy against each other."

"No," Pax said, putting an arm around each of them. "Never against each other. Not us."

"Okay." Libby hugged him again and then hugged Hope. "I have to go. I'll call when I get to Montana." She ran out of the room, still crying.

Hope ground a palm into her eye. "I can't believe this." The Seven weren't bad, or Garrett and Logan wouldn't be part of them. "What are we gonna do?" They had to figure out a way to get the shifter nations to change their minds. They were a part of the Realm.

Pax shrugged. "I don't know. Maybe if we kicked the Seven out, then we could all align again."

Hope shook her head. She wanted to tell Pax everything she'd dreamed and figured out so far, but sometimes he made judgments without all the facts, like he had with Drake the Kurjan. She didn't want Pax mad at her right now, especially since Libby had just left. "Why do grownups goof everything up all the time?"

Pax patted her shoulder with his bony hand. "Maybe the grownups are right. Your dad is really smart and he knows how to protect the nation, so we should trust him. Let's ask him what he thinks about the Seven."

It was a good plan.

Her dad walked into the room right then, a scowl on his face. Pax took a step back.

Hope picked up the present from Libby. "Dad? Do you think the Seven are bad?"

Her dad paused, his eyes greener than usual. "What do you know about the Seven?"

Her stomach rolled over. "We've been hearing rumors that the shifters are leaving because of the Seven, and that maybe they're bad, but they might be good. What do you think?"

"I think they're a disaster," her dad growled. "I need to figure some things out before I make a decision."

In other words, he knew that Uncle Logan was a member of the Seven and he wanted to get Logan out. But there was no getting out, as far as Hope knew. She kept quiet, though. Sometimes fate wanted secrets kept, and since the adults kept screwing things up, she wasn't going to say a word. Right now, anyway.

Zane looked at Paxton. "You ready to go see your uncle?"

Pax's eyebrows rose. "We're still doing that today? With everything else going on?" He sounded kind of nervous.

Zane nodded. "Yeah. I could use some air and am planning to walk back to demon headquarters. Do you want to come with us, Hope?"

"Yes," she said, wanting to reach for Pax's hand but feeling weird about it. They'd kissed, and it was nice, but they were just friends. Hopefully Pax knew that, too. "Dad? Can't you make the shifters stay in the Realm?"

Her dad reached for her coat on the sofa. "Honey, I'm not even sure I can make the demon nation stay in the Realm right now."

* * * *

Paxton felt skinny and slow as he walked along the lake by the demon leader. Zane was silent on the journey, no doubt trying to figure out how to fix the Realm. Change sucked. It totally sucked that Libby and his other shifter friends had to leave Idaho. It wasn't fair that the kids all suffered because the adults kept screwing things up, just like Hope had said.

She knew more about the Seven than she'd admitted. He'd been able to read her for a long time, because she wasn't very good about keeping her expressions hidden.

Not like him.

He couldn't believe she'd let him kiss her the other night. It was the best night of his entire life, even though his dad had nearly broken his hip this time. But he'd gotten out, and he'd kissed his girl, and he was like a guy in a movie. Well, except that he wasn't tough. Yet.

His gut ached at the thought of staying with his uncle, but the demon couldn't be worse than his dad had been. His memories of his demon uncle were hazy but seemed pretty cool. If he turned into a jackass who hit, Pax was out of there. He'd spent enough time feeling scared, and he was old enough and big enough to make it on his own.

They reached the demon subdivision and walked through the snowy streets to a small home, all brick, at the end of a drive.

Pax couldn't breathe.

Zane slid an arm over his shoulder. "Your uncle is a decent guy. I wouldn't let you stay with him if I hadn't checked up on him." He rang the doorbell.

The door opened, and Uncle Santino stood there, much bigger than Pax remembered. He had pure white hair and midnight black eyes, showing him to be a pure-bred demon. His chest was wide and his smile wider as he yanked Paxton in for a hug. "Man, you've gotten tall," his uncle said.

Pax awkwardly hugged him back. "Thanks." The house smelled like chocolate cookies and pepperoni pizza. Boxes were scattered in every direction, evidence of his uncle's recent move. His stomach growled.

Santino winked at Hope. "Hi there, sweetie. You've gotten taller since I last saw you, too. Man, these kids grow up fast."

She smiled. "Hi."

Zane slipped his arm around her shoulder. "We'll let you two get acquainted. Pax? Give me a call tomorrow and check in, would you?"

Paxton nodded, wanting to ask them to stay. But he might as well man up now. "Sounds good."

They left, and Pax looked around. A comfy-looking sofa faced a crackling fire, while the biggest television he'd ever seen took up another entire wall. Boxes covered it for now. A puppy bounced out of the kitchen and made a beeline for him, wagging his tail wildly.

Pax dropped to hug the dog, laughing as the pup licked all over his face. "What's his name?"

"You get to name him." Santino chuckled. "I figured if you lived here, you'd want a dog. All boys should have a dog. He's a cross between a yellow lab and a collie and probably a few other things. A stray, like you and me." He grinned. "Figured we'd all do just fine together."

His uncle had gotten him a dog? A real dog? Pax cleared his throat. "Thank you."

"Sure." Santino jerked his head toward the kitchen, just past the television. "I ordered pizza with dessert. I should probably confess right now that I'm not a good cook. This is the first time I've bought an actual house and planned to stay in one place. I can make spaghetti and toast, and I order in a lot. We can order in healthy stuff, if you want."

"Um, okay." Pax scratched his head.

"Your room. You should see it." Santino lumbered in the other direction from the kitchen and down a hallway to push open a door.

Pax followed with the puppy tripping over his feet on the way. The room was big with a bed covered in a thick blue comforter. A television was set across from it with a brand new X-Box and a bunch of games piled next to it.

Santino winced. "Those came this morning, and I set them up for you. I should've asked. Do you game?"

Pax's heart leaped. "Yeah. I love to play."

"Oh, good. Me too. I have the new Mars Four, Galaxy Battle over there and thought we could play." He pointed to the stack.

Pax blinked. "That doesn't release for three more months."

Santino grinned. "I have a buddy who has a buddy, you know? Got an early copy."

Oh, man, this was too good to be true. A desk sat over by the window with a new laptop on it. Pax didn't deserve any of this. He frowned.

Santino stilled. "Oh. The walls. Yeah, sorry. They're blank, but I didn't know what you liked. You know. Movie posters, pictures of lakes, pics of girls? Not sure. You can put anything you want on the walls. I started an account for your allowance, and I was thinking, what? Maybe five hundred a week?"

Pax made a garbled sound.

Santino's lip twisted. "Too much? Not enough? Dude, I'm new at this." He scratched his head. "I can talk about butterflies all day. But allowances?"

"Way too much," Pax whispered. He got to put things on the wall? Whatever he wanted?

"Okay. Then two hundred. If you have extra, maybe you could play the stock market or something. But you're in charge of your dog, and you gotta buy him food. I read that responsibility is good for kids." He smiled. "I loved your mom, as you know. She was sweet and took good care of me and didn't mind that I get lost in my head sometimes. I'm starving. Let's eat pizza."

"Okay." Pax followed him, stumbling a little. What was happening? Did his uncle really want him here? Not just like out of duty? The guy seemed a little lonely.

He sat at the table in the comfortable kitchen, accepting the huge piece of pizza Santino dropped on his plate.

"I travel a lot for work and leave on Tuesday for a week. Going to Africa, and you should come with me. You ever been there?" Santino shoved a large bite in his mouth.

Pax shook his head. He bit his lip, looking down at the panting puppy.

Santino followed his gaze. "Oh, he can come. You never leave family behind, right?"

Even the dog could come? Pax breathed out, feeling as if bubbles of excitement were popping inside him. He took a bite of the pizza, and it was the best he'd ever had. "This is good."

"I'm glad," Santino sighed, wolfing down another piece. "We'll settle in here, and I think you should see that shrink. The pretty blonde?"

"The prophet Lily?" Pax chewed thoughtfully. "Sure." If that made his uncle happy, he'd do it.

"Good. It'll help to talk about everything you've gone through."
His uncle shrugged. "Probably."

Pax grinned, looking at the hand-painted picture of a butterfly
on the counter. "What do you do?"

"I'm a researcher. I research different animal environments and
ecosystems." Santino's eye sobered. "I also have a mission. We're
family, Pax, so I don't ever want to lie to you, especially since it
has to do with your friend. The pretty girl."

Pax dropped his pizza on the plate. "Hope?"

"Yeah. I know you've heard the scuttlebutt about the Seven lately
with the shifters taking off and all." Santino chewed thoughtfully.
"The Seven are horribly mistaken, possibly evil, and have to be
stopped. If they're not, Hope is going to pay the price. She's a
prophet and must be protected. No matter what."

Pax took his pizza again and chewed slowly. It was weird being
trusted with the serious stuff. "Hope is all that matters," he agreed.

Santino grinned. "It's about the girl, huh?"

Pax's face heated. "I've always known it's about her." He sighed.
"It's gonna be bloody and painful." Every once in a while, rarely,
fate gave him a glimpse. "Is this Seven the real enemy?"

"One of many, and when we stop them, it's gonna be ugly,"
Santino said. "You have to choose your own path, and you don't
have to choose mine. But I wanted you to know the truth."

"My path is protecting her, and always has been," Pax said.
"No matter the cost."

Santino lifted his soda. "To the girl."

Pax lifted his, clinking them together. "To Hope." Finally, his
mission, his destiny, was clear.

He was home.

Chapter 33

Another storm blanketed the world with snow outside, so Grace waited inside the main lodge as Adare finished loading the helicopter Benny had landed on the road.

The King strode down the hallway and stood next to her, sighing. "Did he have to land on my damn street? I have an entire airfield just down the road with, you know, landing areas and runways."

Grace grinned. "Benny likes to make a statement."

"Benny likes to be an ass," Dage returned, tension rolling from him.

Grace faltered but reached for her bag. "I have a present for you." She dug inside and drew out a file folder holding photographs, handing him one of Emma she'd taken days ago and developed while at the cabin. The queen stood in her lab, in her white lab coat, looking over her shoulder at the camera.

He took it, his mouth opening slightly. "It's Emma," he murmured. Then he grinned. "I know it's of Emma, but it's really *Emma*. My Emma." He studied the photograph, his gaze softening. "You captured her. Her brilliance and her heart. Her determination and sheer kindness." He breathed out, his smile now gentle. "If I were fanciful, I'd say you caught her soul."

Grace shuffled her feet. "Adare thinks this is my enhancement. Catching a moment or seeing to the heart of a person."

Dage looked up, his silver eyes intense. "I think he's correct. Thank you for this. I'll cherish it always." His phone buzzed, and he looked down at the face. "Damn it." He patted her shoulder. "Good luck, Grace Cooper. I'm sure I'll see you soon." Taking his photograph, he strode purposefully down the hallway toward the conference rooms at the other end of the lodge.

The air in the vestibule relaxed slightly. Being the king of immortals was probably a rough gig.

Emma emerged from the medical wing, her hair piled high and a cookie in her hand. "I wanted to say goodbye."

"You just missed your mate," Grace said, nodding her head in the opposite direction.

Emma finished off the snickerdoodle. "He's in a mood. The possibility of the Realm's falling apart again doesn't sit well with him." She leaned in for a hug. "I'm going to miss you and your sister."

"Me too." Grace hugged her back. "Is Adare really going to be all right?"

Emma nodded. "Yeah. I rechecked his blood, and his cells have strengthened. The only drawback is that the process is going to take some time, maybe a week or two, until he regains all his power. Bursts of training, of adrenalin and high energy will speed up the process. Other than that, he has to take it easy between trainings, and that's going to be tough. Immortals are used to healing much faster."

It was a good thing they were heading to the cabin for some relaxation. Grace would make sure he took it easy, which would give her time to put her plan in motion. Proving to him that love existed was one thing; making him see that he was in love with her was another.

Emma tilted her head. "That's a very determined look on your face. What's up?"

Was there time to grab a cookie? That snickerdoodle had looked good. "Just a plan I have in mind. An impossible one."

"Those are the best kind," Emma said, smiling. "Keep in mind that you're going through some major changes genetically, too. It'll take you a few months to regain all of your strength, but then it'll be amazing. So give yourself some time."

Faith had already warned her about how tired she'd be. "Thanks, Emma."

"Also, I looked at the blood sample I took from you the other day, and I still haven't identified that foreign material in your system."

Grace felt fine, albeit a little tired. "Is it something to worry about?"

"No, but I'd like to know what it is, and if it has something to do with being a Key. I'll keep at it." Emma reached for another cookie in her jacket pocket.

Grace had more important things to worry about than Emma's research at the moment. "Hey. Do you have an unlimited supply in there?" Grace asked.

Emma grinned and handed it over. "No, but I can get another one from the kitchen."

Grace accepted the treat before Emma could change her mind. She worried her lip for a moment. "Do you think the Realm will really declare war on the Seven?" It didn't seem like a fair fight, but what did she know? The Seven had powers nobody realized, she was pretty sure.

"No," Emma said, sobering. "Too many family members are part of the Seven. But I think the Realm might have to distance itself for a while, just to get things back on track. If we can." She glanced at her watch. "I have to go. Already said goodbye to Faith and the rest of the gang. Stay safe, Grace." With that, the queen turned and headed back toward the kitchen, no doubt for another cookie.

Grace munched contentedly on the pastry. Her burner phone buzzed, and she lifted it to her ear. "Hello."

"Hey, friend. How are things?" Bobbi sounded a little frazzled.

"Good. How about you?" Grace dusted her hand off on her jeans.

Bobbi cleared her throat. "Not great. Brian broke his leg and will have to have surgery, my sister has lost her mind and gone back to her crazy husband, and Rosy has strep throat."

Grace winced. "That's terrible. I'm so sorry." She wished she could tell Bobbi about the Realm splitting up and her mate becoming a possible enemy of the strongest immortals on earth, besides him, of course. Keeping this friendship one-sided was difficult. "Can I do anything to help?"

"Well, yes. I hate to ask, but I'm desperate. Is there any way you could come stay with Rose for a day or two while I take care of Brian in the hospital? I feel so torn—I don't know what to do."

Grace dropped her head, staring at her boots, considering various possibilities. She wanted to be a good friend, and it meant so much to her that she'd found Bobbi and Brian after all this time. "When are you thinking?"

"Tonight and tomorrow," Bobbi said, hope filling her voice. "The surgery is later today."

Grace exhaled, her shoulders heavy. "Oh, Bobbi, I'd do anything to help you, but I can't right now." Adare needed her, and he had to come first. They had to get settled into the cabin so he could heal, and he'd just worry if she wasn't there. His protectiveness was kind of sweet, and she had to make sure he was all right before leaving him for the baptism.

"Why not? I really need your help," Bobbi said.

"I know, but I have to be somewhere else," Grace murmured. "Adare has been, well, ill, and he needs me right now." The stubborn Highlander would deny he needed anybody, but she was going to care for him whether he liked it or not. "The same way Brian needs you."

Bobbi sighed. "Well, I can't argue with that. I hope Adare feels better. Keep me in the loop."

"You, too. I know it'll all go well. Give me a call after the surgery." Grace said her goodbyes and then slipped the untraceable phone back into her pocket.

Adare opened the front door and snow swirled in around his boots. "Are you ready to go?"

She slung her pack around her shoulder. "Definitely."

* * * *

Adare finished setting the security at the cabin while Faith and Ronan settled into Benny's suite. Benny had taken different transport to meet with his family about the new split between the Realm and the Seven. Many of his family members worked for the Realm, but others didn't, and Benny wanted to keep the family from splintering. He wasn't confident of his chances.

Satisfied that all of his security measures were at full go, Adare skirted the kitchen and headed through his quarters to the master bath. He'd designed the shower himself, years ago, so it was wide and tall enough for him, in addition to being surrounded by natural rock that held in heat. A wide bench ran along one wall, and he liked to sit there when the steam unit was going.

He dropped his clothes and turned on the spray, stepping beneath instant heat and letting out a low groan. His blood moved sluggishly—he'd have to talk Ronan into sparring later to speed up the healing process.

The swish of clothing being dropped warned him the second Grace strode around the rock wall, buck assed naked.

His slow-moving blood turned hot and fast, really quick. He drew her under the stream, watching as the water sluiced over her body to land by her tiny feet and circle the drain.

She ran her wet hands up his chest. "Rumor has it you'll heal faster if your blood gets pumping."

He grinned, gathering her hair in his hand and leaning down to kiss her luscious lips. "Are you going to heal me?" She tasted of chocolate with a hint of whiskey. Had she and Faith had a hot toddy?

"Yes." Her eyes were a luminous green in the steamy shower. "I'm going to heal you in all sorts of ways." Pushing up to her tip-toes, she nibbled beneath his jaw, sinking her teeth into his collarbone. Her belly brushed against his erection, and he growled, the vibrations sparking down his legs.

He yanked her head back and kissed her, pushing her against the wall and settling a knee between her legs.

She mewled and scratched his chest and abs, her small nails biting in with a force he felt to his balls. He grinned and lifted her, pinning her to the wall with his body and licking her neck to kiss the bite marks he'd left the other day. She shuddered against him.

He leaned back, looking his fill. The female truly was magnificent with desire darkening her eyes and her lips swollen and dark pink from his kiss. "This is the only way to heal," he murmured, edging his cock between her legs.

She caressed the sides of his neck with both hands, letting him hold her aloft with both hands on her butt. "Good. I need you on the way to recovery before I head to Colorado the day after tomorrow."

"Colorado?" He settled his hands more securely across the fleshy part of her butt.

"Yeah." She leaned toward him and licked his nipple.

Shocks zipped through his system, and he struggled to keep his mind on the conversation. "We're not going to Colorado."

She gently bit his pec and then leaned back, setting her head against the stone. All of that glorious curly hair cascaded down, sliding over her shoulders and dripping more water. "I know you're not. You can stay here and spar with Ronan to speed up the healing process. I'm just getting you started here." She headed for the other side of his chest, and he snagged the back of her neck with one hand, sliding his other across her ass to maintain balance.

"Grace."

She blinked and licked her lips, still looking at his other nipple. "What?"

He tightened his hold on her nape just enough to catch her attention.

She looked up, meeting his gaze. "Adare?" Her breathy tone amped up his desire.

His cock jumped against her core, wanting inside her. Now. He settled his stance to keep them balanced. "You're not going anywhere for the next week or so, when we head to Seven headquarters." The team would need to meet and decide on a plan of action, depending on the decisions made by the Realm nation. But they had this week to heal and rest, and they needed it. Why was Grace talking about Colorado?

"Sure I am." She caressed his arms, pinched his wrists, and rubbed her palms back up. "I promised Bobbi I'd be there for Rose's baptism, and they're gonna need help. Brian is having surgery." She pressed both thumbs against his collar bone. "Why are we talking about other people while naked in the shower? Let's concentrate on us." The last was a purr.

He'd love to concentrate on them. Every nerve in his body, every predator's instinct, demanded he take what she was so generously offering.

They could talk later.

Yet he had to be straight with her. "No."

She stopped her exploration, and her gaze snapped up. "No? You don't want to concentrate on us?" She wiggled her butt, stroking her wet heat across the tip of his dick.

His control started to shred faster than a log in a woodchipper. "Oh, I want this," he rumbled honestly. "But I also want you to understand what I'm trying very hard to say." The words were difficult to form when all he had to do was shove forward, and he'd be surrounded by her.

She sighed, need in the sound. "How about we talk after? This is going to end up with us fighting, and I'd rather do that, you know, later."

So would he, but that wasn't how he worked. "I feel like I have your attention now."

"You feel?" she snapped. "Well, that's a new one."

Apparently the fight would begin at once. Steam rose around them, cocooning them, even as tension began to permeate the fog. "I've never hidden who I am, nor have I ever given you an idea that you'd come and go freely while there's danger out there."

"I've come and gone fine the last five years," she said, her clit pulsing against the head of his cock.

"That was before you all but announced where you were to the Kurjans," he retorted. "It was also before you willingly committed to being my mate. Welcome to matehood."

Chapter 34

Grace could not believe they were fighting while naked and surrounded by erotic steam. Her temper mixed with her incredible need, ratcheting up every emotion. Her legs were spread around his thighs, one of his hands supported her entire weight by holding her ass, and the other hand all but controlled her head by the nape. The vulnerability of her position propelled her desire even higher, much hotter, and that only pissed her off more. "If we're gonna fight, let's do it outside the shower." She was at too much of a disadvantage here.

"No."

Her nostrils flared when she took in the heated air. "That is rapidly becoming my least favorite word in your vocabulary."

"I'm thinking you might need to get used to it." His hold was absolute, and he stood there as if he could maintain their positions all day. His gaze wandered down her chest, and her nipples hardened as if he'd licked them with his rough tongue. "You have the prettiest pink nipples."

She smacked him on the nose.

Adare's head jerked up, and her eyes widened. What in the heck had she just done? It had been pure instinct, just a gut reaction. "I didn't think hitting was on the menu," he murmured.

She should apologize and get out of this situation. "It is when you deserve it," she snapped instead.

"I see. Good to know." Faster than she would've imagined possible, he turned them, lifted a knee onto the bench, tossed her over it, and slapped her butt with his huge hand. Before she could cry out, he turned again and she found herself back in place, the smooth rock cooling her back and the controlling immortal holding her in place, her legs still spread.

Her mouth gaped open. "You. *Ass*." To punctuate the words, she punched him right in the neck.

His eyebrows rose. "Well, okay." This time, when she found herself over his knee facing the rock, he smacked her rear end three times. Hard. Then he lifted her back into place, his cock against her clit, his hand spread across her burning butt. Then he waited.

Tingles spread from her punished flesh to her sex, warming her and making her clit fire with more than need. She bunched her fist.

"I could do this all day," he warned her. "Your ass is already a lovely pink, and I have no problem turning it red. You'll end up right in this position, every time. Feel free to punch me now."

Oh, she wanted to. She'd give almost anything to see the shock on his face if she punched him right in the eye. Or maybe the nose. She breathed out, her mind reeling, her hand ready to fly.

His eyes morphed to a dark silver, burning and alive. Color filled his high cheekbones, making him look like a warrior from times long gone by. "Are you finished with the hitting, Grace?" His rough voice slid beneath her skin, igniting every nerve.

She might be angry, but she wasn't a complete moron. "I'm reserving the right until later." She had to keep some dignity.

His smile was slow. "Sounds like a date, then. It wouldn't hurt for you to be reminded every time you sit that you don't want to challenge me."

Oh, he did not. "It's like you want to get punched," she muttered, her body aching so badly her stomach hurt.

"Whatever it takes, *Leannain*."

Seriously. She grabbed his neck and yanked his head down. If the only way to get him to shut up was to kiss him, she'd do it. She shoved her tongue inside his mouth, tasting male and mint, rubbing her sex against his engorged penis. He overtook her, going deep, mastering the kiss like he did everything else.

Slowly, still kissing hard, he penetrated her, inch by inch, his speed steady and sure. She gasped into his mouth, her body stretching, controlled by his mouth, his hand, and his cock. He gave no quarter, holding her in place, pushing insistently into her until he was embedded all the way.

She jerked her mouth free, sucking in air, impaled against the wall.

Then nerves inside her fired and flared, hurting and needing. He was so big and so much. "You could come with me to Colorado," she whispered, clenching around him.

He nipped her nose. "Neither of us is leaving this cabin until my strength is completely restored." He pulled out and pushed back in, slapping one hand on the rock by her head to keep his balance. "We can argue about it all the time you want, however."

Her eyelids fluttered shut from the exquisite pressure, and she forced them back up, feeling wide open to him. "I don't take orders from you, Adare," she rasped.

"Yeah, baby. You do now." He pulled out and shoved back in, setting up a hard rhythm that echoed around the steamy shower with the sound of flesh on flesh. He took her out of her head, even out of her temper, fucking her hard in the shower and not holding anything back.

Her thighs ached, they were stretched so far apart, only adding to the desperate desire ripping through her like sharp blades, cutting every nerve into several more. They all fired, for him, just waiting to detonate. She held her breath and her thighs tightened against his hips as she climbed, fighting falling over. It was too much.

He shifted his angle, hitting her clit. Pleasure detonated inside her, and she cried out, arching against him. The climax stole her breath, and she held on to his arms, her body shaking with the force of her orgasm. A million stars exploded through her body, flashing white behind her eyes.

She bit into his pec, drawling blood, trying to keep from screaming his name.

He ground against her, jerking several times inside her and shuddering with his own climax.

She kissed the bruise she'd just left on his chest and leaned back, panting wildly. Okay. Maybe fighting with Adare wasn't so bad. She chuckled to herself.

* * * *

The woman was nothing if not tenacious. Adare fought the urge to fuck her again and instead held her close in the sprawling bed while the storm beat ice and snow against the windows. "We need sleep. Stop talking," he ordered.

She wiggled her bare butt against his groin. "I'm just saying that we have to live normal lives, and my attending my friends' baptism is part of that."

"We are not normal, we will not have normal lives, and you will not attend." Maybe he should spank her for real. She had to understand he was serious about her safety. "I'm finished discussing this with you and suggest you call your friend tomorrow and let her know, just to be polite."

Grace yawned, her shoulder blades brushing his chest. "Listen, buddy. A guy who doesn't have emotions doesn't get to be boss."

"Says who?"

"Everybody knows that." She settled her chilly feet on his calves and moaned softly.

Interesting. "I have emotions; they just don't dictate my life."

"Ha. What emotions do you have?"

Who knew she'd be so chatty after sex? "I like you and have vowed to protect you throughout eternity. I promise to keep you safe and make sure you want for nothing." That was what he had in him and what he had to give. "That's my job."

She was quiet for a moment. "What's my job?"

"To enjoy life and stay safe. It's up to you if you'd like to have children someday." It was her decision, really. A little boy with her eyes would be endearing. "Though you should probably know that vampires only have males. You knew that, right?"

She yawned again. "I knew that but thought that maybe it had changed because Hope is part vampire. Because of that virus everyone caught way back when, right?"

"Something like that." He hadn't paid attention, to be honest. "But I don't think the proclivities of our species have really been changed. So far, parents with vampire blood have only created males. Something for you to think about."

She stiffened slightly. "Do you want children?"

"Yes. Someday." Not for quite a while, however. Anyway, it usually took centuries for immortals to conceive, although there were definite exceptions, obviously.

"What if I decide to go to the baptism, anyway?" she asked.

"You're not going. Take that in any way you wish," he said, his eyelids closing. It was time to sleep. They'd gone over this enough times, and either she got it or she didn't. He was done.

"You can't watch me every minute of every day for the rest of eternity," she countered.

His eyelids popped wide open. "I would prefer not to." The workings of her mind were truly fascinating. He waited, wondering where she'd go next.

"I'll make you a deal."

Not his usual course of action, but what the heck. He flattened his hand over her abdomen, smiling when her stomach muscles clenched in response. "What's the deal?"

She audibly swallowed. "I will promise to keep my safety at the top of my to-do list, and you promise to open yourself up to emotion and to love. It doesn't mean you have to love or anything, but that you are open to it. That's all we can do."

What a sweetheart. "Fine. I will open myself to love." How hard could it be?

She relaxed against him. "Good. I'm glad we got that taken care of."

"You're still not going to Colorado."

"Damn it, Adare." She shook her head, and her hair fluffed across his face. "Why are you so impossible?"

That was a question for another day. He kissed the back of her head. "Sleep. Now." Shockingly enough, she soon did. He let himself relax finally and drifted off, his body content.

It was just past dawn when her burner phone buzzed from the bedside table. Who in the world would be calling so early? Grace flipped on the light and sat up, holding the sheet to her bare breasts. "Hello?" she answered, blowing hair out of her eyes. She stiffened. "When? How? Are you sure?"

He sat up, his body going on full alert. "What has happened?"

Grace shook her head. "We'll be right there. Tell Adare what's happened." She handed over the phone and slipped from the bed, fetching her pack from the chair by the small fireplace. Hurrying back to bed, she dumped out the contents and flipped open a file folder holding photographs. "I knew there was something weird about her." She tapped her finger on a picture of the lady who'd answered the door at her old apartment when Adare and Benny had visited, looking for Grace. It was a photo of the woman who'd had the toddler in her arms.

"Hello?" Adare said.

"Hi. It's Bobbi." A crying woman sniffled, panic in her voice. "My daughter has been taken by my sister and her crazy boyfriend, and I don't know what to do. Brian is in the hospital after his surgery, and I'm alone, and they said they'd kill Rose if I called the police. I need a million dollars."

Adare straightened. "Your daughter is being ransomed for a million dollars? Do you have a million?" It didn't make sense to demand that amount from parents still living in an apartment complex. What was going on?

"No, but they sent a text with a picture of Grace at the restaurant. They know who she is—that she's a famous photographer. They said to ask her for the money. I don't have it." Bobbi's voice rose to shrill.

"So your sister knew all about Grace?" he asked, tossing the covers from the bed and standing up to fetch his jeans.

"Yes. I've always been so proud to be Grace's friend," Bobbi wailed. "I'd call the police, but the kidnappers will kill Rose. She's only two years old. How scared she must be. I don't think my sister would hurt her, not really, but her boyfriend is nuts. He's on meth and I think he'd be happy to hurt Rose. Or sell her for money for drugs. What should I do?"

Adare drew on his pants and turned to Grace. "Go awaken Ronan. Now." He headed for the closet to get his shirt and weapons. "Tell me everything about your sister, her boyfriend, and where you're supposed to go with the money."

"I don't have any money," she sobbed.

"I do. Now start talking."

Chapter 35

Grace paced the kitchen, wringing her hands. "Let me go with you. Bobbi will need help."

"No." Adare clipped several weapons into place on his side and even in his boot. "You're safe here with the security engaged, and something about this doesn't smell right."

"At all," Ronan agreed, pulling a jacket on over his shoulder harness. He turned and read the panel by the door. "We're secure and the missiles are armed. Nobody is getting in here." He leaned down and kissed Faith on the cheek.

Adare paused in the middle of strapping a knife to his leg. "You should stay here. I can go alone."

Ronan shook his head. "You're not at full strength yet, and like you said, this is off. Ransom for a toddler whose parents don't have money? Yeah. Right."

Adare looked at his watch and nodded. "All right. Benny is en route and will be here in about an hour, so you two just hang tight until he arrives. If there's any hint of trouble, run downstairs and shut the door. They won't be able to find the underground room."

Grace hovered. "Promise you'll call as soon as you know anything." The idea that little Rose was in trouble sent ice through her veins. Grace had known something was off with that woman, the sister. Why hadn't she said anything?

"It's only an hour flight via the helicopter. We'll have the baby soon," Adare said, his eyes veiled.

What wasn't he telling her? Grace craned her neck to look at the blustering storm outside. "Should you fly in this?" There was zero visibility.

"Sure." He pulled her in for a hard kiss and then let go. "Don't disengage any of the security measures until Benny is at the gate and you see his face on video. Understand?"

She nodded, trembling.

"Let's go," Adare said, striding out the front door and not looking back. Ronan followed.

Faith, dressed in yoga pants and one of Ronan's over-large T-shirts, turned toward the coffee maker. "I'll put on a pot. Tell me again what Bobbi said to you."

Grace repeated the story again for her sister. "I mean, my photographs have been selling well, and I guess her sister knew that, somehow. I saw the darkness in her, Faith. I saw it." Or rather, all around her.

"This isn't your fault." Faith took two mugs out of the cupboard. She waited as the coffee flowed out and then poured two mugs, bringing one over to the table and motioning for Grace to sit. "Ronan and Adare will do what needs to be done."

Grace wrapped her hands around her mug, letting the brew warm her. "This all seems odd, right?"

Faith blew on her coffee and then took a sip. "Definitely."

Grace stiffened. "Do you think it's a trap? That the Kurjans got to Bobbi? Or that the Kurjans have threatened Rose because of me? That I led them right to Bobbi and Brian? This is my fault." She started to stand and jerked in surprise when her sister yanked her back down. "What are you doing?"

"We have no idea if it's a trap or not. What we do know is that our mates are over a thousand years old, have fought countless enemies, and are still standing." Faith took another sip. "Either way, that baby is who matters right now, and they'll do whatever they have to in order to save her."

Grace released her mug. "How can you be so calm?"

Faith set her cup down. "Oh, I don't know. My sister was in a coma for two years and I could do nothing to help her. Then I met a vampire-demon hybrid from another world who was around fourteen hundred years old, and then I had crazy sex with him and got all mated and immortal. I guess after a while, you learn to trust that things will work out."

The sarcasm was new but kind of funny.

"Fair enough, but I'm still worried. If it isn't a trap, then Rose is in danger. If it is a trap, then Bobbi and Rose are in danger, because they're being used." Her body ached.

"I know." Faith finished her coffee and stood to pour herself another cup. "I need to take a shower before Benny gets here, just in case we end up fleeing once again. Are you okay for a few minutes?"

Grace took a drink of her coffee, letting the caffeine jolt her system. "Go ahead. I'm fine. Take your time." She'd forgotten how Faith liked to drink coffee in the shower. Grace had tried it once and had just ended up with watery coffee. She waited until her sister had left before grabbing the manila file full of pictures and looking again at the one with Kim and Rose. Shadows all but swallowed them both up.

Why hadn't she said anything?

Forget the fact that she didn't have details. A simple warning would have alerted Bobbi. God, Adare had to find that baby, and she had to be all right.

Grace flipped through to the image of the happy family sitting on the sofa, and then one of Bobbi and Brian outside in the bright sunlight with the snow sparkling all around. More shadows seemed to reach out to them from the trees. Was the entire family in danger?

Something wasn't right.

She went through all the photographs, her instincts flaring wide awake. There was no doubt in her mind that her old friends were in danger. Horrible, horrible danger. She stood and paced some more. Beneath one of his smiles, Brian looked contorted, as if he was being tortured. Was it an omen?

Thunder crashed far in the distance, and she could swear she felt the house move. The storm must be getting worse. Hopefully the weather had cleared up toward Denver for the guys. She glanced at her watch. They'd been gone nearly two hours. Had they found anything?

The sensor from the gate dinged and she whirled around, running to the control panel. "Yes. Benny?" She flipped the switch to turn on the video. Only garbled noise came back. "Benny?" she asked again, tapping on the screen. Nothing happened. She took a deep breath. "Benny, if that's you, let me know. I can't disengage the security unless I know for sure."

A blue mitt wiped snow off the camera by the gate, and then a face came into view. "Grace? It's Bobbi." Her friend was pale with her light hair whipped around by the storm.

Grace stepped back. "Bobbi? What in the world are you doing here?"

Bobbi coughed, her cheeks red from the cold. "Adare sent me and said to stay here. That it was the only safe place, but to make sure you saw me so you could do something with some sort of sensor?" She coughed again, her lips turning blue. "Would you turn off the sensor?"

Grace frowned, looking at Bobbi through the camera. None of this was making sense. "Wait a sec. You met with Adare in Denver and he sent you here? How did you get here?'

"Some guy piloted me here, dropped me off, and then turned right around to go back. I don't know what's happening. Have you heard anything about my baby?" Tears gathered in her eyes. "Anything about Rose?" She wiped more snow off the camera. "Please, let me in. I'm scared, Grace."

"I—this doesn't make sense," Grace muttered. How could Bobbi be at the gate so soon?

"I'll explain everything once I'm warm. It's freezing out here,' Bobbi said, coughing again. "Let me in, okay?"

Grace studied her, looking beneath the surface. The hazy camera and snowy weather hid too much, but she had a brain, and she had instincts, and she went with them. "No."

"No?" Bobbi shrieked. "Are you crazy? Your boyfriend sent me to the middle of nowhere, into a snowstorm for help, and you won't even open the gate? My baby is *missing.*" She leaned in, her blue eyes bloodshot and her nose running. "Have you gone crazy? Lost your damn mind?"

Maybe. Was Grace just getting paranoid? Her head hurt but she pushed through the pain. She trusted Adare and she'd start there. He'd said to keep the security in place until she saw Benny. If Adare had sent Bobbi here, he would've also sent word that she was coming. It only made sense. "If I've lost my mind, I'm really sorry. We have a friend coming to the gate shortly, and then we'll talk." Although Benny was late. Where the heck was he?

Bobbi stared into the camera for several beats. Then her expression smoothed out. "Your friend isn't going to make it."

"What?" Grace asked, realization slithering down her torso.

"We might've blown him up." Bobbi smiled then, the sight garish.

That far away thunder? That had been an explosion?

"Who are you?" Grace whispered.

Bobbi sighed, her breath heating and fuzzing the camera. "Long story. How about you just come out, so we don't have to come in and get you?"

"No." Grace panted out air.

As if on cue, a multitude of explosions ripped up the driveway. The sputter of electricity arced through the air, lighting the falling snow.

Bobbi laughed, the sound strange. "We're coming in, Grace. I know you're there, and I'll tear that place apart, or maybe blow it apart, to get to you. There's nowhere for you to hide for long. But go ahead and make this as difficult as you want. I'm okay with it." She lifted a weapon and fired right into the camera. The screen fuzzed and went black, all sound disappearing at the same time.

Shit. Grace dropped her mug and ran toward the living room, where Faith was emerging from the other bedroom, dressed in jeans and an overlarge sweater, her hair wet around her shoulders.

"What's happening?" Faith asked, her eyes wide. "Is Benny blowing things up again?"

"No." Grace grabbed her sister's arm and dragged her toward the hidden door right past the fireplace. "Bobbi's here blowing things up."

Faith stumbled and then righted herself. "Bobbi is here? What?"

"Yeah. She's the bad guy." Grace jumped up and clicked the button to open the keypad. What were the numbers? She closed her eyes, remembered Adare repeating them in his strong voice, and then reopened her eyes and typed quickly.

Three more explosions rocked the world outside.

The door opened, and Grace nudged Faith inside.

Faith partially turned. "What are you doing?"

Grace panted out air, her nervous system misfiring with fear. "They know I'm here, and they'll burn this place to the ground to find me. They don't know you're here. You have to hide."

Faith's shoulders went back. "Oh, hell no. You come in here." She made a grab for Grace's arm.

Grace pushed her hard enough that Faith had to back down several steps before she could regain her balance. "I love you. Tell Adare I love him, too." She slammed the rock door shut. Adare had said it locked from both sides, and she didn't think anybody had told Faith the combination She waited, hovering in case she had to reason with her sister, but nothing happened. No sound came from within, either.

Considering there was no doubt Faithie was pounding on the door, the lair must've been nicely soundproofed. Good.

Grace turned to run into Adare's room to find a weapon when the front door burst open, splitting into several pieces. A man stomped inside, and it took her a second to recognize him. It was Brian but not really Brian.

He was still tall and slender, but his eyes were purple and his hair long and black. His face was stark white, but his features were the same as before. Had he been wearing a wig and contacts?

Bobbi stepped up behind him, smiling. "There now. See? I told you we'd be right in."

Grace's knees wobbled, her mind reeling as she gaped at Brian. "Bu-but you're a Kurjan!" She shook her head, trying to see the good-natured friend she'd thought he'd been, but instead a monster stood before her. "I don't understand. I saw you in the sun. You spent a lot of time in the sun."

"Yeah. Things have changed." His fangs dropped, sharp and yellowed. "Surprise."

Chapter 36

Adare sat on the park bench, watching the sun sparkle off the snow in every direction. A walkway stretched between his bench and a rushing river that was going so fast it hadn't iced over completely. Not even the birds were out. The storm from down south hadn't reached Denver yet.

He kept his body relaxed while his mind was on high alert. The place was isolated enough that it'd be a great trap.

He took his phone from his pocket and speed dialed the king.

"Dage Kayrs," the king answered.

"Hey, King. It's Adare O'Cearbhaill. Do you have any news on a hit out on Ronan or me?"

Dage was quiet for a moment. "No, why? Are you being shot at?"

"Negative. I'm fairly certain we just walked into a trap and was wondering if you could provide any intelligence." He leaned down and pulled his gun from his boot.

"No. The demon and witch nations have decided to stay with the Realm for now, and the shifter nation wouldn't set a trap. They'd come at you head on, and my sources say they haven't voted on that possibility yet." Papers shuffled as Dage did something on the other end of the line. "If it's a trap, it must be Kurjan and Cyst."

"Not possible." Adare looked at the deep blue sky and bright, albeit weak, sun. If the Kurjans were dumb enough to attack on a sunny day like this, they deserved to fry.

"Okay. Well, good luck." The king disengaged the call.

Adare spoke into his earpiece. "I think he's starting to like us a little."

Ronan snorted. "Whoever was supposed to pick up the money is an hour late, so I'm thinking it's humans who got stupid. Let's go talk to that Bobbi and find the sister and boyfriend. This has fucked-up humans written all over it."

"Agreed." That didn't mean the baby was safe, however. Adare had looked at a few of Grace's pictures, and the little girl was a cutie. They had to save her. He couldn't break Grace's heart by failing, and he couldn't stand the idea of an innocent little toddler being hurt. He stood and tucked his gun away before slinging the backpack full of cash over his shoulder.

He loped down the walkway to meet Ronan, who'd taken point from behind a tree. "Have you heard from Benny?"

Ronan shook his head and settled his gun back beneath his jacket. "No, but he's not the best about checking in." He clipped his knife back at his thigh. He looked at the backpack. "You and Benny just store millions in your lair?"

"Stop calling it a lair, and yes, we store millions. Sometimes it comes in handy." Adare lengthened his strides, wanting to get back to Grace. "Do you believe in love?"

"Sure. It's fundamental."

Adare frowned. "I don't see you skipping through meadows and singing sonnets."

Ronan chuckled. "Love hurts a lot more than that, my friend."

The breeze lifted, tossing powdery snow over the walkway. And the scent of moldy lemons. Adare's head jerked up, and he looked around. Forest on one side, rushing river on the other. Good place for an ambush. But the sun shone down, bright and brilliant.

The breeze came off the water again.

Ronan halted. "I smell—"

The Kurjans attacked from the forest first, and then a squad rose from the river, having hidden in its depths just under the ice. Adare immediately pivoted, putting his back to Ronan's and whipping out his gun. He hit the first Kurjan in the neck and the second in the eye, but took several bullets to his torso. The lasers turned to metal and dropped harmlessly on the ground. Then a round hit his arm, and he winced as pain flew along his bicep and blood spurted out.

What the hell? The Kurjans weren't wearing protective gear. The sun glinted off the nearest Kurjan's skin, turning him pink but not burning him to death.

"I've got two down and six coming," Ronan hissed.

"Two down and two coming," Adare said, looking for a way out. How was this happening? "Forest or river?"

Ronan's shoulder jerked, hitting Adare's arm, and he groaned. "Fuck. The river. On three."

"Three," Adare bellowed, ducking his head and running full bore for the first soldier as Ronan turned and ran for the other. Bullets struck his back and legs, but he kept going, tackling the asshole into the ice and through to the freezing depths.

He slashed and diced with his knife, finally plunging it in the Kurjan's neck and sticking him to a rock at the bottom. Ronan crashed into him, and Adare turned them both, staying under the surface and letting the current take over.

The Kurjans ran along the river, firing wildly.

Bullets pierced the ice, several impacting Adare's other leg. Blood flowed around him, but they kept going. The water punished them, smashing them against rocks, but they stayed under until they reached a large pool where the water slowed.

He shoved himself up, along with Ronan, and they both gasped air into their lungs.

Adare looked around a fairly busy park. The pool was deep but the water kept moving around a bend toward the city. The Kurjans were gone. Adare partially stood, his legs protesting. Blood poured from several wounds along his arms and legs as well as one in his neck. He sent healing cells immediately to the injuries, stomping across river rocks to the bank.

Ronan slugged along beside him, bleeding from a wound in his cheek.

A woman walking a baby all bundled up in a stroller paused and then screamed.

"Shit." Ronan held up a hand. "We're okay. We were working upstream on the electrical grid and fell in. The rocks did a number on us."

"Electrical grid?" Adare muttered under his breath.

Ronan shrugged. "She stopped screaming."

They climbed up the decorative rocks to the brick walkway that led to several stores and restaurants. In the late afternoon, the coffee shop to the right was busy, and most of the patrons watched them with wide eyes.

Adare nodded at the crowd and kept on walking. "We need to get out of here."

Ronan hustled up to his side. "Can you run?"

"Yep." He might be a little dizzy, but he'd get to the helicopter. They'd hidden it in the forest, far from the meeting place. "We have to go by that Bobbi's apartment. The Kurjans have obviously gotten to her." It was probably too late, but for Grace's peace of mind, he needed to check.

Ronan ducked his head and loped into a jog. "We'll go by there, but it's a waste of time." He was quiet, his speed increasing. "The Kurjans were in the sun."

"I know," Adare said, keeping pace and running toward the sun. The sheer magnitude of that fact was too much to comprehend right now. The Kurjans had somehow modified themselves so they could venture out in the day—which altered things considerably. In the Kurjans' favor.

Everything had just changed. Again.

Ronan's phone buzzed, and he drew it from his pocket, halting in a parking lot for a movie theatre. Water dripped from the device, but he pressed the button anyway.

Adare stopped and scouted the area for threats.

"Hello." Ronan put the phone on speaker.

"Ronan? It's Emma. I just received an email from Faith saying she's stuck in Adare's lair and that Grace is gone."

Everything inside Adare froze and then heated. "Gone?"

* * * *

Her hands were tied, but Grace managed to lever herself up and look into the back of the SUV where Benny lay on his side, blood pouring from a wound in his neck. Half of his hair was burned off, and his jeans still smoldered. He wasn't moving. "What did you do?" She fell back to her seat, her heart aching and fear making her legs shake.

Bobbi shrugged next to her, holding a gun pointed at her ribs, while Brian the Kurjan drove. "We blew him up. He wasn't expecting a missile."

Grace gagged. She could even smell the burned flesh. "I don't understand. Any of this. Who are you?"

Bobbi flicked snow off her shoulders. "I'm Yvonne, the chosen one."

What? Grace rolled her eyes and tried to loosen the old-fashioned rope scraping against her skin. "Seriously? Give me a break." She ignored the blonde and looked at the driver, who apparently held the actual power. "We really dated, right?"

Brian nodded. "Sure did. Just long enough to determine you didn't know what a Key was or where the others were. Then I was going to take you in."

She remembered the purple eyes she'd seen when she was attacked. Her voice shook. "You put me in a coma, asshole," she spat.

"Yeah. Sorry about that." He smiled, his face a garish exaggeration of the Brian she thought she'd known.

She swallowed, looking outside, where the snowstorm kept most people off the streets. Hopefully Faith had gotten word out somehow. What where they going to do to her? She couldn't stop talking. "Are you somehow special? In being able to tolerate the sun?" She'd been told that was impossible. She had to somehow warn everyone.

"No," Brian said. "Thanks to Yvonne."

Yvonne winked at her. "It took years. I expanded on research the Kurjans have been conducting for a century, but I finally came up with a virus."

Another fucking virus? "This one makes it so Kurjans can go into the sun?"

"Yes. I had to actually conduct genetic manipulation that you wouldn't understand. My virus is the delivery mechanism." Her hand remained steady on the weapon.

"How old are you?" Grace burst out.

"Thirty-two," Yvonne said, waving the gun. "I graduated from high school at twelve and college for the first time at fourteen. I knew I was the chosen one long before that."

The chick had been watching too many sci-fi movies. "This is probably the biggest scientific breakthrough for any species, well, ever." Grace edged toward the door, but if she jumped out, she'd leave Benny at their mercy. He needed help.

Yvonne licked her lips. "My intended will be pleased."

"Who's your intended?" Grace asked, searching wildly for a way to escape.

"Ulric, of course," Yvonne said.

Grace coughed. "You know, they say genius and madness are the flip side of the same coin." Grace listened carefully for any sound of movement from Benny. She had to get him to a medic. "It'd be really nice if you stopped talking like you were from the dark side of a howling moon."

Almost casually, Yvonne struck Grace with the gun.

Grace's head flew back and she gasped, pain bursting through her cheekbone. "You bitch."

Yvonne laughed. "That's nothing. You should see what Terre can do when he's motivated."

"Terre?" Grace asked, her face pounding as hard as her heart. Her lungs felt too full, and her hearing was fuzzing out from fear.

Brian turned around. "My real name."

Grace shook her head to focus, ignoring the ache throughout her entire face. "What was the point of this complicated ruse? Dating me and then the two of you acting like a young family and my friends? You could've taken me any time that day."

"You're not the only prize," Terre said, his long hair dark against his pale skin. "We were hoping you'd lead us to the other Keys."

"How did you find me?" she asked, feeling the rope on her right wrist give a little bit.

Brian, or rather Terre, sped up, driving onto the Interstate. "Enough talking." He flipped the visor down to protect his face and reached for dark sunglasses. Maybe his exposure to sunlight still had to be limited. "After we discovered your location here, our guys went to work on the security system. It's good. We needed the full time you were away to drain it to the point we only needed a few explosives to get through the electric fence. Now shut up while I drive."

Grace sat, quietly working on her wrists while listening for signs of movement from Benny. Nothing. Had he sustained a head injury? When she'd looked, she'd only seen the back of his head. He had to be healing himself. She'd be ready for the moment he lunged over the seat.

Darkness was beginning to fall before she spoke again. "Where are we going?"

"Secondary location in New Mexico," Yvonne said, sounding tired. "We have a small headquarters and a much larger holding just a few miles away. We moved the Cyst there because it's better defended, and they must be protected until Ulric returns."

The woman was all in, that was for sure. "You're human?"

"Yes. Enhanced. Like you, but better." Yvonne smiled.

"Then this plan Ulric has for enhanced females, whatever it is, will kill you, too." The skin around Grace's wrist was bleeding, so she set her hands on her jeans and kept working away.

Yvonne shook her head. "No, I won't die. You will, however." She leaned to the side. "How much longer, Terre? I need to use the facilities."

"Half hour," Terre said, taking off the sunglasses.

Grace's heart rate hadn't slowed down any. She felt like a coke bottle that had been shaken up, and her skin prickled. Was it adrenaline? Terror? "Adare is a good fighter, Terre. One of the best. Are you sure you want to piss him off?"

Terre laughed. "Adare's dead by now, pretty Key. He wouldn't have expected an ambush in full sun, would he?"

A rock, sharp and solid, dropped into Grace's gut. Nobody knew that the Kurjans could go into the sun, and Adare never would've seen them coming. He wasn't in top shape right now, either. *Oh, God.* Her shoulders shook and her teeth chattered.

"I think you terrified her," Yvonne said to Terre.

He looked at Grace in his rearview mirror. "Don't pass out on me, girlfriend. We have a lot of talking to do later."

"Talking. Right," Yvonne clicked her tongue. "So that's what you kids are calling torture these days." She leaned to the side as if telling a secret. "I've seen him work. He can make it hurt so bad you can't even scream."

Grace reacted without thought, dropping her head and smashing her forehead onto Yvonne's nose.

There was a pop and blood burst forth. The blonde yelled, clapping a hand over her nose. "You fucking bitch."

Grace's ears rang. They were going to torture her and then save her to kill when they got the other Keys. Reasoning with them wasn't going to work. Might as well make them bleed first.

Chapter 37

Adare burst through the destroyed front door of his cabin a step ahead of Ronan. "Grace?" he bellowed, running for the hidden door and keying in the code.

Faith dashed out, bounced off him, and headed straight for Ronan. He held her tight, breathing her in, his gaze tortured. Faith pulled back, tears on her face. "They came to get her, and I think she's gone. They destroyed most of the security system, but I watched the cameras downstairs, and they tied her up and put her in a back seat of a green Suburban."

"Who?" Adare growled, his body settling into fight mode, even while he bled from one leg. The blood pooled on his boot, dripping onto the wooden floor.

"Bobbi and what looked like a Kurjan in the front seat," Faith said, wiping her face off. "But the snow had stopped and the sun came out. I don't understand. Maybe he was wearing a mask? But he looked like a Kurjan. A real one."

They'd passed the burnt-out shell of Benny's truck, and the hybrid was nowhere to be found. If he'd survived the attack, he would've gotten word to them. Or maybe he was tracking Grace. It was unlikely he would've gone without leaving word, but it was a hope to hold on to. Benny had to be okay.

Fury raced through Adare so quickly, he swayed. "How the hell did Bobbi find her? Find this cabin?" He grabbed his phone from his pocket and quickly dialed the Realm. The device had somehow survived the dunking in the river.

"I take it you didn't die in the ambush," Dage Kayrs said absently instead of a greeting.

Adare dug deep for patience. "Listen up, King. The Kurjans have developed the ability to withstand the sun, so you might want to send the word out. They're probably ambushing anyone they want right now."

"Bullshit," Dage returned.

Adare pinched the bridge of his nose. "It's true. We were attacked from two sides in full sun." He pulled the phone away from his face, focusing on Ronan. "Why do you think they had a bigger force in the trees than the water?"

Ronan kept Faith plastered against his side. "I'm not sure. Maybe the water amplifies the sun?"

That was a good thought. It took Adare a beat to realize the king was yelling into the phone. "What?" he growled.

"If they're able to go into the sun, why did the force you attacked the other day need to use protective gear?" Dage asked. "You described their equipment well, and we've been researching their uniforms around the clock."

"How the fuck should I know?" Adare snarled. "Maybe the new ability is limited to special forces. But I'm telling you, two full squads attacked in the sun earlier, and the light didn't seem to slow them down any. We got out of there fast. Also, Grace was taken by another Kurjan, but I haven't reviewed the video recording yet."

"Grace was taken?" The king's voice lowered.

Adare swallowed, fighting a pain dead center in his chest. "Yes. And we need to know how they found her here. The only way would be if we were followed from Realm headquarters, either by a force or satellite. How shitty is your security?" He wanted to shake the king by his arrogant hair.

Dage was silent for a moment. "Our security is flawless. You weren't followed from here."

"Wrong. That's the only way it could've happened," Adare countered.

A soft voice murmured on the other end of the line, and the phone was muffled. Then the king returned. "Emma's here and she might have an idea. Hold on for a few minutes."

"I don't have a few minutes. Get your satellite guys on it and track any vehicles that left my cabin today. Call me back." Adare clicked off, already shucking his damaged pants and shirt to suit up for another op. He had to find Grace. His legs still hurt, but he shoved the pain away and tried to speed up his healing cells. He didn't have time for weakness.

"They won't kill her, Adare," Ronan said, still holding Faith. "They'll want all three Keys."

Yeah, but they'd have no problem hurting her. Maybe torturing her for information about the Seven, the Keys, and even the Realm. His stomach rolled over and his chest hurt even worse. If anything happened to Grace, he'd scorch the earth to destroy the entire Kurjan nation. He hustled into his room and pulled on fresh winter-camo cargo pants and a shirt, reaching for his weapons.

Ronan stepped inside, a bruise healing across his jaw. "We don't know where to look."

"Dage will get his satellite guys on it, and we'll have a direction," Adare said, his hands shaking. He felt like throwing up. What was happening to Grace right now?

"Benny hasn't called in, so he's probably tracking her."

Adare didn't look up. "He would've gotten word to us, so he's a prisoner, too. You saw his rig, Ronan. It'd be a miracle if he was even conscious." Which meant he was as good as dead if they didn't find him soon. Anybody dumb enough to take Benny Reese hostage would soon realize the eccentric immortal wasn't worth the struggle. There was no way he'd give up information, no matter what they did to him.

Ronan put a hand on Adare's shoulder. "I'll gear up and be ready as soon as we have a direction." His green eyes were tortured.

"She's strong, and we'll figure out how to find her, brother. I promise."

Adare nodded. Dage had the best satellite experts in the business, so if there was any sign of that green suburban, they'd find it. He needed a break. Anything. "Go suit up."

Ronan pivoted and disappeared.

Adare finished inserting knives and guns throughout his clothing, his movements deliberate, his mind calculating, and his chest bursting. Whatever was flowing through him was something new. Something desperate and dark. An image of Grace, her eyes teasing, flashed across his mind.

The sound of her sweet voice echoed in his head. *"Do you believe in love?"* Those words, asking the bigger question. Was this love?

This desperate, furious, riotous energy nearly ripped him apart. The fact that the Kurjans had her, that she might be frightened or hurt, brought the beast at his core fully to the surface, growling and ready to destroy. A thought caught him and he rushed into the kitchen, dropping to examine the pictures Grace had spread over the table.

Ronan moved in behind him, already dressed in winter camo. "What are you doing?"

"Just looking." Would he be able to see what she did? He just saw people. Then he found the picture of the woman with the baby, and he picked it up, holding it to the light.

"What?" Ronan asked.

Adare held it higher. *Holy shit.* How had he missed it? If she wasn't Bobbi's sister, who the hell was she? "What do you see? On her neck?"

Ronan leaned in. "Oh. Bite marks. Deep and old. That's a mating mark." His voice rose in surprise, and he leaned back. "I can't believe it."

The woman was a Kurjan mate. And Adare hadn't had a clue. He hadn't focused on the female that day, and he hadn't gotten any sort of tingle or vibe from her that she was mated. Yet the mark looked very old, so the evidence should have been there. "I've never met a Kurjan mate, have you?"

"No," Ronan breathed. "Whose toddler do you think that is? She's female, so she's not Kurjan." The Kurjans only had males, just like vampires.

"Maybe Bobbi's?" Adare shook his head. "I know she was human, and by the time I showed up at the restaurant, Brian was gone. I never imagined he could be a Kurjan, because of the sun. But could he have been? That would explain why he left before I got to the restaurant. I would've sensed him."

Ronan nodded. "I guess it makes sense that they'd try to use Grace to lead them to other Keys before taking her. The Kurjans of old wouldn't have played such games. They weren't strategic enough." Ronan had been gone from this world for centuries, so he was still catching up.

"They changed and evolved," Adare said grimly. Obviously they'd changed more than even he had realized, considering they were no longer burned by the sun. It was a situation he never thought he'd see. The Realm's advantage in battle situations had just disintegrated faster than the ability to teleport had. "Our lives just became even more dangerous, if that's possible."

He'd never once been afraid of giving up his life for the cause. But he wouldn't give up Grace. Never. He had to find her. She had to be okay. New energy, wild and angry, teemed through his blood, strengthening him.

The sound of vehicles pulling up outside had his head snapping up. He drew his knife and stalked through his doorway and the living room to the porch.

Males jumped out of several vehicles. Quade Kayrs, Ivar Kjeidsen, Logan Kyllwood, and Garrett Kayrs. All wearing winter combat gear and fully loaded with weapons, their expressions determined and strong, their gazes on him. There was understanding and an indescribable loyalty glimmering in their eyes.

His brothers.

The full contingent of the Seven, minus Benny, whom they'd find soon.

He rocked back on his heels as if he'd been punched. Emotions broke free like a torrent from a cracked dam, flooding him.

Ivar reached him first, clapping him on the back in a fierce hug. The Viking felt solid and strong, and Adare knew he'd give the mission all he had. "We'll get her back, brother. You have my vow." He moved inside as one by one, his brothers issued the same promise before entering the house.

Quade planted a hand on Adare's shoulder, his gaze clear and his face hard. "We've faced worse, and we've won each time. As a force, we're stronger than this entire world, and your mate is a Key. She has power and protection we can't even imagine—I know that in my very bones. Trust me, brother." He nodded and moved on into the house.

Garrett's hug was strong, and his words few. He was a Kayrs, and he had the power of that entire lineage in every hard muscle. "I'm ready to hunt. We'll find her."

Logan was the last one, a newly mated vampire, one with ties to the Realm, the demon nation, and to the Seven. "We'll do what we need to do, brother." He wore more knives across his chest than he had pockets. "I have the demon nation looking, and Garrett has the Realm. We've reached out to the witches and the shifters, and even though they're pissed right now, they won't let the Kurjans take a mate. We will find her, and we're ready to go the second we get word. She will be all right."

Adare swallowed, his body settling. They'd come. The second he'd needed them, they'd immediately come, no matter what. That kind of loyalty, that kind of brotherhood, was exactly why and how they were going to win this thing in the end.

His phone buzzed, and he lifted it. "King?"

"Hey, Adare. Emma heard us talking and got an idea. She just returned from testing—"

"Hi, it's Emma." The queen's voice came clearly over the line. "There was a substance I couldn't identify in Grace's blood, and I figured it was something to do with being a Key, so my tests went in that direction. But when you were arguing with Dage about how she was tracked to your cabin, I had another idea."

"Hurry it up, queen," Adare growled.

"Right. Okay. It was tracking dust. Also known as tracing dust. We've dealt with it before in other ops, and this was sophisticated stuff, but that's what it was. They somehow got it into her blood stream. Probably her lungs, too. Maybe liver."

Adare stood stock still, anticipation licking through his veins. "Can you track it?"

"Already have," the queen said quietly. "I'm sending the coordinates to your phone. Happy hunting and good luck."

Chapter 38

Grace struggled against Terre as he dragged her from the vehicle and into a large rustic lodge set amongst many smaller wooden cabins. The area looked like a camping facility or corporate retreat rather than the hellhole she'd imagined. He pushed her through a doorway and down several cement steps. The air cooled even more, and she shivered, trying to look behind him. Were they bringing Benny too?

Terre turned down a corridor, blowing past several closed doors to what looked like a cell with some type of Plexiglas wall on one side. Using a keypad, he opened it and pushed her inside. She backed away from him. There was nothing in the cell but a small door to the side that revealed a bathroom.

Two Cyst soon followed, lugging Benny. They threw him into the cell, and he landed on the cement with a hard thud, not moving on his own, not even a little bit.

Terre shut the cell and stood on the other side, watching her.

She ran for Benny and turned him over, wincing at the burns across his face. One was so deep, she could see singed parts of his skull and maybe brain matter.

"He's lucky the blast didn't take off his head," Terre said, his voice coming clearly though a set of round holes across the glass.

Her legs shook, but she stood to face him, keeping Benny behind her. "What's your plan? Why did you bring him?"

Terre crossed his arms, still looking so much like Brian that the perversity was frightening, especially since Brian didn't really exist. "Benjamin Reese has been a member of the Seven since the very beginning. He's one of the few originals, and he has a lot of information in that crazy head of his. Information we need to extract before cutting it off."

Bile bubbled in her stomach. "I suppose you think I have information in my head."

"I look forward to finding out." He licked his lips.

The bile rose and burned her throat.

Heavy footsteps sounded and another Kurjan joined Terre, this one a couple of inches taller. His black hair was tipped with red. "This is the Key?" His faced was angled and his skin pasty, but he had a sharpness to him that was compelling. His voice was deeper than Terre's and his stance more casual, but he had an aura of power around him that was almost physical.

Her fingers itched for her camera. She wanted to capture him on film and now.

"Yes, brother. We've found one." Terre lifted his chin, satisfaction flaring his nostrils.

The other Kurjan stepped closer to the glass. "I'm Dayne, leader of the Kurjan nation. Show me your marking."

Words escaped her, so she stood tall, all the while wanting to curl into a ball behind Benny and make him wake up and deal with these assholes.

Dayne tilted his head to the side and smiled. At the sight, her legs almost gave out. Her breath shortened, and she allowed her lips to open slightly so she could breathe out of her mouth. He was oddly intriguing, definitely imposing, and with that smile he should've been handsome.

But she saw beneath the surface—and the vision of who he really was chilled her flesh as if she'd been stuck in a freezer all day.

"She's stronger than she looks," Dayne said.

Terre nodded. "Definitely. I've known that for a while."

Dayne slipped his hands in the pockets of his black pants. His shirt was a black cotton button down and showed a muscled chest. "You were right about the approach. Plus, you liked the undercover work."

Terre laughed. "I really did. I think I have a new calling."

They were joking around right in front of her? She'd never been dismissed or treated like nothing before, and a sputtering of anger percolated through her terror. But she had to find out what had happened to Adare. If she asked straight out, they wouldn't tell her. "When Adare gets here, he's going to take off your head." She held her breath, waiting for a response. Was Adare alive? He had to be.

"Nobody knows you're here, little Key," Dayne said, almost gently. He lifted his head and sniffed the air. Sighing, he stepped up to the glass and flattened his hand on the separation. His fingers were long and thick. "You've mated. I can sense it." He looked over his shoulder at his brother. "You didn't mention that fact."

"New development," Terre said, sighing.

Dayne let his hand drop. "Sorry. I know you had plans for her, but you'll need to find someone else. Plan B?"

Terre nodded. "Yeah. I decided on Plan B, anyway. I've had my eye on her for a while, and all we need is the virus."

"We could give this one the virus, once we get it," Dayne offered.

Fire ripped through Grace. "Stop talking about me like I'm not here. I'm a Key, damn it, and that means something even in your fucked up little world."

Dayne's eyebrows rose. "She's got a mouth on her."

"For now," Terre said, stepping up next to his brother. "I may cut her tongue out. She'll only need it long enough to give me the information I want. Then she's useless until we find the other Keys."

Dayne winced. "Can you imagine living without a tongue? Pizza would be a thing of the past."

Now they were joking about her?

Terre laughed. "Stop looking so angry. We're just messing with you. If I cut out your tongue, which probably will happen, by the way, then you can heal yourself and grow a new one."

If she had those skills. She still didn't know if she could actually heal herself. More importantly, they hadn't answered her about Adare. She couldn't do this life without him.

Now she realized she loved him?

Terre palmed the glass. "I think we scared her too much. She just turned stark white." He patted the glass. "Relax, Key. You're immortal now and will probably survive anything we do to you. You might not want to, but you will."

"All right." She put her hands on her hips, faking bravado. "Enough with the threats. Why don't we just exchange information?"

Dayne pursed his lips. "Interesting. Okay. Where are the other Keys?"

"I have no clue. Where's Ulric? Is he back?"

Dayne sighed. "*No clue* doesn't help me, and I'm sure you're lying, anyway. Besides, we wouldn't want to deprive Terre of his plans, would we? He's definitely earned some fun time after pretending to be human all this while." His chin lowered. "Now, I'm not going to ask you again. Show me the Key marking."

"No." Her voice shook, but she held her ground.

Seeing a Kurjan roll his eyes was an experience she never wanted to have again. Dayne reached to the wall on the side of the glass, pushed something, and an electrical current ran through the floor. Just enough to make her yelp and jump up. She turned to see Benny still not moving.

Dayne returned. "That was a tickle. The next one will shock you to the roots of your hair, and who knows what it'll do to him."

"Fine." She jerked her shirt to the side, revealing the perfect mark of a key between her heart and her collar bone.

Dayne's nostrils flared. "Excellent." He turned to his brother. "We have work to do. Meet me in the war room in fifteen minutes." He turned on his combat boot and strode away, hands still in his pockets.

Grace swallowed. "Your brother is the leader of the entire Kurjan nation?"

Terre nodded. "Yep. I'm the spare." He grinned and his fangs were partially revealed.

They'd been friends once. Could she get through to him? Or had it all been a game? "I really liked you as Brian. Was there any of the real you in there?"

"You didn't like me that much," Terre said. "We went out a few times, hung out a lot, and I still couldn't get you naked."

Oh, thank God. She hadn't wanted to ask, because she hadn't wanted to know. "We didn't sleep together?"

"No. I lied about us living together, too. We didn't." He shook his head. "For an artistic type, you were surprisingly prudish."

"More likely my instincts were on track, even if I didn't realize it." She breathed out, eyeing the floor. Where did the electricity come from? Would there be a way to somehow divert it to the door? "Was any of it real? Any of our friendship?"

He rubbed his smooth chin. "Sure. It was fun playing human for a while, and you were a challenge." He stepped away from the glass. "Not enough to keep me from extracting information from you now, however."

"Hey. I'm happy to tell you anything you want," she said. It wasn't as if she had any classified information or knew anything that they didn't, apparently.

"How will I know you're not lying?"

She drew in air. He was playing with her like a cat with a goldfish, and she was done being agreeable. "Didn't your brother order you to a war room? You should probably obey him." She put her back to him and leaned down, checking on Benny to make sure he was breathing.

Terre laughed. "I'll send food down to you. You'll want to keep your energy up."

She paused. "Terre? What happened to Rose? Whose baby is she?"

"Oh, I have no clue. Yvonne found the baby and took her because she looked like Yvonne. Little thing is enhanced, though. We'll probably keep her." He turned and the sound of his footsteps receding echoed back down the hall.

God. Where was that toddler? Surely the Kurjans were keeping her somewhere in this compound. Grace needed to wake Benny up and find the baby before they escaped. They had to get the baby to safety. "Benny?" She nudged his shoulder. "Wake up, would you?" Shouldn't his skull be stitching itself together? She'd thought that injuries to an immortal's most important organs healed first. That had to be his brain. She leaned in, her ear over his nose, to make sure he was breathing.

He was, slow and sure.

Good. That had to mean he was healing.

A scuffle sounded down the hallway, and Grace stood, instinctively keeping Benny behind her. If they tried to take him, she'd fight to protect him, but her chances sucked. A woman came into view with a tray in her hands. She keyed something on the pad, and a small opening appeared in the bottom of the glass.

Grace stepped closer. It was Bobbi's sister. "Hey. I know you."

Except today the woman wore a long dress, covering even her shoes, with her blond hair tied back in what looked like a tight ponytail. "Yes. Here. The food is healthy and will give you strength." She pushed the tray through the opening and it smoothly slid shut again.

"Wait. What was your name? Kim?" Grace didn't look at the food.

"No. That's what they call me. My name is Karma," the woman said, looking up. Her eyes were a light brown, almost topaz.

Right. Grace moved closer to the glass. "You have to help us." She now saw there was kindness in the woman as well as fear. Grace realized the shadows in the photographs hadn't come from her. They'd hovered all *around* her.

"I can't." Karma pointed to the food. "You have to eat to keep strong. The food is good and not dosed with anything." She turned to go.

"Wait," Grace said. "What about Rose? The little girl. Where is she?"

Karma clasped her hands together and turned back. "She's safe right now." She angled her neck to study Benny behind Grace. "He needs blood to heal." Then she looked up at the corner, ducked her head, and scrambled back down the hallway.

Grace glanced up to find a camera mounted in the corner. Great. They were being watched. She pulled the food toward Benny and sat next to him.

"Okay, Ben," she whispered. "Karma was right." She'd have to force blood down his throat somehow. The food was simple oatmeal, accompanied by a couple of spoons and juice boxes. No knives. How was she going to cut her wrist? It wasn't as if she had fangs.

She gingerly opened Benny's mouth and pushed on his damaged gums. Nothing. She looked around the cell. There was nothing sharp anywhere. Her gaze caught on the bathroom. She suddenly had to go. Bad. Wincing and feeling self-conscious, she hurried over to take care of business. Hopefully the bathroom wasn't visible on camera, but just in case, she barely took her jeans down and covered herself with her sweater. She flushed, and partially turned to view the toilet. It was standard.

She took off the lid as the water slowly filled the tank.

The stopper was held in place by a thin chain. That'd do it. She unhooked the chain as fast as she could, just in case there were other cameras around.

Nobody came running, so she sliced into her wrist, scratching more than cutting. Darn it. Holding her breath, she cut as deep as she could, pressing her lips together as the pain increased. Soon she had a decent wound. Holding her wrist to her body, she hustled over to Benny and sat on her knees, spooning some of the oatmeal at the same time. She bent over his body, her back to the camera. "You have to eat this oatmeal," she said, shoving it in his mouth and following with her wrist.

Her blood mixed with the oatmeal in his mouth.

That was so gross.

She reached for the juice box and ripped open the side tab, pouring it in his mouth as well. The mass finally slid down. "Okay, good. Eat some more. You have to wake up." She kept her voice loud so that any observers could hear it.

She spooned up more oatmeal and added her blood, hoping the camera wasn't catching any of her actions. This time, more blood soaked into the oatmeal, and she didn't need the juice.

The lumps slid down his throat again.

He still didn't move.

Chapter 39

For the first time, Adare didn't have to plan a Cyst attack around the time of day. It no longer mattered. He half-hung out of one of the two attack helicopters belonging to the Seven, his weapon held with ease in his hands. It was snowing again, and ice crystals battered his face and the craft, but they flew true and close to the tree line.

Ronan hung out the other side, and the second they set down, he'd launch into motion.

They landed within a gulley between two sloping hills, about ten miles from the compound to which Emma had tracked Grace. While New Mexico was high desert, there was as much snow here as there had been in Colorado. He tucked his head and hit the ground, sinking to his waist in the powder and immediately pushing himself into a run.

The schematics of the compound ran through his brain, as did the plan they had created on the flight there. With only six of them, they couldn't leave anybody to guard the helicopters.

He ran between trees, his pack heavy on his back but not slowing him. Nothing could slow him. The sense that Grace was near and in danger fought with the certainty that she was all right. For now.

The mating mark pulsed and heated on his palm, demanding he go faster.

So he did, his brothers keeping pace, all silent and ready for battle. Today there would be no mercy. No vacillation on whether to kill or question to gain information.

The only goal was rescue. Whatever he had to do to save Grace and Benny, he would do. Quickly and instinctively. So when he came across the first guard patrol, three miles out from the perimeter, he sliced right across the first male's neck without slowing his stride.

Garrett took care of the other.

The storm strengthened, golf-ball sized hail pummeling them as if Mother Nature wanted to help but couldn't figure out where to aim. One chunk of ice hit him on the cheek, and he blinked, running even faster through a series of tall trees, their boughs heavy with ice and snow.

He reached out with his mind, searching for his mate.

Only a sputtering response came back. It wasn't a surprise, considering they'd just mated. Telepathy took time. But his heart warmed, thumping harder, and he sensed her near. He could *feel* her.

So this was love. Ronan had been correct. It hurt more than he would've thought. His leg ached, but he banished the pain, moving even faster. There was no feeling, no indecision. Yeah, he loved her. The ah ha moment didn't slow his stride.

He reached the snow-covered security fence and paused, ducking to look ahead. On the other side lay a wide cleared space that led to two metal buildings and the rest of the facility, which appeared to be log cabins. Anybody crossing the clearing would normally be visible, although the snow camo they wore would conceal them in the snow. At least for part of the way.

Logan crouched next to him, studying the nearly invisible wires. "Good security," the young demon whispered. "The snow is coming down too thick for them to have detected us via land triggers, and any cameras will be covered with snow. They don't know we're here yet."

Ronan and Garrett took point behind them, watching their backs for any movement.

Ivar crouched on Adare's other side, withdrew his hands from the gloves, and set his pack on the snow. He drew out dark glasses that glowed a neon blue and leaned in to study the wires. His movements sure and economical, he reached in the pack for a box and leads to attach to the wires, and then keyed in several commands on the face of the box. "If we can disengage this without explosives, we'll have a better chance of making it across that clearing." Cold-weather warfare was the Viking's specialty. A small beep came from the box.

Ronan put his back to Adare. "The second they know we're here, they'll call for backup from the main Cyst facility to the west. Remember to set your watches for ten minutes—that's my guess on how long it'll take for reinforcements to arrive."

They'd be so far outnumbered at that point that it wouldn't matter. "We can get it done in ten minutes," Garrett said grimly.

Ivar removed the leads and replaced the provisions in his pack. "It's disengaged. We go over and not through. All set."

Adare didn't wait. He stood and jumped straight up, tucking and rolling in the air before landing on the soft snow and sinking down on the other side.

Then he waited. Nothing happened. No sirens, no alarms.

His brothers followed suit, all landing near.

Ivar handed out goggles. "They're set to detect land mines, but the snow might conceal the glow, so proceed carefully."

Adare pulled his goggles over his head, tucked his gun at his waist, and dropped to his belly. The ice chilled his skin, and he ducked his head down, using his other senses to keep him heading forward. Any movement, any lifting of his head, might alert guards in the control room.

Only the wind and falling hail could be heard. His brothers moved as silently as he did. If he didn't sense them, he wouldn't have known they were there. Even the younger members, Garrett and Logan, had been exceptionally trained.

He'd never be able to thank them enough.

The closer he got to the buildings, the stronger he felt the pull of his mate, and the stronger he became.

Finally, he edged out of the snow and crab-walked to the first metal building, not surprised to find his brothers in step with him. He reached for explosives in his pack, setting them along the perimeter. These ones would work. "Let's get in as far as we can before lighting up the world."

Then he took a deep breath, stood, and turned the corner around the building.

A guard looked up, gasped, and lifted his weapon.

* * * *

Grace finished wrapping the napkin around her bleeding wrist, trying to send healing cells to the injury. Nothing happened. She really needed some time to figure out this immortal stuff. Still on her knees, she patted Benny's face. "Ben? Wake up, now. I need your help."

His breathing seemed to deepen, but he didn't twitch a muscle other than that.

"How was dinner?"

Grace swung around to see Yvonne on the other side of the glass. The woman had changed into designer jeans and a sparkly top with fur-lined boots. "What do you want?" Grace stood to face her.

Yvonne craned her neck to look beyond Grace. "I was just curious whether he was awake yet. I've never seen a hybrid blown up before." Her blond hair curled naturally around her shoulders, and intelligence shone bright in her eyes. Or maybe that was insanity.

Grace tilted her head and studied her. Really studied her. The air wafted around her, not sparkling but not clear. She had an aura of shadows, light gray, maybe silver. Interesting. "You said you were the chosen. What exactly does that mean?"

Yvonne arched one eyebrow. "How do you not know your destiny? Everything about all of us?"

She'd been kind of busy healing from a coma and living her life for the last five years. "Maybe you didn't interest me before now." The shadowy sparkles were certainly intriguing. "There are many enhanced females, three Prophets, three Keys, but only one Chosen? I don't think so." She moved closer, going for the body blow. "If I had to guess, and I do, then I'm thinking you're one of many hoping to be chosen."

Yvonne's smile held certainty. "Cute. Trying to make me angry, are you?" She flicked a piece of invisible lint off her cashmere sweater. "I don't mind talking to you, Grace. We were kind of friends for a couple of days." She tucked her hands in her jean pockets. "I had fun."

Fun? Grace stepped even closer. Was the woman lonely? It had to be difficult living with Kurjan soldiers all the time. "You don't have to do any of this, you know. If there's something decent in you, you have to see how wrong all of it is."

"No, it's fate." Yvonne turned around and lifted her sweater to reveal a baroque symbol centered on her spine. The design spread out like the wings of a butterfly with a symmetrical pattern of symbols in each wing. Beautiful and complex.

"Wow." Grace tried to memorize the marking. "You were born with that?"

"Indeed." Yvonne turned back around, facing her. "You're right that I'm not the only one. Each generation or so, another is born, just like with the Keys. If you die, another will take your place. Same with me, but it's my time, and Ulric is coming back for me. I dream of him. He dreams of me." She clasped her hands together as if posing for a picture. "Fate talks to us all, if we just listen."

That would sound nut-job crazy if Grace wasn't sitting in a jail cell with a demon-vampire hybrid who'd had part of his face burned off. "I think fate gives us options, and we choose from there." Grace flattened her hands on the glass. "If you believe in destiny, you believe in the afterlife. Shouldn't you give that some consideration? Let us go. Give yourself a chance in the next life."

Yvonne chuckled. "I'm not leaving this life. When Ulric mates me, when he finally comes home, I'll live forever."

Huh. All right. "What about Rose? Where is the toddler?"

Yvonne shrugged. "We sensed she was enhanced and took her as part of my little family charade for you. You have to admit that seeing Brian and me with a baby kept you off guard. It was a good move. Plus, it was fun."

Fun? They'd kidnapped a toddler and thought it was fun? Grace's stomach rolled over. "Where is the little girl now?"

"Who cares? She's around here somewhere. I think we should either leave her in the snow or at a church," Yvonne muttered. "But since she's enhanced, I'm sure the Kurjans will want to keep her. Somebody will want to mate her when she's an adult."

Grace swallowed. "Forget what I said. You're definitely going to see hell someday."

Yvonne sighed. "You're as much fun as that old hag, Karma."

Grace's chin dropped. "Old hag? She looks around twenty, maybe twenty-five at the oldest."

"No. She's ancient. At least a couple hundred years old and a total wallflower. No fun whatsoever." Yvonne scratched her wrist. "We're going to try the virus on her first, before using it on others. At least she'll be good for something. Plus, Terre needs a mate. The guy needs heirs."

Benny coughed and stirred.

Grace whirled around. "Ben?" She dropped to her knees to lift his head. "You with me?"

His skull had already stitched itself together, and the skin on his forehead was mending quickly. He opened his metallic eyes, and blood dripped out of one. "Ouch." He mended his eyeball and sat up, groaning like an old man. "Shitballs," he muttered, seeing the cell.

Grace patted his shoulder. Relief ticked through her. Thank goodness she wasn't alone any longer.

Benny leaned around her. "Who's the hot blonde?"

Grace stood and tried to help him to his feet. "Long story, but she's not on our side."

Benny wavered but remained upright. "Did I get blown up?" He shook out his right leg and winced. His growl was both pained and pissed off. "Did you blow me up, Blondie?"

Yvonne smiled. "I'll go let Dayne and Terre know you're ready to chat, Benjamin Reese. We can talk more later, Grace. I'm sure we'll end up becoming great friends through the years." She turned and strode gracefully away.

"What a wench," Benny complained, leaning back against the rear wall. "Everything hurts. Are you okay?"

"I'm fine."

An explosion rent the night, and she jumped, adrenaline pumping fast though her veins.

Benny smiled. "My brothers have arrived. Good." He opened his eyes and looked around the cell. "Any idea how to get out of here?"

She gulped down panic as more explosions and then gunfire erupted outside. "An electrical current runs through the floor if they push a button outside the cell. I figure that we could maybe short the circuit?"

Benny glanced toward her. "Do you know how to short a circuit?"

"No. You?"

"Not really." He wiped blood off his neck. "I could try to run through the glass, but it's probably fortified, and I ain't at a hundred percent yet."

A swish sounded down the hallway, and Karma ran up with Rose in her arms. She reached way up, ticked some buttons, and the door opened. Her eyes were wide and frightened. "You have to go. Now." She handed the baby over to Grace, who took her before Rose could protest.

Karma reached into the pocket of her dress and brought out a sharp kitchen knife for Benny. "It's all I could get. You have to go. Two soldiers are at the top of the stairs, both armed."

Chapter 40

Adare slashed the soldier through the neck, moving on. Shouts erupted from every direction and an alarm blared through the night. Bright lights, flood lights, lifted into motion, highlighting the entire area with enough illumination to make it visible from space.

He motioned for Garrett, Quade, and Logan to go left, while Ronan and Ivar went right. He charged straight ahead, right for the main lodge, feeling the strongest pull from that building.

A helicopter instantly lifted from behind the lodge, and he ran faster, bellowing at the top of his lungs. Two soldiers barreled out of the lodge, guns up, and he tackled them both back inside, slashing with his knife and his fangs, fighting with all the fury he'd ever own.

"Grace!" he yelled, fighting to get to the back of the lodge. He went through two more guards, more animal than soldier, reaching the back door and kicking it open with one boot. Running outside and sliding across an ice-covered deck, he looked up at the lifting craft.

Two Kurjans sat in front, while a blonde was in the back. No Grace.

The Kurjan in the passenger side leaned out his window and fired. Bullets pinged up from the deck and snow, and one pierced Adare's left arm.

He turned back to the lodge just in time to duck as a machete swung perilously close to his throat. He edged back, dodging and weaving, as a Cyst soldier forced him back onto the deck. Snow piled up to his waist, and he kept his arms in defense position, trying to keep the sharp blade from taking off his head.

The Cyst had to be about seven feet tall and wide as a barn, his swings powerful and his movements inexorable.

Gunfire and explosions continued to sound from the other side of the lodge, along with cries of pain and the smell of smoke and blood.

The Cyst plunged the blade, and Adare jumped back, sucking in his gut out of pure instinct. The Cyst smiled, his bald head gleaming in the harsh light, except for the strip of white down the center of his scalp that ended in a long braid to his waist. "Never thought I'd be the one to end a Seven." His garbled voice cracked like a whip.

Adare set his stance. "Don't think it now." He yanked his knife from its sheath.

The Cyst laughed. "Mine's bigger." He lunged again, and this time Adare kept his hands at his sides and let the enemy's blade hit him center mass, right in his solar plexus. No doubt the Cyst planned to rip up, beneath the rib cage, and slice Adare's heart.

Instead, the blade rang loudly, vibrating as if it had hit solid steel. It snapped in two, no more dangerous than a child's toy.

Adare lunged, shoving his knife up beneath the Cyst's jaw and going right to the brain. The Cyst fell back onto the snow, his purplish-red eyes wide, his lungs gurgling as blood bubbled from his mouth. "It's not the size of the knife, asshole," Adare said, ripping to the right as far as he could and splitting the Cyst's neck open. "My torso is a shield. Remember?"

Pulling his blade free, Adare glanced at the useless machete and sighed. He didn't have the time necessary to decapitate the Cyst solder with his knife, and the machete would've come in handy.

He stood, wiping his knife on his pants leg, staining the white red. "Another day, then." He had to find Grace. He barreled through bloody snow to the lodge, as the sounds of a massive battle came from the property outside. "Grace?" he yelled, running down a hallway and kicking open doors. He shot three Kurjan soldiers, barely stopped himself from shooting two female Kurjan mates in time, and kept moving.

A bullet ran right through his left wrist, and he growled, turning toward the threat and throwing his knife as he moved. The blade spun end-over-end and struck a Kurjan soldier's neck, ramming right through to pin the asshole to the wall. His eyes widened and he struggled to pull the knife out.

Adare jumped forward, grabbed the handle and yanked it free, only to plunge it in the guy's eye. He gurgled as he went down to the ground. Kurjan flesh was easier to pierce than was Cyst. Figured.

He moved past the downed soldier and spotted stairs leading down. *Grace.* He ran forward, only to be tackled from behind, right into an office past the stairs. His head smashed into the desk, going right through to the steel chair on the other side. Pain flashed hot and bright in his brain.

Rolling over, he punched out, ready to fight.

A knife flashed just as a Cyst swung it down, right for Adare's neck.

* * * *

Grace held the baby close and followed Karma down the hallway.

Benny pulled Grace behind him, blood coating the back of his jeans. "If you see a way out, take it. I'll buy you as much time as I can." He ducked his head, limping, the simple kitchen knife looking small in his hand.

The little girl wrapped her arms around Grace's neck and snuggled her nose into Grace's hair, whimpering.

"You'll be okay," Grace soothed her, patting her back and running after Benny. "We'll get you home, sweetheart. Just hold on."

Karma stopped at the bottom of the stairs, her eyes wild. "She's enhanced, and they'll fight for her if they figure it out. But they want you worse, so run. Whatever you do, don't look back."

Benny grabbed her arm. "Come with us. You don't have to stay here."

Karma's smooth skin blanched. "I can't. This is only a small stronghold. They've taken more women and children than you can imagine, and I don't know where they are. I have to find out before leaving." She looked at the toddler in Grace's arms. "I memorized your number from the card you gave me. I'll call you." A red rash washed up from her chest to cover her neck.

Benny drew back his arm as if shocked. "Ow." An identical rash covered his hand. "You're mated."

"Yes," Karma said, scratching beneath her chin. "Go. You have to go now. Reinforcements are only a few minutes away. Dayne called them in before leaving in the helicopter. Run." She pushed Benny toward the stairs.

Grace stumbled but moved. "What about you? They'll know you let us out."

"Don't worry about me." She dodged in front of Benny, agile despite her long skirt. "Let me check if the hallway is clear upstairs." She ran, her footsteps silent, leading the way.

Benny followed her, almost on her heels, the rash spreading up his arm and around the back of his neck where the burned hair still hung.

"Doggie," the little girl whispered.

"We'll find a doggie. I promise," Grace whispered. "Shhh for now. We have to be quiet." What would she do if the girl started screaming? They couldn't give away their position. Not that the noise of the firefight going on outside didn't drown out all other sounds.

They reached the top of the stairs and Karma leaned out. A monstrously large Cyst soldier yanked her up and tossed her against the other wall. She yelled as she hit hard, dropping with a thud.

Benny leaped out and tackled the Cyst, head in gut, sending them both crashing down the hallway.

Another soldier, this one Kurjan, raced in from the open front door, gun up and already firing. Grace dropped into a slide toward Karma, who was sitting up, her lip bleeding. "Here. Hold her." Grace handed the girl over, turned, and stuck her leg out just as the Kurjan went by to attack Benny.

His arms windmilled and he tripped, falling on his stomach.

Sucking in air, panicking, Grace lunged forward and grabbed his gun, then stood and backed up. Her hands shook so badly, she could barely hold the gun.

The soldier flipped around and stood, well over six feet, his fangs sharp and his eyes a bright purple.

Oh, God. Grace glanced to the side to make sure Karma had the little girl tucked against her neck, her face hidden. Then she turned, and before the Kurjan could attack, she squeezed the trigger several times. Green lasers shot out and turned to metal the second before they impacted his face.

He came for her, his head down and his face bleeding.

She screamed and fired off several more shots, hitting his chest and neck. He reached her and fell on her, flattening them both to the floor. Hissing and yelling, she twisted her wrist and fired the gun as many times as she could into his body. The Kurjan yelled and rolled over, bleeding from multiple spots, grabbing his groin.

Benny stumbled out of the office, bleeding. "What is up with you shooting folks in the balls?" he muttered, weaving toward them and smashing his boot into the Kurjan's face several times. The soldier went limp, finally unconscious.

"I've been training," Grace gasped.

"You okay?" Benny held out a hand to help her up.

She took it, her head spinning. "Yes."

A Cyst soldier flew out of one of the doorways by the stairs, fracturing the wall all the way to the rebar. Adare followed him, bloody and battered.

"Adare!" Grace cried.

He turned, his eyes a deadly black rimmed with silver. "Grace." Relief softened his face just as the Cyst jumped up and rammed him back into the office. They rolled out, kicking and punching, damaging the doorframe. The Cyst grabbed a knife from his boot and slashed, faster than Grace could see.

Adare locked his legs around the Cyst, spun them over, and landed on the soldier's chest. In one smooth move, he took the knife, flipped it around, and drove the blade through the Cyst's neck to the floor. The soldier grabbed the knife, kicking, and Adare stood to stomp on his nose and face until he went unconscious.

Grace swallowed. He was alive. He was okay.

Another Kurjan soldier burst around the corner, gun out and firing. Benny took one in the jaw, and Grace reacted without thinking, shoving him out of the way.

A bullet pierced her neck and she cried out, slapping a hand to the wound and going down fast.

The roar from Adare was animalistic and raw. He was a blur of speed as he raced past her and took the enemy down, his bare fists breaking bones and cartilage. Blood flew in every direction until the Kurjan soldier stopped moving.

Benny leaned down, his gaze concerned. "What the hell were you doing?" His words came out garbled with the bullet hole still in his lower jaw.

Grace gagged. Tears filled her eyes.

Adare rushed toward her, dropping to his knees. "What in the hell were you thinking?"

"I forgot," she whispered. She'd reacted without thought when she'd seen an injured Benny in trouble.

Adare ripped open his wrist and shoved the wound toward her mouth. "Drink."

She did so, taking in his strength and imagining the cells going to her neck. The bullet popped out and plopped onto the floor. Her skin stitched itself together, and the pain slowly ebbed. She removed her hand. "I love you. Totally. Want to let you know."

Then, even though her wound was healed, the entire bloody room spun around.

As she passed out, the last thing she saw was Adare's eyes turning from black to silver.

* * * *

Adare hefted his unconscious mate over his shoulder and rushed for the door as Benny helped Karma up with the child in her arms. They ran outside, where Logan was setting down one of the two fighter copters, with Quade shooting out the other side.

Garrett leaned over, holding out a hand. "We have about two minutes until reinforcements arrive," he yelled.

Adare took his hand and jumped into the helicopter, sitting in the middle as Garrett leaped into the front seat and Ivar came in hot on the other side with Ronan on his six, firing wildly behind him. Adare settled Grace on his lap, cradling her. "Grace? Wake up."

Benny climbed in and turned to reach for the woman and child.

Karma shoved the little girl toward Benny, and he grasped the child, pivoting and handing her to Ivar. Then he turned back and grasped the woman's arm, pulling her in.

She brought her elbow down on his wounded arm, and he released her. She fell back into the snow, rolled, and turned to run back toward the lodge, her skirt catching in the ice.

"No," Benny growled, grasping the side of the craft and preparing to jump out.

Bullets winged the side of the helicopter, hitting him, and he fell back in. Adare bunched his body over Grace's to protect her while Ivar did the same with the child.

Logan lifted the stick and the copter rose high and fast, while Ronan fired out the side at the Kurjan soldiers. They skimmed over the treetops, and once they reached the other helicopter, Garrett and Ronan jumped out to take it. "See you at our headquarters," Logan called out, lifting his craft again into the stormy sky.

"They'll pick up Faith at your cabin and bring her, so we can strategize from there."

It'd be nice to have them all in one place. It had been too long.

Adare reached down and lifted Benny to the seat beside him, leaning across the healing male to shut the door. Ivar shut his door and settled with his legs out and the tiny blond human on his lap, sucking her thumb.

"You okay?" Adare asked Benny.

"No." Blood poured from most of Benny's body, but he flipped his hand over to reveal a mating mark, R for his last name, clearly black beneath all the blood.

Adare jerked. "H-how?" He frowned, looking at Benny's battered and bewildered face.

Benny shook his head and lifted both shoulders, scattering snow and blood. "I don't know. I mean, she's mated, right?"

Adare could only nod. It was unheard of, really. "Did you touch any other unmated female? Any female at all?"

"No."

"Was there one around somewhere?" It didn't take touch. Maybe there had been an enhanced female close and Benny's body had reacted?

Benny wiped blood off the marking with his other thumb. "No. I felt it happen when I touched Karma. It burns like a hot poker. I don't understand."

Adare set his head back and caught Ivar's concerned gaze. It didn't make any sense. Wasn't possible.

Grace stirred in his arms, and he held her tighter. She blinked. "Adare?"

"Yeah." He leaned down and kissed her cute nose.

She swallowed, looking around the craft. "I'm confused. I healed myself, was fine, and then passed out?"

"Yes." He reminded himself that getting angry at her for jumping in front of a bullet for Benny was counterproductive. They'd have that discussion later, over hot chocolate and a few more kisses. "Your body basically took a kill shot. As a human, that would've killed you. So when you were healed, your body still reacted. The response goes away after a while." Although she wouldn't be taking kill shots, so it wouldn't matter. "What the hell were you thinking?" So much for waiting for hot chocolate.

She poked at her healed neck. "I wasn't thinking. Benny had been hurt, so I was in protection mode. I just reacted." Lifting herself up, she looked at Benny. "Benny, are you all right?"

"No." He looked at her. "Tell me everything you can about Karma."

Grace's eyes widened, and she looked over her shoulder, relaxing when she spotted the little girl. "Is she okay?"

Ivar nodded. "Falling asleep, believe it or not. Who does she belong to?"

Grace shook her head. "I don't know. We have to find her parents."

"We will." Adare ran his hand down her wet hair, indulging himself. "I'm truly sorry about this, Grace. I never thought I'd leave you in danger." He might never forgive himself.

She snuggled closer, patting his chest. "Wasn't your fault. I never did figure out how Yvonne and Brian, I mean Terre, found me."

"Tracking dust," Adare said, pausing. "Wait a minute, Logan. We can't go to our headquarters yet." How could he have forgotten the tracking dust? Nobody knew the location of the Seven headquarters; not even the king. "Can you get a direct line to Emma?"

"Affirmative. What do you want me to ask her?" Logan yelled back.

"Ask her how long tracking dust stays in the body," Adare said. There was no way it could be permanent.

Logan communicated with the queen and then made a course correction before answering. "Emma said that the tracking dust is probably already out of Grace's blood but not her lungs. She said that oxygenated air would help, and she'll have a room set up for us."

Ivar rubbed the little girl's back as she slept against his chest. "We should go to Realm headquarters. The Kurjans already know its location, so we wouldn't be giving anything away. Plus, the king's resources will help us find this little one's home."

"Sounds good," Adare said.

Benny had fallen into a disturbed silence, staring at his bloody palm. Adare didn't have any words of wisdom for him, so he didn't give any. They'd have to figure out what to do once they were safely back at their own headquarters, and whatever Benny decided, Adare would have his back.

He leaned in and kissed Grace, being gentle but making a claim. "You said something to me. Something that mattered."

She yawned. "I said I loved you. Meant it, too." She caressed the cords in his neck and snuggled closer into his chest, sighing. "You don't have to say it back. I'll work on you until you know you feel it."

He rubbed his chin against the top of her head. "I already feel it. I love you too, my stubborn little mate."

* * * *

Grace finished the last hour in the weird, dark tank of water, a snorkel in her mouth and her head calm. The door opened, and Emma stood there, her eyes gleaming the way they did when she got to do experiments. Grace was beginning to dislike that look. She climbed out and accepted the towel, wrapping it around her simple swimsuit.

"Well?" she asked.

Emma read the screen on her tablet. "You're clean. No tracking dust in you or on you."

Grace's shoulders settled. "Finally." They'd been at headquarters all day, and Adare was itching to get out of there. "I wish I could figure out how it got in me." It wasn't as if she'd been unconscious around Yvonne.

Emma tapped her lips. "We've gone over your time with them, and nothing comes to mind. I feel like everything you ate was okay. I mean, even if you did ingest the dust, it wouldn't have ended up in your lungs. You had to have inhaled."

Grace thought back. "Wait a minute. There were sparklers on a dessert we had, and when Yvonne blew hers out, I coughed. I definitely inhaled something from them." She tied the towel to the right of her chest and squeezed water out of her hair.

"Ah ha. There you go. Sparklers, huh? That's a good delivery mechanism. I'll have to remember that." Emma made a quick notation on her tablet, humming to herself and then muttering a bunch of numbers that didn't make any sense. "Of course, you'd have to get the person to sit still while you blew out. It'd make more sense to have the subject suck it in somehow."

Speaking of memories. "I'm remembering more of my childhood, but still nothing about the two months before I went into a coma. Will I ever remember that time?" Grace asked.

Emma lifted a shoulder. "There's no way to know, but if other memories are coming back and those aren't, maybe not. At least you know most of what happened during that time."

Grace nodded. She'd rather have her memories of her childhood with Faith, anyway.

A male, tall and broad, entered the room. He had shaggy black hair, sharp features, and nearly translucent green eyes. There was something very compelling and familiar about him, but Grace couldn't quite place him.

"Sam." Emma straightened. "I thought you were resting."

Resting? A guy with a body like that didn't rest much. Oh, Grace was mated, not dead.

Sam ran a hand through his thick hair. "I can't stop the dreams. It's too much, Emma." He nodded at Grace. "I'm sorry to interrupt." Then he tilted his head, and his eyes flashed aqua and then back to green. "You're a Key."

Grace took a step back, while Emma slowly turned her head. "Grace? This is Sam. He's Zane and Logan's middle brother. Sam, this is Grace, Adare's mate and Faith's sister. What is a Key?"

Adare entered the room at that moment. "A Key? What? For like a door?" He slipped an arm over Grace's shoulders and hauled her into his side. Since they'd landed, there hadn't been any time just for the two of them. He'd said what she'd thought he'd said in the helicopter, right? Or had she been dreaming?

"Right. For a door." Emma looked at Sam, her expression contemplative.

Adare turned to Sam. "You know, you should come with us today. We're just going to explore mountains and maybe do some skiing. It'd probably be good for you to spend some time with your brother."

"He is," Emma interjected. "He's staying with Zane."

"Your other brother," Adare said, his smile not quite right. "I'm sure Logan misses you."

Sam hadn't looked away from Grace. "Yeah, okay. I wouldn't mind skiing with Logan for a while."

Emma frowned. "I'm psychic, you know. Sometimes."

Grace leaned around Adare to look at the queen. "What are your abilities telling you right now?"

"Nothing." The frown deepened.

"Welcome to the club," Grace murmured, wondering what in the world was going on.

Adare leaned down and kissed her, his lips firm and delicious. Then he released her. "Oh. I have good news."

"About Rose?" Grace's breath caught.

"Yeah." Adare brushed her wet hair away from her cheeks. "She was kidnapped from an orphanage, and Dage has said she can stay here. He'll find her a family. Hope and Paxton are playing with her now, and she seems to have latched on to Pax. He's cute with her."

Emma nodded. "We've already checked her out, and she hasn't been harmed in any way. She's also young enough that hopefully none of this will stay with her. That Karma took good care of her, somehow."

"That's great, and I'm so thankful she'll find a family here," Grace said, finally relaxing.

Emma nodded. "She will. Also, I checked on Janell Lewiston? The little girl with cancer that you befriended at that hospital? Her doctors are top notch, and her prognosis is very good. I'll keep an eye on her for you."

Grace smiled and hugged the queen. "Thank you," she whispered. Then she stepped back.

Adare maneuvered Grace toward the door. "Let's get out of here before the king decides to declare war on us. Especially since we're taking Sam."

They had to be alone at some point. Grace either had to bask in his love or start her campaign to get him to realize that he did love her, just in case his earlier words had been spoken in the heat of the moment.

"Let's go," she agreed.

Chapter 41

Adare finally relaxed once they arrived at Seven headquarters. Ivar had spent the last several years creating the perfect place in the Wyoming mountains, letting each member of the Seven know, without a doubt, that if this place burned down, he was done. The rest of them could live in shacks in the middle of nowhere, because he was never rebuilding.

Should Adare carry Grace across the threshold? It was an oddly human thing to do, but when they reached their log cabin, he swept her up anyway.

She laughed, sliding her arm along his shoulders. "We've been mated for years," she said, her voice happy and her body relaxed.

He needed to take it easy on her—she'd been shot just the day before. In fact, they could both use some rest. Their house had three bedrooms, a sparkling stainless steel kitchen, a great room with stone fireplace, two darkrooms, an office, and a gym. Of course, it also had entrances to hidden tunnels that would take them deep into the mountains should the private subdivision in the valley of two imposing mountains ever be attacked.

With their track record, that was a very real possibility.

He shut the door with his boot and set her on the sofa, his hands suddenly damp. Was he nervous? No way. Not in him.

She settled and instantly kicked off her boots to place her stocking feet on the table. "Why did you invite Sam Kyllwood to this new lair?"

Not her, too. "This is not a lair." He went about making a fire, starting the kindling easily.

She laughed. "Okay. The lair is in the mountain, so this is the entrance to the lair? Anyway, answer my question."

Bossy, wasn't she? He turned and caught her coat as she threw it, discarded his own, and set them both near the now crackling fire. "The ritual to kill Ulric will take the Seven, the blood of the three Keys, and the Lock, who is Hope Kayrs-Kyllwood."

"What does the Lock do?" Grace asked.

"There's some debate about that, but I think her blood is like a catalyst that gets yours and that of the other Keys going." Then all four females could remain safely out of the final ritual, which suited him just fine. He moved to the sofa and settled beside her, contentment flowing through him.

She reached for the pack of her belongings that had been sent from the cabin Adare and Benny shared and drew out a file folder. "So, Sam?"

Oh yeah. Adare looked over at the folder. "We don't know where the ritual takes place. Sam does. Or rather, it's his job as keeper of the place to find it. Apparently he's struggling." He grinned when she gave him that look that said she was doubting his grasp on reality. "I know it's a lot." So was gravity or the Earth being round if someone had been raised to believe otherwise.

She breathed out. "I want to talk to you, but do we need to go check on Benny?"

Adare shook his head. Night was falling, and Benny needed sleep. "No. Garrett is going to keep an eye on him tonight, since everyone else is reuniting or celebrating with mates. Tomorrow we'll gather and figure out a plan. First, we need some rest, and like you said, we need to talk."

She swallowed and drew out a photograph. Of him. "What do you see?"

He tugged her closer to look. "It's me, maybe five years ago?" He was standing outside, near a lake. Maybe at Realm headquarters.

"Look closer."

It hit him then. He was seeing himself through her eyes. He looked strong and fierce, impossible and in love. Definitely in love. That had to be the light glinting in his eyes. "I see."

"Do you?" She set the picture down and slid over him, straddling him, her eyes an impossibly stunning hue.

"Yes." His throat closed.

She leaned in and kissed him, her lips sweet and soft. "I love you." Then she leaned back. "What you said before was sweet but it's okay if you're not really there yet, and it's okay if we have to wrench open your emotions with the jaws of life. Apparently I'm now immortal and have centuries to make you realize what you feel."

The jaws of life? The female did have a way with words. As much fun as it would be to get her to spend lifetimes teaching him that he loved her, he already knew. When he'd thought she was hurt, he'd nearly lost his mind. He would've lost his soul. Life could be short, even for his kind, so he gave her everything. "I love you, Grace. Have since the first moment I held you in my arms."

* * * *

Grace stilled, her entire body going on full alert. It was too good to be true. "You love me."

"Yes." His smile held amusement and something else. Something real. Love. "I don't believe completely in fate, as you know. But there's a reason I was able to mate you without sex, and there's a reason my marking appeared on my hand the second I touched you."

Yeah, but there could be all sorts of biological reasons for that. "You were doing a favor."

He kissed her, going deep but being playful. Fun and light. Gentle and teasing. Then he leaned back, his gaze full dark silver. "Don't get me wrong. I'm fine with you spending all the time you want getting me to love you more, but it's impossible. I can't imagine there being more love. It's not all roses and rice, either."

She smiled, cuddling into his massive chest. "Of course not." Roses and rice were just symbols. They had something deeper. "Thank you for coming to get me." It didn't matter which time. They all counted.

"I'll always come and get you." He kissed her again, expressing every emotion she could ever want. Apparently when the Highlander let go, he did it completely. Figured. "The times ahead aren't going to be easy, but I know we'll always make it through."

She smiled, her hand over his heart, right where she wanted to be. "I know. You're a great soldier."

He nipped her lip. "Even so, I have what other soldiers could only dream of having." He kissed her again, sending desire and something deeper, something true, through her very veins.

She lifted her head, feeling at home for the first time in her life. "What do you have?"

"I have you. Grace."

Please read on for an excerpt from the newest Romantic Suspense novel in Rebecca Zanetti's bestselling Deep Ops series.

DRIVEN

Prologue

Six months ago

Thunder bellowed a distant warning while the wind rustled dried leaves along the lake path. Angus Force stumbled over an exposed tree root and somehow righted himself before falling on his ass. Again. The mud on his jeans proved he'd slipped at least once already.

Roscoe snorted and kept scouting the trail, his furry nose close to the rocky ground. His snort held derision.

"Shut up," Angus said, surprised his voice didn't slur. He'd started the morning with his fishing pole and two bottles of Jack. Now it was getting dark, he had no fish, and the bottles were empty. The forest swirled around him, the trees dark and silent. He glared at his German shepherd. "Be nice or I won't feed you."

The dog didn't pause in his explorations. His ears didn't even twitch.

Angus sighed. "I should've left you with the FBI." Of course the dog had a slight problem with authority and probably would've been put down at some point. Angus brightened. They had that in common. "All right. I guess I'll feed you."

Roscoe stopped suddenly.

Angus nearly ran into him, swerving at the last second and slipping on the leaves. "What the hell?"

The fur on Roscoe's back stood up, and he stared straight ahead down the trail. He went deadly silent, his focus absolute.

Angus dropped his pole and the sack containing the bottles. Damn it. He hadn't brought a gun. Of course, he'd been more concerned about having enough alcohol to get through the day.

He gave a hand signal to the dog and veered off the trail, winding through a part of the forest he could navigate blindfolded. The scent of fresh pine and dead leaves commingled around him, centering his focus. Soon he approached his lone cabin from the side, so he could see front and back.

Nothing.

Roscoe stayed at his side, his ears perked, his fur still raised.

The woods around them had gone silent, and a hint of anticipation threaded the breeze. Roscoe sat and stared at the cabin.

Yeah. Angus remained still. There was definitely somebody inside. He angled his head to study a black Range Rover parked in front of the cabin. So his visitor wasn't trying to remain hidden.

Angus's shoulders relaxed, and he waited.

Waiting was what he excelled at. Well, waiting and drinking. He'd become a master at downing a bottle of whiskey. Or several.

Ten minutes passed. Something rustled inside the cabin. Now he was just getting bored. So he gave Roscoe a hand signal.

Roscoe immediately barked three times.

The front door of the cabin opened, and two men strode out. Government men. Black suits, pressed shirts, polished shoes. The older one had a beard sprinkled with gray and the worn eyes of a man who'd already seen too much.

The younger guy was a climber. Even when he stood still it was clear he was on his way to the top and had no problem stepping on bodies to get there. His shoes were expensive and his blue silk tie even more so.

Angus crossed his arms. "You're trespassing, assholes." Was it a bad sign he could sound and feel sober after the amount he'd imbibed all day? Yeah. Probably.

The older man watched the dog. The younger man kept his gaze on Angus.

The older guy was obviously the smarter of the two.

The younger guy smoothly reached into his jacket pocket and withdrew his wallet to flip it open. "Special Agent Thomas Rutherford of the HDD." His voice was low and cultured. Confident. He was probably about Angus's age—in his early thirties.

"You're lost," Angus returned evenly.

"No. We're looking for you, FBI Special Agent Angus Force," Rutherford said, his blue eyes cutting through the space between them.

"I'm retired." A true statement, which had made nosing around lately a little difficult. However, he'd obviously shaken something loose, considering these guys were now standing on his front porch.

The older guy cocked his head. "That's a tactical Czech German shepherd," he said thoughtfully.

Angus lifted an eyebrow. "Nope. He's a mutt. Found him last week in a gulley." Was he drunk, or did Roscoe send him an irritated canine look? Angus jerked his head at the older man. "You are?"

The guy also took out a wallet to flash an HDD badge. "HDD Special Agent Kurt Fielding." Rough with an edge of the street—no culture there.

Angus crossed his arms. "There is nothing the Homeland Defense Department could possibly want with me." The agency was an offshoot of the Department of Homeland Security; one of the offshoots the public didn't really know about. The name alone made it easy to divert funds. "Go away."

Agent Rutherford set his hands in his expensive pockets in an obvious effort to appear harmless. "We'd like a few minutes of your time."

"Too bad." Angus wanted another drink. They stood between him and his bottles. That was a bad place to be.

Agent Fielding had deep dark eyes that looked all but hangdog. He finally looked away from Roscoe and focused on Angus. "We know you've been contacting witnesses from the Henry Wayne Lassiter cases."

Heat flushed down Angus's spine. "The last person who said that name to me got a fist in the face and a broken nose."

"We're aware of that fact," Rutherford said. "FBI Special Agent in Charge Denby still has a bump on that nose."

Yeah, well, his former boss had known better. Angus shrugged

Agent Fielding tried again, his gruff voice matching his weary eyes. "We just want to talk."

"No," Angus said softly. "You're here to warn me off the case. I was just playing around." If the agents hadn't shown up, he probably would've chalked up his theory that Lassiter was still alive to an overactive imagination. But now that they were here, he was inspired. Finally. "I know something is up, and I'm not going to stop until I know what." He'd been a damn good tracker for the Behavioral Science Unit until that case, and then he'd fucking lost everything. Maybe even his mind. "A source reached out and told me Lassiter isn't really dead." Yeah, he'd shot Lassiter, and blood had sprayed all over. But he'd been shot as well, and he'd passed out before he'd been able to check the body for a pulse. Apparently his recent nosing around had ruffled some feathers.

Rutherford smiled, showing perfectly straight white teeth. The guy probably had them bleached. "We understand that a former file clerk contacted you, but you have to realize that the FBI forced Miles Brown into retirement, and he was trying to make trouble by contacting you and drumming all of this up. He apparently succeeded. Lassiter is dead. You killed him."

Apparently the HDD still wanted to keep secret the fact that one of the most prolific serial killers in history had been a low-level computer tech for the agency. Why? Who the hell cared?

Miles had been a great record keeper, and the only thing his message had said was that there was a problem with the Lassiter file and Angus should call him immediately. "Fine. Then let me talk to Miles." Brown's phone had been disconnected, and so far Angus had been unable to find him.

Agent Fielding winced, his salt and pepper eyebrows drawing down. "Miles Brown suffered a stroke and is in St. Juliet's on the east side of DC. He has no family, so we're putting him up."

That explained why Force hadn't been able to reach him. "I'd like to see his office and all of his records."

"His office was cleared out," Fielding said, his gnarled hands clasped together. "Per procedure. Nothing out of the ordinary there."

Right. Except that Miles had called, and there had been a sense of urgency in his voice. "Yet you're here," Angus murmured.

Agent Rutherford sighed, looking as if a bartender had served him too many olives in his martini. "We know you've been through an ordeal, but—"

"Ordeal?" Angus growled. "Are you kidding me?" He'd give anything for his gun.

Fielding held up an age-spotted hand. "We're very sorry for your loss, but this is important."

Loss? Had the fucker really just said the word "loss" to him? Angus took two steps toward the agents, and Roscoe kept pace with him, low growls emerging from his throat. "Leave. Now." He still hadn't dealt with what had happened. Loss didn't cover it. Not by a long shot.

Rutherford eyed the dog warily. "We want you to stop pursuing the issue. Lassiter is dead. Let him lie."

Angus snorted. Roscoe stayed at attention but stopped growling. "Why are you here, then? If the case was really closed, you wouldn't bother." Homeland Security had barely been able to shut down news of Lassiter's previous employment before it became public. Of course the agency wanted this dropped.

Fielding shuffled his feet, his gaze descending to his scuffed shoes.

Angus straightened. His gut churned, and his instincts flared to life. "Say what you need to say."

Rutherford swallowed and looked toward the older agent.

Fielding sighed and glanced up again, experience stamped on his square-shaped face. "Let it go. We're not going to give you a choice."

Ah, shit. Lassiter really was alive. No way would two HDD agents have sought Angus out if he wasn't getting close to something. Or maybe they were afraid he'd let the public know about Lassiter's former employment. Governmental agencies had definitely taken a beating lately in the press, and Homeland Security wanted to keep HDD as under wraps as possible.

Angus stood perfectly still, his mind focusing through the booze. "Well, then. We all know you don't want me talking to the press

I guess for now this gives me leverage." Just how much? How worried were they?

Their silence gave him even more confidence. It also helped him pursue the nagging feeling that had never really left him. The Lassiter case had never felt...finished. Sometimes his instincts were all he had. Well, his instincts and his dog. What else did a burned-out, obsessive drunk of an ex-FBI agent really need?

He rubbed his jaw and let whiskers scrape his palm. "Let's see. Either I work on this myself along with a couple of really good investigative journalists I befriended during my years with the FBI, or you give me the resources to do a little investigating. That seems fair."

The wind tousled Rutherford's blond hair, and he scoffed. "Not a chance."

"Bull," Angus returned instantly, reading the men. Oh, they were seasoned and pretty good, but he hadn't lost all of his abilities. "Try again."

Fielding shot a hand through his thick hair, making the gray stand up more through the brown. "You know we can't have you at HDD looking into a closed FBI case."

Fair enough. "You could have me at HDD working on other cases while I quietly pursue this one. I'm a reasonable guy, and I'm sure we can negotiate some sort of agreement."

"Lassiter is dead," Rutherford gritted out between perfect teeth.

Angus shrugged. "Then you have nothing to lose. You do, however, have everything to gain. One year."

There was no doubt HDD would try to get rid of him. Even so, he couldn't give this up. He looked down at the dog. "Wanna go back to work, boy?"

Chapter 1

The swirl of red and blue lights exposed the taut crime scene tape in a back alley outside of DC. Rain blasted down, pinging off battered metal garbage bins at the rear of businesses long closed for the night. The bastard had dumped the victim near a pile of litter the rain had mangled into a sopping mess of paper and take-out cartons.

Angus kept his face stoic as he ducked under the tape and flashed his badge to the uniformed officer blocking access. It felt kind of good to show the badge, even though he worked better without it.

It would be the only good feeling of the night, without question.

HDD Special Agent Kurt Fielding was the first to reach him, skirting several numbered yellow evidence markers placed on the wet asphalt. Fielding was pale and looked even grizzlier than the first time they'd met a year before. "I heard the call go out, got the details, and figured you'd be here." His T-shirt was wrinkled and his brown shoes scuffed. He grimaced. As an HDD handler, he wasn't so bad. "The locals don't want us at the scene, just so you know."

"The FBI will take over soon enough." Unless there was a way HDD could force itself in, which didn't seem possible. Federal agencies rarely played well together, regardless of the party line. Force straightened, acutely aware of his men at his back. West and Wolfe had both seen some rough shit in their time, but this was something new. He needed West's mind clear so he could run the office for now, but when he turned his head to give an order, West was already shaking his head at him, his gaze direct. No way would he be left behind.

Angus turned back around and started to focus, speaking as much to himself as to his team. "Everything is relevant. Any sign on a piece of garbage, any scratch on the building, any glint of anything shiny."

Agent Fielding shook his head, sliding to the side and putting his body between Angus and the scene. "You're not understanding me. This is not your case. Hell, it isn't even *our* case. Never will be." He scratched his chin. "Not that it matters. Time is up."

Fire ripped through Angus so quickly his ears burned as if he'd been flicked with a poker. "Lassiter killed this woman, which makes it my case. Period." He had to get to the body and make sure, but his gut never lied.

Special Agent Tom Rutherford, his blond hair mussed for the first time ever, reached them next. Fielding's partner was usually impeccably put together, although his too-blue eyes were as pissy as ever. "You're not supposed to be here. Neither are we."

"I still have some sources in the FBI and was contacted immediately about the crime," Angus muttered, his hands itching for his gun. "Now get out of my way."

"This scene isn't the same as the others," Rutherford said, his eyes bloodshot.

Wolfe rocked back on massive boots, spraying water. "What do you mean?"

Rutherford slid a manicured hand into the pocket of his perfectly creased dress pants. Who dressed up for a crime scene at midnight? "I've studied your old case files on Henry Wayne Lassiter. His MO was unique. This crime scene is different."

Angus swallowed. "Where's the note?" The psychopath had always left a note.

"No note," Fielding said as the local techs moved efficiently around.

"Look again," Angus said evenly, his gut aching so bad he wanted to bend over and puke.

Rutherford planted a broad hand on his shoulder. His law school class ring dug into Angus's skin through his T-shirt. "Please leave before I have you escorted away."

Wolfe shoved Rutherford's hand off before Angus could grab it and break a finger or two.

Angus probably owed Wolfe for that. "There are two options here. Either you get the hell out of our way so we can view the scene, or we get in a fight, beat the shit out of the two of you and then we go and view the scene." His voice had lowered to a hoarse threat. Once the FBI showed up, he was definitely going to be thrown out of the alley. His exit from that agency hadn't been cordial.

Wolfe tensed next to him, while West drew up abreast, his shoulders back.

They were ready to fight alongside him, if necessary. Angus would reflect on how much that warmed him later. His team was good. Better than good. He had to keep them in the game somehow.

Rutherford smiled, no doubt wanting payback for when Raider, another team member, had broken his nose a few months ago. "I'm ready. You hit one of us, just breathe wrong on us, and I'll plant your ass in a jail cell. You're done, Force."

West cleared his throat, his blue eyes piercing through the dark. "If you're so sure Lassiter didn't do this, give us a minute with the scene. Force will know the truth."

Rutherford began to shake his head.

"Okay," Fielding said, stepping aside. He shrugged at his younger partner. "Why not? Lassiter is dead, right?"

"Right," Rutherford gritted, his gaze promising retribution.

The stench of puke, garbage, and worse filled Angus's nostrils as he stepped past the agents to penetrate deeper into the alley. "Lassiter kidnapped women and tortured them until their hearts gave out. We'll need an autopsy on this one, but we probably won't know much about her heart."

"Why not?" West stopped short as the body came into view.

"That's why," Angus said, trying to shut down his humanity. So he could analyze the crime scene and not lose his fucking soul.

West's breath caught. "Oh."

Yeah. Oh. A tarp had been erected above the body to protect it from the elements. The woman lay naked on the pavement, her eyes open and staring straight up. Long dark hair, milky brown eyes, petite form. Her arms were spread wide, hands open and palms up. Her legs were crossed and tied at the ankles with a common clothesline rope found in a million places. Her chest gaped open, the ribs and breastbone spread, leaving a hole. The crime signature was similar but not exactly the same. What did that mean?

West coughed. "Her heart is gone."

Angus went even colder. Rain dripped off his hair and down his face. The scene was...off. "He eats it. Says it makes them stay with him forever." Nausea tried to roll up his belly, and he shoved it down.

Wolfe came up on his other side, his movements silent. He didn't gasp or go tense. He just stared at the body, his jaw tense. He pointed to the victim's arms. "Burn marks?"

"Affirmative," Angus said crisply. "There will be both cigarette and electrical burns." Outside and inside the woman. "As well as whip marks, ligature marks around the neck, and knife wounds. Shallow and painful—not enough to let her bleed out. The cuts for the heart here were rough—not smooth the way Lassiter liked to do—which was why the press dubbed him 'the surgeon.'"

Yet the heart was gone.

West coughed. "Raped?"

"Probably," Angus said.

Agent Rutherford approached the scene from the far end, carefully stepping over water filled potholes with his shiny loafers. "There's no note, and she's not blond. In addition, the cigarette marks are too large—almost like he used a cigar." He looked around as if worried the FBI would catch them working outside their purview. The Homeland Defense Department didn't deal with serial killers.

Angus breathed in and out before responding. He much preferred Fielding to this guy. "Lassiter is very choosy about his cigarettes and would never use a cigar." Angus dropped into a crouch, closer to the woman. Lassiter also loved blondes. Were the victim's features Asian? This close, her skin looked dusky and not pale. Lassiter had liked them pale. "Are you sure there isn't a note?"

"No note," Rutherford snapped. "Told you it wasn't him."

Everything inside Angus insisted it was Lassiter. But was that because he needed it to be? Needed to be on the case and hunting the evil psycho down—finally? He looked around, noting the alley had been cordoned off and blocked from the view of neighbors or the press. In a different situation, he'd be fighting with Rutherford right now about the media. It probably killed the guy that he couldn't chase the cameras—especially since HDD didn't have jurisdiction. "Once you get an ID, track down her medical records."

"No ID," Rutherford said, glancing down at his shiny phone. "Her prints came up empty, and this isn't our case. Time to go, gentlemen."

Wolfe scouted the alley, his gaze sharp. "You think Lassiter did this?"

Yes. "I don't know. The MO is close but not perfect, and he was a perfectionist." Frustration tasted like metal in Angus's mouth. "If it isn't Lassiter, it's a copycat, and I was the best profiler the FBI had."

"Until you drank the entire wagon," Fielding said, his bushy eyebrows rising.

Something on the victim's hand caught Angus's attention. "Glove?" He gestured toward a couple of techs.

One tossed him a blue glove, and he slid it on, gently turning the woman's right hand over.

"Shit," West said, leaning down. "Is that what I think it is?"

Angus swallowed. "Yeah." A perfect tattoo of a German shepherd with strong markings had been placed right beneath the knuckles on the back of her hand.

Wolfe swallowed. "Looks like Roscoe."

"Could be a coincidence," West said, his lips turning down.

"Probably is," Angus stood. But he knew that was his dog. "Fielding? I want this case. Lassiter or not. FBI or not."

West gripped his arm and pulled him aside. He leaned in to speak quietly. "Even if the FBI and HDD both allow it, are you sure you want this? Serial killers don't just change their MOs, right? Especially ones like Lassiter."

Angus nodded. "You're right."

"You're obsessive and you're just getting your drinking under control. If this isn't Lassiter, and that tattoo is a coincidence, then why take on the HDD, the FBI, and the local DC police force right now?" West released him, his gaze again straying to the poor woman on the ground.

Right now, they were the best chance of justice the woman had.

Fielding slid his phone back into his pocket. "The HDD wants you off this case."

Angus turned on his heel and shoved his hands in his jeans pockets, striding down the alley. The rain increased in force, its cold, angry slash a prelude to a dark oncoming winter.

His team members flanked him.

Wolfe stepped over a puddle. "We're not letting this go, are we?"

"Not a chance in hell," Angus said. "Call everyone in. We have a new case." He ducked under the crime scene tape, walking away from death.

This time.

About the Author

New York Times and *USA Today* bestselling author Rebecca Zanetti has worked as an art curator, Senate aide, lawyer, college professor, and a hearing examiner—only for it all to culminate in stories about Alpha males and the women who claim them. She writes romantic suspense novels and dark paranormal romances.

Growing up amid the glorious backdrops and winter wonderlands of the Pacific Northwest has given Rebecca fantastic scenery and adventures to weave into her stories. She resides in the wild North with her husband, children, and extended family who inspire her every day—or at the very least give her plenty of characters to write about.

Please visit Rebecca at: rebeccazanetti.com
Facebook: RebeccaZanetti.books

Printed in the United States
by Baker & Taylor Publisher Services